THE ROMAN EMPIRE
14 A.D. - 117 A.D.

Roman Miles   English Miles

0 50 100 200 300 400   0 50 100 200 300 400

Emery Walker sc.

The Fight for Rome

Also by James Duffy
Sand of the Arena

THE FIGHT
FOR ROME

A Gladiators of the Empire Novel

By James Duffy

McBooks Press, Inc.
Ithaca, New York

Published by McBooks Press 2007

Copyright © 2007 James Duffy

Cover painting by David Palumbo © 2007.

Dust jacket and interior designed by Panda Musgrove.

ISBN: 978-1-59013-112-1

Library of Congress Cataloging-in-Publication Data

Duffy, James, 1955-

The fight for Rome : a gladiators of the empire novel / by James Duffy.

p. cm.

ISBN 978-1-59013-112-1 (alk. paper)

1. Rome—History—Nero, 54-68—Fiction. 2. Gladiators—Fiction. I. Title.

PS3604.U378F54 2007

813'.6—dc22

2007001367

Distributed to the trade by Independent Publishers Group

814 North Franklin Street, Chicago, IL 60610

(800) 888-4741

Additional copies of this book may be ordered from any bookstore or directly from McBooks Press, Inc., ID Booth Building, 520 North Meadow St., Ithaca, NY 14850. Please include $5.00 postage and handling with mail orders. New York State residents must add sales tax to total remittance (books & shipping). All McBooks Press publications can also be ordered by calling toll-free 1-888-BOOKS11 (1-888-266-5711).

Please call to request a free catalog.

Visit the McBooks Press website at www.mcbooks.com.

Printed in the United States of America

9 8 7 6 5 4 3 2 1

For Greg, Kris, Nina & Bill

Acknowledgements

I am grateful to Alexander Skutt and his staff at McBooks for their support of the Gladiators of the Empire series. Once again, I offer a special note of thanks to my editor, Jackie Swift, for her uncanny attention to detail in plot and characters. To Caroline Upcher for her valuable contributions to this story and her words of support. To the master of ancient sources and all things Roman, Sander Van Dorst.

To all the friends and family who offered their valuable feedback and suggestions, especially Mike Schafer, Greg Duffy, June Poole, Norma Whitt, Larry Casella, and the most supportive parents in the business. And most of all, my love and thanks to my wife and in-house editor, Kristina, whose support, help, and love continue to get me through the hard parts.

Major Battle Locations in the Year of the Four Emperors, AD 69

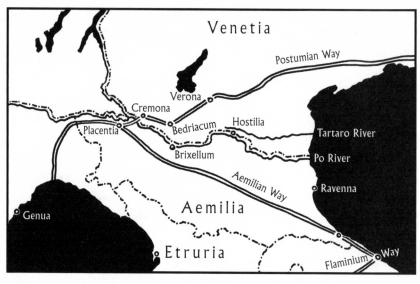

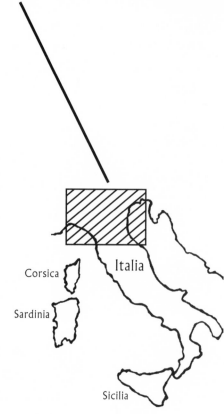

The Fight for Rome

I

December AD 68

THERE WAS NOTHING Taurus liked better than the roar of the crowd when he cut into flesh. The adversary he studied through the grated eyepieces of his Thracian helmet now had a ribbon of blood running down his left arm. And the mob loved it.

The stench of offal from the morning animal hunts, the noxii criminal executions, and the preliminary gladiator bouts hung in the crisp air of the December afternoon. But the smell didn't bother Taurus. It was simply the vestige of another successful day of games in the Pompeii arena. The familiar coolness of the sand beneath his feet gave him comfort, even as he occasionally stepped through the dampness of warm blood. The harenarii—the arena attendants—had been too hasty in their raking between bouts, he thought as he toyed further with his opponent.

He kept the late afternoon sun at his back, forcing his adversary to squint through the glare. There was no need for the amphitheater's vellarium roof on such a beautifully cool day, so the view of Vesuvio and the green hills to the northwest provided a dramatic backdrop to the action in the arena. But Taurus knew the attention of the twenty thousand spectators was not on the landscape. He could feel their eyes pressing upon him. The boisterous crowd showed no sign of tiring on this first day of the Saturnalia festival. Even after a full slate of hunts, executions, and fifteen gladiator bouts, they still called for blood.

The brute facing Taurus was Livius, a massive hoplomachus of top primus palus ranking. Taurus had sparred against him often on the training field of their Pompeii ludus. He knew the man well. He knew how he wiggled his small shield ever so slightly before he lunged high for the shoulder with his spear. He knew how he dug his right heel into the sand just before a low thrust to the thigh. Of course, Livius was not aware of these tells. But Taurus made it his business to know them all. Most heartening, he knew Livius did not have near the speed or agility that he himself was able to muster. Even with the extended reach of Livius's six-foot pike, not a trace of anxiety crossed Taurus's mind.

Although his heart had been pounding hard for more than five minutes, Taurus continued to stalk his prey, waiting patiently for the slightest mistake that would give him the split-second advantage he sought. He saw the hoplomachus's helmet turn ever so slightly to the left. He knew his opponent was glancing at the fresh gash on his arm, worrying about how slippery the blood would be when it reached the handle of his shield. That was all the information Taurus needed. The time had come.

His sica shot forward. The curved sword beat once, twice, three times against the wooden spear handle. Taurus heard the wood start to splinter. Livius backpedaled across the sand. Taurus pursued his adversary, his sica now a blur of silver as it windmilled toward Livius's right, then left shoulder. He augmented the threat of his blade with the bottom rim of his square parmula shield, catching Livius on the thigh, then in the chest. Taurus had mastered the concept of using his shield as much for offense as for defense.

Although wounded, Livius did a good job of blocking the assault with his own small bowl-shaped shield, which would have seemed terribly inadequate to a lesser fighter. He attempted a lunge to back Taurus off and stall the advance. But Taurus had his own shield in place before the metal spear tip came close to his chest. Taurus pressed his advantage and swung his razor-sharp blade in blinding arcs. The speed came from somewhere deep inside; Taurus didn't understand it, but the power was there when he needed it.

As his sica beat against the shield again and again, he sensed the tiny protective disc shift ever so slightly. The blood had reached Livius's hand. He saw panic in the eyes behind the grating of his opponent's face mask. And he knew the match was won.

He sliced sideways at the shield. Livius's bulky arm glistened as the muscles tightened. But he could not hold on. The slickness of the blood, combined with the crushing power of Taurus's blow, forced the gladiator's only protection to sail from his hand and clang against the arena wall. The small dagger he held in place behind the shield as a backup weapon also slipped from his grasp. Before the hoplomachus could recover, Taurus went to work on the spear. Two more blows and the metal tip fell to the sand, leaving Livius waving a splintered pole half its original length. He swung the pitiful remnant in an attempt to parry Taurus's sica. But on the next contact the curved blade sliced through the wood like a loaf of bread and buried deep into Livius's left bicep. The hoplomachus screamed and dropped to his knees. He grabbed his arm to try to stem the torrent of blood, his fingers disappearing inside the gaping wound. Taurus placed the tip of his blade on Livius's chest.

The referee stepped forward and used his five-foot rod to halt the match. Taurus looked at the smile on Julianus's face. As chief trainer at the ludus, it was Julianus's job to also referee his troupe's arena battles, using the rod to beat some sense into the more cowardly tiro gladiators. But there was little need for the pole in these late afternoon matches with only the top fighters and crowd favorites on the sand.

"Another fine fight, Taurus," he said quietly as the crowd roared. "You, too, Livius. I know it's hard to match that speed of his."

Pleasing Julianus and his lanista, Titus Cassius Petra, was a key ingredient in Taurus's passion for arena combat. It ran a close second to the adulation of the mob. Ironically, the only part of arena combat he hated was the killing. The *art* of the fight was paramount to Taurus, not the taking of a brave man's life—although he had had to do it on occasion.

"I just hope we don't lose Livius," Taurus replied. "He's a good man."

The trembling in Livius's body was transmitted to Taurus's arm through the sword touching the man's chest.

"His fate is in the hands of the magistrate," Julianus said.

All three turned and looked across the arena at the old man seated on the podium. The magistrate was studying the reaction of the mob.

Taurus scanned the cavea and was relieved when a sea of white handkerchiefs fluttered in the late afternoon light—the sign of mercy. He glanced back at the podium. The old magistrate reached inside his draped sleeve and pulled out a small white cloth which he waved briskly twice across his chest.

"*Missio!*" Julianus shouted. He pushed Quintus's sica aside and helped Livius to his feet. Two harenarii arrived quickly to escort the bleeding fighter to the tunnel.

Taurus dropped his shield and touched the tiny terra-cotta figurine that hung from the thin leather strip around his neck. He raised the effigy to his lips and planted a quick kiss on the icon that embodied three beloved spirits: his late mother and father, and his murdered friend and childhood bodyguard, Aulus Libo. He let out a wild victory cry and hurled his sica, blade first, into the sand. The victory ritual was more dramatic with his trident when he fought as a retiarius, but the sword worked almost as well. As it swayed at his feet, he raised his arms and incited the mob of twenty thousand to a deafening crescendo. A chant of "Taurus! Taurus! Taurus!" swept around the oval cavea. He absorbed every second of it, bathing in the adulation as if it were a warm pool in the local baths. He wondered what other vocation could bring such hero worship to a young man barely twenty years old.

"Funny how they know you only as 'Taurus,'" Julianus said with a smile as he retrieved the remnants of the broken spear and readied for the final bout. "Yet at the ludus we have the pleasure of knowing both Taurus *and* Quintus."

"Ahhh, but is it not Taurus who makes the money for Dominus Petra?"

the fighter replied without taking his eyes from the crowd. "So you tell me which half of me he prefers."

Julianus laughed and slapped his back. As he scanned the cheering faces in the crowd, Taurus considered how he was able to leave Quintus Honorius Romanus in the tunnel before each bout. The process wasn't clear to him, he just did it. He always managed to assume the persona and herculean fighting tactics of his alter ego, *Taurus*. This was how his legions of fans knew him best: as the showman and *always* the victor—at least so far in his three-year arena career. But Taurus was much more than a stage name fabricated to instill fear in his opponents and excitement in the mob. Taurus was a state of mind. It defined the swift, aggressive, calculating warrior that Quintus was able to muster from deep within his being each time he stepped onto the sand. Taurus could do the things that Quintus could not. And he proved it with each appearance in the arena.

"I think it's time to visit the podium," Julianus said, pointing his stick toward the magistrate.

With his usual flare, Taurus pulled the griffin-topped helmet from his head and dove for his sica. He tumbled through the sand and rose a second later in a theatrical pose, left arm stretched forward and curved sica arching gracefully over his head. The crowd screamed its appreciation. The sand that stuck to his sweat-drenched torso did little to cover the beautiful black stigmates that had become his trademark. The ornate bull head on his chest stared defiantly forward with wicked eyes bordered by elaborate curved horns, its wide-set, ringed nostrils set above a row of pointed teeth. Taurus's broad back was adorned with the face of Medusa the Gorgon, her hair a nest of vipers and her evil white eyes daring any foe to attack from the rear. Both images did their job in distinguishing Taurus the Bull from every other helmet-clad fighter in the arena.

After a few more poses highlighting his solid physique, Taurus crossed the sand and stood before the magistrate. It took a few moments for the old man to quiet the crowd. As Taurus waited, he relaxed and took a few deep breaths. The rush of adrenalin ceased and his pounding heart began to slow. Once again, he was Quintus.

"Each time you appear, you prove yourself a true hero of the arena, Taurus. I congratulate you on your twelfth victory." Shouts and applause from the crowd briefly interrupted him. "May Hercules continue to protect you." A bag of coins landed at Quintus's feet, followed by a green palm frond, the traditional symbol of arena victory. Quintus bowed with a smile, gathered up his spoils, and trotted toward the arena tunnel, waving the palm above his head. The cheering of the crowd followed him into the passageway and echoed off the rough stone walls.

As he rushed through the portal, he almost ran into a female fighter who was securing her helmet and readying for her first fight in more than a year. Her statuesque form was enhanced by the shape of her murmillo helmet. The crest of scarlet-dyed horsehair made her appear even taller than her six-foot height. The silver flare at the rear of the helmet matched the graceful shape of the auburn locks hanging across her bare shoulders. Her well-oiled body, naked but for a small red loincloth and black leather belt, glistened even in the dim light of the tunnel. It was easy to see why the lanista had decided to pluck her from a life of prostitution and slavery. Although this would be only her third arena battle, it was clear she was already one of the top arena draws of the Empire. She was known to all as The Gladiatrix Amazonia.

But on this late afternoon, Quintus noticed her normally self-assured stance and confident swagger was missing. "You're ready for this, you know," he said to her quietly so her opponent, a slim Thracian, could not hear.

"I know, I know. I just want to get it over with," she snapped back.

She shook her arms again and shifted her weight from side to side. The jittery moves betrayed her nervousness to Quintus. He knew this was her first bout since the near disaster in Rome a year earlier. Not many fighters could have recovered from a deep puncture wound, a fight with a lion, and an almost fatal infection all in the span of one week. The wound came at the hands of a crafty Germanic hoplomachus in a featured bout. She had lost her concentration and paid the price with his spear tip buried deep in her thigh. The lion came later that same day. It had been one of ten sent into the arena to dispatch Quintus. While gladiators did not fight beasts—that job was left to the trained venatores like their Ethiopian comrade, Lindani—this fact was lost on the games' editor, Lucius Calidius. Such a breach of arena protocol was not about to stand between Lucius and the death of his lifelong rival, Quintus Romanus. To this day, it pained Quintus to know that his closest friends, Amazonia and Lindani, had both almost been killed helping him defeat the lions sent to destroy him.

Quintus looked at the ugly scar on her left thigh that marred an otherwise flawless limb. He thought about the horrid infection that had set in. The head ludus physician, Agricola, felt it might have been triggered by the lion's blood, which had entered her gaping wound and mixed with her own. She had recovered from the high fever but almost lost the leg. Only constant vigilance by Agricola—and Amazonia's own perseverance—had saved it. She endured months of painful recuperation, followed by many more of therapy, herbal remedies, and excruciating exercise. Finally, the ludus physicians pronounced her physically ready to return to the arena. *But was she ready mentally?* Quintus wondered as he watched her twitching arms.

"He's small but light on his feet, this thraex," Quintus warned. "You know he always feigns right before going for the left shoulder."

Amazonia did not respond. On the podium the praecone stood for his final announcement of the day.

"Fellow Romans and guests, in honor of our esteemed new emperor in Rome, his Imperial Majesty Servius Sulpicius Galba, our benevolent magistrate, Publius Aurelius Capito, presents the final bout of our first day of Saturnalia." He paused for the expected swell of voices from the cavea. "For your amusement, we present the thraex Priedens. And fighting for the first time in more than a year, the most beautiful murmillo in the Empire, the magnificent Amazonia!"

Amazonia stepped into the dim light of the afternoon as she and her opponent began their walk across the sand to where Julianus stood waiting. Quintus stepped forward and crouched at the tunnel entrance. He leaned against the rough stones of the arena wall and let their coolness soothe him. The cheering that had sent him from the sand returned in earnest as every pair of eyes in the amphitheater now followed the magnificent semi-nude figure floating across the arena. Although female gladiators had appeared here before, none came close to the beauty of Amazonia. And certainly no other had the skill and power to be matched against a male fighter.

Before the battle began, Quintus felt a presence beside him. He turned to see Lindani next to him, still wearing the leopard-skin loincloth from his morning animal hunt. The flexibility of the man's lanky frame was evident as he sat motionless with his feet flat on the tunnel paving stones and his knobby knees almost at shoulder height. His skin, the color of polished ebony, was rimmed with a copper highlight by the late afternoon sun. The colorful beads braided into his long locks of black hair clicked gently as he moved his head. His bright eyes held the intensity Quintus had come to know well when the African was keenly focused.

"She is nervous, no?" he said in his melodic Ethiopian accent.

"I've seen her on edge before," Quintus replied, "but never like this."

The moment she stepped from the cold hard stone into the sand of the arena, Amazonia's senses began to tingle. It had been so long since the softness of the sand caressed her feet, quite different from the hard packed earth of the ludus training field. She was surprised at how much it soothed her rattled nerves. But in the back of her mind she wondered if she was truly ready for this. Her leg felt fine, but would it tolerate the extreme test of an arena match? More important, could she herself still endure a match?

The roar of the crowd grew as Julianus motioned Amazonia and Priedens into position.

"Be on guard . . ." he yelled as he dropped the rod between them.

Amazonia crouched slightly, sliding the bottom edge of her large scutum forward and positioning her gladius along the right edge of the scarlet shield. She watched the tip of her opponent's sica as it wavered, ready to thrust, and felt a chill rush up her spine. She checked her position behind the scutum and lowered the shield a bit further. She needed to protect her leg.

Julianus's pole jerked back. "Attack!"

Before Amazonia had a chance to move, Priedens thrust forward. His sica struck her scutum and glanced off the top edge. Her left shoulder stung. The razor-sharp blade had cut a small gash. She had lowered her shield too far, and her experienced foe had exploited the error.

She ducked sideways and struck back hard with two slashes that collided with her opponent's small square shield. The parry halted his initial advance. But only seconds into the fight she was pumping blood down her shield arm. Her mind flashed back to Quintus's fight just moments earlier. The blood that had run down Livius's arm had had devastating consequences. Was she done for already?

Wasting no time, Priedens came at her again. His sica swung with a force that belied his small frame. Although Amazonia stood a head taller, she had difficulty blocking the blows as she retreated. How could this be happening? Her usual aggressive offense was quickly deteriorating into a sloppy and ineffective defense. Panic began to overwhelm her.

Priedens pressed forward. His arm moved quickly. First an assault from the right, then three blows from the left. Amazonia continued stepping backward, using the scutum as best she could to impede the attack. Although the afternoon breeze was cool, she felt sweat bead on her forehead. It would soon be running into her eyes. The clamor of the mob echoed in her helmet. Within the cacophony, she detected Quintus's voice across the arena.

"Attack him! Take a stand and attack him!"

She tried to heed his advice, but Priedens would not allow it. The thraex was almost on top of her, hammering away. His aggressiveness forced her to give ground, and she shuffled backward through the sand that had given her comfort earlier. Now the softness worked against her. She stepped into a shallow depression and began to fall. In panic and frustration she struggled to thrust her shield forward and managed to catch Priedens on his advancing leg. The sudden jolt, combined with his momentum, tossed him forward. He landed in a heap on top of her, his sica pinned between his own body and her scutum. She wrapped her long legs around his lean torso and pulled him close. It was a move she had used often in her days as a prostitute when a client became a bit too aggressive. And it brought a mixed reaction from the mob: some cheers, some jeers. But she didn't care. All she wanted was time. Held tightly, Priedens was helpless to move or swing his weapon. Unfortunately, his close position also prevented Amazonia from finding flesh with her own gladius. The sand and dust churned as she wrestled desperately to keep her opponent pinned and stay alive.

"What in Hades is wrong with you?" a voice screamed from the side.

She glanced through her helmet eyepiece to see Julianus lying chest down in the sand next to them. Fury raged in his squinting eyes.

"You think this crowd's going to spare you with this kind of performance? You think just because your tits are bouncing around out here they're going to let you live? You'd better save yourself, woman, because you're as good as dead. Now *fight!*"

The final shouted word acted like a hammer breaking a cask of wine. All of the emotions—nervousness, apprehension, frustration, and anger—came flooding out of Amazonia in a torrent. Her right hand tensed on the hilt of her gladius. She released her leg lock and with the power of Hercules in her arms, she pushed Priedens off her with enough force to send him flying backward in an arc. Before he hit the ground, she was on her feet with a fluid move that brought her legs under her and her torso upright in the blink of an eye.

Priedens landed hard on his back, but rolled quickly and got to his feet as Amazonia reached him. As if it had a mind of its own, her gladius swung in a series of slashes and thrusts that forced her opponent into an immediate retreat. The faster she slashed, the quicker he retreated. She matched him stride for stride, her attack growing more forceful with each step. Finally, she saw him wobble. It was now his turn at a misstep in the uneven sand. It was just the opportunity she was looking for. With her next step, she twisted into a kick that sent her long right leg spinning. As it came around, her foot crashed into the side of her challenger's helmet. A roar rose from the crowd. It was the move they had been waiting for, Amazonia's signature.

Priedens staggered. Amazonia launched another spin kick, this time aiming low. Her foot connected, knocking her opponent's legs out from under him. He hit the sand with a thud, and she was on him quickly, gladius poised under his quivering chin.

Julianus grabbed her arm and peered through the helmet grating. His calm, pleasant smile helped settle her racing heartbeat.

"See . . . all you needed was a little motivation."

Amazonia returned the smile and looked toward the tunnel entrance where Quintus and Lindani stood cheering. She nodded to the two friends who meant more to her than anyone else.

On the podium, the magistrate abided by the crowd's wishes and allowed Priedens to leave the arena alive. Relieved, not only by the win but by not having to take the man's life, Amazonia dropped her helmet and shield and raised her gladius in triumph. She whirled in a brief victory spin that had the crowd on its feet, every man and woman in the cavea straining to see the exotic charm she radiated. Her elegant face, framed by the mane of reddish-brown hair, almost seemed incongruous on the muscular body that was beginning to carry the array of cuts and scars so common to gladiators. She knew what the people of Pompeii wanted from her, and she was happy to oblige as long as the coin purses continued to fall from the podiums of the Empire. As a prostitute, all the money went to her pimp father. But here in the arena, what was awarded to her by the editor stayed in her own pocket. She swaggered toward the podium, pausing once, then twice for another spin, each ending in a pose designed to accentuate the remarkable curves of her body.

"An interesting wrestling match, Amazonia," the editor called to her as she approached. "I thought you had had it there for a moment, but you pulled it out. Congratulations."

He tossed the palm and coin purse to the sand. As in her previous arena win, she retrieved the money first. She clutched the bag to her bare breasts, bowed toward the podium, then stepped toward the tunnel entrance.

The magistrate addressed the crowd. "People of Pompeii . . . I thank you for helping me honor both Saturn and Galba, our revered emperor in Rome. May he bring us out from under the dark cloud of Nero's reign, and may the Empire return to its path of strength, culture, and learning. All hail Caesar."

The cavea responded with a boisterous salute to the new emperor, signifying the end of another long day of games at the busy resort town.

Quintus winked at Amazonia as she passed. "Good save," he said. He glanced back through the portal and noticed that not a single person left the cavea until the stunning gladiatrix was well out of sight in the dark tunnel.

"She holds their attention, no?" Lindani said with his bright smile.

"You didn't do so badly yourself," Quintus responded as they followed Amazonia down the dark passageway. "Picking off thirty antelope with thirty arrows, then finishing up with two bears skewered on a single spear seemed to hold their attention pretty well, too."

Lindani shrugged. "It is what I do."

As always, Quintus was struck by how unassuming his friend was about the miracles he performed during his hunts. But as modest as he was in the passageways and holding cells deep under the amphitheater, his flamboyant style and incredible skill in the arena made him a true legend in the Empire. In the few years Quintus had known him, he had witnessed this young Ethiopian doing battle with hippopotamus, crocodile, bear, boar, auroch, lion, and leopard, usually with little more than a hunting spear in hand. In his astounding displays with bow and arrow, Quintus had seen stag, antelope, gazelle, and ostrich dispatched in bizarre and imaginative ways, always to the total delight and fascination of the crowd.

The tunnel led to a large holding room, now bustling with activity at the games' end. The gravelly voice of Titus Petra, one of the two Pompeiian lanistae, rose above the noises. From his tone, it was obvious he was not happy.

"What was that, Amazonia? You call that a good bout? I thought you were ready." The stocky lanista approached her with authority, despite the fact that he had to tilt his bald head back significantly to look her in the eye. The plentiful scars that marred his aged arms and legs spoke of considerable combat encounters of his own. He stared past his broken nose, waiting for a response.

"I *am* ready, Dominus," Amazonia replied. "It was a bad start. I lowered the scutum to protect my leg and he came over the top. It won't happen again."

"It better not happen again. You need to forget about that damn leg of yours. It's healed. Understand me?"

"Yes, Dominus."

"You want to keep getting those coin purses?"

"Yes, Dominus."

"Then get your mind off that fucking leg and into the fight."

"Yes, Dominus," she replied, but Petra had already pushed past her, on his way to count the substantial sum he and his ludus partner, Facilix, would split for providing the fighters for the day's games.

Amazonia threw her gladius into the weapons box with a crash. The attendant grumbled, then kicked the lid closed. From the rough wooden bench she snatched the scarf Petra had provided to cover herself. Quintus stepped forward and took the ends to tie them behind her.

"He just wants to see you do well," Quintus said quietly from behind, although he sensed her anger was directed more at herself than at the tough lanista.

"I know. Just protecting his investment, right?" she replied dryly.

"Is that so wrong? If the dominus loses a draw like you, that's a serious blow to the ludus. You know we all incur his wrath when we fuck up out there." Quintus finished tying the knot and spun her gently to face him and Lindani. "But that's not what this is about, is it?"

He watched her eyes flicker between him, Lindani, and the floor. The spark of life he used to see in her radiant emerald eyes seemed dim. He knew it wasn't just the faint torchlight of the holding area. There was more to it than that.

"It's hard, Quintus. I just can't muster the fight anymore." She pulled away and sat on the wooden bench. She continued, but spoke to the stone wall. "I keep seeing that fucking hoplomachus with his spear in my leg. I thought I was dead. The euphoria of living through it got me through the next few weeks. But the more time passes, the more clearly I keep seeing that damn spear in my leg. I can still feel it puncturing my skin and tearing my muscles apart." She finally looked up at Quintus. "I lost my concentration for a split second that day in Rome, and it almost cost me my life. Then, because I was uneasy about it, I did exactly the same thing here today. If Julianus hadn't been there, I'd probably be dead now."

Quintus thought for a moment. "Maybe. Maybe not. What's important is that you overcame the fear, you mustered the fight. The instinct is still there, and that's what matters most."

Lindani sat down next to her. "I have looked into the jaws of death many times. They snap so close to me I smell the beast's last meal. On those nights I, too, refight the venatio in my head many times. I, too, wake up cold with sweat. But then I remember that my life is with the

Fates. When they say I die, I die." He shrugged and flashed his gleaming smile at her. "But until then, I live, no?"

For the first time in a few days, Quintus saw Amazonia smile. Lindani's simple approach to life always seemed to open eyes once clouded by troubles and self-doubt.

The loud clang of a helmet falling into the weapons box startled them all. Julianus, their head trainer and arena referee, stood over them looking at Amazonia, a squint still etched in the eyes astride his aquiline nose. He wiped the sweat that matted his curly black hair to his forehead.

"I guess you already heard it from the dominus, so I'm not going to say it again. Just get your fight back, Amazonia. I can train your mind and body, but I can't train your spirit."

"I know, Doctore. Like I told the dominus, it won't happen again. I'm just glad you were out there with me. I'm glad you got back in time."

"Believe me, I'd rather be here than still in Africa. The dominus's old ludus in Thysdrus does not compare well with our schools in Pompeii and Britannia."

Lindani nodded. Having spent many months in Petra's African ludus before being shipped north, he knew its horrors well.

"I will agree with that, Doctore." Lindani looked at Quintus, and his wide smile returned. "It is not a good place for the people of Rome."

The four of them laughed at the simple statement, none harder than Quintus. Although it had been more than a year, he always laughed as he remembered the wagon rolling out of Rome with Julianus at the reins and Lucius Calidius locked in the back. He remembered Lucius's wailing cries floating over the hills of Rome when he learned his fate. To Quintus, it was more than justice. It was almost spiritual. To see his one-time slave, who had stolen his identity, manipulated his relatives against him, and turned his family's good name to one of shame . . . to see him locked in the back of a ludus wagon and dragged off as a latrine slave to one of the toughest, filthiest, most remote gladiator schools in the Empire was blissful.

As the ludus attendants gathered the weapons and equipment, and the other fighters lined up for the march back to the nearby barracks, Quintus stared at the wall. He mindlessly rubbed the tiny icon that hung from his neck. His mind was a thousand miles away in a steamy, tropical environment.

He wondered what his ex-slave was doing that very moment in the African ludus.

II

December AD 68

PICK THAT BUCKET of shit up right now, or by the gods, you'll be eating it for supper tonight!"

The shrill voice of the dispensator pierced Lucius's ears like a knife. From the day he had arrived at Titus Petra's ludus in the remote North African town of Thysdrus, Lucius had hated the short, depraved superintendent and his womanly voice. In fact, he hated everything about the ludus: the squalid cells, the inedible food, the foul temperament of the entire work staff. But mostly he hated the vile chores that were his responsibility.

He knew he was running behind schedule in his afternoon rounds of the ludus latrines. But he had taken a moment to rest on the edge of a latrine seat, his back aching badly from a day spent hauling timbers for the construction of new barrack cells. That is how the superintendent had found him on his surprise inspection.

"You want a rest? Is that it?" the little overseer screamed.

"No, sir. I'm sorry."

The forced apology made Lucius bite his tongue with anger. It took every ounce of strength for him to stand up and lift the overflowing buckets. Ever since the cook had changed the recipe for the troupe's miselania, now adding a powerful cumin-like spice to the gruel, the latrines had been even more revolting than usual. While most of the men's prodigious waste ended up in the troughs beneath the line of stone seats, there were some men—mostly the criminals from regional nomadic tribes—who insisted on defecating while squatting on the floor. They had been beaten for it often, but continued the practice as a form of protest against the harsh treatment dealt out by the trainers and guards. The more civilized fighters and ludus workers simply shook their heads in disgust and steered clear of the reeking piles. But Lucius had no such luxury. Just as he did in the horse stables every morning, he had to shovel the feces into buckets and dump it into the dung pit outside the ludus gates. As he headed for the door, a full bucket in each hand, he heard the high-pitched voice from Hades again.

"You missed a pile, asshole," the dispensator screeched, pointing toward a far dark corner.

Lucius put the buckets down and reached for the shovel he had left leaning against the cracked wall.

"Fucking animal," he mumbled. The statement was meant as a slur on the nomad who had left the pile. But the superintendent misinterpreted.

"What did you say?" he screamed. "Fucking animal? I'll show you a fucking animal, you vermin scum!"

"No, sir. I meant . . ."

But before another word reached Lucius's lips, one of the buckets was sailing through the air at his head. He tried to duck, but it was too late. The foul bucket hit him hard in the face, spilling its repulsive contents across his chest and into his nose and mouth. Lucius gagged, wiping frantically at his face. The overwhelming stench forced him to double over and vomit. He fell to his knees, gasping for breath while he continued to wipe the wet feces from his face. He saw red streaks in the brown filth and realized his nose was bleeding. The stinging twinges that shot through his face when he wiped at the nostrils told him it was most certainly broken. Out of the corner of his eye he saw the black leather boots of the dispensator walk up beside him.

"I didn't mean you," Lucius gasped between more dry heaves.

He did not expect an apology from the short man, but neither did he expect his day to get even worse. It did. A searing pain shot across his back, accompanied by a loud crack. Lucius was sure his spine had snapped, until he saw half the pole from his shovel fall on the floor next to him. A second whack with the now shortened stick followed.

"You ever talk to me like that again and I'll kill you on the spot," the dispensator squeaked. His foot delivered a sharp blow to Lucius's side for added emphasis. "Now clean up this mess before I get back, or this little episode will be the highlight of your day."

Lucius heard the other half of the shovel hit the stone floor and the man's footsteps fade into the distance. He could barely muster the strength to open his eyes. He pushed himself to a sitting position, trying to ignore the throbbing that grew in his head and the welts he felt rising across his back. The thought of another go-around with the mad superintendent motivated him to block out the pain and use the remaining half of the shovel to finish his job. Luckily, the rapid swelling in his nose impeded the stench. He refilled the bucket and used rags and water to sop up the last remnants from the floor, after first wiping what he could from his mouth, hair, and what was once an oatmeal colored tunic.

He lumbered out the door and across the vacant training field, lugging his two pails. A guard pulled open the rear gate and hastily waved him past, not wanting to smell either the slave or his payload. Lucius made his way down the small hill to the edge of a deep cesspool and emptied both buckets. He walked back up the hill and stood for a moment to take in the surroundings. Although his swollen nose blocked the pleasant scent he knew was there, the cool breeze drifting across the green hills was a heavenly change from inside the ludus walls. On more than one occasion he had considered dashing for freedom across the venator training field and into the olive groves and vineyards that ringed the ludus grounds. But in a town as small and isolated as Thysdrus there would be few places to hide. And the punishment for a runaway slave was usually crucifixion. The chance of making it safely to the Mediterranean coast twenty-five miles away without being recaptured was slim at best. And even if he got that far, where would he go? He knew well that there was no future for him anywhere beyond the walls of this ludus.

He turned and walked back through the gates, concerned that the enraged dispensator would once again seek him out for tormenting. He kept as low a profile as he could for the rest of the evening. He ate quickly and quietly with the other slaves. But being the lowest of the slaves, his day did not end with supper as most of the others' did. He cleaned the staff mess area, helped the kitchen workers with the pots, and made sure everything was ready to begin the monotonous cycle again in the morning.

A few hours after dusk he finally trudged to his cell and was locked in by the night guard. As the bolt was thrown, he thought about how low his life had sunk when the best part of his day was being locked away in a two-person cell that was barely big enough for one person. But that was only on the nights when his cellmate, a brawny one-armed Bedouin slave named Bersuq, was too tired for sex. Yes, nights at the ludus could bring their own special kind of hell. Although Lucius had grown physically in the past year due to the never-ending manual labor, he had never been able to fight off the Bedouin. Thankfully, Bersuq's loud snores told him tonight would be a peaceful night.

Lucius lay on the dirt floor. His curly brown hair was matted with dried waste and his brown eyes were red with weariness. The dim orange light from a torch in the corridor filtered through the barred window in the door and flickered on the rough timbers that made up the ceiling. As he watched the dancing shadows, the coolness of the sandstone foundation helped relieve the burning of his welts. He wondered how many more days like this he could endure. The only certainty to his future at the ludus was that things would never change. While other slaves eventually moved up in their standing, the worst of their responsibilities eventually passing on to the newer unfortunates, Lucius knew he would not be so lucky. When Julianus had delivered him to the remote ludus over a year ago, he had left explicit instructions that Lucius was not to be promoted in any manner. His rank would always be considered the lowest of the low and his chores would always be the worst of the worst. This was a directive from the head lanista himself, Cassius Petra.

Lucius rolled over quietly, so as not to wake Bersuq and end the day with even more humiliation. He swatted at a rat which had crawled close, attracted by the smell of his tunic. His broken nose had cleared a bit, and the reek made it hard to sleep but he dared not remove the garment, lest Bersuq misinterpret the action as an invitation. As he lay there watching the rat scurry back and forth, the events in the latrine replayed in his mind. He did not blame the dispensator for the smell on his tunic or the welts on his back. Just as he did not blame the armorer who had struck him the previous day, or the gladiators who threw food they did not like at him, or the rat who had gnawed at the open sore on his arm while he slept the week before. No, there was only one person to blame for all of this pain, suffering, and humiliation: Quintus Honorius Romanus.

Lucius did his best to block the memories of his past life from his head. The thought of rising from common household slave to magistrate of Aquae Sulis to Imperial Advisor for Britannia Affairs under the Emperor Nero himself was fine. But the part where he was forced to return to a slave life a thousand times worse than his original role in Rome was too much to bear. He readied for mental battle, as he often did when he became depressed in his cell. For as much as he wanted to blame Quintus Romanus for his situation, his subconscious would constantly struggle to remind him that his quandary had more to do with his own actions than anything Quintus had done.

He rolled over again and tried to push the thoughts from his mind, but he knew they would come anyway. Once it got this far, there was no turning back. The "what if" scenarios were about to parade once again through his head like a gladiators' pompa, cornu horns blasting so loudly he could not understand why Bersuq did not hear them.

What if that cursed storm had not shipwrecked them on the way to Britannia? What if he and Quintus had not been the only two to survive? What if he had not used the opportunity of an injured and unconscious

Quintus to convince the boy's aunt and uncle in Britannia that he himself was Quintus Romanus? What if he had not been pushed onto the first rung of a political ladder by those new relatives? Then his life would never have crossed again with Quintus Honorius Romanus. The events that led Quintus to become a gladiator were still a mystery to him. All he knew was the overwhelming shock he had felt looking into the arena from the editor's podium in Rome—during the games he himself had sponsored—and staring into the eyes of the only man in the Empire who knew his true identity. The thought of that incident made him curl up and hug his legs. He knew he had had no choice on that day in Rome. He had to eliminate this threat once and for all. But his rage had blinded him to rational thinking. After the lions had failed to carry out his sentence, Lucius had pushed aside the arena manager and attempted to release more beasts himself. But the yank of that single cage bolt—the *wrong* bolt—resulted in this ludus cell. The instant he had mistakenly let those three bulls loose in the seats of the amphitheater rather than the arena floor, he had become *persona non grata* in Rome. He rocked back and forth on the filthy cell floor as his mind raced. What if he had pulled the right bolt? What if the bulls had simply dispatched his rival? Then Quintus would not have been able to track him down, toss him into that cursed ludus cart, and have him shipped to the armpit of the Empire.

Despite the cool evening, Lucius was sweating now. His muscles were tight knots and his nerves discharged in shakes and spasms. He rolled over again, agitating the rat, as he tried to drive the images from his mind. Each time he was depressed, each time he put himself through this mental torture, it became worse and worse. His hopelessness fed on his regrets, his despair fueled by the stupid mistakes caused by his own blind rage. He once tried to console himself by thinking of the disgrace he at least had brought to the name Quintus Honorius Romanus. But it didn't help because Quintus was no longer known in public by that name. He was now "Taurus" to his hordes of fans. And those in the ludus close to Quintus who *did* know his true name were well aware that he was not the maniac who had destroyed the sanctity of the games on that dark day, causing the deaths of dozens of innocent spectators.

Lucius's realization that he had not even succeeded in tarnishing Quintus's name drove him further into despair. It was a despair that had visited him often lately. He knew that these thoughts were, quite simply, driving him mad. The past few times he had undergone this self-inflicted anguish, the only images that finally brought reprieve were those of his own death. Seeing himself hanging in his cell, or dropping onto one of the kitchen knives, or being trampled by one of the stabled horses brought him a strange sense of calm. But once sleep came, the dawn of a new morning always seemed to wash away the will to die. By the following day, he could never muster the courage it took to commit the suicidal act. Perhaps tomorrow would be different, for the way he felt—and even smelled—on this night was far worse than any other over the previous year.

The bang of the door bolt being drawn back jolted Lucius to an upright position. If he had fallen asleep, it could not have been for long. No morning light spilled through the door when it was pulled open, only the slightly brighter flicker of the torch in the corridor.

"Lucius, on your feet!" yelled one of the guards.

As he stood up, his head spun with a combination of weariness and physical pain from his bruised and battered back. Bersuq grunted but didn't wake. Lucius stepped over his cellmate, and his mind raced. Was the dispensator about to dole out even more punishment? How much pain would he have to endure for a single misunderstood comment?

The guard reached in to grab his tunic to hurry him along but thought better of it when he saw and smelled the brown stain across his chest.

"Hurry it up, shit crust. The magister has called for you."

Lucius wondered why the ludus master was summoning him at this time of night. He shuffled down the corridor, feeling the blunt end of the guard's staff prodding him in the back to keep moving. They emerged from the slave quarters, crossed the dark practice field, and entered the colonnaded portico on the far side. As they approached the door of the magister's office near the front gate, the guard pushed Lucius aside with the rod, stepped forward and knocked on the door.

"Enter," came a voice from inside.

The guard pulled open the latch and shoved Lucius through the portal. Didius Fronto, a stocky middle-aged man with a mop of curly brown hair, was seated reviewing notes on a wax tablet on the well-worn table before him. A single oil lamp sent a warm halo across the desktop and onto the administrator's wide torso. An ex-gladiator himself, trained personally by Petra, Fronto acted as the lanista at the Thysdrus ludus in Petra's absence. But the sight of the tough administrator grabbing at his nose as Lucius approached the desk was almost comical.

"Jupiter's holy ass! What in Hades have you been doing to smell like that?"

Lucius tried his best to keep the venom from his voice. "There was a bit of a misunderstanding in the latrine today."

"Well, that doesn't surprise me. You've been nothing but a pain in everyone's ass since you got here. I don't know if this rather . . . odorous situation changes anything . . ." The magister paused and glanced over Lucius's shoulder, then shrugged. "It appears this handsome woman has requested the company of someone like you for the evening." Raising an eyebrow and averting his eyes down to the tablet, he finished in a mumble ". . . although the gods only know why."

Lucius thought for a moment that he was still in his cell dreaming. Only the top gladiators were rented out for orgies and sex. He was a lowly latrine slave. He turned and glanced over his shoulder. In the shadows at the corner of the room he could barely make out the figure of a woman. She seemed attractive in stature, but it was too dark to make out any features. Lucius was certain she would resemble the horses he dealt with in the ludus stables.

"I tried to talk her into one of our fine fighters," Fronto said as he scratched some additional notes into the wax with a stylus, "or even an

African hunter, but she insisted on the lowest slave we had in our ranks." He paused and looked toward the guard who stood beside Lucius. "Everyone's into their own little games, I guess . . . bizarre as they may be."

Lucius heard the guard snicker beside him. The magister returned his attention to the tablet.

"Anyway, everything's in order, madam. If you would just sign here. You're pledging to keep him under lock and key and that he'll be returned in the morning. Is there anything else you need?"

Lucius heard her step forward.

"No, this one will do just fine."

The shock hit Lucius's body with the force of a large hammer. Although he had not heard the voice in what seemed like a decade, he knew it very well. It was the voice that had coaxed him and comforted him over many years, had screamed at him in anger and sighed with him in passion, had whispered both trivial tidbits and critical affairs of state into his ear. He turned and watched Julia Melita step from the shadows.

She was even more striking than his faded memory had pictured her over the past year. Her dark hair was pulled back with a black and gold band and tied in a bun, a few strands out of place, perhaps from the long ride to Thysdrus from wherever she had landed in Africa. Her long white stola and green palla showed signs of dust, but the low-cut neckline distracted the male eye from any imperfection.

As she stepped forward, the look in her eyes told Lucius to keep quiet and not acknowledge their relationship. He marveled at how, after more than a year apart, their nonverbal communication was as fine-tuned as ever. It was as if they had just been apart for a few nights.

"I'll have the guard escort you to the gate," Fronto said as Julia bent forward to mark the tablet, providing an ample display of her full breasts in the process.

"That won't be necessary," she said with a smile. "I'm sure he won't be giving me any problems. Will you . . ." She made a point of glancing down at the notes in wax, as if reading his unknown name. ". . . Lucius?"

This was the "Aunt" Julia he remembered so fondly—calculating, scheming, and using her best assets to her advantage. "No, madam. No trouble at all," he replied.

Julia placed a good-sized bag on the magister's table. The sound it made as it hit the mahogany told Lucius it contained a substantial sum of money.

"That will be all, Paetus," the magister said to the guard, his gaze never leaving the bag of coins.

As the door closed behind the guard, Fronto sat forward and untied the string at the top of the purse. Lucius saw his eyebrow raise as he looked into the bag. He knew at that moment he was a free man.

"This seems to be substantially more than we discussed, madam."

Julia smiled. "Yes, it is. In fact, it's exactly four times more than we discussed."

There was an awkward silence as the two simply looked at each other. Finally, the magister spoke.

"Am I to interpret this as a bribe then?"

"Not at all." Julia leaned further over the desk. Lucius watched Fronto's eyes dart up and down between Julia's face and chest. "Let's just say it's payment in advance for the death of a lowly latrine slave. I'd say there's more than enough there to replace him, plus put a few hundred dinarii in your own pocket for your time and trouble."

Fronto smiled at her. "But the slave isn't dead, madam."

"No, but he soon will be." She leaned on Fronto's desk and used her upper arms to squeeze her breasts together as she whispered, "I enjoy a little violence once in a while. Don't you?" She punctuated the question with a wink and a depraved grin.

Lucius had known from the moment he saw Julia step forward that she would have a plan worked out. His death was perfect. It would prevent the inevitable search for an escaped slave and allow them the time needed to flee the region, probably back to Britannia.

The magister cleared his throat and glanced up at Lucius. "I don't know what it is about this slave, but it seems he's always at the center of one intrigue or another. Petra left explicit instructions on his future here. I can't risk the wrath of my lanista over something like this. He could make my life as difficult as that of the slaves." He pushed the bag of gold coins back across the table. "I'm afraid the answer is no."

Lucius felt his muscles tensing. He was not about to walk back to that dismal cell, not after coming this close to freedom. He would dive across the desk and beat some sense into the magister. Of course, he knew he would die in the process, but right now that would be preferable to returning to his one-armed cellmate, the womanly dispensator, and all the other miserable ludus dwellers. Julia's voice interrupted his rising fury.

"Wait outside, slave," she said in a harsh tone. "The magister and I have business to discuss." She leaned further forward, placing her elbows on the thick leather-bound volume at the edge of the desk and dipping her fingers into the bag, the gold coins clinking as she toyed with them. Fronto was about to speak, but Julia continued. "Your gates are well guarded."

The magister stared openly at her breasts, her nipples now fully revealed in the swoop of her stola. He glanced at Lucius and gruffly pointed toward the door with his chin.

Lucius hid his smile. He turned and walked out the door, latching it securely behind him. He sat in the dirt, gently resting his tender back against the rough wood to be sure Julia's "negotiations" were not interrupted by another ludus worker. While the muffled voices behind him progressed to stifled grunts and groans of passion, Lucius let his mind wander. His time in Hades was about to come to an end. His mind drifted to thoughts of freedom. What will his first meal be? How will fine woolens and Egyptian cotton once again feel against his skin? How long will he float naked in the warm waters of the baths? What will a proper bed feel like? Behind him, the rhythmic cries of lust intensified. In an odd way, he was jealous. He knew well the sensual pleasures that the uninhibited Julia was capable of delivering to a man. He remembered their first liaisons behind "Uncle" Sextus's back at the Britannia villa. And he could picture her in action at Nero's massive orgies in Rome, as well as their own private parties with select senators and wives. Yes, Julia was a connoisseur. And she knew how to use her talents to get what she wanted. But what *did* she want? The thought suddenly cut short his fantasies of freedom. Why was she here, after all? Why would she spend a substantial sum for a long sea voyage and pay such a hefty fee to rescue him from a North African ludus cell? He knew her well enough to know that it wasn't simply for the pleasure of his company. Not Julia. She always had a motive, and it always focused on Julia.

The muffled, passionate cries from the office came to an abrupt end. After a moment, he heard the latch click above his head and stood to face a damp Julia and a sopping wet Fronto. On the desk behind them, Lucius noticed two bags where one had been before.

"Guard, allow these people to pass," the magister yelled toward the front gate. He looked toward Lucius. "As of now, I'm considering you dead and out of my hair. Enjoy your final night, asshole."

With that, the door slammed in Lucius's face. His blood began to boil, and he reached for the latch. Julia's hand grabbed his wrist with authority.

"Don't you even think about it," she hissed. "I just screwed that pig's brains out to get you out of here, and you think you're going to fuck it up because he insulted you? What kind of an idiot are you?"

Before he could respond, she pulled him by the arm to the gate. The guard lifted the beam and kicked open the large door. He chuckled as they passed.

"Enjoy your evening. Hope you clean him up a bit first," he said, fanning his hand in front of his face as they passed.

Lucius heard the laughs of two other sentries come from inside the guard shack. But now that he was past the gates and on his way to freedom, he knew the last laugh belonged to him.

As they approached a waiting coach, an elderly driver jumped from his seat and pulled open the door. He offered his hand, and Julia took it as she stepped up into the lush interior. The driver staggered back a step when he saw and smelled Lucius approaching.

Lucius sneered at the slave. "Just drive, old man."

He pushed past and stepped up into the coach. The interior was about the same size as his cell, but the contrast in ambiance could not have been more striking. He sat on the wide upholstered seat across from Julia. Next to her, a short white tunic edged with bands of geometric patterns was laid out on the seat.

"Please put it on and get rid of that shit-covered slave garb," Julia said. She stared at him for a moment. He almost detected a look of sympathy in her eyes. "What in Jupiter's name happened to your nose?"

In his euphoria, Lucius had forgotten all about his broken nose. He touched it and winced at the pain and its swollen size. "A bit of a dis-agreement with the dispensator . . . a foul man whose balls should shrivel and fall off, if the gods are listening."

The horse-whip cracked, and the coach lurched forward. Lucius laughed as he pulled the oatmeal tunic over his head. He sat back naked, opened his arms, and gave Julia a leering smile.

One edge of her mouth curled up, dashing Lucius's hopes. "Not until you clean up a bit. We're heading for Carthage, where my ship is docked. They have a spectacular bath house. We should be there just before dawn. We'll get a physician to look at that nose, too."

"What baths will be open at that time of the morning?" he said as he balled up the soiled tunic and cocked his arm to throw it out the window.

"I slipped the manager of the baths a few dinarii to open early for us." She grabbed his upright arm. ". . . And I wouldn't toss that here. It's too close to the ludus. Wait until we get outside of town."

Lucius dropped the old tunic on the floor and donned the new white one, savoring the feel of the fleece-like Egyptian cotton against his bat-tered and aching body.

"It's always the simple things you miss," he said as he closed his eyes and leaned back into the soft cushions of the coach seat. "You cannot imagine the misery I've been through. Tasks unfit for an animal, beatings every day, inedible food, snakes and vermin everywhere . . ." He paused to open his eyes. "It would have been good of you to come a little sooner."

The sarcastic tone annoyed Julia. "You think it's been easy for me? After your debacle in the amphitheater I was lucky to get out of Rome alive. The mob was out for my blood just as much as yours. I had to pay a cart driver two hundred sesterces to lay under the garbage in his cargo bed all the way to Ostia. Thank the gods one of our ships was in port delivering textiles from Alexandria. The captain hid me belowdeck until he set sail the next morning. It cost me a fortune to re-route him to Britannia. Luckily, news of our little escapade never reached Sextus or anyone else in Aquae Sulis. I told him Nero sent you on a special mission to Dalmatia, so I returned without you. Thankfully, he didn't ask a lot of questions."

"Ah, Sextus . . . How is the old man?" Lucius asked, not really caring. "Still up to his ass in the Aquae Sulis shop?"

Julia looked down at her lap. "He's dead, Lucius."

The news took Lucius by surprise. While he had never really been close to Sextus, the man did take him in, teach him the textile business, and finance his run for the magistrate's seat.

"I'm sorry to hear that. How did he die?"

Julia's head stayed low. "You know he always liked his food. He grew heavier and heavier until he just couldn't handle it."

It had been obvious to Lucius and anyone else who had known them in Britannia that Julia and Sextus had never enjoyed a loving relationship. She always seemed to view it more as a business arrangement, a way to finance her social climb. Sextus was happy building and running textile shops in the provinces, while she wanted the lavish lifestyle of Roman high society. Yet Lucius could see she was clearly affected by her husband's death. She finally looked up at him.

"That's why it took me so long to get here. I had a lot of affairs to put in order. I not only had the textile business to deal with, but remember, we took over the entire Romanus shipping fleet after his sister died."

Lucius knew the story well, for she had died in the same shipwreck that killed his own mother. It was the night that had changed all their lives.

"So are you running the businesses yourself now?"

"Not on your life. I brought in a managing partner, another textile merchant in Aquae Sulis. He runs it day to day, but the majority of the profits are mine. And I have to say . . . the shipping business, combined with three large shops, is a very lucrative arrangement." A sly smile crossed her lips. "How else could I afford to bribe lanistae and bath house managers?"

"I'm glad to see you're putting your millions to good use," Lucius said, returning the smile. "I think you'll get a good return on this investment."

The coach rolled past the small houses that made up the outskirts of Thysdrus. A full moon hung low on the horizon, backlighting the rows of olive trees, wheat heads, and grapevines that covered most of the surrounding landscape. Julia picked up the reeking brown slave tunic from the floor and tossed it out the window.

She smiled at Lucius. "You can kiss that life good-bye . . . again."

Lucius interlaced his fingers behind his head, lay back on the soft cushions, and studied her round, attractive face. Although she now approached forty, it seemed she had not aged a day in the twenty months since he had last seen her. Even under a layer of dust kicked up off the African roads, she was still a remarkably beautiful woman.

"Why?" he asked.

Her smile broadened. "Why what?"

"Why did you come?"

She finally broke his gaze and looked out the window before she answered. "Would you believe me if I said I needed you?"

That was a generic answer, he thought. He closed his eyes and sighed. "Mhmm . . . And what is it you need from me?"

There was no response. He opened his eyes. She had turned and now looked directly into his face. There was hurt in her eyes and possibly the glisten of a tear. The full lips that had just held a smile now trembled slightly. But he knew this woman. He knew what an actress she could be when it suited her.

"I need you, Lucius. With Sextus, I had to be the woman he wanted me to be. But with you and me, it was different. I wasn't just the doting spouse, or the bedmate, or the stepping stone. I was your *partner*. During the last few months in Britannia I realized I want that again. I need that." The sorrowful look in her eyes turned sadder still. "I need you."

Lucius was shocked. In all the years he had known her, he had never seen her like this. Her voice and her eyes reflected nothing but honesty. But was it another brilliant performance? After all, she had managed to fool him for three years, never letting on that she had known all along he was not Quintus Romanus. At least not until it suited her. He had vowed then never to trust this woman again. But tonight she seemed different. Alone in this coach, on this lonely North African road, this strong-willed, independent woman seemed vulnerable, almost broken.

"Let's take it a step at a time." He knew it was a lame response, but he was not yet sure how to deal with this side of Julia. He looked to change the subject. "Will we stay in Carthage?"

Julia studied him for a moment before responding. "I do have an export office there with a few workers, but I don't think it's a good idea. It's too close to the Petra ludus. I was thinking about Alexandria."

"Really? Sounds exotic."

"Well, it's probably best we stay out of Rome for a while. We certainly can't go to Pompeii. And by the gods, I've had enough cold, damp Britannia weather to last me a lifetime."

"Where will we stay in Alexandria?"

"I hear the Romanus shipping fleet has a large office and a rather nice apartment there. I inherited it with the rest of the line, so we might as well put it to use."

It was the best arrangement he could have hoped for. Not only was he free of the horrid ludus, but he was crossing the threshold to a totally new world, ripe with unlimited possibilities and the financial resources to make them happen. What had started out as another miserable day, had certainly turned into one of the best days of Lucius's life. He couldn't help but laugh.

"What's so funny?" Julia asked.

Lucius could not answer. His laughter grew until it spilled out onto the road and echoed across the rolling green hills. The contagious nature of his bliss started Julia giggling like a little girl. Lucius finally took a breath and wiped a tear from his cheek.

"A little while ago I was lying in a cell, covered in shit, with a one-armed nomad and a rat, trying to decide on the best way to kill myself. Now I'm riding to the baths of Carthage in a luxury coach with one of the richest women in the Empire." Julia's giggling escalated to laughter. He closed his eyes and enjoyed the sweet sound and the softness of his surroundings. "I couldn't even dream about something like this in that shithole."

The swaying of the coach as it headed north on the Hadrumentum Road soothed Lucius into the first peaceful sleep he'd had in almost two years.

III

January AD 69

TITUS PETRA STEPPED from his cluttered office onto the open training field of the Pompeii ludus. He saw Oppius Facilix, his co-lanista, already inspecting the new fighters they had purchased the previous day at the slave market. Even after two years of working together running the large ludus, Petra still did not totally trust his partner. It was hard to forget the lies Facilix had handed him when Petra's troupe first arrived from Britannia for the well-promoted North vs. South games the two had arranged. Facilix's claim that his ludus barracks were suddenly full, forcing Petra's troupe to camp in a field outside Pompeii, was designed to demoralize Petra's fighters before the games. Then Facilix's last-minute substitution of a seasoned veteran to fight Amazonia—he had not wished to be the first lanista whose gladiator fell to a gladiatrix—caused a near riot in the amphitheater. But despite the rocky start, the two had come to terms on merging their respective ludi into the largest and most respected gladiator school outside the Ludus Magnus in Rome. Still, Petra viewed everything his partner did with suspicion. Facilix's beady little eyes, gaunt features, and devious manner didn't help the situation.

The clash of wooden practice weapons filled the air as Petra crossed the training field. "Already deciding their fighting disciplines?" Petra asked, annoyance clear in his tone.

Facilix looked up with his usual smirk. "Not without consulting my partner first."

"Right. I want Julianus to put them through their paces first. Then let him decide." Petra turned to walk toward the venator field, but Facilix grabbed his arm.

"So long as Justus agrees," he said, the false grin still plastered on his face. Both lanistae relied heavily on the advice of their head trainers. The problem was, their two head trainers distrusted each other more than the lanistae distrusted each other.

"Fine," Petra replied as he yanked his arm free. Despite the friction among the administrators, the Pompeiian ludus still managed to turn out some of the best fighters in the Empire, a testament to the top-quality doctores—the training staff—at the school.

Before he turned away, Petra's attention was drawn to a worker running toward them from the front gate. The excited slave approached Facilix.

"Dominus! There are a group of soldiers at the front gate demanding to speak with you. One is a tribune."

Facilix looked at Petra, a puzzled look now replacing the smirk. "What's this about?" he asked. "Requests for fighters aren't delivered by a tribune."

"Show them in," Petra said to the slave. "Bring them to my office."

"Better use my office," Facilix said. "A bit more room." His smile returned.

The two lanistae crossed the field quickly, calling for more chairs to be brought to the office, along with some bread and wine. Facilix had just a few moments to straighten some scrolls and volumes on his desk, when the door opened and the Roman tribune entered. Two centurions flanked the portal outside and closed the door behind their officer, remaining on the portico. It seemed the tribune did not want this meeting disturbed.

The man's military bearing commanded their immediate attention. His silver and brass muscle cuirass was aptly named, as the breastplate conformed well to his considerable chest. His helmet, matching the brilliance of his breastplate, sported a squat angular crest on top, an ornate brow plate trimmed in gold, and wide cheek pieces that tied under the

stubble of his chin. A long scarlet cloak draped his left shoulder and gathered gracefully behind his legs. From below the edge of his breastplate
hung a row of white lappets, covering most of his short white tunic, except
for the narrow band of purple signifying his rank. Maroon knee breeches
extended below the tunic and his feet were clad in the famous caligae open-
strap boots that defined a Roman soldier. The hobnails beneath the thick
soles rapped loudly on the tiled floor as he approached Facilix's desk.

"It's been a long ride from Rome, gentlemen," the officer said as he
pulled up a chair. "Some wine would be appreciated."

"We have some coming now, Tribune," Facilix said, settling behind the
desk. Petra pulled a chair to the side and sat, watching the tribune remove
his helmet and drop it on the floor next to him. The creases in the warrior's
face, combined with his bulbous, slightly purple nose, revealed a hard life.
Two slaves entered through a side door with a tray of bread and sliced
cheeses, a tall flask of wine, and some terra-cotta goblets.

Before Facilix could reach for the wine, his guest helped himself to the
decanter, pouring a full goblet. He downed half the contents in one gulp,
then ripped a handful of bread from one of the loaves and began stuffing
his mouth. He seemed in no rush to get to the point.

Petra let the man swallow, then leaned forward. "What can we do for
you, Tribune? We're a bit busy today with some new acquisitions."

The tribune looked at Petra as if noticing him for the first time. "Who
are you?"

"My name is Cassius Petra. This is Oppius Facilix. We're co-lanistae of
this ludus. And you are . . . ?"

"Co-lanistae, eh? That's an interesting arrangement. How does that
work?" The officer took another bite from his hunk of bread.

Petra was beginning to lose patience with the man's blustery attitude.
But Facilix spoke up before he could say any more.

"It's a unique business arrangement we worked out in order to join my
Pompeii ludus with Petra's Britannia ludus. We've developed a very powerful troupe of fighters and hunters here with our combined doctores."

The tribune, chewing and nodding, continued to stare at Facilix. There was an awkward moment of silence until Petra spoke up again.

"Like I said . . ." He waited again for the man's name.

"Martius Macer," the tribune finally disclosed, "senior tribune with the First Adjutrix Legion."

"We're busy here this morning, Tribune Macer. Is there something you need?"

Macer studied Petra for a long moment before he spoke. "Actually, there *is* something I need." He leaned back in his chair and propped his feet up on Facilix's desk. "Three hundred of your best fighters."

Petra looked at Facilix. It was clear his partner was as puzzled as he was.

"Why would the Roman army want three hundred gladiators?" Facilix asked.

Macer shrugged nonchalantly. "Because our emperor needs them."

"If Emperor Galba is looking to hold games, why send to Pompeii?" Facilix asked. "Is the Ludus Magnus running low again?"

The tribune tossed back his head in a blustery laugh, spraying bits of bread into the air. He let his chair fall forward as he reached for the wine flask again.

"Not at all. First of all, Galba is no longer emperor. He died two days ago . . . an unfortunate victim of assassination, I'm afraid."

"What?" both lanistae replied together. Petra sat forward, his mind calculating where this conversation was heading.

"So who is emperor?" Facilix asked.

"Marcus Salvius Otho has taken command of the Praetorian Guard. And we all know that whoever controls the Praetorians, controls Rome. So my money is on Otho."

Petra could tell something in this news did not sit right with his business partner.

"Why should he need the Praetorians to assume power?" Facilix asked warily. "I thought Otho was already considered next in line for the throne." Petra realized that his co-lanista's penchant for political gossip was an advantage in this conversation.

Macer finished a long swig from his wine cup and sneered at Facilix. "You and most of Rome. That decrepit bastard, Galba, was in his seventies and never had a son. Everyone assumed Otho would be adopted and named heir to the throne based on his long relationship with Galba. But the old fart shocked everyone and adopted that snot-nosed asshole, Piso. Otho won't stand for it. He knows he deserves the honor more than Piso." The tribune leaned forward and lowered his voice, the effects of the wine now starting to slur his speech. "Let's just say he took matters into his own hands."

"So if Otho controls the Praetorians, why do you need us?" Petra asked.

"Because the legions at Germania and the Rhine have pledged their allegiance to another . . . their own commander, Aulus Vitellius." The intensity grew in the tribune's eyes. "The man is an incompetent, fat buffoon. If Otho wouldn't stand for Piso claiming the principate, he certainly won't stand for an idiot like Vitellius claiming it."

It was exactly what Petra was dreading. He'd heard of gladiators being sucked into the legions before, but it had not happened for many decades. He had to try to discourage this idea. The thought of his prime fighters on the front lines of a bloodbath did not appeal to him in the least. There was no telling how many might die in the uncontrolled butchery of a battlefield.

"What good are three hundred gladiators going to do against the legions of Germania?" he asked.

"Three hundred alone . . . nothing. But your three hundred will be joining fourteen hundred from the Ludus Magnus in Rome and three hundred from Capua. A force of two thousand well-trained fighters could certainly augment the Praetorians and the Italian legions that have pledged allegiance to Otho. Besides, this is a temporary force. Your men just need to hold the Vitellians away from Rome long enough for the legions from Moesia and the Danube to arrive. They, too, have pledged for Otho."

Petra looked at Facilix. "So the slaughter of our men will be used simply as a diversionary tactic to slow down the Vitellians," he said to his partner. "I don't like it."

The tribune leaned forward with a hard look at Petra. Before he spoke, Facilix interjected the question that was always foremost on his mind. "How much?"

The tribune sneered at them both. "You should be doing this for the benefit of your new emperor, not for financial gain."

Facilix smirked at him. "Tribune, we are businessmen first and patriots second. How much?"

Macer leaned back in his chair with a loud laugh. "By the gods, when they call you lanistae 'pimps,' they're not kidding."

Petra bristled at the slur, but Facilix grabbed his arm before he did something they would both regret.

"Alright, alright," Macer continued, still laughing, "Otho has authorized me to offer you standard legionaries' pay for the use of your fighters. That's 900 sesterces per fighter—270,000 sesterces in all. But for that, we want only the best men, no tiros. And remember . . . we've been to the games; we know who they are."

"That's quite a bit less than our normal fee for our top fighters and hunters, Tribune," Facilix negotiated. "How long would the men be in your service?"

"For up to a year."

Facilix began shaking his head and Petra jumped to his feet. "After a year on the front lines, there will be no one left!" he yelled. "You must be joking." The lanista looked at his partner as he stepped toward the door. "I have to get back to the training field. I want to—"

Macer bolted off his seat and kicked the chair across the room hard enough to break it against the office wall. He grabbed Petra by the front of his green tunic, pulled him close, and looked down into the stocky man's face. The lanista's flat nose touched the tribune's purple, hooked beak.

"Look, you fucking pimp! This matter is not up for discussion."

Petra clenched his fists and prepared to swing at the officer. The situation reminded him of a fateful day many years earlier when he was a centurion in the legions. His violent reaction to a similar egotistical tribune in Britannia had cost him dearly. The memory sobered him, and he held his swing in check.

"When the lanista at Capua gave me a hard time yesterday," Macer continued, "he lost his administration building to an unfortunate fire. Then he saw things my way." The tribune looked around the well-used office. "You wouldn't want this fine building to end up a smoldering pile of ash, would you?"

Petra glared at the man, refusing to answer. Facilix spoke up quickly. "We can see you're well committed to Emperor Otho. We'd be honored to supply you the fighters you need. The rate you offered is acceptable."

"Fine," Macer answered as he released Petra with a shove. "I want murmillones, secutores, thraeces, provocatores, and your best hunters with spear and bow. And I want them trained for frontline combat. I'm the one who has to lead this fucking band of rabble into battle." He spat the words, obviously unhappy with his assignment. "I want killing machines. No fancy, drawn-out swordplay. I just want Vitellian guts at the end of each gladius." He snatched his helmet from the floor and reached for the closed door. "Have them ready in ten days." He threw open the door and strode out past his centurions, who fell into step behind him.

"Say good-bye to our ludus, Facilix," Petra said as he stepped forward and watched the soldiers push their way through the front gate. "I've been on the front lines against the barbarian hordes. It was like living in Hades. But that was nothing compared to what these battles will be. Now both sides possess the best-trained fighting force in the world."

They re-entered the office and shut the door. "We have no choice," Facilix said. "Plus, I seriously doubt there will be any games with all this going on. At least we'll make enough to cover our expenses for a while."

Petra looked at his partner and shook his head. "Don't count all your money yet, Facilix. I'm going to need some of that to bring in a trainer, one who understands the tactics of the legions." He turned and reached for the door.

"Where will we find a legionary instructor on the eve of civil war?" Facilix asked with some exasperation. "We have only ten days."

"I know just the person," Petra said as he left the office and headed toward the stables. "I'll have him here tomorrow."

IV

January AD 69

LUCIUS WATCHED the sparkling light on the horizon. In the past few moments he had noticed that it flashed in beat to the ship's rocking.

"What is that?" he called to the captain who stood atop the deckhouse.

"That's the lighthouse on the island of Pharos. It will guide us through the shoals by reflecting the sun with a polished metal disc. As night falls, you'll see the great flame lit." The captain ordered the two helmsmen to come about and they began the run into Alexandria's main harbor.

Lucius took a deep breath and closed his eyes, letting the late afternoon breeze caress his rejuvenated body. Although still hesitant to board a ship after the ordeal that had claimed his mother's life off Britannia, he welcomed any mode of transportation that took him far from the vile ludus of Thysdrus. After these days of luxurious freedom, he vowed he would never spend another day in servitude for the rest of his life.

He heard the creak of wood behind him and turned to see Julia emerge from the door of the deckhouse. The setting sun behind her added a warm halo around her dark hair. With a white handkerchief she patted at the beads of perspiration that clung to the top of her breasts, which overflowed the white stola she had just put on. They had spent much of the two weeks of their journey belowdeck, making loud and passionate love in the luxurious cabin Julia had added at the stern of the merchant vessel *Juno*. The past two hours had been no exception.

She grinned as she approached him at the railing. "Had enough for a while?" she asked as she stepped between him and the railing, grinding her backside into his crotch. He wrapped his arms around her, pressing his chest against her back and slipping his hand down the front of her stola.

"I thought I was the one who spent the past twenty months isolated in a ludus cell," he said as he kissed the back of her neck.

"My days in Britannia were just as lonely. Caring for an overweight, ailing husband on his deathbed doesn't breed much of a sexual appetite."

"Well, you're making up for it now," Lucius said as he continued to nibble at her neck. ". . . not that I'm complaining."

She reached behind her and began stroking him through the soft Egyptian cotton of his white tunic. "Glad you got your strength back so quickly," she said with a giggle in her voice. "And that physician gave you a nice new look." She leaned back and kissed the squat nose that now spread wider across his olive face, then whispered into his ear. "It's exciting. It's like fucking some handsome stranger."

Lucius laughed, then breathed a contented sigh. "You know what makes it all so much better? Knowing that this very ship should have been inherited by Quintus Romanus, and instead it's ours. We can use it to take us anywhere in the Empire, while he fights for his life in arenas and lives like an animal in the ludus."

Julia's hand stopped its pleasurable work, and she turned to face him. "Don't tell me you're going to start this again. For Mars' sake, your obsession with that gladiator consumes you. Let it go, Lucius. It's over." She turned and looked back over the rail toward Alexandria. "We've won. We're back on top. Leave it at that."

Lucius did not respond. The ember that smoldered inside him could not be extinguished. He knew, no matter where he went or what he did the rest of his life, the spectral thought of Quintus Romanus would be with him always.

They stood quietly, listening to the dark waves wash the hull of the ship. As the sun dipped below the horizon, a colossal fire came to life atop the Pharos lighthouse directly ahead of them.

"What a sight that is," Julia said, the wonder evident in her voice. "It's so much more than an aid for ships. It says to the world: this is a city of wealth and power." She leaned back again into Lucius's arms. "There's so much to see in this Empire, and yet there are so many who never leave the safety of their walled town. What a waste of life."

Lucius didn't respond. He was mesmerized by the massive fire.

"Let's get married."

Lucius continued staring at the inferno for another moment before the words he had just heard sunk in. His arms twitched with a shiver. "What?"

She turned and looked up at him with a grin. "Let's . . . get . . . married," she repeated slowly, as if teaching a foreign language.

It took him a second to catch his breath. "Why? We have everything we could ever want right now. Why change things?"

"Because it will make things easier for us. How am I supposed to introduce you to my shipping managers tomorrow? These are people whose respect I need. They operate my shipping line on a daily basis. They hold my fortune in their hands."

Julia's words echoed in his ears, mingling with the loud thumps of his increased heartbeats. *What's gotten into her?* he thought. This was certainly not the wild, carefree Julia he knew in Britannia and Rome.

"Listen," she pressed on. "Do you remember in Rome how everyone laughed behind our backs at the aunt and nephew relationship we hid behind? I hated that they respected our money, but they didn't respect *us*." She paused to let the words sink in. "We have an opportunity to start fresh now. Let's do it right." Her eyes took on the serious glint they had held in the coach a few weeks earlier. "Lucius, I don't want to be laughed at anymore. I want to be respected. I want to stand with my head high, with nothing to hide anymore. No more lies. No more deceit. Just a new life . . . together."

Lucius could not have been more uncomfortable with a knife at his throat. What in Hades did this woman really want? He thought he had learned to detect the agendas hidden in her words and actions. But now she seemed so damned sincere. Was it another fine performance? Or was it truly a heartfelt dream of a better life together? Either way, the fact that he had to wrestle with this question gave him the answer to his dilemma. *How could he possibly marry a woman he could not trust?* But if he said no, would he be sealing his own fate? Would it be as if he hopped over the railing in front of him and drowned? Would he be throwing away a golden opportunity to live a life far beyond his wildest dreams? His mind raced, searching for a way to buy time. Time to learn her real agenda.

"Well," he heard himself say, stalling. "How about this . . . ?" A clear thought finally began to materialize. "How about if you introduce me to your managers as your husband? They won't know any better."

"But—" Julia began to protest. Lucius touched his finger to her lips and continued.

"Then we'll give ourselves a few months to settle in at Alexandria. If we decide that's really the best way to proceed, then we'll have a small private ceremony . . ." The next few words stuck in his throat for a moment. ". . . and we'll do it." He smiled a congenial smile, trying desperately to appear enthused about the idea.

Julia's pout turned to a grin beneath his finger. She ran her tongue up the length of his forefinger and sucked playfully at the tip. A deep-throated laugh came from her as she turned back to face the approaching lighthouse, wrapping Lucius's arms around her and replacing his hand on her left breast. Lucius felt as though he had stood beneath a rain of arrows and managed to dodge every metal tip. He took a deep breath of salt air.

It took hours of slow progress to navigate the dangerous shoals off the Egyptian coast, even though the ship's captain had pulled into Alexandria's port dozens of times, delivering and taking on goods for the Romanus shipping fleet. His confidence showed as he calmly but firmly issued orders to the crew as they approached the harbor entrance.

Lucius and Julia gazed up as the towering lighthouse passed to their starboard side. The white limestone building was constructed in three sections: a rectangular base supporting an octagonal tower, which in turn supported the enormous circular cupola that housed the inferno. A colossus of Jupiter adorned the dome of the cupola. Small licks of flame drifted off to the southeast like a thousand fireflies dancing in the starry sky. Before they realized it, they were tied up along the seawall that ringed the wide harbor.

As the crew prepped to off-load the cargo in the morning, Lucius and Julia spent the night in their comfortable cabin. They left the windows open, allowing the powerful flame of the lighthouse to illuminate the heated passion in their bed.

Morning brought the tang of rotting seaweed and the shouts of dockworkers through the open portals of the cabin. Lucius woke to find himself alone in the oversized bed. He dressed and climbed the stairs to the deckhouse door. He opened it and was taken aback by the sight of the sprawling city in the bright early light.

Past the curved neck and head of the swan that adorned the prow of the *Juno* lay a busy access road and a canal that flowed just outside the harbor area. A wide bridge spanned the channel, supporting the road that ran toward a massive gate. The entire city was encircled by a substantial wall that spread for many miles in either direction. Above the fortification, a spectacular array of white and earth-toned buildings could be seen, most topped with russet-colored terra-cotta tiles.

"Quite a city, isn't it?" said a male voice Lucius did not recognize.

He looked toward the gangway where Julia stood with the captain and another man dressed in a brilliant white tunic with a red pallium draped over his shoulder like a toga. Behind them, the ship's crew was busy off-loading amphora and a variety of crates.

"Lucius, this is Aelius Marinus. He runs our fleet office here in

Alexandria." Julia's face lit up as her eyes met Lucius. "Aelius, this is my husband, Lucius Calidius." Her introduction came with nonchalance, as if she had been saying it for years. But the words shook Lucius out of his morning stupor. His discussion with Julia the previous evening replayed in his head.

"Welcome to Egypt," the friendly man said as he gripped Lucius's forearm.

"Aelius is going to show us the Romanus apartment in the city," Julia said. "Ready to go?"

"So long as Master Marinus can provide us with good wine and a hearty breakfast," Lucius said with a smile. He set his mind for the new husband/wife charade to begin. The story seemed more plausible than the old aunt/nephew ruse, despite the nineteen-year difference in their age. Luckily, Julia managed to keep herself looking at least ten years younger than her true age. And he had certainly aged at least five years in his twenty months of misery at the ludus.

"I was informed last night you had arrived," Aelius said. "We have a banquet laid out for you and Mistress Melita. We are at your service." The fleet manager bowed and raised his arm toward the side of the ship. As Lucius approached the gangway, he saw a coach with two beautiful white horses waiting for them on the pier. Julia winked at him before she stepped down the walkway. He had to smile to himself. Things were quickly returning to the way they should be. Somehow, in the light of a new day, the thought of actually taking Julia as his wife seemed a bit more appealing. They entered the well-appointed coach and waited for the driver to climb aboard.

"Those are some of our warehouses," Aelius said, pointing out the window to two large buildings with hipped roofs alongside the pier. "They have easy access to the canal that links the harbor with Lake Mareotis on the south side of the city. From there, it's a short voyage to the Nile and into the heart of Egypt. It's a very efficient layout. And we're paid well, whether we're transporting by sea or by lake."

Lucius watched the stevedores muscle the cargo from their ship's hold onto wooden palettes and into the warehouse. Three overseers studied each load, tallying the count in ledgers and wax tablets. Then the reins snapped and they rolled smoothly down the pier and across the bridge linking the port to the mainland, and on toward the main city gate.

"Alexander the Great wanted his city to have a dramatic impact on newcomers," Aelius said as they passed through the gate, revealing a paved boulevard wider than any Lucius had ever seen. The immaculate street, at least ninety feet across, was lined with palm and date trees. "Did he succeed?" Aelius asked with a smile. This was obviously a ritual he had gone through before with new visitors.

"I think he did well . . . for a Greek," Lucius said with a wink.

The diversity of the inhabitants surprised him as much as the city's scale and layout. Romans mixed with Egyptians, Greeks, Jews, Phoenicians, Berbers in their strange headdress and striped robes, and black Africans from the southern regions of Nubia and Ethiopia. It was a cosmopolitan city in the truest sense of the word.

The carriage stopped as it approached a large intersection. "Here we are," Aelius said as he opened the coach door and assisted Julia out. "Best location in the city."

Lucius stepped from the carriage and walked into the middle of the intersection in awe. Although there were horses, carriages, and people everywhere, there was no sense of overcrowding or the claustrophobia one felt in Rome. The cross street, which ran from one end of the city to the other, parallel to the coastline, was even wider than the entrance road. A series of low, rectangular fountains adorned with relief images of trade ships divided the boulevard down the center, adding another touch of elegance to the exotic surroundings.

"Come upstairs for an even better view," Aelius called to him.

They entered a large corner building faced in white Egyptian granite and framed by dozens of Doric columns. Next to the door was a sign reading: Romanus Shipping and Transport. Lucius bristled at the name and pushed quickly through the door behind Julia. The first floor contained a nicely appointed set of offices, bustling with the activity of twenty or so workers. Each stopped and bowed his head with a smile as Julia and Lucius passed the work spaces.

They climbed a set of marble stairs at the far end of the building, which led to the owner's suite. The large foyer was beautifully decorated with a tall cedar wood chest flanked by two chairs. The trim of all three furniture pieces was inlaid with colored glass, accentuating the dark and medium hues of the wood. An alabaster vase with green and gold floral garlands graced the top of the chest, alongside a black varnished jackal with golden ears. The slender chair legs ended as lion's paws and stood atop an impressive mosaic floor medallion featuring the great pyramids.

Lucius was anxious to see if the rest of his new apartment lived up to the promise of the entrance hall. But as they stepped into the living quarters, he was distracted by a chorus of voices that rose from the open air patio at the far end of the room.

"Welcome to Alexandria!" a small crowd shouted in unison, followed by enthusiastic applause.

"These are many of your managers and shipping clients, Mistress Melita," Aelius said with a smile. "They wanted to all welcome you personally." The fleet manager stepped forward and raised his voice. "May I present to you the Lady Julia Melita and her husband, Lucius Calidius."

The applause resumed in earnest. Lucius glanced at Julia. As the new company owner, she clearly enjoyed the fawning of her staff and customers. She waded into the crowd with a gracious smile, planting kisses on many cheeks. These were, after all, the people who would be making her millions over the coming years. Lucius thought back to his days as magistrate of Aquae Sulis and imperial advisor in Rome, when this sort of flattery was directed at him. But so long as Julia kept the money flowing, for the moment he was willing to allow her a bit of celebrity.

He stepped out onto the patio, marveling at the view across the wide boulevard toward the brilliant city buildings and the lake. Along the low wall at the edge of the patio was a row of food platters brimming with figs, dates, cucumbers, grapes, onions, pomegranates, a variety of shell fish, emmer-wheat and barley breads, wild duck, sweetmeats, and an assortment of local delicacies he had never seen.

"Try the mehiwet cakes," came Aelius's voice from behind him. "They're sweetened with honey."

"Sounds delicious," Lucius replied, lifting a sticky round cake from the tray.

Aelius stepped forward and pointed to a large three-level building to the south. "That's our famous library, a gift from the Ptolemys. They felt knowledge is power, so they brought together all the learning of the world under their exclusive control. Needless to say, Greece was not too receptive of the idea."

"Nor should they be," Lucius replied as he downed the cake and licked the honey from his finger tips. "How can a single culture have possession of all the knowledge in the world? That's a dangerous prospect."

"True," Aelius responded, "but perhaps a convenient resource for future generations."

Lucius shrugged, wanting to absorb more of the city's sites rather than engage in debate. "I could see myself living here," he said as he leaned on the patio wall. "This city seems alive, like Rome, but without the throngs and congestion. Tell me about the administration. Does the magistrate keep his people happy?"

Before Aelius could answer, Julia stepped through the doorway. "Already considering another run for office?" she said with a smile. "Lucius was a local magistrate before he became one of Nero's advisors," she said to Aelius. She took Lucius's arm and pulled herself close to him. "He was nothing short of a hero. Averted a major clan uprising in Britannia without losing a single soldier."

"Ahh, a remarkable track record, Master Lucius," Aelius replied. "Do you think you'd consider an administration position here in Egypt? It could certainly open more doors for the company."

Lucius snickered. "No thanks. I'm done with the petty issues of local politics. I'd only consider another imperial position."

"I see," the fleet manager responded with a nod. He then turned toward Julia. "Mistress Melita, I know it's been a while, but I wanted to mention how sorry we were to hear of the horrible shipwreck at Britannia. I'm sure that was a blow to your family."

Lucius glanced at Julia, then looked out over the city again. "Yes, it most certainly was," Julia replied, lowering her head a bit.

"Caius and Politta were wonderful people to work for," Aelius continued. "I'd been with Caius since we crewed together on the ships of Marcus Didius. He was a fine man."

"You're right, Aelius," Julia said. "They were good people." She did not further the discussion, and Lucius, too, was happy to let the matter drop. It irked him that he could not tell this man how his own mother had also lost her life that night five years ago. But it would raise too many questions.

"I heard that Caius's son, Quintus, survived," Aelius said.

Lucius turned his gaze from the city and looked at Julia. He cursed himself for not having prepared better for this eventuality, especially knowing they would be meeting senior Romanus business associates.

"I heard that Quintus, too, had a run at politics for a while," the shipping manager continued. He then lowered his voice and leaned closer. "Rumor has it that it didn't go so well for him."

The panic that had begun to rise in Lucius subsided as he realized Aelius did not connect the two stories. The manager had no way of knowing he was actually speaking of *Lucius's* exploits during his impersonation of Quintus Romanus. It dawned on Lucius that he had nothing to fear from his past life. Before Julia could answer, he spoke up. "You mean that amphitheater fiasco? I'm afraid the rumor is true. It seems young Quintus went a bit mad after the loss of his parents."

Julia's eyes flashed a warning at him, but the opportunity to drag Quintus's name and reputation further through the mud was just too irresistible. "How he managed to obtain a position in Nero's court is beyond comprehension. His debacle at the games that day was a disgrace."

Lucius dared not look at Julia. He could feel her eyes burning into him like a firebrand. The fleet manager shook his head. "By the gods . . . It's so hard to believe that the young boy I once bounced on my knee could turn into such a lunatic."

The word stung Lucius for, after all, the man was speaking of him. But he remained calm and shrugged. "Power corrupts some more than others, I guess," he said with a sigh.

"What ever became of him?" Aelius asked.

Lucius's mind raced, but before he could open his mouth, Julia answered. "He disappeared after the arena incident. Most in Rome assume he was arrested and put to death. Quietly, of course, to minimize embarrassment to the emperor."

It wasn't the story Lucius would have gone with, but it worked. Julia pulled him toward the food display. "But enough of this depressing talk," she said as she selected one of the small honey cakes. "Tell me more about the business, Aelius. What opportunities are there for growth here in Alexandria?"

The manager's eyes lit up at the prospect of expansion. More profits for the fleet meant better wages for him and his staff. "Well, our ships come and go with their holds full, and we often turn cargo and passengers away. Our grain carriers haul at least three hundred tons of wheat and barley out of Alexandria on every voyage. Oil amphoras, crates of fruit, and your textile shipments, especially the Egyptian cotton, keeps our cargo freighters overloaded. I would think we could easily fill two more of the bigger freighters for the sea crossing to Italia. And I could fill at least three more smaller vessels toting goods across the lake and down the Nile."

Julia nodded. "Draw up some cost and profit figures for me. Let's look into it. Any business that doesn't grow eventually dies. That's how Sextus and I always ran our textile company."

The man's spirits rose dramatically. "Yes, madam. Right away."

"Where else should we be looking, Aelius?" Julia continued. "Surely there are more opportunities on the eastern shores of the Mare Internum than Alexandria."

The fleet manager's eyes became even wider. "There certainly is," he said excitedly. "Caesarea . . . I was just speaking of this port to some of the captains and managers but a week ago."

"In Judea?" Julia asked. "Isn't there trouble with the Jews in that region?"

"Perhaps, but the governor there, Vespasian, is a strong military man. Rumor has it he's a rising star in the political world, although he's had some rough spots in his past. They say he'll have the Jewish revolt completely subdued soon. When he does, Judea will prosper." Aelius lowered his voice again and took a step closer to them. "That could be very good for us, since Vespasian has a history with Romanus Shipping."

"Really?" Julia asked with a raised eyebrow. "What sort of history?"

"I heard he helped Caius win some of his early transport contracts," the manager explained. "That allowed him to expand the fleet quickly."

Julia looked at Lucius, but he could only shrug. The name rang a bell, but he couldn't place it.

"What sort of trade could we expect in Judea?" Julia asked.

"It has much to offer in the way of olive oil and wine. But more important, it's the gateway to the Far East. As you know well, Mistress Melita, the Far East is famous for outstanding silk textiles. I have no doubt Caesarea will be the next Alexandria, and those who get there first will capture the wealth of the eastern Empire. We already have a small office there to coordinate our olive oil shipments. In my opinion, that operation should be expanded immediately."

"How much would the fleet need to be increased to capitalize on this?" Lucius asked.

"Perhaps three or four large freighters to begin with," Aelius answered. "From there we could see."

Lucius looked at Julia. He could tell by the vacant stare that she was calculating the additional profits based on the additional tonnage. He already knew the answer. If the fleet manager was correct, it could double the profits of the company within two years.

"Add those projections to the ones I've already requested," said Julia. "We'll discuss this next week."

"And Aelius . . ." Lucius added with a sly smile. "We can already see there's potential there. No need to pad the estimates."

The manager seemed to take offense for a moment, but his excitement overpowered any umbrage. "The figures will be accurate, sir. You can count on me." He scurried away with a broad smile on his face.

"And I was just saying how I could get used to living in Alexandria," Lucius said as he turned back to the outstanding view toward the lake.

"We'll be here for a while. But Caesarea sounds promising. So does this provincial governor . . . What's his name? Vespasian? Sounds like he's got some aspirations."

Lucius smiled as he looked at Julia. "Our kind of man."

V

January AD 69

QUINTUS HELD HIS TRIDENT secure as he readied the net in his right hand for another throw. The secutor he faced was one of the newer acquisitions, so Quintus knew the training bout would not last long. The two men circled, jostling for position and kicking up a small cloud of dust on the training field. Although Quintus worked at half his normal speed and aggressiveness, the inexperienced secutor could not find a safe avenue of attack. Quintus took the opportunity to enjoy the cool fresh air as he worked stripped to the waist and without a helmet. It was the thing he loved most about fighting as a lightly armored retiarius.

Before the weighted rete left his hand to envelop his opponent a second time, he heard Julianus call a halt to all practice sessions on the field. Glancing at the sun's angle, Quintus knew it was too early to be released for the day. It had to be a general assembly.

Petra, Facilix, and a third man stepped onto the low wooden platform at the far end of the training field. They waited for the group of five hundred fighters and venatores to gather in front of them.

Quintus looked for Lindani and Amazonia. The hunter's stark black skin and the gladiatrix's long reddish locks made them easy to spot as they stood near the east portico.

"What's this all about?" he asked as he approached them. Both friends shrugged.

"The third man has the bearing of a soldier," Lindani replied as he studied the body language of the guest.

"I saw him come through the front gate a while ago," Amazonia said. "He's been with the lanistae ever since."

"Alright, ladies, listen up," came the raspy voice of Petra. "This is my old friend, Marcus Livius Castus. We served together in the legions as centurions many years ago. While Castus here went on to a brilliant military career and retired to a nice villa on the slopes of Vesuvio . . . well, let's just say my career went a little differently."

Quintus was surprised at this revelation. He had never heard the tough old lanista mention that he was once part of Rome's army.

"Now, unfortunately, many of you will be going away for a while," Petra continued. "Castus is here to train you for that journey." He paused for a moment as the murmur of questions grew within the ranks of gladiators. He glanced at Facilix before he continued.

"This can't be good," Quintus said quietly to his two friends.

"Three hundred of you will be trained as auxiliaries and temporarily attached to the legions on campaign," Petra said. "You leave in nine days."

"*What!*" Quintus yelled, louder than he knew he should have. Luckily his shout was overridden by the outcry of hundreds of other fighters on the field. The ludus guards stepped forward from under the portico, whips and rods poised for action.

"Settle down!" Petra roared in a voice that commanded obedience. "You are all the property of this ludus, and you will fight for whoever you are told to fight for. Is that clear?"

"Yes, Dominus." The weak reply came from less than half the fighters.

"Are we understood?" Facilix screamed in a louder voice than Petra could muster.

"Yes, Dominus!" came a thunderous response.

"Alright, then," Petra continued. "The following gladiators and venatores will line up on the west side of the field when your name is called . . ."

Quintus listened intently as Julianus stepped up on the podium and began reading the roster from a long scroll. He was not surprised when his name came near the top of the list, followed closely by Lindani's. He was relieved to see Amazonia remain at her original position near the portico columns after the final name was read. She was not on the list. He also noticed that none of the retiarii, dimachaerii, and other specialty fighters were called. He assumed his work as a thraex with sword and shield, rather than his retiarius skills put him into the auxiliary group.

"All those whose names I did not call, clear the field and return to your cells immediately," Julianus called out.

Quintus watched Amazonia look toward him and Lindani. She threw her wooden gladius against the equipment rack, then turned and walked away.

Marcus Castus stepped forward. Lindani's initial assessment of the man's military bearing proved accurate. Although his stocky build and aged face mirrored Petra's looks, his stiff back and confident manner betrayed his long military career. Quintus could easily picture him in the plumed helmet, mail shirt, and chest medallions of the centurion, rather than the simple blue tunic he currently wore. He noticed his feet were shod with caligae, ankle-high military sandals he would probably wear the rest of his life.

"Alright," Castus shouted, "I want all those who fight as murmillo, secutor, and provocator to pick up your training weapons and pair off in the middle of the field. The rest of you stand aside and pay attention. Julianus, put your best murmillo in front of me."

"Memnon! Front and center!" Julianus yelled.

Castus stepped from the wooden platform and picked up one of the large shields and a wooden practice sword the length and shape of a gladius. Quintus noticed the slight smile Petra had on his lips as he watched from the podium. Castus turned and faced the heavyset brute stalking toward him, who was equally well-armed and half his age. Memnon exaggerated the swagger of his bulky, hairy body as he approached the older man. His silver helmet was tucked under an arm as wide as most men's thighs.

The smug murmillo grinned one of his famous intimidating sneers before donning his head gear.

Castus didn't seem to notice. He pointed the wooden rudis at Memnon as he spoke. "I'm going to show this man the difference between fighting for show in the arena and fighting for your life on a battlefield."

Memnon secured his chin strap, then cocked his head. "You think we don't fight for our lives in the arena?" he said, the clipped tone showing his annoyance.

"Not like this you don't," Castus replied with a smile. "Attack when ready."

Memnon took a step forward. But before his next step was completed, Castus charged. The old man crouched low behind the shield as he advanced with the force of a bull. Memnon held his ground. As Castus came within striking range, the gladiator attempted to thrust down over the top of the scutum into the old man's shoulder. Castus raised the shield just enough to counter the blow. But the old man never slowed. The metal boss on the front of his red scutum smashed into Memnon's shield. The gladiator, used to fighting at arm's length, staggered backward trying to gain a foothold. Castus never let up the press. He pushed hard against the large retreating gladiator, using his shield as an effective offensive weapon. Memnon continued to hack and thrust but could not find a way past the shield just inches from his face. With the speed of lightning, Castus finally thrust with his wooden gladius. But rather than strike at Memnon's exposed arms, his thrust came from a low angle. The weapon slipped under the bottom of Memnon's shield and directly into his groin. Memnon howled in pain and fell to the dirt. He rolled back and forth, his hands between his legs, until a cloud of dust obscured his large body. Howls of laughter erupted from the assembled fighters.

"What the fuck are you laughing at?" screamed the old centurion as he spun toward the group. "If this blade had been metal, that man would be dead—his guts and blood oozing from where his prick used to be." The fighters quickly quieted down. "That is a standard legionary attack move.

You will learn to defend against it over the coming days."

The statement struck Quintus as odd, and he decided to speak up. "Doctore, if you don't mind me asking, why would we be concerned about that? We'll be fighting *with* the legions, not against them."

Castus looked toward Petra for a response. The lanista took his cue and stepped forward on the platform.

"Actually, you'll be fighting both for and against the legions. Rome stands on the brink of civil war." The murmurs quickly returned within the gladiator ranks. "Galba has been assassinated and Salvius Otho, the governor of Lusitania, has claimed the principate. Unfortunately, Aulus Vitellius, the leader of the Lower Rhine military district, has also claimed the throne." Petra paused and glanced at Castus with a sigh. "We've been hired by Otho to bolster his legions against the Vitellians. You will be part of a band of two thousand gladiators fighting for Otho under the command of a tribune named Martius Macer."

As the words sank in, there was silence in the crowd of three hundred fighters and hunters. "So we will be killing fellow Romans," Quintus said, more as a statement than a question.

"You'll be killing whoever we're hired to kill," Petra responded. "For now, you'll take your orders from Castus." He abruptly turned and walked from the podium, followed by Facilix.

The news of civil war settled like a dark cloud over the now quiet training ground. Lindani leaned toward Quintus. "The dominus washes his hands of this ordeal. He was forced to this decision."

"I've never seen the dominus forced to do anything he doesn't want to do," Quintus said as he brusquely grabbed a rudis from the weapons rack. "Why didn't he just say no?"

"Venatores, line up here," Castus yelled. "You will work with your regular doctores. I have given them instructions for your new drills. Now move out to your training field."

"There is more to this story," Lindani said to Quintus before he walked toward the rear gate. "I am sure of it."

Castus gathered the remaining gladiators and doctores. He assisted Memnon to his feet and smacked him on the back. The gladiator gave the old man a sharp look as he rubbed his aching genitals.

"Look, I'm not here to insult any of you or your skills." Castus spoke in a more conciliatory tone, but still with an unmistakable air of authority. "With Cassius Petra running this ludus, I know you're all excellent, well-trained fighters with a good heart. My purpose here is to keep you alive. As I just demonstrated, battlefield tactics are different than arena tactics. You prisoners who have fought against our legions know that. Those who haven't need to accept that if you want to return to this ludus alive someday."

Quintus sensed the attitude of the men change rapidly as Castus continued to speak. The old man certainly had a way of gaining the trust and respect of the men in his charge. Quintus figured that was a critical trait in a good centurion.

Castus used Memnon once again to illustrate his first lesson. "There are three points of attack for the legionary. Here . . ." He pointed the rudis again at Memnon's groin. The gladiator's hands instinctively jerked to cover his crotch, soliciting smiles from the other fighters. ". . . here . . ." Castus continued, now pointing at Memnon's neck. ". . . and here," he said, pointing at Memnon's flushed face. "Legionaries do not have face guards on their helmets like a gladiator, so the face is vulnerable. These are the three areas where you will deliver the quickest and most devastating blows. Remember, this is not for show. We don't want to drag these fights out. The name of this game is: kill 'em quick and move on."

As Castus continued his training, Quintus could not stop thinking about these blows being dealt against fellow Romans on a battlefield. He knew many of the prisoners-of-war at the ludus would be more than happy to face off once again against a front line of legionaries. But he was a Roman citizen, born and raised in Rome itself. Never in a million years would he have envisioned himself lining up in battle against Roman soldiers. He had been taught to respect the legions. They were, after all, the protectors of Rome, not to mention the most powerful fighting force in the world. He knew nothing of the politics of Otho, or Vitellius, or even the late Emperor Galba. In the isolation of a ludus, news of Rome's politics rarely trickled down to the fighters. Nor was it important to them. He was here to fight arena battles, to savor the adulation of the crowd, not to be conscripted into the army. His opponents were supposed to be prisoners, slaves, and criminals, not the heroes who defended Rome. The more he thought about taking up arms against legionaries—fellow countrymen— the less interested he became in these new lessons in death.

For the rest of the day, Castus drilled the men in the ways of the legions and the art of battlefield killing. Quintus and the other Thracian fighters were issued large scuta. At more than three times the weight of his small parmula, Quintus would need to get used to maneuvering the heavy shield. But the desire to work for this cause simply was not in his heart. By the middle of the afternoon, after hours of going through the motions, a miserable reality finally struck him. Without the desire, his inner energy would not flow. And without the energy there was no Taurus. Quintus's focus and reflexes would still help him take on any adversary, but without Taurus, the chances of him leaving the battlefield alive were just slightly better than fifty-fifty. The odds sobered him.

As night fell, Castus joined his old friend, Petra, and the head trainer, Julianus, for dinner in Petra's quarters. The spacious room, kept neat and orderly by the lanista's staff, easily held the large table and six chairs carved of elm wood. Petra had always preferred the practicality of table dining to the ritual of couch dining. The neatly cut stone and tile floor reflected the flickering lamps hanging from tall stands in the corner. The scent of the burning oil blended with the aroma of roasted poultry.

"Macer is an asshole," Castus stated between bites of his chicken leg. "I've served under him. The men don't respect him because he's too concerned about covering his own ass with the legate than in planning and fighting his battles."

Petra nodded. "I sensed that when he was here yesterday. He's all bluster and no game."

"Your men can do well on the battlefield. I can see that after working with them just a few hours. My compliments," he said, nodding toward Julianus. "But they need a true leader. Someone they respect amongst themselves. What about Memnon? Could he watch over them?"

Petra shook his head. "He's a brute. A hell of a fighter, but no brains."

Julianus nodded with a smile on his greasy lips. "Taurus is your man. No question."

"The one with the Minotaur on his chest?" Castus asked.

"And the Gorgon on his back," Julianus said as he attacked another chicken breast. "That's the one."

"I've heard about him," Castus said. "But to be honest, I didn't really see any spark in him on the field today."

Julianus nodded slowly as he ate. "I saw that as well. He wasn't himself today."

"Did any of the fighters have their usual energy today?" asked Petra. "The thought of fighting a civil war in a few weeks came as a shock to all of them."

"There's no question that would weigh heavier on Quintus than the others," Julianus agreed.

"Wait. I'm confused," Castus interrupted. "Who's Quintus?"

"Quintus is Taurus," Petra explained. "He calls himself 'Taurus' in the arena. If you ever saw him fight a match, you'd know why."

"Why would fighting the Roman legions affect him more than the others? What would a criminal or prisoner-of-war care who he fought?"

"He's neither," Petra said, perhaps a bit too harshly. "Quintus is a citizen of Rome, here as a volunteer. He's our best fighter and sharp as a pugio dagger. He has an interesting background, but that's not important now. What's important is that all the men respect him and look up to him, even though he's younger than a lot of them. I have no doubt they would follow him into battle."

"Sounds like he's our man," Castus said with finality.

Julianus looked across the cluttered table at Petra. "I agree, but I'm concerned about his feelings on Roman fighting Roman."

"Let me deal with that," Castus said. "Let's get Quintus in here. There's something I need to discuss with all of you."

Quintus leaned his elbows on the sill of the barred window, watching the glow of a quarter moon sparkle on the rushing water in the stream behind the ludus. The relaxing sounds of the brook usually helped lull him to sleep. But on this night his mind was too distracted by the news of his involvement in a civil war.

The echo of footsteps in the stone hallway caught his attention. He turned toward the window in his cell door, although now that he was ranked "primus palus"—the best of the best—his large room could hardly be considered a cell any longer. The comfortable cot, table and chair, woven rug, and small accessories he had purchased in Pompeii's markets lent the room an almost cozy atmosphere—a far cry from his original tiny cubicle and bug-ridden sleeping mat. His numerous victory palms lined one wall, the newer ones still green, the older awards now brown and brittle. The laurel wreath with its gold medallion, awarded for his dramatic victory in the Britannia vs. Pompeii match two years earlier, sat higher on a shallow ledge. But his most treasured possession resided in the alcove common to all ludus cells. The shallow depressions were meant to house icons of the fighter's personal god. Most of the men honored small statues of Hercules or Mars, the patrons of all gladiators. But Quintus's alcove housed a terra-cotta figurine of a ship captain—the same icon he wore around his neck in the arena. The figure was the only remnant of a beautiful miniature galley bought for him by his father at his first naumachia. The souvenir of the arena ship battle had been viciously smashed by Lucius Calidius in a jealous rage. For Quintus, the tiny figure now held the spirits of those who were once most dear to him. It was a welcome reminder of his past life and a tangible connection to his roots in the city of

Rome—the same city he was now being asked to fight against.

The footsteps in the hallway grew louder, then stopped outside his door. The latch opened and Julianus stepped inside. Quintus was surprised at the rare, late night visit from the head trainer.

"The dominus wants to see you."

By Julianus's flat tone, Quintus could not tell if the news was good or bad. Curiosity got the best of him.

"Something wrong?" he asked casually as they left the cell and headed toward the offices near the front gate.

"Castus has some information he wants you to hear," Julianus replied.

They walked across the training field and entered Petra's office. Quintus noticed that one of the bronze lampstands had been slid closer to the table at the center of the room. The three oil lamps hanging from it cast an orange glow across the lanista and ex-centurion who were already seated. A decanter of wine and four cups sat before them. Quintus stepped toward the table and a flash of red caught his eye, conspicuous against the earth tones of the office. A long-stemmed rose teetered on top of the tall lampstand.

"Do you know what that means, Quintus?" Castus asked.

"Yes. It means this meeting is sub rosa—cloaked in secrecy. Everything we say here remains at this table."

"Good," Petra said. "Take a seat."

The lanista poured him a cup of wine. Between the rose and the wine, Quintus assumed the news was going to be bad.

"Castus here has something to say to us," Petra continued, "and he wanted you to hear it."

"I've heard a lot about you, Quintus. Or . . . I guess, I've heard a lot about 'Taurus,'" Castus said with a smile. "I have to say, though, you didn't impress me much out on the field today."

Quintus looked at Petra and Julianus, not sure how to react.

"Say what you feel, son," Petra said. "It's one of the few times you'll get to do it in the next few months."

"Well, Doctore, I can't stomach the thought of us fighting Romans. Frankly, the thought of civil war nauseates me."

"It should nauseate all Romans," Castus replied. "The gods know, we've seen enough of Romans killing Romans over the years. But let me ask you this . . . If the cause was the right cause, and it was worth fighting for, wouldn't you prefer to be on the front lines yourself, rather than letting weaker men fight the battle?"

The question cut to the heart of Quintus's self-imposed mandate to always control his own destiny. "If I believed the cause was right, I suppose so," he finally answered.

"How about leading those men in battle?" Castus pushed.

Quintus immediately shook his head. "I know nothing about battlefield tactics. That would not be a wise move."

"You wouldn't set the battle plan. That would be left to the legates and the tribunes. But there are men of courage who lead the soldiers to carry out those plans. In the legions, they are the centurions. Now, I don't believe Macer will place Roman centurions with the gladiators. I believe he'll try to control them all himself, with the help of his junior tribunes. This is a bad idea, but I think that's the way it will play out on the lines."

Quintus was stunned with the direction the conversation was taking. "So, you're saying you want me to lead the gladiators in battle?"

"The dominus and Julianus feel you're the man for the job. The men respect you, you're probably the best fighter in the ludus, you're better educated, and they feel the men will follow you into battle." Castus paused and leaned forward a bit. "You would still need to follow orders from Macer, but you'd make the decisions in the heat of battle. Trust me, you won't find Macer there."

"What about the other seventeen hundred gladiators?" Quintus asked.

"I don't give a shit about them," Petra interjected. "I just want my fighters back in one piece . . . at least as many as I can get."

Quintus now saw why Petra had poured him the wine. He lifted the cup and drained it in one gulp. He looked at the three men who sat waiting for his reply.

"I'm a gladiator, not a centurion," Quintus said. "Facing a man alone in an arena is one thing, but facing hundreds or thousands of well-trained soldiers on a battlefield is another. In the arena, I'm responsible for my own life, nothing more. I don't want the responsibility of leading all these men to what may be their deaths."

Castus leaned back and looked at Petra. "Sound familiar?" he asked the lanista. Petra nodded. "This is the classic self-doubt struggle of every new centurion in the army," he said to Quintus with an unexpected warmth. "Nobody wants to lead men to their deaths. Nobody wants all that blood on their hands. But here's how I looked at it . . . I know my own abilities. Do I want to put my life in the hands of some asshole I don't even know? It's bad enough when the battle plan is not considered carefully enough. But when you compound it with some idiot centurion who couldn't find his ass in his tunic trying to execute that plan, that's when young men die. And die in big numbers. I didn't want to feel the sting of a gladius in my gut because of some other asshole's mistakes. I wanted to control my own destiny." He leaned closer to Quintus. "I wanted to lead. And I think you're that kind of person, Quintus. I think you want to lead, too. You're not the type to blindly follow some idiot to your death. You want to control your own destiny, don't you?"

Quintus studied Castus for a moment. Just like he had pointed out the vulnerable strike points that afternoon on the practice field, the old centurion knew exactly where to strike at him. Quintus had sworn years ago, after Lucius Calidius had managed to get him tossed into slavery, that he would never again allow another person to control his life. But this was different. This was much larger. Certainly *too* large a proposition to consider. Another dilemma suddenly flooded his mind. Even if he were to agree to this madness, which part of him would lead his men? Would it be Quintus or Taurus? He would need the speed and strength of Taurus on the battlefield, but would he be able to summon the warrior spirit on command if his heart was not in the battle?

Quintus did not hide his exasperation as he looked Castus in the eye. "By the gods, Doctore, I don't know what I'm fighting for. I don't even know *who* I'm fighting for! Who in Hades is Otho? I know nothing of this man. It's hard enough for me to put my own life on the line here, let alone lead others into this madness. I cannot do what you ask of me."

Castus took a deep breath before he spoke. "Your point is valid, Quintus. I've gotten ahead of myself. You need to know about Otho." Castus looked at Petra and Julianus, then glanced at the door to be sure it was closed. "This is what I wanted to speak about with all of you together," he continued. "I served in Lusitania years ago, when Otho was governor there. Gentlemen, this is *not* the man to lead our Empire into the future. Otho is an arrogant, self-absorbed megalomaniac. Things will be no different than they were under the crazed incompetence of Nero. What's more, Otho does not have the military support that Vitellius has. This is why he needs the gladiators. But even with the additional fighters, his legions are tremendously outnumbered."

Quintus looked at Petra and Julianus. Their bewildered looks mirrored his own feelings. He shook his head in frustration. "Great. So we're fighting for the wrong side."

"Not exactly," Castus answered. "Vitellius is no better. From what I hear from my contacts within the Lower Rhine legions, Vitellius is a lethargic oaf of a man, more interested in betting on the chariot races and consuming vast quantities of food and drink than in running an Empire."

Julianus leaned forward, his face wrinkled with puzzlement. "Then why in Mars' name do his legions support him for the principate?"

Castus laughed. "It's very simple . . . money. If their own commander becomes Emperor, who do you think would become the new Praetorian Guard? Many of these men would be transferred from their remote and dangerous frontier posts in Germania to comfortable palace duty in the heart of Rome. And at twice their current wage. So, who would *you* pledge allegiance to if you were in Vitellius's legions?"

Petra shook his head in disgust. "I can't believe these morons would jeopardize the future of the Empire for higher wages and a better post. What good will it do them if the enemies of Rome sense weakness and move against us?"

Castus shrugged. "Many soldiers think only for today, never tomorrow." Quintus felt the old man's intensity change at that moment. "I, however, *am* thinking of tomorrow," Castus said in a low, serious tone. "There is one who can lead this Empire out from under the dark shadow of civil war and into a bright future." He looked around the small table to be sure he had the attention of each man. "He is a simple man, not given to gluttony and greed and the insanity of so many past Emperors. This is a strong man who can take control of all Rome. He will win over the Senate, the people, the military, and subdue the enemies of Rome, both inside and outside the city gates." He looked at his old comrade-in-arms. "You know this man, Petra. We fought together with him in Britannia, when we defeated the Belgae and the Atrebates."

Quintus looked at Petra, who suddenly showed a hint of recognition. "Vespasian?" the lanista asked.

The name came as a thunderbolt to Quintus. He sat forward, but said nothing.

Castus nodded. "Ever since you came to me yesterday with news of Galba, Otho, and Vitellius, I cannot get the man from my mind. He is the one to put things right."

"But I thought he was still in Judea suppressing the Jewish revolt there," Petra said.

Castus nodded. "He is. But once he learns of Galba's death, and Otho's undeniable involvement in the assassination, I think he'll see that Rome is ready for new leadership."

"Who is this Vespasian?" Julianus asked.

"He's the finest commander I've ever had the honor to serve with," Petra answered, his voice almost reverent. "He was fair to his officers, to his men, even to the tribes we conquered. His heart was always with the Empire. He did what benefited Rome, never what benefited himself. He's a damn good man."

"He's more than a damn good man," Quintus suddenly said. "Titus Flavius Vespasianus is a savior."

All three men stared at Quintus. Castus finally broke the silence. "You know Vespasian?" he asked. His eyes were wide, and deep wrinkles creased his forehead.

Events and stories from a decade earlier flooded Quintus's mind. "He and my father were friends and business associates."

"Really?" Castus asked. "When was this?"

"About ten years ago. When my father started his own shipping line, Vespasian was one of his first customers. They met when he booked passage to Sicilia on my father's first ship. They became friends, which didn't surprise me; they were both cut from the same cloth."

"This was after Vespasian's military retirement and consulship," Castus said to Petra and Julianus.

"Yes it was. In fact, once my father learned of Vespasian's background, he hired him as a business consultant to help grow his shipping company. Vespasian convinced many of his contacts to ship their goods with my father's company. He even managed to secure shipments of surplus military equipment. Both he and my father did very well. It allowed my father to add two new ships to his fleet within two years of starting the business." He paused and looked around the table. "So you don't have to convince me that Vespasian is a good man."

Petra's face held a rare smile. "Did you ever meet him yourself, Quintus?"

Quintus nodded. "Quite often, actually. He used to come to our house for meetings with my father." Quintus smiled as memories long forgotten drifted through his mind. "He was a fan of the games as well, so each time he stopped by, we'd talk for half the evening about the latest matches in the Amphitheater of Taurus. Then I'd demonstrate the latest sword techniques my bodyguard, Aulus, had taught me. No matter how much work he and my father had to do, he always made time to offer some tips or show me a new move."

As he pictured himself so clearly with his parents and Vespasian in his home in Rome, a thought long suppressed suddenly filled Quintus's memories. The smile drifted from his face and the sting of a tear touched his dry eye. "So . . . yes, I know the man." He lowered his gaze, and Castus picked up the conversation.

"Gentlemen, what we have here is an opportunity to help guide the future of the Empire." He paused for a moment to allow the gravity of the thought to sink in. He looked at Quintus. "This is much more than bloodsport, Quintus. This is Rome's destiny."

Quintus looked up and studied the unfaltering intensity and sincerity in the old centurion's eyes.

"This is why I need you, Quintus," the man continued. "There's no question you're needed to bring as many of Petra's men back alive as possible. But *I* need you for something much bigger. I have a plan . . . a plan to deliver Rome into competent and honest hands for a change. Hands that you know well." Castus looked at Petra. "Hands that we all know well."

Petra winced slightly. "Jupiter's balls, Castus. I see why you placed the rose above us. It sounds like a plan that borders on treason."

"What one man sees as treason another sees as an act of loyalty to the Empire," Castus said with a sly smile. He returned his attention to Quintus. "But I can't make it work without someone like you on the front lines."

Although he had known Castus for less than a day, Quintus could see he was an insightful man, not given to flights of fancy. Quintus had come to learn that any friend of Titus Cassius Petra came from the same mold as the lanista himself. All were truthful, sensible, and able to deliver on promises. He had no reason to think Castus was any different. He reconsidered the old man's earlier comment about the futility of following a poor leader into battle. There was no question the argument was valid.

And he was now being asked to control not only his own destiny and that of his men, but the destiny of Rome itself. It was certainly a level of duty that could beckon Taurus from his lair. And, after all, wasn't that what he now needed? The *desire*. As his tutor from the Orient, Master Sheng, had taught him so many years ago: without desire, there is no movement. Perhaps Castus's plan would provide the missing link that would allow Taurus to emerge and lead the men to victory.

And Vespasian would certainly be someone worth leading them to. The man had placed an indelible mark on Quintus's life. Not only had he helped his father successfully launch a risky business undertaking, but he had comforted his family through one of the most difficult periods of their lives. The thought of it continued to press on Quintus's mind.

Petra's office was suddenly silent and still. Quintus took another long swig from his refilled cup.

"Alright. I'll lead them."

Petra breathed a sigh of relief, and a smile broke across Julianus's face.

"You're a good man . . . Taurus," Castus said as he slapped Quintus's back. "Let me tell you what I've been thinking."

"I'm listening," Quintus responded as he sat back and looked up at the blood red rose dangling above their heads. "But with talk of treason, I hope we're the only ones listening."

Quintus closed the door of his cell and lay on his cot. He looked at the terra-cotta ship captain figurine for a moment, then brought his arm across his face to cover his eyes. He pictured every detail of his original home in Rome. Not the larger house they eventually moved into once the shipping company grew, but the original dwelling off the Clivus Salutis in the more claustrophobic part of the city. It was a modest four-room apartment on the second floor.

He clearly saw Politta, his beautiful mother, through the open archway leading to his parents' bedroom. She was lying across her bed, the sound of her sobs echoing off the bare russet walls and assaulting his young ears.

The light of morning had crept through the two small windows of the main room, but it made little difference. The dark shadow that hung like a funeral veil over their home was not about to be displaced by the mere presence of the morning sun. This had been the way most days had begun for the past few weeks—ever since his mother had become convinced that her husband, Caius, was dead.

Her worry had not been without reason. Quintus's father was long overdue from one of his first sea voyages to Egypt. He had returned late before; ship captains always sailed at the whim of Neptune and the other gods of the natural world. But this had been different. The return date Caius reckoned had passed more than three months earlier. Each morning after his departure, Politta would mark the calendar Caius had created on wax tablets. As the marks grew, so did the family's anticipation. But now, the marks had extended far beyond the due date, and Politta had become convinced that her husband would never return. Her anguish was evident on the calendar itself, where her neat "X's" had become horrid slashes and smudges. The image of those calendar tablets was burned in Quintus's memory, as if his mother's stylus had etched the marks directly into his brain.

Quintus's bodyguard, Aulus, had done what he could to encourage the family, but his well-intentioned support had little effect.

The only salvation, the only ray of sunshine, that made a difference had been the visits from Titus Flavius Vespasianus. Every few days, he would make time in his busy schedule to stop by the apartment and visit with Quintus and Politta. He always brought some small gift for Quintus and extra food for the family. But most important, he brought hope. He would tell them stories of his adventures across the Empire, each one ending with some unexpected twist that resulted in a delay of schedule for him or his legions. Now, as he lay on his cot, Quintus wondered whether they were true adventures or fables Vespasian had invented to soothe their fears. Either way, they had worked miracles. His and Politta's outlook would improve for a few days after Vespasian's visits. Then, as more damnable time passed and their spirits began to fall, he would show up at their door once again, as if he had some mystical sense of their well-being. This had gone on for many weeks. And never once did Quintus sense Vespasian losing hope.

Then, one evening, as Quintus had worked with Aulus on his lessons and Politta busied herself mending a tunic that was hardly worn, they had heard Vespasian's booming voice in the distance. Excitement was evident in the man's tone even before he had reached the stairwell. The family had rushed to the top of the stairs. Quintus never forgot the man's words: "Your husband is alive! His ship is undergoing emergency repairs in Creta. Quintus, your father says he misses you dearly." Even at ten years old, Quintus had known he shouldn't cry. But he had hugged his mother tightly as they both wept joyously for what seemed an eternity.

Vespasian explained how he had put word out across the southern reaches of the Empire, looking for Caius. A friend had returned from Creta that day and brought the good news. Apparently, a message Caius himself had sent to the family telling them not to worry had gone astray.

To celebrate, Vespasian took Quintus and Politta out that night to one of Rome's nicest eating houses. As they ate, Vespasian made a prediction as to when Caius would return. He was off by just two days.

Caius let his first mate take charge of the next voyage, and he spent the next few months with Quintus and Politta. They traveled through northern Italia, spending many wonderful weeks in the hilly countryside. It was one of the happiest times of Quintus's young life. Ten years later, he still remembered every detail of the trip.

But what he remembered most was the kindness, concern, and caring of Titus Flavius Vespasianus. He owed this man, and he now had the opportunity to repay that debt.

Quintus rolled over in his cot and yawned. The thought of helping Vespasian, while saving Rome from yet another megalomaniac despot, put his mind at ease and kindled a peaceful sleep.

• • •

Castus continued to work the gladiators and venatores hard over the next week. Gradually, they began to grasp the new close-order fighting drills and the other battlefield tactics the ex-centurion taught. Those venatores who had previously worked only with hunting spears were drilled in the use of the bow. All the hunters were trained in the art of the sling, a challenging weapon few had ever attempted. Although Lindani was one of the venatores who had never fired a stone from a long leather strap, the skill quickly became second nature to the young African. Within a few days, he was repeatedly striking his straw mannequin in the head from a hundred feet.

Macer had three hundred pila delivered to the ludus. Castus made sure that gladiators and hunters alike became proficient in tossing the long, heavy javelins. On the morning of the eleventh day, Macer arrived to take delivery of his mercenaries.

Quintus and the other selected fighters and hunters stood at ease with pila and scuta at their sides. Castus had set them in smart formations of three full centuries of eighty men each and one under-strength company of the remaining sixty. Behind them sat a train of carts loaded with supplies and weapons.

Soon the sound of hooves drifted over the ludus walls. Quintus watched the gates open and about a dozen military men rode into the training yard. Castus called his fighters to attention with an impressive bellow. As one, three hundred pila snapped to a uniform upright position, legs came together, and a roar of *"Victory!"* echoed across the training field.

Macer nodded with a smirk as he dismounted. Quintus decided he disliked the patronizing man already. "They look good on the parade ground, gentlemen," the officer said to Petra and Facilix, "but are they in fighting form?"

"I think you'll find them more than suitable, Tribune," Facilix replied. "Castus has done an exceptional job training them."

The officer turned and looked at the old centurion who stood alongside the lanistae. "Livius Castus, isn't it? You served with us in Lusitania years ago, didn't you?"

Castus gave a short bow. "Yes, sir. That's correct."

"A wise choice for trainer," the officer said as he walked down the front line of gladiators. "He was a good centurion." He got to the end of the line and looked up at the vexillum banner held aloft on a hunting spear by Priedens the Thracian. The image of a black gladius over a gold laurel wreath stood out on a crimson background. Underneath were the words: Cohors Gladiatorum. Macer smiled.

"I think he likes your work," Quintus whispered to Lindani.

"Well, you're not quite a full cohort," Macer said loudly, "but I like your spirit. Carry that banner proudly, vexillarius," he said to Priedens. He then turned and faced his new auxiliaries. "My name is Martius Macer." His booming voice easily carried across the yard. "I am your tribune. Think of me as your new lanista." His smirk returned. Quintus glanced toward Petra, and he could see the muscles in his lanista's arms go tight. "I understand you are good fighters and venatores. Is this true?"

In unison, the men shouted, "Yes, sir!" The response was loud enough to startle the horses. Macer seemed surprised by the troupe's fervor.

"Well, alright then. Maybe you'll return here quicker than we thought, and you can go back to hacking the shit out of each other." A mutter of laughter rose from the cavalry troopers still seated on their horses.

A snort came from beside Quintus. He glanced at Riagall, one of the veteran fighters. "No matter how well we fight," the Celt muttered, "we'll never be taken seriously by these assholes."

Alongside Riagall, Drusus the thraex nodded. "We could show these pretty boy troopers a move or two."

Quintus knew they were both right.

Macer nodded to his escort. Four of the troopers struggled to remove bulging saddle bags and dropped them at Petra's feet. There was a loud jingle of coins as each bag hit the dirt. Payments to the lanistae were

usually made in private, certainly out of sight of the fighters and never cal-
lously tossed from horseback. Some of the gladiators glanced at each other.
Quintus was sure they all wondered the same thing: How much were their
lives worth? Petra's face turned red with anger at Macer's tactless action.
He looked toward his men.

"Your shares will be waiting for you when you return," he called out to
the ranks of fighters and hunters.

Macer grinned again. "How generous of you, lanista."

It looked to Quintus as if Petra was about to lash out at the tribune, but
Macer turned his back on the two lanistae and remounted his charger.

"I hope you are prepared to march, gentlemen," Macer yelled. "It's a
long walk from Pompeii to Rome. To break you in easy, you'll be carrying
only your scutum. Your weapons and extra equipment will follow in the
carts." His face suddenly grew stern as he looked down on the ranks from
his horse. "And I certainly hope none of you have any thoughts of escape.
These troopers will run you down before you get twenty steps. The penalty
for desertion is death. Keep that in mind before you try anything stupid."

He nodded again to his escort, then kicked his horse toward the open
gate. Castus stepped forward before the horse got too far and spoke quietly to the tribune. They both turned and looked at Quintus. Macer gave
a quick nod and rode on.

"Flank left!" one of the troopers shouted. "Move! Lay your pilum in the
empty cart as you pass."

The fighters began filing out of the ludus four abreast. Quintus was in
the first row, Lindani by his side. He nodded with a quick smile and a
wink as he passed Petra, Castus, and Julianus.

"May Hercules be with you all," Castus replied, raising his hand.

As the column left the ludus and marched down the Via dell'
Abbondanza behind their Cohors Gladiatorum banner, Quintus was
surprised to see so many Pompeiians lining the wide street. At first he
thought they were there to cheer them on and bid farewell, but the mood
was more angry than festive.

"So who fights for us while you're off playing soldiers?" a man yelled from the crowd. A chorus of voices shouted in agreement.

"We're left with the shit!" a ragged woman called out, prompting a louder cry from the crowd.

"Shut your mouth, you fucking whore," a cavalry trooper called down from his horse. "They'll be back when we're done with them . . . at least the ones the sagittarii don't shoot in the back as they run screaming from the battlefield like women."

The other troopers laughed raucously as they rode on. Quintus glanced back at the riders flanking their column every thirty to forty feet. He noted that Macer made no attempt to silence the public ridicule. An odd way to gain the favor of new fighters, he thought.

The column turned right on the Via di Stabia and headed out of the city through the Vesuvio Gate. Quintus was already thankful that Macer had sent three hundred pairs of caligae along with the javelins. The thick, hobnailed soles would certainly ease the ache of many feet on the long trek. But as they circled the base of the great mountain and approached Capua after a few hours of marching, the heavy shield began taking its toll.

"I'd love to toss this scutum up on that cart," Quintus said quietly to Lindani.

"That would not be wise," Lindani replied, "especially since you might hurt someone."

Quintus looked at him, unsure of his meaning. Lindani grinned a broad smile. "Look closely at the cart," he said.

Quintus studied the wooden transport wagon ahead of them loaded with crates of swords and other weapons. At first nothing seemed out of the ordinary, but then he saw what Lindani meant. Toward the front of the cart bed, just behind the high driver's bench, was a tuft of reddish brown hair.

"Oh, don't tell me . . ." Quintus began, then leaned over and snatched a loose pebble from the surface of the Via Annia as he walked. He glanced over his shoulder and saw the closest cavalry trooper was staring off into the distance. He casually lobbed the stone into the cart bed. The tuft of hair jerked with the sudden noise, and the emerald eyes of Amazonia peered out at him from behind the crate of swords.

VI

February AD 69

LUCIUS AND JULIA stood near the curved swan's neck at the prow of the *Juno*. They watched their crew secure the last line and lay the gangway to the dock at Caesarea. The morning activity in the port was lively, with ships coming and going and dozens of cargo holds being loaded and unloaded with wooden hoists.

"It's like Alexandria in miniature," Lucius said, scanning the harbor and the small city beyond. "Even the lighthouse looks like the smaller brother of the Pharos light."

"It's much nicer than I expected for such a remote part of the Empire," Julia replied as she leaned on the deck rail.

The collection of white stucco buildings that made up Caesarea was dominated by a massive temple that faced the harbor. The town was enclosed by a low wall that arched in a semicircle from the rocky beaches on either side of the port. An aqueduct pierced the wall on the north side and ran far up the coastline in a series of delicate arches.

"Welcome to Judea. May I come aboard?" The pleasant voice with a foreign accent came from a middle-aged man standing at the foot of the gangway. His long black hair was partially hidden under a tall head wrap. The pointed beard and layered Syrian robes of white, brown, and gold were exotic to Lucius and Julia but native to the region where they now found themselves. "I am Aram Kalyndu, your representative here in Caesarea."

"Of course, come aboard," Julia called to him.

He approached them at the prow and bowed deeply with a sweeping hand gesture. "I am at your service, Mistress Melita. The captain of our last ship from Alexandria told me of your arrival."

"Our thanks to you, Aram," Julia responded with a smile. "This is my husband, Lucius Calidius."

Lucius was almost getting used to the "husband" title. He smiled as the Syrian bowed to him.

"We have much to discuss about our operations here," Julia said as she walked toward the side rail and looked out across the wide harbor. "I wasn't sure what to expect in Caesarea. But this could be quite pleasant."

"Our city is magnificent, madam, I assure you," Aram said in a proud voice. He pointed toward the mammoth colonnaded building in the city center. "As you can see, our temples rival those of Rome. That one honors the mighty Caesar Augustus, a gift from our King Herod. It was built almost a hundred years ago."

Lucius had turned and was inspecting the southern end of the town. "It appears your palaces rival Rome's as well," he said, nodding toward a dramatic sprawling structure that topped a green promontory jutting into the sea.

"Ahh, that is the palace, also built by Herod the Great," Aram said with a wide smile. "Now it is the residence of our governor, Vespasian."

"Yes . . . Vespasian," Julia said. "We must try to arrange a meeting with the governor very soon."

"He is a good and wise man, madam. I am sure he will be pleased to meet the two Roman nobles who will be increasing trade to his province."

Lucius glanced at Julia and had to stifle a laugh. They both knew that Lucius was far from "noble." In fact, as a slave, he was not even a citizen of Rome. However, the masquerade was so much easier to keep up in the remote provinces, where as long as he dressed well and acted the part, no questions were ever asked. And being introduced as Julia's husband perfected the façade.

"Is that a theater there by the palace?" Lucius asked. "It looks—"

His words were cut short by the ship's captain, who approached with deliberate speed. "I must speak with you both right away," he said quickly to Lucius and Julia. Lucius was about to chastise the man for interrupting, but the ominous look on the captain's face stopped him.

"What is it, Captain?" Julia asked. Aram stepped back a few feet.

"This freighter that tied up next to us . . . it just came from Ostia. The captain tells me Emperor Galba is dead! Assassinated! They say it's civil war."

"By the gods!" Lucius said.

Julia grabbed Lucius's arm. He saw that her mind was already at work.

"We can use this to get to Vespasian," she said, "but we need to move quickly." Lucius stepped back as she kicked into action. "Captain, run and get the captain of that freighter and tell him if he wants to earn an extra week's salary for only a moment's work, meet me on the dock *now*. Aram, is the carriage ready to go?"

"Yes, madam. I just need to turn it around."

"Do it," she said as she headed for the deckhouse. She pulled the door open and called down the stairs to her ornatrix. "Bring my gold palla right away. And the master's toga." She walked quickly back toward Lucius. "I want you to present this news to the governor, if he hasn't yet heard. It will leave a lasting impression of our first meeting. Let's go."

They grabbed the outer garments from Julia's handmaiden at the top of the stairs, then headed down the gangway. Their captain was just arriving with the freighter captain in tow.

"Tell us everything you know of the events in Rome," Julia said quickly. "I'll make it well worth your while, so long as you keep the news contained here on the docks for a while."

The man rambled through a litany of facts, rumor, and personal speculation on the intrigue and uncertainty that was gripping the capital. When he was finished, Julia and Lucius hastily boarded the open carriage.

"Thank you, Captain," Julia called down to him.

"Make haste to the palace, Aram," Lucius said as the fleet manager climbed aboard to drive. "A bonus for you as well if we are the first to arrive with this news."

"I'll settle with you this evening," Julia called to the freighter captain, left standing on the dock. "My ship's captain will vouch for my word."

Once clear of the loading cranes, Aram snapped the reins hard and the horses responded. The pair kicked into a full gallop, as stevedores, sailors, and warehouse managers scattered across the harbor promenade to get out of the way. Some called obscenities to Aram in a variety of foreign tongues. The carriage passed under the harbor's entrance arch, then turned right and rushed along the wide boulevard that flanked the shore.

"This is good," Julia said, not seeming at all concerned about the carriage's speed. "This will make an impression with Vespasian and introduce us as people who can deliver more than just trade products to his province."

Lucius held tightly to the top edge of the carriage, the end of his white toga blowing back along the side of the coach. "Assuming of course we make it to the palace alive."

Aram looked back with one hand on his tall head wrap and the other on the reins. "Not to worry, Master Calidius! I will get you there quickly and safely."

To counter his point, a woman carrying a large bushel of produce balanced atop her head dove for cover as the horses thundered past, their hooves trampling many of her brightly colored fruits. The chargers seemed to take notice of the hippodrome stadium to their left and increased in speed as they galloped alongside the large horse racing arena.

Lucius was happy to see they were almost at the palace entranceway. Four legionary guards stood outside the gate to the peristyle courtyard at the entrance to the palace complex. They lowered their javelins as the carriage rolled to a stop. Lucius stood up in the bed of the open coach.

"I am Lucius Calidius, former Imperial Advisor to Nero. We seek an immediate audience with the governor. I have urgent news from Rome."

One of the legionaries motioned to the junior guard, who drew back the bolt on the metal gate and disappeared behind the peristyle walls. As they waited, Lucius glanced over his shoulder to see if any others were making for the palace with the news. The road was clear except for a few strolling pedestrians. So long as the news had not already arrived by courier or on an earlier ship, they would be assured a good first impression with the governor.

The gate swung open again and an older man stepped through, followed by the junior guard. Although he wore no armor, the broad purple stripe on his tunic signified the rank of senior tribune.

"What is it you need?" the officer asked with authority. "The governor is in a meeting and cannot be disturbed."

"I have news from Rome that must reach the governor immediately," Lucius said, matching the tribune's fervor. "It is a matter of State urgency. It concerns the well being of the emperor. Tell the governor that Lucius Calidius and Julia Melita, owners of Romanus Shipping and Transport, seek his audience." Lucius figured Julia wouldn't mind him taking part ownership in the business for a day if it got them access to Vespasian.

The tribune raised an eyebrow, studying Lucius for a moment, then turned to the guards. "Search them, then escort them to the audience hall."

Lucius stepped from the carriage as one of the legionaries ran a quick hand under his toga and around his midsection in search of hidden weapons. They all looked at Julia as she rose and stepped from the carriage. The guards seemed unsure what to do.

"Let's go, boys. Get it done," she said as she pulled her draping palla to the side. The long stola underneath hugged her alluring body tightly.

"I'm sorry, madam," the junior guard said quietly as he ran a quick hand across her waistline in back and front. "There are many in Judea who cannot be trusted."

"I understand, legionary," she answered with a smile.

Lucius and Julia followed their escort through the entranceway as

Aram spun the horse and carriage around and pulled to the side of the entrance path to wait. The rectangular peristyle they entered was large, easily the size of the training field at Lucius's old North African ludus. But rather than brown earth, this courtyard was carpeted with a perfectly manicured lawn of emerald green. In the center of the verdant oasis was a statue of Juno, painted in exquisite lifelike detail. They walked along the portico surrounding the yard, filing past dozens of Doric columns supporting a barrel-tiled roof. The escort led them toward the north corner of the peristyle, where an opening in the outer wall allowed a spectacular view of the rocky edge of the promontory and the deep blue sea beyond. Breakers crashed against the rocks, sending a fine spray over the north face of the palace.

As the mist touched his face, Lucius felt a wave of nostalgia. He was suddenly back in Nero's Golden House in Rome, where a fine mist of perfumed water would periodically cascade from the ceilings. He felt a sudden sense of belonging and reveled in the luxury. The imperial dwellings of the Empire were where he was destined to be. He leaned toward Julia and spoke quietly as they walked. "We'll be back in the halls of power soon. I know it. I can feel it."

Julia glanced at him but did not respond.

Before they reached the opening, the escort ushered them into a large audience hall adorned with muraled walls and a geometric floor created in shades of blue, green, and beige tiles. The furnishings were sparse but elegant: a bronze armchair with a small matching footstool and a few couches of wood and blue cushions. Narrow windows high on the far wall allowed in just enough of the Mediterranean sun to bathe the murals in a soft light.

Lucius walked toward the back mural and had just begun to study the details of a vivid seashore scene when the echo of footsteps swept into the room. The tribune appeared in the doorway, followed by a balding man of average height and powerful build. His compressed lips and arched eyebrows lent him a strained expression, although his voice came in a friendly manner as he addressed Lucius.

"I am Flavius Vespasianus, governor of Judea. I'm afraid you've caught me in the middle of a finance meeting. But my tribune tells me you are with Romanus Shipping and have important news from Rome."

The governor made no attempt to sit, so Lucius knew this would be a short meeting. "Yes, sir. I am Lucius Calidius, former magistrate and Imperial Advisor. This is my wife, Julia Melita, owner of Romanus Shipping." He paused and glanced at the soldiers who stood in the arched doorway. "May we speak in private?"

Vespasian glanced over his shoulder. "Legionaries, leave us," he said and the two soldiers stepped out to the portico. "My tribune stays," the governor said as he returned his attention to Lucius.

"Of course. Sir, I'm afraid the tidings from Rome are not good. Emperor Galba has been assassinated."

The look on the governor's face assured Lucius and Julia they were the first to deliver the news. Lucius almost smiled with relief.

"When? How?" Vespasian demanded.

"A few weeks ago. It appears he was the victim of a plot led by Salvius Otho, although Otho put his freedman, Onomastus, in charge of the intrigue. They rallied the Praetorians against Galba and attacked him in his litter as he tried to escape the palace. A soldier from the Fifteenth Legion struck the fatal blow and the rest hacked him to pieces."

Vespasian was quiet for a moment, looking toward the patterned floor. "Had the Emperor named an heir?" he finally asked.

"Yes, he had adopted Calpurnius Piso," Lucius said. "Unfortunately, Piso, too, was struck down that same night. Otho made no secret that the adoption of Piso is what prompted his action." Vespasian listened with interest as he paced the tiled floor. Lucius let the news sink in for a moment, then continued. "There's more. The legions of Aulus Vitellius in the Lower Rhine have rejected Otho's claim to the throne. They're supporting their own commander as emperor. Rome is now bracing for civil war."

The governor nodded as he absorbed the information. He summoned the tribune over, and the two spoke quietly for a moment.

"There is some good news to report," Lucius continued, interrupting the private conversation. "Otho has named your brother Flavius Sabinus to be Prefect of the City of Rome."

Vespasian shook his head slowly with a tight grin. "He's a shrewd rogue, Otho is," the governor said more to himself than anyone in the room. "He made that appointment as a gesture of peace to me. He wants me and my legions behind him." He resumed his private discussion with the tribune.

Lucius glanced at Julia. She gave him a quick wink of reassurance. As usual, she had offered much more than moral support in this endeavor. When they had decided to make this journey a few weeks prior, Julia had put her staff in Alexandria to work researching Vespasian's background. *Always know the players,* she had said. It was the same approach she had used to help Lucius become the youngest magistrate in Britannia. The information they had gathered about Vespasian's past might or might not be important, but Julia made note of every detail they had uncovered: His closeness with both his mother and the grandmother who helped raise him; his distinguished military career in Britannia; his two bright sons, the eldest assisting him here in Judea and the younger one still in Rome; and his reputation of fairness and honesty during his consular appointment in Africa. Apparently, he had returned from the rich province with no more money than he had before, a testament to his integrity in a position that invited graft and corruption. As a result, the years following his consulship were hard. He had raised livestock and started a transport contracting business, earning the nickname "the Muledriver." He had come into favor with Nero, as had his brother Sabinus, who Nero appointed Prefect of the City—the position he resumed now under Otho. Vespasian had been invited to join Nero on his trip to Greece. But the excursion resulted in further hardship after Vespasian had made a serious tactical error—not during any military action, but during one of the

Emperor's lengthy musical recitals. Vespasian had fallen asleep. He was banished from Nero's entourage and, for a while, appeared in jeopardy of execution. Instead, the Emperor sent him to Judea to quell the Jewish Revolt. Some called it an exile. But by all accounts, Vespasian considered it an honor and duty he took most seriously.

But what Julia and Lucius found most interesting was Vespasian's ties with Romanus Shipping and Transport. Lucius had finally remembered why Vespasian's name had such a familiar sound. The memory brought difficult childhood images from his days as a slave in the Romanus household. But through the haze of time, he recalled seeing this man when he would visit the house. It was well after Vespasian's involvement in helping Caius develop the business, but the two men had remained good friends. The most disconcerting memories were those of Vespasian joking and engaging in mock combat with a young Quintus Romanus. The two obviously had some sort of close bond that Lucius could never figure out. Perhaps it had formed before he and his mother were purchased by the Romanus family.

"Check all this out and report back to me here," Vespasian said to the tribune. "And tell the finance staff our meeting is concluded." The officer saluted and left the room. Vespasian returned to Lucius. "My eldest son, Titus, is in the midst of a sea journey to Rome. He sought to offer our allegiance to Galba. Hopefully he has heard this news at a port-of-call and returns here now. I can use his counsel."

"We have ships in many ports-of-call in the Mare Internum," Julia said, stepping forward into a shaft of sunlight from the high windows. "If we can be of assistance, our fleet is at your service."

Vespasian studied her for a moment, as if just noticing her presence in the room. "I'm well aware of that, Mistress Melita. I helped establish that fleet."

Julia smiled. "So I've heard, Governor. That must have been quite an undertaking."

"It was Caius who did all the work. I just helped steer some business his way. So, you are now the owner of Romanus Shipping?"

"Yes, sir, I am. My first husband died last year. He was the heir to the fleet after the loss of the Romanus family."

Vespasian's eyes became distant and he lowered his gaze. "What a tragedy that was, to die in such a storm. That poor family. At least Quintus survived . . ."

Lucius could feel the hairs on the back of his neck rise. Was there nowhere in this Empire he could get away from the name "Quintus Romanus"? Did everyone in the fucking world know this kid? Lucius's heart began to pound, but Vespasian continued before he had the opportunity to speak.

". . . although I hear his life did not turn out well after that." Vespasian looked up at Julia. "I assume that's why your first husband inherited the fleet rather than Quintus?" Lucius almost detected a hint of suspicion in his eyes.

"Quintus became . . . shall we say . . . a bit impetuous after the loss of his family. He didn't cope well. My husband, Sextus, agreed to look after the business until Quintus was old enough to take it over."

Lucius decided he wanted to complete the story. "But he was in no condition to run a business. He tried to run his own arena games and look what happened." Lucius suddenly felt the pressure of Julia's foot on top of his. Her long stola hid the motion from Vespasian.

"Yes, that was another tragedy," Vespasian replied. "Do you know where he is now? Seems he vanished like a ghost after that incident."

Julia spoke quickly. "He was estranged from the family by then, but I heard he was arrested and put to death. His appointment to the imperial court shortly before the incident made Nero look bad, so it seems they kept it quiet."

Vespasian nodded. "Yes, well, we all know how Nero handled staff members who didn't please him." Knowing Vespasian's background, Lucius saw the irony in his statement. "Still, Quintus was a terrific kid. I'll try to always remember him that way."

There was silence for a moment. Lucius pondered another barb he could throw at Quintus without incurring the wrath of Julia. But she spoke first. "We've just arrived to begin expanding our operations here in Caesarea. We're ordering the building of three new freighters that will call at your port."

"Our fleet captains make excellent couriers," Lucius added, picking up on her thoughts. "When the winds are favorable, communication is quick. Please consider us at your disposal if you need documents or information ferried to Rome or any port cities."

"My flagship is outfitted with outstanding passenger accommodations as well," Julia continued. She paused for a moment and made a show of glancing toward the doorway to be sure they were still alone. ". . . should you have any senior officials looking to travel with a lower profile than a navy galley or trireme might offer."

"Any senior officials . . . or governors," Lucius added, to be sure Vespasian fully understood the offer.

Vespasian looked at the two visitors and nodded with a tight smile on his thin lips. "Thank you for the offer. Your services might well be needed before this ordeal is finished. We shall see how it plays out."

The sound of hobnails came from the portico, and the tribune re-entered the room. "Some of our men from the port are arriving with similar reports from Rome. Another ship just docked from Ostia and confirmed the news."

Vespasian nodded. He looked toward Lucius and Julia as he moved to the doorway. "You'll excuse me, but I have urgent matters to attend to. Tribune, see them to the door." As he reached the portal, he stopped for a moment and looked back one last time. "Thank you," he said.

The governor of Judea then stepped out onto the portico and disappeared down the hallway.

VII

February AD 69

T HE CARAVAN OF GLADIATORS pulled to a stop in a field halfway between Herculaneum and Capua. Macer ordered the supply
wagons pulled toward the center of the field for unloading, and
the weapons carts pulled downwind, away from the camp.

Quintus wondered if it was to keep the malodorous oxen farther from
the camp or the weapons farther from the gladiators. Probably both. But
he was not about to let the weapons cart in front of him out of his sight.
The more he thought about its hidden human cargo, the more he seethed
with anger. He had enough to worry about on this trip without the added
responsibility of an untrained stowaway. He glanced at Lindani, and the
hunter nodded.

"This man is good with animals," Quintus said, pointing Lindani out
to the nearest cavalry trooper. "He can deal with the oxen. I'll get him
started."

He didn't wait for an answer. He was the appointed leader of the
Pompeiian gladiators, and he wanted to begin testing the boundaries of
his authority. No protest came from the trooper, although Quintus could
hear two horses walking behind them as he and Lindani followed the last
cart toward the tree line.

When it came to a halt, they busied themselves unhitching the pair of
oxen, casually scanning the area around them. The two guards rode past
them, then dismounted and began directing the lead driver in securing
his cart for the night.

"What in Hades is wrong with you?" Quintus whispered near the left ox's rump. "This is the stupidest stunt you've pulled since you decided to fight a lion in the arena with a gladius."

Amazonia's husky voice came from the blackness of the cart bed. "I saved your asses then. I'm here to save your asses now. You two can't seem to get it right without me."

"This is insanity, Amazonia. Lindani and I will cause a distraction. Jump from the cart and make your way back to the ludus. You'll be there by morning."

"That's not going to happen," she said firmly.

Quintus looked at Lindani. The African shrugged with his wide grin. "The woman has a job to do. Who are we to argue?"

The frustration built in Quintus. He knew they were about to enter a world of violence on a much different scale than the arena. The thought of this beautiful woman in the middle of a titanic battle between the legions had his stomach in knots. But what frustrated him most was knowing there was nothing he could do about it. As much as he hated seeing her in harm's way, it was useless to argue about it. He had considered revealing her presence to Macer earlier in the day, as soon as Lindani had spotted her behind the crate. But she would never have forgiven him for such a betrayal. She always insisted on pulling an equal share of responsibility and proving her worth. Whether she desired to prove it to the other fighters or to herself, he wasn't sure.

"They'll find you eventually," Quintus whispered as he loosened the straps on the oxen. The two beasts shifted their weight and slapped their tails toward Quintus.

"I doubt it. They won't unload the weapon wagons at night," she whispered back.

"So you will spend the entire war in this cart?" Lindani asked. "I think there is little action you will see from there, no?" His wide grin was almost too bright in the evening darkness.

"I'll climb out when we reach Rome. By then it'll be too late for

Macer to send me back to the ludus."

Quintus rolled his eyes at Lindani. "Brilliant plan."

"There's only one problem," Amazonia whispered. "I really have to pee. Is there anyone in sight?"

Quintus glanced around. The closest troopers were still working with the cart driver about thirty feet away. "Go over the right side and make for the trees," he murmured.

Amazonia pushed with her shoulder and slid the crate of swords forward enough to squeeze from her cramped hiding space. She lifted the tarp, scrambled over the side planks, and dropped down on the far side of the wagon. Her right foot landed in the soft grass, but her left snapped a dead oak branch in two. "Shit," she grumbled.

The loud crack split the night air. Quintus glanced at the cart driver ahead of them. The driver's head jerked up. His reaction caught the attention of one of the troopers.

"What's happening there?" the guard yelled out as he started toward their cart.

Lindani looked up nonchalantly from unfastening the leather straps. "The oxen are nervous. Perhaps a snake is nearby."

Amazonia crouched low, ready to sprint the ten feet into the brush, but Quintus grabbed her shoulder and held her down. She never would have made it without being spotted by the guard.

In a few seconds, the trooper was at the back of the cart, scanning the contents suspiciously. "Why is that crate moved?"

Nobody answered. Amazonia remained crouched against the wheel.

"And why is the tarp thrown back like that?" He eyed Quintus standing next to him.

"I was—"

"Pulcher!" the trooper suddenly yelled. The second cavalryman ran toward the wagon, drawing his sword in response to the alarm in his comrade's voice.

"It's nothing, trooper," Quintus said calmly, trying to diffuse the situation before it got out of hand. "The crate slid during transport, and I was simply readjusting the load."

"That's horseshit," yelled the jittery guard, now drawing his own weapon. "A weapons crate is too heavy to slide around on its own. You were going for the swords."

Lindani moved to Quintus's side. "You are wrong. He sought no weapon," he said calmly.

"What's going on over there?" Macer called from across the camp.

Quintus groaned. "It's nothing, Tribune. I was just—"

"Looks like he was going for the swords, sir," the second guard yelled.

Macer trotted toward the cart, followed by four more guards. The remaining troopers quickly swung to face the tired gladiators setting up camp and drew their long spatha cavalry swords.

"No, no. I wasn't," Quintus said. "I was just—"

"He was just trying to protect me." Amazonia stood up and stepped from the far side of the cart.

Macer's ruddy face grew two shades darker. "What's this? You brought along a whore?"

"No, Tribune," Quintus replied quickly. For a brief second he debated whether to insist she get sent back, but the look in her eyes told him otherwise. "She's a fighter and a damned good one."

"I'll have you flogged, bitch," Macer yelled in her face. "How dare you stow away in my caravan? Who do you think you are?"

Amazonia did not back down. "Like he said, I'm a fighter and I belong with these men."

Macer studied the curves of her short tunic. After a moment, he spoke again, lust now replacing the anger in his voice. "Perhaps it *would* be a shame to waste you. You will stay with me and my men." The troopers' eyes grew wide with anticipation at the order.

Amazonia laughed. "I'll do no such thing," she said, raising her chin. "I'm a gladiator, and I'll stay with the other gladiators from Pompeii."

"She's one of our best fighters, Tribune," Quintus said. "Our lanista pairs her against male opponents. Her skill with a gladius would be an asset for you."

One of the cavalry troopers stepped closer to Macer. "I've seen her fight, sir, at the Pompeii Challenge last year. Her name's Amazonia. She's a bit unorthodox, but a good fighter."

"Ahh, so you're the famous Amazonia," the tribune said with a sneer. His condescending tone irritated Quintus. "Well, you may be a popular attraction in the arena, but the battlefield is no place for a woman. You wouldn't make it past the opening charge of our first engagement."

"It'll give me great pleasure to prove you wrong about that, Tribune. Allow me to stay. If you're right, then I'll be killed quickly and out of your hair. If you're wrong, you've picked up an extra fighter at no cost to the emperor."

Macer seemed enthralled by her deep voice but then shook his head. "You didn't train with Castus. There's no time to train you in the basic legionary drills."

"I watched everything Doctore Castus showed these men," she answered. "I practiced in my cell at night."

Macer continued to study her body. As his eyes eventually worked their way back up to her face, his expression became more serious. "Alright, you'd rather be a fighter than a whore? Fine. Then you'll conform to Army regulations." His malevolent grin returned. "And that begins with your hair. Pulcher!"

"Yes, sir?" the trooper yelled.

"Give this recruit a regulation legionary haircut. Let's see how badly she wants to be a part of this army."

The guard's smirk matched his officer's. "Yes, Tribune."

Pulcher grabbed Amazonia's arm and led her toward the fire that had been built near the center of camp. Quintus knew his own shoulder-length hair, as well as most of the other gladiators' locks, were much longer than what was stipulated in army regulations. But he had discovered that, beneath the crusty surface, Macer seemed a bit intimidated by the male gladiators. Humiliating a female fighter was a much safer way to flaunt his power.

As Quintus watched her being led away, another thought—one he hated to admit to himself—crossed his mind. He felt a small sense of satisfaction at the penance Amazonia would now have to endure for her stupid actions.

"Back to work," Macer yelled at Quintus and Lindani. He turned and pointed menacingly at the first guard. "And *you* are supposed to be watching these men. Now, get up there and secure that weapons crate." The guard snarled at Quintus as he climbed into the cart, muscled the crate back into place, and retied the tarp.

Quintus and Lindani finished unhitching the oxen and led them to the makeshift corral, where they were fed and watered. They then hurried toward the center of camp, where Amazonia was seated on a short stool beside the campfire. Pulcher stood behind her, the leer still etched on his face. He ran the fingers of his left hand through her long hair. His right hand grasped crude iron shears from his horse grooming kit. He was milking the event for all the attention he could muster from the dozen other troopers who were now cheering him on.

Quintus circled around the fire and locked eyes with Amazonia. Her face was impassive, but she managed a wink at him. He could read her like an oracle. Although it would pain any woman with such beautiful hair to have it shorn so mercilessly, she was not about to give Macer and his troopers a hint of satisfaction. In the arena, the auburn tresses spilling from beneath her murmillo helmet and onto her bare shoulders had become as much a part of Amazonia's persona as her explosive fighting style. But her hair—like her beauty—was just a tool, not the *real* her. He knew she felt this initiation was a small price to pay in order to fight this war with the men of her ludus. Still, he watched the warm glow of the fire enhance the brilliance of her red highlights for the last time.

The first snip brought louder cheers from the guards. In their midst, Macer smiled and nodded as her locks touched the grass.

"Come on, get on with it, ornatrix," Amazonia said, taunting Pulcher with the term for a woman's handmaiden and beauty assistant. The insult sparked howls of laughter among both the guards and the gladiators who had gathered to watch. Quintus looked at Lindani and laughed. The bravado of this woman never ceased to amaze either of them.

Pulcher grumbled and began hacking away with the horse shears. Amazonia's hair drifted down around her like auburn snow. She stared ahead without the tiniest flinch, even as the intimidating shears came dangerously close to her face and scalp. Pulcher walked around her while he cut furiously. Within moments it was over. The trooper had left her with the tightly cropped style that adorned the heads of the new legionaries.

Pulcher stepped to the side, and Quintus stared in amazement. The transformation was remarkable. The subtle softness that her flowing mane had once afforded was now gone. Her look was more severe, her overall image much tougher. Yet her beauty was still intact. Perhaps it was the slim, slightly pointed nose. Or the emerald eyes. To Quintus, she still possessed the beauty of Venus and the vigor of Minerva, goddess of war.

"Can I go pee now?"

The words knocked the divine images from Quintus's head.

"Go on," Macer said, leaning his head toward the tree line. "Then help finish setting camp with the rest of your stinking gladiators."

"Let us hope her strength was not in her hair, no?" Lindani said as they watched her walk away, rubbing at her new stubble.

"Her strength, like her beauty, is too deep to be affected by a haircut," Quintus replied.

It took the gladiator caravan seven days to reach Rome. They had stopped at Capua to pick up the additional three hundred fighters Macer had extorted from that ludus. All six hundred mercenaries were now housed within the giant complex of the Ludus Magnus in Rome, near the Amphitheater of Taurus. But even the Empire's largest gladiator training facility did not have enough cells and barracks for all the new fighters. Most of the Pompeiians and Capuans were forced to pitch tents in the sand of the oversized training arena, sleeping eight to a tent—the standard contubernium, the subunit of a century of soldiers.

Quintus joined Lindani, Amazonia, Memnon, Riagall, Drusus, Valentinus, and Roscius in a goat-hide tent near the center of the arena. The sand beneath him made for a comfortable sleeping surface, and the bodies of the eight veteran fighters huddled together generated enough heat to ward off the winter chill. He decided it was a much better arrangement than sleeping on the hard ground under the stars, as they had done on their trek from Pompeii.

Amazonia was awakened by the sound of cornu horns shortly after sunrise. She glanced around the cramped tent and smiled to herself. Even during her years as a prostitute, she had never slept with seven men at once. She was almost insulted that not one reached for her in the night. The men obviously still took Petra's warning about touching her seriously. The sting of the whip was a potent deterrent.

She stretched and threw back the tent flap. The morning sun blinded all eight tent mates. Macer stood on the podium of the small cavea that surrounded the arena. His voice echoed in the morning stillness.

"I hope you got on well with your tent mates last night. Look at those men." Macer paused, and Amazonia realized the statement was more than a metaphorical suggestion. It was an order. She glanced at Quintus and Lindani first, then the other five men.

"Each is your contubernalis," Macer finally continued. "You will sleep, eat, shit, and live with these people for the rest of this war, or until you or they are killed. You will come to learn why the word *contubernalis* means much more than 'tent mate' to a legionary. It is a term of comradeship. It is a term of affection. You will look out for these men, and they will look out for you."

Amazonia knew she could not have chosen her tent mates any better.

Although she hadn't heard the word before—and despite the axiom that gladiators should avoid friendship in a ludus—she knew that every man in her tent understood the meaning of *contubernalis* long before they were conscripted into this army. It was the reason she, herself, left the safety of the ludus to join her fellow fighters in this civil war. This was her familia, and she was not about to abandon them. Certainly not Quintus and Lindani. Especially not Quintus.

"Today," Macer continued, "you will commence training under Rome's elite: the Praetorian Guard. In terms a dim-witted gladiator might understand, these men are the primus palus of Rome's army. Each is loyal to Emperor Otho and will defend to the death Otho's divine right to the principate."

As Macer slowly walked to the other side of the podium, Amazonia thought back to the gossip and rumors about Otho that had spread like a plague through their camp over the past week. Most were instigated by the Capuans. Tales of Otho's bizarre excesses and maniacal ambition for power did little to separate him from the parade of irrational predecessors. In fact, it seemed he might be worse. She had wondered why they were here in the first place, but then she heard the story of the mysterious fire that destroyed much of the Capuan ludus after their lanista balked at Macer's request for fighters. She considered the wisdom of fighting for a man who needed to recruit supporters through intimidation, extortion, and blood money. But she concluded any rational thought during the outbreak of civil war was a waste of her time.

"This morning you will be issued your kit and armor," Macer continued. "Gather them and assemble on the drill field where you'll find your weapons. Venatores assemble on the west side of the field; you will be issued a kit, but no armor. All of your weapons are waiting for you on the field. Do it now."

The arena gate opened, and at the end of the entranceway were long rows of tables covered with military equipment. Amazonia and Quintus slowly made their way along the queue, each acquiring a red tunic, a

T-shaped pole with a variety of pots and leather pouches attached, a cuirass of articulated metal bands, a helmet, a groin guard of studded leather strips, a wide belt, and scabbards for their sword and dagger. She looked uneasily at the protective chest armor. Awkwardly she hauled the load, which she estimated at more than forty pounds, out to the training grounds. Shields, javelins, swords, and pugio daggers were set neatly in hundreds of piles across the drill field.

"And we thought carrying our shields from Pompeii to Rome was tough," Quintus said quietly as they selected two piles of weapons and dropped their gear.

"Lindani has the right idea," Amazonia said nodding toward the venatores across the field. "They just carry their kits, bows, arrows, and slings. I knew I should have fought animals rather than people."

"Tell me that the next time he faces a few bears or lions in the arena with just a hunting spear in his hands," Quintus replied. "I'd rather carry this shit across the Empire than do that."

"Alright . . ." Macer shouted from a podium of crates that had been set at the north end of the field. "Off with your old tunics and on with the military tunics."

Quintus glanced at her. "I'll shield you," he offered.

Amazonia smiled. "You've got to be kidding. I'm half naked in front of twenty thousand spectators in the arena. You think a few hundred gladiators are going to bother me?"

With that, she casually pulled her blue tunic over her head and dropped it on the ground in front of her. She could feel many of the fighters' eyes upon her as she stood clad only in a small brown undergarment tied at her waist. She noticed even Quintus glance at her breasts, although he'd seen her naked before. A shiver ran up her spine, and her nipples stood erect in the cool morning air. She bent over and plucked the new red tunic from the ground.

"I hope this is big enough," she said as she dropped it over her head and shoulders. The wool fabric was rough and pulled tight across her chest, but she gave a firm tug and it dropped into place.

Amazonia noticed that Quintus caused almost as much of a stir among the Capuan fighters when he pulled his green tunic from his body. Few had seen decorative stigmates before, and obviously none had seen images like the elaborate Minotaur and Gorgon that adorned his chest and back. From the corner of her eye, she could see nudges and pointing all round them. Quintus threw the tunic over his head and had an equally tough time getting it pulled down over his massive chest.

"Looks like we could both stand a looser-fitting tunic," she said. "We'll have to see the camp prefect later."

"Armor up and on," Macer yelled. "Help the man beside you in tying the straps, front and back. There should be no gaps in the banding. Do it."

Amazonia and Quintus both pre-tied the rear leather straps. She bit her lip and hefted the twenty-pound iron-banded armor up and onto her torso. Right away, her concerns became well founded. She glanced around and turned partially away from Quintus so he wouldn't witness the embarrassing spectacle about to come. She sucked in her tight stomach muscles and managed to get the ties on the bottom bands secured without too much trouble. Tugging on the top laces, she was distressed to see a gap of at least a half-foot across her ample chest. She glanced over her shoulder at Quintus, who had pulled and shifted his armor into place and was now securing his last two straps. She turned away, slid her hand inside her armor, and pushed on her left breast to flatten it down. Using her other hand, she did the same with her right breast. With grunts that came louder than she had hoped, she struggled to close the gap between the front edges of her armor. She managed to get one more of the seven leather strips tied.

Exasperated, she turned to face Quintus. His teeth bit into his quivering lower lip, as he looked about to burst into uncontrollable laughter.

"Don't just stand there, damn you. Help me stuff these things in here."

Quintus glanced around, then attempted to tug the front straps closed while she pressed her breasts as flat as she could.

"Take a deep breath, then exhale," he instructed.

She blew out a lungful of air, and he pulled the small straps tight and quickly began tying them.

"Okay, breathe again."

The moment she inhaled, two of the three straps Quintus had managed to tie popped open. The third looked as though it would split on the next breath. Quintus bit his lip again. She wasn't sure if she should be annoyed with him, or laugh herself.

"I'd like to see *you* carry these milk sacks around on your chest for just one day," she said, but even the single sentence was a labor. "By Jupiter, I can't fucking breathe." On her final word, the third strap gave way and her armor sprang open with a pop. Quintus could hold it no longer, and a laugh sprang from his trembling lips. The noise attracted the attention of the fighters around them, and the laughing spread. Amazonia flushed with embarrassment.

"What the fuck is going on back there?" Macer yelled. Amazonia looked up at the podium and steeled herself. She was not about to show the irritable tribune any further humiliation. She opened her arms and pointed at her chest armor. "Do these things come in bigger sizes?"

Macer rolled his eyes at one of his aides. "Go help her," he ordered.

As Macer moved on to the beltus and groin guards, the aide approached Amazonia. He stared at her breasts, squeezed together and protruding gracelessly from the armor, then nodded before he looked up at her with a deadpan face.

"Nice tits, soldier."

Amazonia couldn't help but laugh. "I'll bet you say that to all the boys," she shot back. "So what am I supposed to do here?"

"Not a problem," the aide said. He turned to a young camp slave standing nearby, ready to assist. "Bring me a lorica hamata . . . a large size."

She untied the lower straps, removed the banded cuirass, and dropped it in the grass. A few moments later, the boy returned with a ring mail shirt draped over his arm.

"Try this," the aide said, as he helped pull the heavy shirt over her head and shoulders. Although quite heavy to hold, the iron mail seemed much lighter on the torso. It fit similar to the wool tunic, though shorter.

"Much better," she said to the aide, "although the view's not as good, is it?"

The man grunted a laugh and walked away. She strapped on the studded beltus and groin guard, then donned her helmet and tied the strap beneath her chin. The helmet's felt lining seemed coarse against her nearly bald head. She already longed for the day her hair would once again touch her shoulders, although her new look had an unexpected effect on her. Ever since that night in camp the previous week, she had felt different. There was a new toughness in her nature. It almost seemed her female sensibilities had fallen away with each strand of hair that dropped from her head. She wondered if the feminine feel of her full auburn locks had kept her from completely embracing the strength needed in her life as a gladiator. Had the shedding of the locks been the last vestige of the prostitute she had once been, falling away and freeing her? She somehow felt—dare she think it?—more like one of the men.

Perhaps there was a method to Macer's madness after all.

Across the training field, Lindani was troubled.

The venatores were already well into their first drills under the eyes of the Praetorian trainers. The instructors wanted a quick assessment of the quality of sagittarii they were dealing with. Targets were set, and five lines of hunters were established. Lindani stood second on the far left line. As he awaited his turn, he looked down the field and studied his target.

The setup was not unlike a typical venator training ground, although it lacked the elaborate movable target system Petra had built in his Britannia school. But what bothered Lindani were the targets themselves. The trainers had constructed five realistic human forms and placed them two hundred feet downrange. Lindani studied every detail as the hunter ahead of him fired. These were a far cry from the dummies he had fired his arrows and stones at with Castus in the Pompeii ludus. Those were rough, faceless masses of straw in a vaguely human form. These were detailed soldiers, dressed in full battle gear with tunics, armor, weapons, and helmets. A wooden support with a short crossbeam behind the shoulders held the target securely in place.

The venator ahead of Lindani fired his tenth and final arrow, hitting the left leg of the target. Six of his ten shots had struck vital areas. Lindani took a breath, stepped forward, and drew his first arrow from the quiver that hung at his side.

He pointed downrange with his chin as he nocked the arrow on his bowstring. "How do they create such lifelike targets?" he asked a young camp slave crouched beside him, ready to retrieve the first batch of arrows.

The slave looked up with raised eyebrows. "You really don't know?"

Lindani's heart raced. He suddenly dreaded the answer.

"Those are the criminals who were sentenced to be thrown from the Tarpeian Rock a few days ago."

Lindani tried to block the words from his ears. He closed his eyes and prayed to his African gods for strength.

The boy spoke in a low voice. "The Praetorians use the bodies when they're training the venatores . . . you know, to be sure they can fire on a human." He glanced around and dropped his voice further. "Don't worry, they're already dead."

"African . . . fire your weapon!" a trainer yelled.

Lindani understood the logic of this exercise. He, like almost all the venatores, had never fired on a human being before. But he knew he had to do this. He had to protect Quintus, Amazonia, and the others in his ludus. The thought brought him solace. He had to think of these soldiers as wild animals.

He opened his eyes and drew back the arrow. He sighted down the shaft and pointed the barbed tip just above the bowl of the dead man's helmet. He knew gravity would tug the arrow just enough to strike directly between the eyes. He tried not to look any lower, but his conscience forced his eyes down. For a long moment he stared at the face of the corpse. Thankfully, the dead man's eyes were closed, and the pasty white skin looked strange enough to be inhuman. He could do this. He just needed to convince the two fingers that trembled as they held the taut bowstring.

"African!" The trainer's yell startled Lindani. Out of the corner of his eye he saw the man wave his short splayed whip. "Fire that arrow, or feel the sting of twenty lashes."

Determination welled up inside Lindani.

"For Quintus and Amazonia . . ." he whispered, then released the bowstring.

The arrow traveled the distance in a split second. It struck the corpse directly between its unseeing eyes, just below the rim of the helmet.

"Not bad, once you were able to fire it," the trainer said. "Now do it again."

This time there was no hesitation on Lindani's part. He nocked his arrow, drew back the bow, and whispered once again, "For Quintus and Amazonia . . ."

The arrow flew and buried deep into the right eye socket of the corpse.

"Excellent!" yelled the trainer. "I see we have a gifted sagittarius here."

"My gift is to know the beasts," Lindani replied quietly. "I know their thoughts and their actions better than any other." He again pointed downrange with his chin. "*This* I do only to protect my comrades . . . my contubernium, as you say."

"We all have our reasons for fighting, especially in this war," the trainer said in a conciliatory voice. "Now finish your work."

Lindani fired his remaining eight arrows. Each struck a vital part of the target, although one splintered on the chest armor.

After the final shot, the trainer called a halt and sent the two young camp slaves to retrieve the arrows. Lindani winced as his small friend casually wrenched his arrows from the face of the dead criminal. He wondered about the nightmares the child must have suffered after his first day at this task.

He wondered, too, about the nightmares they would all suffer after their first battle.

VIII

April AD 69

THE DARK WOODS alongside the Via Postumia provided Quintus and the other fighters a cool, peaceful setting in which to await their first battle.

For two months they had continued their drills with Otho's Praetorians, exercising, marching, training with a variety of weapons, and engaging in mock skirmishes on the training grounds. Their integration with the gladiators from Capua and the Ludus Magnus of Rome was without incident, although the fighters tended to stick close to their own familia. Finally, they had been given orders to march north to meet the legions of Vitellius headed south from the Rhine. Now, near the tiny town of Bedriacum on the north bank of the Po River, the two armies were close enough to wage war.

Tribune Martius Macer knelt in the damp earth thirty feet to Quintus's right. Quintus watched him scan the road, then strain his neck to check as many of the two thousand gladiators and venators as he could see concealed among the trees for half a mile.

Quintus studied his gladiators. Anticipation showed in their faces and in the way their weapons twitched. Most knew what was coming. He, Amazonia, Lindani, and perhaps a handful of others were the only fighters in these woods who had never experienced such a battle. Most of his gladiators were prisoners from Rome's many enemies and had likely faced off against these same troops before.

"The cavalry riders come," Lindani said quietly as he crouched next to Quintus and Amazonia.

It took another few moments before the sound of hooves on the paving stones of the Via Postumia were discernable to Quintus. He wondered if he would ever grow used to the intensely acute senses his friend had acquired on the plains of Ethiopia. All eyes were on the band of thirty Vitellian cavalry who rode past the hidden gladiators. A Vitellian trap was about to be sprung on the Vitellians themselves. Macer slowly raised his arms with hands and fingers extended, reminding all who could see him to remain still and quiet. They watched the first part of the trap unfold.

A shout arose far to their right, followed by the yells of hundreds of Othonian legionaries. The Vitellians who had just passed returned at a full gallop, pursued by two cohorts of Praetorians marching at the quick-step. Again, the gladiators and venatores remained quietly in place, although Quintus could see the men tightening their grips on swords, shields, and bows. But it was not yet their turn.

As Quintus had heard the story from Macer, one of their spies had infiltrated the nearby Vitellian camp and learned of the trap on the previous night. This small contingent of Vitellian cavalry was the bait to lure the Othonian army into a chase. Down the road, toward the Temple of Castor and Pollux at the crossroads, the brunt of the Vitellian forces waited in ambush for the pursuing Praetorians.

But the Praetorians were armed with a plan of their own. Their pursuit would be slow, hoping to draw the itchy Vitellians into springing the ambush early. They would then retreat, drawing the unsuspecting Vitellians back down the road and into the same type of ambush, with the gladiators waiting in the north woods and portions of the First Legion, two cohorts of auxiliaries, and five hundred cavalry waiting in the south woods. Just around the bend, an additional cohort of Praetorians stood six abreast across the Via Postumia.

Quintus touched the tiny terra-cotta icon of the ship captain that hung around his neck and said a short prayer to Hercules that they would all survive this day.

"This plan is thought out well," said Amazonia in a hushed, husky tone, "but I still don't know why we fight for this maniac, Otho. I've heard nothing but shit about this man since we left Pompeii."

Quintus tried to think of some way to respond honestly. He glanced around and kept his voice low. "Because it's no different here than in the arena. Either kill or be killed." He paused for a moment, then went on. "Plus, every man you kill now is one less you'll have to kill later. I think we'll oppose these Vitellians again, but under a different banner." Amazonia and Lindani both stared blankly at him, as if expecting some further explanation. "That's all I can say."

Lindani's head cocked slightly, and he glanced toward the road. "They return," he said, silently slipping one of the many arrows from his quiver.

Quintus listened as the sound of thousands of hobnails scraping paving stones was followed by the distant clash of metal against metal, as the first hand-to-hand encounters began. From his left, the two initial cohorts of Praetorians retreated past them in what appeared to be an unorganized rout. The soldiers were playing their parts well, for they were closely pursued by the confident Vitellians, shouting taunts and battle cries.

The first thing that struck Quintus about the enemy legionaries was their resemblance to his own fighters. Each Vitellian soldier wore the same bronze helmet, banded cuirass, and studded groin guard as his own. Each brandished the same pilum and bore the same gladius hanging at his side. The only difference he could distinguish was a slight variation in the designs on the large scuta. While his own shield displayed four jagged lightning bolts framed by golden wings on a red background, the Vitellians' shield showed only the four bolts of lightning radiating from the center boss. In the heat of battle, he wondered if such a small detail would be any help in quickly distinguishing friend from foe.

His heart beat wildly at the thought, and he found it harder to breathe.

He clutched his shield tighter. Thirty feet to his right, Macer raised his arms again, this time waving the gladius in his right hand to keep his fidgety men in check. The Vitellians continued to stream past them. Hundreds became thousands. The thunder of their feet rumbled the ground beneath Quintus's knee. The intensity of their battle cries grew, shaking the leaves in the trees above him.

Quintus rocked with anticipation. He was ready for this. Sweat beaded on the faces around him, but the determined look in each set of eyes indicated his men felt the same confidence. Even Amazonia, despite her earlier complaints, had the look of a dogged warrior.

He closed his eyes and visualized himself charging from the forest, down the low hill toward the road. He pictured his pilum leaving his hand, then pulling the gladius free of its scabbard and thrusting into the first of the enemy soldiers he would kill this day. He opened his eyes and saw only victims on the road ahead of him. For he now looked through the eyes of Taurus.

"Archers up," Macer called, just loud enough to be heard by the closest of the venatores. The others took their visual cue from the nearest comrades. Taurus watched a human wave ripple down the forest, as two hundred men stood and drew their bows taut. He saw Lindani line up on a soldier who did not know he was about to die. He wondered if his friend would be able to fire. He had had long discussions with the African after his first target practice using corpses. He knew how difficult it had been for him, even knowing the human targets were already dead. Would he now be able to snatch a life away by simply releasing his bow string?

"Fire!" Macer shouted as his gladius swung downward. A cloud of arrows flew from the cover of forest. Lindani hesitated a moment, then seemed to say something to himself, and fired his arrow. By the time Taurus looked back at the road, two hundred Vitellians had dropped.

The Vitellians halted their advance and turned toward the north woods, instinctively placing their shields between themselves and the new threat. At that moment, hundreds more arrows flew from the south woods and hundreds more legionaries dropped on the road, shafts imbedded in their backs. The instant they spun again, Lindani and his hunters unleashed a second volley. This time the African did not hesitate. More fighters dropped.

"It's a trap!" shouted a Vitellian centurion. "Retreat!"

Taurus knew the time was at hand. But Macer did not give the signal to charge.

"Come on!" he yelled to the tribune. "We'll lose the advantage of surprise!"

Macer delayed further. He looked from left to right, then at the woods across the road. He bit his lower lip. Even from thirty feet, Taurus clearly read the look of indecision on the tribune's face. Beneath them on the road, the Vitellians began to scatter.

"Let's go!" Taurus yelled. "We're losing them!"

Finally, Macer waved his gladius and screamed the charge. Taurus was first from the woods. The heavy scutum he had been concerned about seemed like a feather in his hand. As soon as they cleared the low boughs, each of the eighteen hundred gladiators unleashed their pilum. The javelins arched through the air like a flock of deadly birds. A shout went up among the Vitellians, and the road turned to a sea of red shields as they covered their heads. Pila struck heavy wood, and the thunder echoed through the forest. Many of the weapons found openings between the rims and embedded in arms, legs, and necks. A wail of screams rose from the country road. Even those pila that did not strike flesh did their job effectively. As they struck the shields, the metal shanks at the head bent, just as they were designed to do. Imbedded deep in a scutum, a bent pilum rendered the shield useless.

By the time the javelins had struck, Taurus was at the road's edge. He smashed his shield into two Vitellians, knocking them off their feet. As he passed over them, he thrust at their necks and moved on without looking back. He pressed forward into a mass of blood and confusion, hacking and thrusting his gladius at any soldier before him. Behind the enemy he saw his Othonian auxiliaries and legionaries emerge from the south woods. They charged with a roar and laid into the rear ranks of the Vitellians. As he fought his way through the melee and came closer to his comrades, Taurus took note of the shields. He looked for emblems without gold wings to attack. But the fury of the battle made this virtually impossible. Dust obscured his vision. Bodies pressed tighter against him. A blade came at him from beside a blur of red. Taurus ducked and thrust low. The man fell. Were those wings on his shield or not? Did he just kill a fellow Othonian?

The press of bodies locked in mortal combat became overwhelming. Out of habit, he cocked his arm to swing his gladius. But his elbow caught against another man's armor cuirass. For a moment he couldn't move. He felt terribly vulnerable. He looked around in a panic, but saw only flashes of blood and glimpses of flesh and iron. Another shield flashed before him. Did it have wings or only lightning bolts?

He finally freed his arm. The instructions of Castus and his drillmasters to use short, quick thrusts flashed back to him. A Vitellian charged him with a scream. Taurus blocked the lunging blade. He imbedded the tip of his own sword in the man's open mouth. A gush of blood poured down his shield. Taurus was relieved to see yellow lightning bolts. The dead soldier slipped free of his blade and fell to the scarlet paving stones.

Taurus pressed forward. His foot slid in a puddle of blood as he lunged at another Vitellian. He regained his footing, but tripped on one of the dozens of curved scuta that littered the ground. These were obstacles he had never encountered in the arena. Before his knee touched the stones, he thrust his sword into the thigh of the man in front of him. The challenger dropped, and Taurus finished him with a thrust to his lower back, severing his spine.

He forced himself upright just as another Vitellian charged. Taurus feinted a high strike to the face, then raised his shield high and lunged low. He brought his gladius up into the man's crotch. The studded groin guard covering the lower half of the attacker's tunic did little to deflect the blade. With the power of Taurus's arm behind it, the blade disappeared almost to the hilt. Blood gushed down on his right hand, and the man fell.

One soldier after another appeared before Taurus. Soon they were just a blur of faces, helmets, and armor. If they attacked, he killed them. If they didn't, he tried his best to check their insignia before he attacked. Unfortunately, he couldn't be sure that every man he slaughtered was indeed the enemy.

With a few more steps and thrusts, Taurus fought his way clear of the main battle. He had cut a swath across a hundred feet of dreadful combat, leaving a wake of bodies in his path. Gasping, he turned and faced the fighting. He caught a glimpse of Amazonia cutting down a heavyset legionary. The blow she delivered to the man's neck with a loud scream came close to decapitating him. As the man fell, an arrow streaked past her and landed with a *thwunk* between the eyes of his Vitellian comrade, poised to attack her. Taurus knew only Lindani could have delivered such a precise shot. He was glad the African was watching out for her. But she was still surrounded by threats, any one of which could snuff out her life in a heartbeat.

The thought sent a sudden jolt of energy into his chest and arms. With a roar, Taurus launched himself back into the middle of the skirmish. He delivered a fatal slash to the back of one soldier's neck as the man glanced down at a fallen foe, allowing the rear neck guard of his helmet to rise for the briefest instant. With fewer fighters still on their feet, Taurus now had more room to work. He summoned the full warrior spirit of Taurus the Bull and willed the burst of power into his sword arm. As had happened so often in the arena, his weapon became a blur. He advanced across the road, cutting down everything in his path. His feet now felt for obstacles on their own, and he walked across bodies, shields, severed limbs, viscera, and bloody paving stones as if walking through a country field. His eyes searched out any man without golden wings on his shield. The few surviving Vitellians fought bravely but stood no chance against his one-man onslaught. Many of his fellow gladiators stepped aside and cheered. They knew that, in this state, Taurus could inflict more carnage than a dozen of them put together.

Taurus cut through five, ten, then fifteen Vitellians—as if he was back in the arena, proving to the mob in the cavea he was the best fighter in the Empire. He roared as his right arm and gladius became virtually invisible. With every second, more Vitellians lay dead in the road. He hacked and punched and thrust until there were only trees in his field of vision. He realized he had fought clear across to the north woods once again. He spun searching for another target, but there was none. To his left a few stragglers retreated down the road, pursued by the Praetorians. To his right stood the rest of his fellow gladiators and venatores, all eyes on him. He bent back and let loose a mighty cry. He raised his gladius high, then tossed it blade first into the ground. It stood at his feet like a miniature monument of conquest.

Taurus looked up at his men. The cheering had faded and their expressions now revealed stunned amazement, mixed with a trace of horror. The look caught him off guard. He took a few deep breaths and allowed Taurus to recede. With his head clear, the moaning of wounded and dying soldiers attacked Quintus's ears. He scanned the battlefield. The carnage was undeniable proof of Taurus's lethal proficiency.

Time stopped. Quintus was suddenly inside some hellish painting from the hand of a demented artist. The image was too brutal to be real. Had he really contributed to this catastrophe? Could he have possibly fought this battle even more savagely than the battle-hardened barbarians in his ranks? Could he have possibly taken so many lives? He had thought he knew the power of Taurus, but he had never considered him capable of killing on such a massive scale.

His shield slipped from his grasp and fell beside him, but the sound never reached his ears. It was blocked by the screams of dying men. After an eternity, the ghastly sounds were replaced by a voice he recognized, whispering into his ear.

"Every man we kill now is one less we'll have to kill later." He looked up into the green eyes of Amazonia. A splash of someone's blood dripped from her nose and cheek. "Isn't that what you said?"

Lindani appeared next to her, his bow slung over his shoulder. "We do not know what that means, but you believed it a short time ago."

"Does that justify what we've done here today?" Amazonia asked.

He studied his friends for a moment, then looked back at his men without answering. As their leader, he knew he had to accept the consequence of war if he ever expected them to trust and follow him. In his mind, he sought the only justification for such bloodshed, the only reason he had agreed to lead these men in the first place: He pictured Vespasian as emperor.

His chest swelled, and he punched his fists to the sky. *"Victory!"* he shouted.

Riagall the Celt was the first to break the stunned silence with a war cry. Then the gladiators erupted in a magnificent roar sweeter than any amphitheater crowd could generate. The voices helped soothe the rush of torment that had threatened to overwhelm Quintus.

After a moment, Macer approached him with a wide smile and slapped the shoulder plates of his blood-spattered armor. Quintus noticed that the tribune's armor and tunic were remarkably clean. Castus's comments about Macer leading from the rear flashed through his mind.

"Castus was right," the tribune said.

Quintus looked Macer in the eye, unsure if the tribune had read his mind. "About what?"

"About how you fight. I saw you twitching in those woods, ready to pounce like a tiger. You show initiative. That's good in this army."

"I didn't want to lose the advantage we'd gained," Quintus responded.

Before they said more, a rider approached, followed by a band of bodyguards. Quintus recognized the legate Vestricius Spurinna. He instinctively stood taller for his legion's commanding officer.

"That was an amazing display of combat, gladiator," the legate said. "What's your name?"

"Quintus Honorius Romanus, sir. But in battle, I'm known as 'Taurus.'"

"A citizen gladiator?" Spurinna said with a raised eyebrow. "Are you a volunteer at your ludus?"

"Yes, sir. I've made the arena my world and the ludus my home." Quintus nodded toward the other fighters. "This is my familia."

"This is the one Castus told us about, Legate," Macer said. "From Pompeii. They say he's a hell of a fighter and a born leader."

"He's just proven that to me," the legate said with a nod. "Quintus . . . or Taurus . . . I'm issuing you a battlefield commission. Since your gladiators are a temporary support unit, you can't hold an official rank. But, unofficially, you're promoted to the level of *centurio princeps*—chief centurion. I want you to take charge of all three hundred of your Pompeiians. That's more than three times the number of men under most centurions. Can you handle it?"

"I know these men well, sir," Quintus said without hesitation. "I can do it."

"Good. You'll work directly under Tribune Macer and his staff." The legate raised his voice. "Let all who are present hear these words and abide by my wishes. Understood?"

A thunderous "Yes, sir" came from the assembled fighters and venatores. The legate spun his horse and rode toward his Praetorians, who were gathering prisoners and checking the wounded. Quintus glanced at Macer and found it hard to judge the tribune's reaction. Was he glad to have assistance in leading his mercenaries, or did he feel threatened by the new appointment? Regardless, this was just the opportunity Castus and Petra had told him to seek out. Quintus knew that Taurus's skills with a sword would catch the legate's eye sooner or later. He just hadn't expected it this quickly. Of course, he hadn't expected to wreak havoc at the level he had just managed, either.

"I haven't seen many battlefield commissions in my day," Macer said with what might have been a touch of jealousy.

"I'm here to serve you, the legate, and the people of Rome," Quintus said as diplomatically as possible.

"And what of our Emperor Otho?" Macer asked, his eyes squinting a bit. "Are you here to serve him, as well?"

"It is he who hired us," Quintus said. "We fight for those who hire us."

Macer grunted. He turned to walk away, then stopped and looked at Amazonia, the fresh enemy blood still dripping from her face.

"I guess I made it past our opening charge," she said with a cocky smile. "I told you I'd prove you wrong."

"We'll see how long you last," the tribune mumbled, then walked on.

"Asshole." Amazonia's mutter was just loud enough to reach Quintus's ears.

"Romanus, have your men take inventory of the dead and collect their weapons," Macer called over his shoulder.

Quintus scanned the fighters who stood before him. He wondered if the relief on their faces was a result of the battle's end or the appointment of someone they knew and trusted to make decisions for them.

"What are our losses?" he asked no one in particular.

Memnon spoke up as he wiped the blood that streamed from a gash above his left eye. "I don't know the losses from the other ludi. Of our Pompeiian familia, perhaps ten dead and thirty or so wounded."

The figures did not differ much from a typical two-day arena event. But the fact that the tally resulted from less than a half-hour of combat sobered Quintus. "Carry the most seriously wounded to the medical staff. Then we will bury our dead with honor."

The fighters began moving away, some prodding at the prone bodies, seeking signs of life. Lindani and Amazonia remained beside Quintus. He forced himself to scan the battlefield again.

"I killed more men in one morning here than I've killed in four years in the arena," he said quietly. "But to men like Otho and Vitellius they're nothing but numbers. Expendable slaves for their personal gain."

"But Otho pays us to fight, right?" Amazonia said with more than a little sarcasm. "So we fight."

Quintus looked up at his closest friends. "There are reasons for this. Hopefully, the end result will justify this sacrifice."

"This sacrifice?" Amazonia scoffed. "This is just the beginning, Quintus. There are more legions on the march from Germania, the Danube, Moesia . . . You've heard the talk at camp. There will be eighty thousand soldiers facing each other soon."

"I'm well aware of what's coming," he snapped.

Amazonia refused to back down. "You were horrified at what Taurus did here today? Well, this is a day at the baths compared with what's to come. Will you be ready for that?"

"No!" he yelled, reaching the end of his patience with her carping. "I won't be ready! I'll *never* be ready for this kind of killing."

"Then why are we here?" Amazonia shot back between clenched teeth.

Quintus glanced around, then moved a step closer to her. "*I'm* here to follow a plan that's been set in place. But nobody asked *you* to hide in an equipment cart and be a part of it. So, if you don't want to fight for this man, then why the fuck are *you* here?"

Amazonia's eyes flared. "I have my reasons."

"What?" Quintus pushed. "To prove you're the toughest bitch in the Empire?"

"You know that's not it."

"Then why, Amazonia? Why *are* you here?"

"I'm here because this is my family, and I belong here. And . . ." Her voice quavered, and the flame in her eyes was doused in a sudden pool of tears. She took a deep breath and dashed a tear away with the back of her bloody hand. "I'm here because of you."

She turned away quickly, still wiping at her eyes. Quintus stood mute, both stunned and bewildered. The look on Lindani's face showed equal surprise.

Quintus touched her arm and she turned toward him, but she would not meet his gaze. "If that's the case," he said, "then the best way to prove it is to trust me." He looked once again at the hazy battlefield. "These men *are* a sacrifice . . . an unavoidable sacrifice. You'll see that for yourself someday. But for now, I need you to trust me." He glanced at Lindani. "Both of you."

"I hope the gods are fair after such a sacrifice," the African said.

Quintus nodded slowly, his mind suddenly hundreds of miles away, picturing Castus galloping toward Judea. "We'll find out soon enough," he said as he walked away.

IX

April AD 69

THE COBALT WATERS of the Mare Internum were stark against the low white walls that framed the Judean palace pool and terrace. Lucius sat with Vespasian and his son Titus at the southwestern corner of the oasis. The site offered the best view of the rocky promontory, the churning sea, and the city's port in the distance. But at this moment, all eyes were on Julia, who floated seductively in the clear water above the tiled geometric pattern of interlocking squares at the bottom of the pool.

Governor Vespasian seemed in a jovial mood as he called for more wine. His son leaned back in his chair and closed his eyes, letting the midday sun warm his face and neck.

"It's good to be back in Caesarea," Titus said with a sigh. The breath raised his broad chest under the short white tunic.

"It's good to have you back, son," Vespasian replied with a bright smile. "We have a lot to discuss. How far had you traveled when you heard of Galba's assassination?"

"We'd just arrived in Corinth when we heard the news from a ship captain at the port," he said, his eyes still closed against the bright sunlight.

Vespasian looked at Lucius and grinned. "Another one of your company's gossip hounds, Lucius?"

"Could be. Our men are everywhere," he said with a shrug.

Julia swam toward the steps in front of them and climbed from the pool. She wore a white two-piece swimming outfit she had designed for herself in Alexandria. The bottom looked similar to a gladiator's subligac-ulum loincloth—only much smaller and tighter. The top draped around her neck, crossed to cover her breasts, and tied in the back. Lucius never got tired of seeing her in it, especially when the thin cotton material was wet and virtually transparent. Out of the corner of his eye, he noticed Vespasian nudge his sunbathing son. Titus opened his eyes and smiled as she walked to her towel, the water pouring from her perfect body.

"Like I said, it's good to be back in Caesarea," Titus said as he lay back once again.

"Excuse the interruption, Governor," came a voice from behind them. It was the tribune who worked as Vespasian's personal assistant. "You have a visitor. He says he served with you in Britannia. An old centurion named Marcus Livius Castus."

Vespasian's face grew even brighter. "Castus! By the gods, I haven't seen him in years! Show him in right away." The tribune bowed and went to retrieve the old friend. "This man is one of the best soldiers I've ever known," Vespasian said to his son and guests. "It was an honor to serve with him."

The governor sprang from his seat as the stocky old soldier appeared on the terrace, his blue tunic worn and dusty. "Castus, you old dog! Look at you. Still tough as the hobnails under those boots of yours." They em-braced warmly. "Come meet my son Titus. And these are associates of mine, Lucius Calidius and Julia Melita."

Castus greeted the two men with a hearty grasp of forearms and Julia with a polite nod of his head.

"What in Mars' name are you doing in Judea?" Vespasian asked.

"I've come to see you, Flavius. It's an important matter." Castus's look was serious but haggard. It seemed the long ride had taken its toll on the older man.

"We'll move to the tablinum. But where are my manners? Helvia, bring Castus some food and wine. Right away."

Within minutes, a small feast was spread before the visitor. The old centurion devoured the roast lamb and fresh vegetables as if he had not eaten in weeks. By the looks of him, Lucius wondered if that was, in fact, the case. Castus said little as Vespasian reminisced and laughed about their toughest fights against the hordes of Britannia.

"Do you remember the day we crossed the river at Medway? We thought all their chariots had been put out of commission by the auxiliaries, but that wild Briton came riding at us with his spear flying?"

Castus pointed a greasy finger at a ragged scar on his left thigh. "His mark still aches on wet days."

Vespasian laughed. "I can still see you pulling that spear from your leg and using it to trip his horse as he flew past us. What a move!"

Castus nodded as he swallowed. "And I remember you chasing him down when he got up and charged me. I couldn't move. If you hadn't taken his head from his shoulders I wouldn't be enjoying this delicious lamb right now."

Vespasian waved the statement away with a grin. "I couldn't afford to lose my best centurion."

"That's why the men loved you, Flavius. You were always right there on the lines with us."

Vespasian shrugged. "Well, I couldn't let you bastards have all the fun, could I?"

Lucius and Julia glanced at each other. Lucius knew, in his wildest dreams, he could never imagine what adventures these two men had gone through together in their long lives.

"So tell me, old friend," Vespasian said, "what brings you this far just to see me?"

Castus glanced at the other three seated on the terrace.

"Not to worry, you may speak freely here," Vespasian continued. "Lucius and Julia have proven to be loyal friends over the past months. And if I can't trust my own son, then there's nobody left to trust." He tousled Titus's hair as if he were still a six-year-old.

"Very well," Castus said, his voice still a bit wary. "I assume you've heard the news about Otho and Vitellius both making a play for the principate."

"Oh, yes," the governor answered as he leaned back and folded his arms. "Between my official couriers and Lucius's ship captains, we stay pretty well informed here. What's that got to do with me?"

Castus wiped the lamb grease from his mouth and drained his goblet of wine. "It has *everything* to do with you. I couldn't sit quietly in my villa and let those two idiots fight over the throne, knowing the best damn leader in the Empire is parked on his ass in Judea."

Lucius glanced at Julia. She stopped toweling her hair and looked at the old centurion, as shocked as Lucius at the manner in which he addressed the governor. Titus, too, seemed surprised at the man's familiar tone. Vespasian scanned his guests, then broke into a fit of laughter.

"You must excuse Castus," he said to them, wiping a tear from his eye. "I'm afraid we've known each other way too long. He also seems to have plans for me that are well above my level of expertise."

Lucius glanced again at Julia, and she responded with a nod. The timing of this unexpected visitor with his personal petition could not have been better.

"Castus is a wise man," Lucius said as the slave girl brought another silver tray heaped with exotic fruits. He waited for her to leave before he continued. "Julia and I were just discussing this same notion last evening."

Vespasian scoffed. "This is lunacy. The Judean sun must be baking your heads."

Titus's reaction was hard to read, so Lucius addressed the centurion, pointing toward Vespasian with his chin. "This comrade of yours would make a potent emperor, Castus. He's the type of man the Empire needs right now to pull us from the tar pit that Nero and his predecessors have dragged us into. We've known him only a short while, but it's obvious he's a good, honest man with a strong backbone."

"I've known him half my life, and I can assure you he's all that and more," Castus replied quickly.

Titus sat forward and plucked a dried fig from the tray. He glanced at his father. Lucius saw Julia lick her lips in anticipation. If they could get Titus on their side, he would be a strong ally in their plans.

"You know, Father," he began nonchalantly, "there's a good reason it took me so many weeks to return to Judea after I had heard the news of Galba." Lucius watched the governor carefully. Titus certainly had his father's attention. "I ordered the galley to put in at a number of ports to speak with the eastern governors and judge their support of you." He leaned forward and lowered his voice. "They've all made it clear that they're with you should you decide to make a move toward the principate. Gaius Mucianus, the governor of Syria, was especially enthusiastic."

For the first time that day, Vespasian grew serious. Julia pressed the point further. "That news is promising," she said quietly. "But we all know that true power in the Empire is gained through the support of the legions, as well as the governors."

Titus nodded. "My father has control of all the legions in his domain. They are loyal. Mucianus's legions can also be relied on."

"Probably Julius Alexander's men in Egypt as well," Castus added.

Vespasian raised his hands. "Let's not get carried away. This is not a matter to be tossed about in such a careless fashion. This a subject for serious discussion."

"But you're open to the idea." The comment from Castus was more a statement of fact than a question.

Vespasian looked at his old friend. "Yes, I'm open to the idea." A smile graced his face again. "How can I say no to a broken-down warhorse like you, you old bastard?"

Lucius sat straighter in his chair and breathed the salt air deeply. His spirits soared as the seed he and Julia had figured would take weeks to nurture flowered in a single afternoon, thanks to a like-minded centurion and a son with political ambitions of his own. Of course, it seemed Vespasian had already been carefully considering his options long before this afternoon discussion. A decision of this caliber was not made casually over a midday meal.

Lucius knew that tying themselves early to this respected governor would be the smartest move they'd made since their first meeting with Nero three years ago. The look on Julia's beaming face told him her thoughts were running in the same direction.

"Governor, allow us to be among the first to offer you our full support," she said without missing a beat. "We can provide ships, supplies, and finances if need be."

"Of course, our captains will continue to provide the latest information," Lucius cut in. "Those 'gossip hounds,' as you call them, might come in handy in the coming months."

"Communication is critical," Castus said. He offered Vespasian an impish smile. "That's why I've already established a pipeline right to the front lines."

"You didn't even wait for my answer before you put a plan into effect?" Vespasian sat back with a hearty laugh. "You know me too well, you whore monger."

Castus's smile broadened and the dust on his wrinkled face cracked. "I wouldn't call it a *battle* plan. But I have a group of fighters ready to help. You need just say the word. They are good men with a good leader."

"Really? And who is this rebel leader you trust so well?" Vespasian asked.

Castus glanced at the assembled group on the patio. "I think that name is best kept secret at this point, Flavius."

"Oh?" Vespasian replied.

"His mission is sensitive and his position precarious. The fewer people who know his identity, the better."

Vespasian shrugged. "Very well. I know if *you've* recruited him, he's capable and trustworthy . . . and probably the best there is."

X

April AD 69

QUINTUS HELPED LOAD another boulder into the throwing arm of the catapult. He called out a warning to clear hands and arms, then pulled the rope that released the trigger. The artillery piece jumped two feet off the ground as the arm slammed forward. The rock flew out over the waters of the Po River and struck the wooden tower near the closest span of the Vitellian pontoon bridge. As with the dozen they had already fired, the missile did little damage. It splashed into the water below, and the Vitellian archers reappeared at the castellated parapet and resumed firing.

"Reset the throwing arm," Quintus said. There was little enthusiasm in the order. Behind the sturdy wall they had erected to protect the catapult crew, two of the men grumbled, then strained to winch back the winding mechanism for the fourteenth time that morning.

"We waste time and energy," Lindani lamented quietly to Quintus.

The gladiator looked around and motioned for his friend to follow him. "Keep firing," he yelled to Memnon. Then he and Lindani ran from the forward position toward the rear camp. Away from the security of the wall, they scurried through the woods in a serpentine pattern, arrows whizzing past them. They dove over the protective edge of the ridge that sheltered their camp from the arrows and the occasional boulder hurled by the Vitellians.

"I'm aware that we're wasting time," Quintus said with exasperation, "but this is how Macer wants us to fight this one."

Since being ferried across to the south bank of the Po two days ear-lier, they had watched the steady progress of the Vitellian engineers. The large pontoon bridge was being constructed just south of the Vitellian camp at Cremona. Vitellius needed a way to get his legions across the wide river and into the heart of Italia. The bridge that normally supported the Via Postumia across the Po had been destroyed by the Othonians weeks earlier. And since Otho had gained control of the navy and fleet equipment based at Ravenna, he also controlled the river itself, using small galleys to patrol the waterway and ferry his own forces north and south as needed. Unfortunately, the constant barrage of Vitellian arrows and boulders would not allow his galleys to get close enough to the new bridge to do any damage. The two that tried had been sunk in a matter of minutes. That's when Macer's gladiators were put in position on the south bank with orders to hold the river and prevent a crossing.

"These engineers are smart," Quintus said as he and Lindani studied the defenses from their prone position on the ridge. The enemy bridge builders were protected by a tall tower that floated on wide pontoons. As work progressed, the builders simply pushed the structure ahead of them foot by foot. "I don't know how they reinforced that tower, but I can't find boulders big enough to put more than a nick in it."

They watched the next pontoon—actually a long narrow boat built by the crews downriver—being pulled into place. Near the north bank, a steady stream of legionaries and camp slaves carried freshly cut wood beams and planking across the finished half of the bridge toward the pro-tective tower.

"I can work with some of our archers to harass the men on the far bank," Lindani suggested. "But at this distance, only one or two might drop for every ten arrows we fire."

Quintus shook his head. "That might slow them up, but it doesn't solve our problem of taking the bridge down."

The loud bang of their catapult firing echoed off the ridge. He and Lindani watched silently as yet another boulder pounded the strong wall and splashed harmlessly into the wide river.

"Why do we fight wood with stone?" the hunter suddenly asked. "Are there not better elements to destroy wood?"

"What, fire? The soldiers will douse the flaming arrows before they do any damage. There's certainly no lack of water in the middle of the river. We can't put enough heat on its surface to ignite such a large tower."

Quintus lay on the cool earth and watched the swift currents push at the new pontoon being anchored in place. The long arm of a crane hefted its fifth wicker basket of the morning out over the water and slowly lowered it beneath the surface. Filled to the brim with rocks, the giant baskets were the anchors that held the boats securely in place. The crane released its catch and the anchor rope pulled taut, another pontoon in place and the enemy a few feet closer to a successful river crossing. But as the anchor rope snapped tight against the current, a thought entered Quintus's mind.

"Come with me," he said suddenly. He jumped up and trotted toward the gladiator encampment. Lindani quickly caught up, and they covered the two hundred feet together.

"Tribune Macer," Quintus called as he approached the officer's tent. "I have a plan."

Seated in front of his tent behind a small field desk, Macer held up a hand as he finished a conversation with his three junior tribunes. The pompous actions of this man annoyed Quintus more each day. The officer finally dismissed his aides and looked at the two men. "What is it?"

"Our catapult is having little effect on the engineers' progress, sir. I have a better idea."

Macer raised an eyebrow. The artillery assault had been his plan. "Is that right? And what is your better idea, *gladiator?*" He used the term with an unmistakable condescending tone.

"I'm sorry, sir. I meant no disrespect." Macer nodded with annoyance and waved his hand curtly for Quintus to go on. "Fire, sir, but not with arrows. What about fire onboard a boat?"

Macer leaned forward with his elbows on the desk. "Delivered how?"

"We put a group of men upstream and build a boat, about ten or fifteen feet long. We fill it with dead wood and coat it with pitch. We light it and set it adrift. The current will carry it right into the bridge. The flames will be a hundred times bigger than we could manage with arrows. Once it lodges between the pontoons, the bridge will certainly ignite."

Macer thought for a moment. "There are Vitellians all along the north bank. If they see the flaming vessel headed downriver they could jump in and stop it or steer it toward shore. And what if the boat should miss its target? There's still a gap on our side they haven't spanned yet."

Quintus dropped into one of the seats that had been occupied by the aides. Macer scowled at his breach of protocol. "I'm sorry, sir, may I?" he said, pointing at the chair below him. His freedom and familiarity with Petra and Julianus at the ludus was seeping into his military environment. Macer sighed, waving his hand again for Quintus to get on with it.

"You're right," Quintus said as he thought. "Why just one boat? Why not send many? We have the manpower to build them quickly."

"And why light the flame upstream?" Lindani added. Quintus and Macer both looked up at him hovering over the desk. "We must use the darkness, like the predators of the plain do."

"And how do you plan to light it, African? Swim alongside with a torch?"

Lindani ignored the insulting tone. "I will deliver the fire. You will see."

The tribune finally nodded, and the three worked out the details of the plan. Quintus was confident it would be far more effective than any catapults.

The galley crews waited for the quarter moon to set before shoving off the south bank of the Po. Quintus tapped his fingers on one of the long oars, anxious to get the operation started. He, Amazonia, and fifty other gladiators were still drenched in sweat from building and loading the eight crude boats that bobbed in the water behind the river galleys. A rope held each securely to the low side rails near the stern. The small vessels were piled high with dead branches coated with black sticky pine pitch. The potent smell of the flammable substance reached Quintus's nose as the breeze shifted.

"Both the wind and current are with us," Quintus said in a hushed tone to Amazonia, standing beside him on the deck.

She nodded as she leaned back to feel the breeze. "True. It shouldn't take long for our little gifts to reach the bridge."

Quintus glanced at the western horizon. "The moon is almost gone. Captains, put your galleys in position. Drusus, tell Lindani to keep a sharp eye. His targets will be there soon."

Quintus had put Lindani in charge of the operation near the bridge. He hoped, for both their sakes, the African would put aside his passive, docile ways and take control of the critical task downriver.

Drusus began his mile-long run along the south bank toward their camp. The captains gave the word, and the four small galleys quietly slid free of the bank. Each team of twenty oarsmen expertly maneuvered their ship toward the center of the river and lined up side-by-side, with just enough room between them to keep the oars from fouling. At about half the length of the oceangoing galleys, the undersized ships were the perfect size for a river like the Po.

Aboard the first galley, Quintus raised his arm to be sure Amazonia and the other six gladiators were alert. They all raised their arms in response. He untied the first boat and released the rope, waving his hands to show it was on its way. After a count of five, Amazonia did the same, followed by each gladiator in succession.

Quintus motioned for the crew to take him back to shore, eager to race down the bank and watch his plan come alive. He glanced off the starboard side, but the small boats were already lost in the murky darkness. He hoped Lindani's night vision was as markedly acute as all his other senses.

• • •

The black hunter was nearly invisible as he sat next to the wall that protected their catapult and hid the small fire he had lit earlier. He pulled again on the bow string to warm up his muscles. Beside him lay ten arrows, the tips wrapped with linen saturated with the same sticky pine pitch as on the boats. He heard footsteps behind him and reached for the knife in his belt.

"Firestorm!" The watchword came in a whisper.

"Come, Drusus," Lindani answered, relaxing his grip on the knife hilt.

The gladiator crawled up beside him, breathing heavily after his run. "The targets . . . are on their way . . . Keep a sharp eye."

Lindani laid his hand on the arrows beside him. "When I say, you light the first arrow and hand it to me. I cannot look directly at the fire. It will ruin my vision."

Lindani knew it would take every ray of dim light his eyes could gather to spot his targets on the dark river. He carefully studied the black water upstream from his position. A heaven of stars reflected on its calm surface. Finally, a floating object obscured the reflections for a brief instant. He strained his eyes until he could distinguish the outline of the first small boat drifting lazily toward the pontoon bridge.

"Now," Lindani whispered.

Drusus held the tip of an arrow over the small fire until the linen strip caught. He handed it to Lindani. The hunter nocked the arrow, then drew back the bow and fired. The shaft arched through the night, trailing a plume of flame. It struck the first boat dead center, and the cargo of saturated wood instantly burst into flame. The illumination produced by the fireball lit up the river for two hundred feet. Lindani smiled. The silent procession of seven other targets was now easily visible.

Shouts rose from the tower at the end of the pontoon bridge. Night guards and engineers began appearing at the parapet, pointing and yelling with panic in their voices. The flaming vessel glided closer and closer to the line of wooden pontoon boats that supported all their work. Lindani readied his second arrow. A legionary appeared on the finished side of the bridge, stripped off his helmet and iron cuirass, and dove into the river.

"Sagittarii, stand ready!" Lindani called as he took aim at the second target. A line of fifty archers streamed over the ridge behind him. He fired the arrow, and it struck the center of the next small boat. Another fireball rose, and there were now two fiery vessels floating toward the woodworks. More splashes came from the bridge as three more legionaries dove into the river to try to divert the blazing craft.

"Focus on the river, then the bridge," Lindani said calmly as he nocked another arrow and dipped the tip in fire. From behind him a salvo of arrows flew toward the men floundering in the water. Screams erupted from the river's surface, then all was calm. Four dead bodies joined the procession of boats. As the third target erupted, the first was just a few feet from the bridge.

"Good, we haven't missed all the fun," came a panting voice from behind Lindani. The hunter fired his fourth arrow then looked beside him to see Quintus and Amazonia. "Now, as long as they wedge under the spans, we'll be alright."

A dozen or so Vitellians lined up on the bridge above the first flaming boat. Its bow struck one of the pontoons, then slipped alongside it and under the bridge span. The high pile of burning wood near the rear of the boat snagged on the edge of the bridge, and the floating inferno came to a halt directly under the span. The legionaries tried desperately to disengage the tangle of burning branches. The sagittarii behind Lindani reloaded and concentrated their fire on the group. Of the twelve, four ran screaming with their tunics ablaze and the other eight fell where they stood, arrow shafts buried in their bodies.

"By the gods, it's working," Quintus said with more than a hint of amazement.

"Did the great Taurus lack confidence in his own plan?" Lindani said with a smile as he unleashed another flaming arrow.

"Piling the wood high in the stern was my idea," Amazonia said, nudging the hunter as he readied his final shot. As with the previous seven firebrands, the final one hit the target dead center even though it still floated three hundred feet upstream.

Lindani lowered his bow and watched the second and third blazing boats strike the bridge almost in unison. Once again, the drifting firestorms worked perfectly, snagging the bridge just as most of the flaming debris slipped under a span.

With a sudden roar, the span where the first boat had struck burst into a wall of flames. The soldiers and engineers still in the tower and on the bridge saw their only avenue of escape cut off. Some dropped their weapons and made a run for it, leaping through the inferno trying to reach the north bank. They emerged on the far side totally engulfed in flame. They fell to the ground, screaming in agony. Lindani watched for a moment, then grabbed a handful of arrows from his quiver. He fired across the river and struck one of the burning men squarely in the back, mercifully putting him out of his misery. Following his lead, many of the sagittarii behind him did the same, though only a few struck the writhing targets at such a distance.

The fire from the second and third boats now took hold, and soon the bridge was ablaze in three sections. Soldiers streamed from the tower. The bravest ones futilely attempted to extinguish the fires with the buckets they kept close to douse firebrands shot at the tower. The ones in full panic dove into the water without first removing their iron cuirass and promptly sank to the bottom. But they fared no worse than those who did remove their armor and were killed by the rain of arrows from Lindani and his sagittarii. A few defiant Vitellian archers remained atop the high tower and fired in the general direction of the Othonians. But, unable to see their adversaries in the dense black forest, their arrows flew harmlessly overhead.

"We need one of the boats to strike under that tower," Quintus said.

Drusus shook his head. "It looks like these next two will miss completely."

As predicted, the fourth and fifth boats slid through the gap directly in front of them and continued downstream until they beached on a small island in the middle of the river. But the three final vessels found their marks well. Two struck the bridge just north of the tower, and the final boat wedged tightly under the tower span itself. With the wood already dried to kindling by the intense heat, the east face of the tall fortification erupted within a moment of the boat's impact.

Lindani raised his arm to cover his face as a tremendous blast of heat reached their position. He looked up at the trees above them, wondering if the entire forest and gladiator camp would soon be ablaze. The loud cries of men burning to death drifted over the thunderous roar of flames.

"I have brought Hades itself here tonight," he said bitterly. He lowered his head and tried to block the screams from his ears. "Hercules, please take the spirits of these brave men quickly. Let them suffer no longer."

He felt Quintus's heavy hand on his shoulder and looked at him. He knew the flames lit the tears that streamed down his dark cheeks. "What have I done, my friend? I am a hunter of animals, not men. I did not consider that so many would find such a horrible death by my hand tonight."

Quintus seemed unsure what to say. Amazonia leaned toward the shaken hunter. "Men die in war, Lindani," she said softly. "It's no different than the battle at Bedriacum."

"To me, it is much different," Lindani replied. "On that day I used my bow to protect you and Quintus. But now, I protect no one. I just kill."

Amazonia seemed to understand his emotions. She rubbed the back of his neck. "Then just be content it's the enemy dying and not us tonight."

Quintus nodded and spoke quietly. "I had many nightmares after I helped clear that battlefield at Bedriacum. But you know how I dealt with it? By believing in my heart that one of the men I killed that day would have killed you, or Amazonia, or Drusus here, or any of our men when we met in the next battle. I feel the same way tonight."

Lindani looked at the ground. But a gasp from Drusus brought his attention back to the blazing tower. Two soldiers, fully aflame, fell from the parapet. Burning skin peeled from bones as they fell, leaving a trail of flaming relics fluttering in the breeze as the charred bodies struck the bridge. Lindani felt their suffering as clearly as if the flames blistered his own skin. The hunter prayed to every god in Africa and Rome that one of those two might have taken Quintus's life tomorrow. It was the best he could do to justify his monstrous deed.

With a loud creak, the tower suddenly shifted. The yells and panic on the bridge grew as the sound of snapping timbers filled the air. Slowly, almost gracefully, the massive tower toppled to the right and splashed into the Po. A burst of steam rose from the waters with a shrill hiss, temporarily obscuring the devastation in the river. As the breeze cleared the air, the Othonian archers continued their barrage.

But Lindani fired no more arrows that night. He had had enough of death.

XI

THE SUN CLEARED the eastern horizon, and the pleasant smell
of charred oak filled the cool morning air. From their ridge over-
looking the Po, Quintus and Macer surveyed the scorched relic
that was once a bridge. A few small fires continued to smolder in the debris that had washed toward both banks.

"So the plan worked," Macer said, almost reluctantly.

"It looks like the Vitellians will remain north of the Po for a while
longer," Quintus said with a contented smile.

"Legate Spurinna was more than pleased with my report this morning," Macer said in his usual pompous manner. "And just so our story is
straight, it was *I*, of course, who redirected our strategy to the burning
boats." Quintus looked at the tribune without saying a word. "A battle
record means nothing to a gladiator," Macer continued in a condescending tone, "but to a tribune looking to soon command his own legion, it's
an important tally."

Quintus stared at the arrogant officer for a moment. He had known
from the start that serving under this man would test his patience. But
he forced himself to focus on the larger plan. Without a word, he turned
his attention back to the river. The four small galleys they had used to
set the fire boats adrift were visible through the smoky haze, tied to the
shoreline below the ridge. The boat crews milled about, awaiting their
next orders. An increase of activity on the north bank caught Quintus's
attention. Blustery voices and shouts drifted across the river, although

only a few legionaries and auxiliaries could be seen.

Macer laughed. "It looks like reality is finally setting in over there. That was weeks of work I destroyed in one evening."

The clamor from the north bank came louder, and the soldiers' shouting was now in cadence with the distinct thump of military boots on the march. Macer's laughter subsided as the first ranks appeared from around the bend, advancing toward the river bank.

"What in Jupiter's name are they doing?" Quintus asked.

"Those are the Batavian and Germanic auxiliaries," Macer said slowly, studying the blue oval shields and the standard carried by the signifier. Quintus heard the tension rise in his officer's voice. "By the gods! They mean to cross!"

"Without a bridge or boats?"

"These men are renowned as riders and swimmers. I don't know what they're planning," Macer said, "but prepare the men for battle. I'll not be caught flat-footed."

Quintus turned and ran toward the gladiator camp. "Cornicen! Call the men to arms!" he shouted. The aide grabbed his circular cornu horn and trumpeted the warning. Within minutes, seventeen hundred gladiators and hunters assembled in their designated formations, armor and helmets in place and weapons in hand. Quintus stood in the front rank of the three centuries from Pompeii. He now wore the helmet of a centurion, the bright red crest arching over the top of the bronze bowl making him easily distinguishable to his men in battle.

"They're crossing!" hollered one of the advance guards stationed on the ridge.

"We'll advance to the clearing on the south bank," Macer yelled to his men. "When we get there, I want sagittarii and slingers to the front. As soon as they're within range, I want a barrage raining down on that crossing. At my order, you will then move to the rear and the infantry will advance and defend the south bank. Now move!"

As they advanced toward the water's edge, Quintus considered the logistics of the Vitellians' surprise move. The water was far too deep and wide to ford with armor and weapons, even for skilled swimmers. How were they planning to cross with no galleys?

They arrived at the clearing just as the first line of Vitellians waded into the water across the river. He noticed many of the men had removed their iron cuirasses and had slung their large shields over their backs.

"Sagittarii and slingers stand ready," Macer yelled as he and his aides took a sheltered position behind a thicket of trees to the right of the gladiators.

Lindani and two hundred others nocked their bows and loaded their slings. Quintus stood at the centurion position on the right side of the front rank of infantry. He watched the water level rise on the enemy from knee to waist to neck as they moved deeper into the river. Without their helmets and armor, the warriors took on more the appearance of the barbarians they were. Heads with long hair and beards bobbed in the water.

They swam with an odd paddling motion, remaining afloat even under the weight of the heavy shields. The force advancing in the water appeared to be about cohort strength—480 men. The remaining 1,500 or so men lined the far bank and began cheering the swimmers. Quintus glanced at Macer. The tribune was shaking his head in disbelief.

"What are those idiots doing?" the officer asked no one in particular.

The bobbing heads began to rise as the auxiliaries reached the small rocky island close to the north bank. The first rank splashed ashore and gathered near the center of the island. Rather than continue on across the river, the sodden warriors waved their weapons and jeered the Othonians. The taunts were indistinguishable to Quintus and his gladiators, since they were yelled in the native Germanic tongue of the auxiliaries. The jeers grew in intensity as more and more of the Vitellian cohort reached the island. The widest and deepest portion of the river was still ahead of them, but the enemy seemed content to remain on the island, hurling insults rather than stones, arrows, and other missiles.

Macer turned to one of the aides at his side. "Have the captains move their galleys up to this clearing."

Quintus overhead the order and stepped toward Macer as the aide took off at a run. "Why bring the ships up, sir? This is just a feint. There's no way they can swim the entire span of the Po with their weapons."

Macer's eyes never left the Vitellians on the small island, now hopping and jumping with near comical bravado. "I want them off that island," he said matter-of-factly.

Every instinct told Quintus this was another of Macer's bad ideas. He spoke quietly, so as not to inflame either Macer or the anxious men behind him. "But that's exactly what they're looking for us to do. Let them have the rocky island. What does it matter?"

Macer turned to Quintus. His eyes burned like the inferno that had brought down the tower. "It matters to *me*. That island is my territory and they have occupied my territory. I want them off. Do I make myself clear . . . Centurion?" The title was spat in a mocking tone.

"But, Tribune, there is no room for the men to disembark and fight on that tiny island. We'll be slaughtered before we begin." Quintus's mind raced for a viable alternative. "Allow the sagittarii to rain their missiles on them. It's a long distance, but if we put enough arrows on the island, we'll eventually drive them back."

Macer leaned close enough to Quintus for their noses to touch. "Listen to me, you fucking gladiator. You will get back in that line. You will load each galley with fifty men. You will go to that island and kill those fucking Germanic pigs. Or by Mars' holy ass, I will have you flogged for insubordination." A thick finger poked Quintus's iron cuirass hard enough to make him take a step back. "And don't you *ever* question my orders again."

Quintus looked deep into the man's eyes and flushed with hatred. This would be a futile waste of good men. And for nothing better than the ego of a sadistic lunatic blinded by visions of military splendor. Perhaps this was even to punish him for developing the fire boat strategy that accomplished what Macer's tactics could not.

Without a word Quintus turned and rejoined the ranks. Within moments, the galleys were rowed into position and the gangways laid to the bank in front of them. Wild cheers rose from the auxiliaries on the island, who banged their shields with swords and axes.

Quintus turned toward his men to organize the boarding. He was struck by the look of disbelief on most of the faces. He kept his voice steady and confident, despite the rage that festered inside him. "I want ten sagittarii and forty gladiators on each galley. From the front ranks, board!"

He saw the hesitation in his men, something that had not happened since they had left the Pompeii ludus.

"What's the point in taking this damned island?" Drusus murmured as he passed, headed toward the first galley. "What do we gain?"

Riagall nodded as he lined up behind him. "This is insanity. Look at their numbers."

Quintus knew he needed to give them hope or they were already dead men.

"The numbers are meaningless," he shouted as his men slowly began boarding. "Our arrows and pila will devastate more than half their ranks as we approach." Quintus figured if Macer would not allow him to execute his plan on shore, he would do it from the galleys. "All sagittarii not boarding, give your quivers to those who are going."

On board the first boat, Lindani distributed the extra arrows. Quintus was torn over his African friend's involvement, but if there was one archer that could make a difference in this ill-conceived plan, it was Lindani.

"Swordsmen, the moment our ships touch that island, I want every one of you over the side. The water will be shallow, and you'll gain a quick foothold."

Out of the corner of his eye, Quintus saw Amazonia step forward to board the second galley, pushing her way forward from the middle ranks to join the landing party. Quintus held out his arm to block her and signaled for the gangway to be pulled up.

"Sorry, all full," he said with a stern look. He turned and boarded the first galley before she could respond. He knew she'd be angry, but he'd rather deal with her rage than tend to her wounds, or worse, her burial.

The remaining gangways were pulled up, and the oarsmen strained at the oars. "By the gods, we will leave a pile of Germanic bodies on that island this morning!" Quintus yelled as the boats slid out into the swift moving water. "Am I right?" A roar erupted from the four ships, further inciting the eager Vitellians waiting on the island.

The galleys lined up abreast and closed the distance quickly. Quintus ordered the archers to prepare to fire. As the bows raised in unison on all four ships, there was a sudden flurry of activity on the island. With a loud yell, the auxiliaries let loose with a barrage of stones and arrows, fired from more than four hundred slings and bows.

Shouts of "Shields up!" came from all four galleys. The boats rocked furiously as gladiators, archers, and rowers scrambled for cover. A deafening rumble erupted as heavy stones struck scuta. Without shields, some of the sagittarii and oarsmen dropped, struck in the head or shoulder by the missiles.

"Sagittarii, fire!" Quintus yelled.

A cloud of arrows arched from the four ships. But with so much movement on the decks, the firing platforms were unstable, a condition never encountered by the veteran arena archers. Most of the shafts flew wildly off course. The few that struck near the Vitellians ended their flight imbedded in shields. Quintus stared in disbelief as not a single warrior dropped.

"Gladiators, stand still! Get your feet, archers," he called, "and fire at will. Keep them on the defensive."

But before another arrow was fired from the ships, the Vitellians reloaded and let loose a second volley of stones and arrows. Quintus clutched the rail as his galley pitched. He grabbed one of the archers who was about to tumble overboard. The gesture proved fruitless when a Vitellian arrow slammed into the man's back. Three others fell around him.

The archers scrambled on hands and knees to grab the arrows that dropped from their quivers. Lindani managed to unleash a vicious counter-attack, firing ten, fifteen, then twenty arrows in rapid succession. The Vitellians finally began falling. But even many of the African's shots flew wide, testament to the difficulty of firing from the rocking boat.

The galleys closed on the island. The auxiliaries' taunts came louder. Only a small number of the island fighters were down, much fewer than Quintus had hoped. He prayed to Hercules the javelins would increase the number of fallen.

"Ready your pila," he yelled to all four boats. But just as his men lowered their shields to throw, the enemy fired yet another round of stones and arrows.

The deck rocked violently under his feet. With the gladiators already off balance in a throwing stance, many went down on a deck growing red with blood. Two were pitched into the river and the weight of their armor dragged them under without a breath.

"Steady . . ." Quintus called. "Fire!"

A hundred long, heavy javelins flew into the sky. But Quintus's hopes of causing more casualties before the landing were dashed. More than half the pila never reached the island and dropped harmlessly into the river with hardly a splash. Most of those that did reach land flew far and wide. Only a dozen or so struck their targets, imbedding in the blue scuta of the auxiliaries, the thin metal shanks twisting and locking to the shields.

With horror, Quintus realized his swordsmen were about to do battle with a force of well-trained Vitellians three times their number. And to make matters worse, he had been so preoccupied in trying to implement his strategy, he himself was not prepared for battle. Quintus had not in-voked the warrior spirit of Taurus. Now it was too late.

"Sagittarii, support the swordsmen as best you can!" he called, getting ready to jump from the bow onto the rocky shoreline.

Before the bow struck, half the Vitellians charged into the water toward the boats. The biggest of the enemy fighters made for the bow and stern. Others made for the oars. The gladiators were paralyzed by the unexpected move. Even Quintus was at a loss for a decision. Should the men jump and risk drowning or remain on board and fight from the deck? Before he was able to issue an order, many of the Vitellians used the oars for leverage and pulled themselves up on deck, swinging their swords, axes, and shields like wild men. The burly auxiliaries in the water at the bow and stern pushed the boats back into deeper water. With men snarled in the oars, the Othonian rowers could do little to control the galleys.

Quintus gave a rallying cry and dove into the melee on his deck. He swung with all his might at the closest adversaries he could find. One fell dead. The second was a much stronger fighter, a gladius in one hand and an axe in the other. Their weapons clashed and clanged. Metal against wood, metal against metal. Quintus finally saw an opening. He thrust his blade into the man's neck. He knew Taurus could have ended it far quicker.

All around him, his men screamed and died. The Vitellians dragged many overboard and held them under in the chest-deep water. He ran his gladius into the gut of one large fighter, then swung down hard and chopped off the hand of another looking to climb on board. As he stood up, an arrow whizzed past his ear and struck the face of a Vitellian behind him. Lindani crouched near the stern, and Quintus knew where the arrow had come from. His friend and the other sagittarii were now firing at point-blank range. But a second later, one of the archers dropped dead beside Lindani, an arrow imbedded in his temple. Quintus spun and saw the Vitellian archers firing from the island, sagittarius targeting sagittarius.

He rammed his shoulder into a charging fighter, knocking him into the water, then spun again to shout a warning. But before the words left his lips, an arrow struck Lindani in the left arm, pinning him to the stern rail. The young African let out a cry.

The sound triggered a surge of fear, regret, and terror inside Quintus.

It also managed to unsheathe the fury of Taurus.

With a roar Taurus cut a path through wood, metal, bone, and flesh toward the rear of the ship. He positioned himself in front of the dazed African hunter, his gladius swinging at a speed only Taurus could muster. He took an arm, then a head from two attackers. He stepped forward and cleared the entire aft section almost single-handedly, throwing bodies—both whole and in parts—off the galley and into the river. He scanned the deck and calculated that at least half his force had already been annihilated. And the auxiliaries continued to stream off the island and climb over the low side rails of all four galleys.

The battle was becoming a rout. Enough was enough.

"Fall back to the south bank!" Taurus bellowed. "Get us out of here! Now!"

The oarsmen who were able pushed hard against the thick oars. But the gangs of warriors still holding the sterns kept the galleys from moving. Taurus called across to his archers on the next boat.

"Sagittarii, kill these men!" He pointed down to the group of five Vitellians manhandling his galley near the rudder. Two of the warriors hacked viciously at the hull and keel with their battle axes. But within moments, all five were floating dead, and the boat began to move.

Taurus redirected three of the archers on his own galley to concentrate their fire on the Vitellians holding back the boat to their right. Soon five more brawny Vitellians were dead, and another galley slowly backed away from the deadly island. Taurus shouted instructions to the last two ships to free each other. But the fourth galley had scarcely an Othonian left alive. The archers on Taurus's ship took careful aim and picked off the men restraining the third galley. It, too, finally began to withdraw from the island.

Taurus turned his attention back to the Vitellians still aboard his ship and still fighting like rabid dogs. He stepped forward to charge the closest and his foot sloshed through river water, which was bubbling up and rapidly filling the aft section of the galley. A quick glance over the side told him the heavy battle axes had opened a jagged hole alongside the rudder.

Water swirled around Lindani's waist. Taurus struggled to reach the helpless hunter, but the rapidly rising water tugged at his legs. He couldn't let Lindani die as his mother and father had died so long ago on the *Vesta*. He was there suddenly, in the bitter cold waters off Britannia, watching his father's flagship sink beneath the waves. The frantic fear he had felt then threatened to overwhelm him once again. He couldn't breathe. He couldn't think. It took all of Taurus's power to protect Quintus and fight the memory back into his subconscious. He had to get to Lindani before the water engulfed him.

"Behind you!"

The African's voice slapped him from his stupor. He ducked and spun to meet a charging barbarian. The man's battle ax swung wildly toward his head. He pulled back just far enough for the curved blade to miss the tip of his nose. His sword arm shot forward and caught the Vitellian in the ribcage. Amazingly, the man laughed as Taurus buried his gladius to the hilt. Then the barbarian's eyes rolled back, and he dropped with a splash into the knee-deep water on the deck.

Taurus turned back to Lindani. His friend struggled with the arrow that pinned him in a crouch against the stern rail. The pain on his face stung Taurus like an open wound. Small waves slapped against the African's chest.

Taurus surged past the few oarsmen who were straining to overcome the growing weight of the sinking galley.

"We're not going to make it!" one of them yelled to him. "What do we do?"

Taurus's mind raced as he searched for an answer. What could they do? In an instant it became clear to him that Taurus was the fighter and Quintus was the leader.

"Centurion, what do we—?" The man's voice turned to a gurgle as his head separated from his body.

"You die, that is what you do!" roared a barbarian, his bloody ax completing its swing. "Now, you!"

He dove at Taurus. The scutum in Taurus's hand seemed to move on its own. The ax blade crashed against the wooden shield, pushing the supporting spars into Taurus's face. He heard the wood split and saw the edge of the blade pierce the shield and cut into his forearm. As in the arena, he felt no pain. But before he could react, the blade disappeared. Through the new slit, he saw the barbarian rear back to come with another blow. Taurus swung his gladius hard. The blade met the wooden ax handle on its way down and cut half way through. The tremendous force sent a dull shock up Taurus's arm. The Vitellian drew back again. The wet sword slipped from Taurus's grasp, firmly imbedded in the ax handle. The Vitellian studied the odd arrangement of weapons in his hand. The moment's distraction was all Taurus needed. His fist flew past the right edge of his shield and connected with the man's stomach. A foul breath blew from the barbarian's lips, and he doubled over.

"Arrows come!" Lindani yelled, the water now to his neck.

Over the heaving man's shoulder, Taurus saw another wave of missiles rise from the island. He was safe beneath his shield. But Lindani was a helpless target still pinned to the rail. He spun and threw the heavy scutum with all his might. It splashed into the rising water in front of Lindani.

He then grabbed the tunic of the gasping Vitellian and fell backward into the water on the deck, pulling the man down on top of him. He heard the muffled thud as two arrows hit the man's back and saw the final bubbles of sour breath escape the dead, cracked lips that floated inches above him.

He pushed up out of the water and looked aft toward Lindani. The hunter's head was barely above water. His right arm held the scutum, which had an arrow imbedded in one of the gold wings. His left arm was still pinned. He choked and gasped for air as a wave washed over him. He released the shield and grabbed at the cursed arrow in his arm. Taurus shoved the dead body aside and sloshed toward his wounded friend.

"Stop rowing!" Taurus yelled as he pushed through the rising water. "It's just forcing the water in faster."

"What do we do?" yelled another oarsman.

It was a critical decision, and Taurus knew he had to make it quickly.

"Fight, then row!" he yelled back at the man.

He surveyed the scene around him. The Vitellians were pouring in as fast as the water was filling their galley. His men did not have a chance. The battle was already lost. His warrior instincts told him to keep fighting, but deep inside he knew this was wrong. Had he made the right decision? Had *Taurus* made the right decision? Or was he sentencing even more of his men to the ghastly sacrificial alter that this battle had become?

A wave broke over Lindani's head, and the African coughed. Taurus screamed in frustration. Quintus was needed now more than Taurus. He breathed deeply and attempted to drive the warrior spirit back to its recesses. The sounds of the battle and the smell of blood continued to tug Taurus back to the surface. But through sheer willpower he suddenly saw the carnage before him through a different pair of eyes.

"Wait . . . I withdraw that order!" Quintus yelled back at the oarsman. "Remove your armor and swim." He raised his voice. "All of you! Remove your cuirass and swim for the next galley."

He reached Lindani just as the African's head slipped under. He could see the arrow, distorted and waving beneath the surface of the water. He pushed Lindani's hand away from the surprisingly thick shaft. With effort and leverage, he snapped off the feathered end, then grabbed his friend's arm. With a quick pull, he jerked him free of the arrow and stern rail.

A rush of bubbles and a muffled cry turned to a piercing shriek as the African finally broke the surface. He coughed up water and gasped for air. Before he could talk, he began slapping Quintus on the back and pointing toward the sky.

Without looking back, Quintus grabbed for the scutum underwater. He spun in a spray of water and brought the large shield down over both of them. A split second later, two more arrows clattered into the splintered red and gold wood.

"You alright?" Quintus asked, throwing the shield aside.

Before Lindani could answer, the deck rolled out from under them. They tumbled against the splintered side rail. Looking forward, Quintus saw all his survivors scrambling over the starboard side as one.

"A few at a time!" he shouted. "You'll capsize us!"

The Vitellians near the shore were quick to capitalize on the mistake. At least twenty hefty warriors splashed forward, grabbed the rail, and pulled. The port side of the galley rose clear of the water, dumping gladiators, hunters, and oarsmen into the river.

Lindani tumbled over Quintus, cleared the railing, and hit the water. Quintus tried to grab the tiller bar. His fingers brushed the well-worn wood but he could not hold on. He followed Lindani into the dark, cold water.

Again he entered his nightmare, reliving the moment he was washed out of the hold of the *Vesta*, forced down deep by the torrent of water. The river bank fell off sharply, and the water was well above his head. He kicked violently, but the surface continued to slip away. It was as if Neptune himself tugged at his ankles, forcing him deeper. His lungs began to burn. The more he struggled toward the surface, the farther away it grew. A hand grabbed his arm but let go again. Panic took hold. He could swim. So why was he sinking?

His armor! The weight of his helmet and banded cuirass drove him down like a stone. His panic rose. He quickly stripped the helmet from his head, but how could he possibly untie the seven leather straps and drop his cuirass before his air was depleted? Already, blackness clouded his vision. His feet touched the rocky bottom of the river. He pulled frantically at the leather ties. The first bow pulled free. Then the second. His chest was aflame. The urge to inhale was overpowering, but he fought to control the impulse. He pulled the third and fourth tie free, one with each hand. But the fifth bow caught. Only half the leather strip pulled free, turning the bow to a knot. He grabbed the front edge of his armor and tugged hard. But he only succeeded in tightening the knot.

His panic turned to anger. So this was how he would die. Taurus, the great hero of the Roman games, was not to lose his life in the glory of the arena, but floundering at the bottom of a river. The black haze became a cloak of darkness. His frantic motion slowed to a crawl. He closed his eyes as the life spirit begin to drift from his body. He became lost in the beautiful silence of the water world.

But the ethereal sensation was violently interrupted by a sharp pain in his head. Then another. He opened his eyes and looked into the face of Lindani. The hunter struck him once again in the temple. A shout escaped the African's mouth in a burst of bubbles. Even underwater, Quintus could understand the muffled word.

"Fight!"

Lindani tugged at the cuirass. The anger Quintus had felt a moment ago returned. But this time it was fueled by determination. A surge of energy he rarely felt—even in his most challenging arena fights—shot through his limbs. He grabbed the front edge of his banded armor and ripped with all his might. The leather straps stretched and tore under the strain. He shrugged the armor from his shoulders and felt Neptune's hands release his ankles. He pushed off the rocky bottom. Lindani tugged firmly on his bicep, dragging him swiftly upward.

He broke the surface and gulped loudly, filling his lungs with the sweet nectar of air. The silence of his underwater world was instantly shattered by the clamor of war. The din shocked him back to reality. Lindani surfaced next to him. Blood poured from the African's arm and clouded the water around them. Quintus scanned the shoreline. Dozens of his men were still locked in combat with the auxiliaries. Others were swimming for the galley next to them. Arrows continued to pierce the water.

"Fall back!" he yelled toward the shore as he treaded water. "Get to the galley!"

The men on shore splashed their way toward the second galley, which was continuing to pull away from the island. The auxiliaries close on their heels were cut down by the archers on deck. But as the first gladiators were pulled aboard the boat, they too were picked off by the Vitellian archers on shore.

"Board from the far side," Quintus yelled as he swam. "Unless you want an arrow in your back."

He and Lindani circled behind the rudder as it drifted toward midstream. The rain of arrows finally ceased peppering the water around them. A dozen hands reached over the side and hoisted them aboard. He turned to haul up the gladiators swimming behind him, but only four or five more heads bobbed in the river. He surveyed the swaying deck; less than half the men from his boat had made it to the second galley.

Keeping low, he peered back at the island. The shore was lined with cheering Vitellians. One held a wounded gladiator in front of him. With a high-pitched wail he sliced the prisoner's throat and shoved the corpse into the river, soliciting louder victory cries from the barbarian mob.

Quintus turned away from the revolting site and tried to block the taunts from his ears. Lindani sat quietly beside him and seemed oblivious to the stream of blood pouring down his arm. Quintus ripped a strip of material from the bottom of a dead man's tunic and wrapped the white wool around the African's bleeding limb.

"That'll do until the physician gets to you."

"Our physicians will be overworked when we touch shore, I fear," Lindani replied, scanning the bloody carnage on the deck.

Quintus sat back against the railing and breathed deeply. He considered what would have happened if he hadn't reversed Taurus's order to keep fighting. He wondered how many more of his men's bodies would have been floating in this river. The thought sent a shiver down his spine.

The shudder caught Lindani's eye, and the hunter stared at him.

"You saved my life . . . again," Quintus said quietly, looking to hide his thoughts.

"It is you who saved yourself. I only knocked some sense into your head, no?" The gleaming smile Quintus loved so much returned.

"Thank you, my friend," Quintus said, grasping Lindani's shoulder. "There is much more that might have died at the bottom of this river than just me."

Lindani studied him for a moment, then looked at the dead body lying on the deck in front of them. "There is always much mystery that dies with each man," he finally replied. "Only the Fates know what might have happened if this man lived while another died in his place." He looked once again at Quintus. "But in your case, I sense there is truly much more at stake, no?"

Quintus nodded but did not offer any of the details Lindani sought. The time was still not right. Plus he needed time to mentally prepare for the other enemy he was about to face on the south bank.

Not wanting to risk a turnaround in the middle of the river with inexperienced oarsmen, the galleys moved backward until the rudder and stern struck the bank with a thud. Quintus helped Lindani to his feet, and they walked down the gangway. The faces of the men and one woman who waited on the bank were grim. Quintus saw Amazonia breathe a sigh of relief, but in an instant, fury raged in her emerald eyes.

"Don't you ever stop me from fighting again," she whispered harshly in his ear as he passed. "I'm here to do a job, too."

He stopped and looked at her. "I was not about to put you in the middle of this mess. This was— "

He was cut short by the manic voice of Macer.

"What the fuck was that?" the tribune screamed as he ran toward Quintus. "You call that a battle plan?"

Quintus motioned for Amazonia to take Lindani's arm, then turned to face Macer. "No, sir. I call that a shameful waste of good men. There's no way we could have won that fight, and even if we had, what would we have gained? A rock in the middle of the river? Would that have been worth the lives of a hundred men?"

Macer's face darkened from an angry shade of red to an enraged purple. His arm sprang up and the back of his hand smacked Quintus's face with a crack that echoed through the forest. Every gladiator and venator stopped in their tracks. Quintus barely flinched. He stood tall facing the tribune, his eyes never leaving the officer's face. A trickle of blood ran from his mouth and mingled with the gore from those he had killed.

"Aides, bring my whip!" Macer yelled over his shoulder. "This centurion needs to be taught a lesson."

Two of the junior tribunes grabbed Quintus, twisting both arms behind him and reopening the wound on his forearm. He thought of resisting but knew it would be as futile as the island battle had been. The murmur of his gladiators grew louder, and he thought he heard one or two draw their swords. He wanted no more bloodshed on his hands this day.

"Do not interfere," he called to his men as Macer's aides ripped open the back of his red tunic. A wave of shame overtook him for a moment as he stood in such a vulnerable position in front of his men. But he fought it back and raised his chin high. "You fought well today," he yelled so all could hear him, "even though we lost good men. Hold your heads with honor. And go about your business. See to the wounded and the dead."

Some of the gladiators heeded his word, but most formed a circle around Quintus and Macer. The tribune scanned their faces as his aide handed him the whip. The metal balls at the end of the black leather strands clicked as Macer tightened his grip.

"Do not interfere," Quintus repeated loudly. "This is not your concern."

One of the aides kicked at Quintus's feet, forcing him to kneel. The rocks of the river bed dug into his knees as he dropped.

"It's wise to listen to your centurion," Macer said, trying to hold firm in the face of a mutiny he would not be able to control. "This man got good fighters killed today because of his insubordination. This justice is for you and your lost comrades."

The murmurs grew in intensity as the imprudent tribune raised the whip. Quintus tensed, waiting for the blow. Nothing came. Perhaps the Gorgon's face staring up from his back gave Macer second thoughts. Or perhaps the rash officer had finally come to his senses. There was a sudden whoosh, and a searing pain tore through Quintus's back. The tiny metal balls cut into him like a dozen needles. He refused to cry out in front of his men. He bit his tongue until he tasted blood. The wet, slapping sound pierced the quiet woods, followed by a roar of disapproval from the hundreds of angry gladiators gathered in the clearing.

Quintus caught his breath. "Hold steady, men," he called out. "This is not important."

As he spoke the words, it took every ounce of self-restraint to hold Taurus deep inside. His warrior spirit wanted out. He wanted to break the arms of the two junior tribunes and rip Macer's head from his body with his bare hands. But Quintus kept his mind focused on the bigger plan. He would not let Petra and Castus down. And he would not let Vespasian down.

The whip came down again on his back. He gritted his teeth and tensed every muscle to bury the pain. A scuffle broke out to his right. He raised his head. Amazonia stood with her sword half drawn, the point of a junior tribune's gladius against her breast.

"Not a wise move, Amazonia," Macer said. "Best you stand aside before you're next."

She looked down at Quintus, and he slowly shook his head. She shoved her sword back into its scabbard. Quintus closed his eyes and braced for another impact of the whip. It came with even more force than the others. Strips of flesh ripped from his back, and streams of warm blood ran down his spine. He tensed, waiting for the next blow. Instead, a thud followed by a high-pitched cry echoed through the clearing, and a loud gasp came from the gladiators and hunters. The aides released Quintus's arms, and he looked over his shoulder. The bloody point of a javelin protruded from the right shoulder of Tribune Macer. The whip dropped from the officer's hand, and he staggered as his aides caught him and shouted for the physician.

From his low vantage point, Quintus looked past the legs of the crowd. A shrub rustled about fifty feet away. The assailant was nowhere to be seen, but Quintus knew of only one person who could throw a spear so accurately from that distance.

"By the gods, I'll have your fucking head!" Macer screamed at the invisible assailant in the woods. "Find him!" he yelled at his aides. The physician's assistants took Macer under the arms, and the junior tribunes ran into the forest, swords drawn.

Quintus smiled as he rose stiffly to his feet. He knew Lindani would never be caught, and Macer would never know who had thrown the spear.

The tribune sneered at Quintus as the assistants walked him to the medical tent. "I want you at the war council tonight. Legate Spurinna promoted you to this position. Now we'll let *him* deal with your incompetence."

XII

April AD 69

THE LEATHER COMMAND TENT at the Othonian camp in Bedriacum was crowded with officers. A hum of speculation hung in the air until the flap was finally pulled back with a flourish and Otho made his entrance. The assembled group jumped to their feet and offered a stiff salute as the new emperor crossed the dirt floor and dropped into the largest chair on the dais. He leaned toward two of the generals seated next to him and held a whispered conference before the war council began.

From his position near the rear of the tent, Quintus studied the man for whom he was reluctantly fighting. It was the first time he had seen Otho and, even with the rather bizarre rumors that circulated about the emperor in camp, he was surprised at the man's appearance. Otho was slighter in size than the rotund Nero but seemed to carry the same self-centered aura about him. He was dressed in a purple toga embroidered with gold, an archaic choice of dress that harkened back to the earliest kings of Rome. The comical wig of curly brown hair atop his head looked absurdly out of place in the military tent. Gossip hinted that the man also scented his feet each day, but from across the spacious tent no trace of that reached Quintus's nose.

The gladiator shifted on the hard wooden bench. Despite the physician's balm, the tender streaks on his back still throbbed. The only good news regarding his ordeal came from Amazonia when she told him his Medusa looked even more frightening with the new raw stripes across her face.

Legate Spurinna called the war council to order. "Before we begin, I understand Tribune Macer would like to make a report about a skirmish on the Po near Cremona today." He nodded curtly to Macer.

The tribune made his way forward, and Quintus's heart pounded. His ride to the headquarters camp with Macer, two of the junior tribunes, and the physician had passed in icy silence. Now Quintus sat in quiet resentment, fighting to keep his temper in check, as Macer spewed lies and exaggerations to the assembled council. From his first words, referencing the shoulder wound inflicted during "enemy action" to his final tirade on the total incompetence of his newly appointed chief centurion, Macer painted a rambling, twisted picture of the morning's disastrous events.

When he was finished, Macer spun and pointed at Quintus. The move made the tribune wince, and he clutched his shoulder. "Therefore," he muttered through clenched teeth, "I call for the immediate execution of Quintus Romanus on the charge of gross insubordination resulting in the unnecessary loss of more than one hundred of my men."

Quintus sat up, shocked. He had known Macer would try to cover up his part in the fiasco, but he had not expected to be brought up on charges that could result in execution. As Macer sat, every eye in the tent turned toward Quintus.

"These are very serious charges, gladiator," Spurinna said. "Do you have anything to say?"

Quintus stood and cleared his throat. He took a deep breath to calm his nerves and get his thoughts in order. "The actual events of this morning are much different than you just heard, sir. First, if that shoulder wound was caused by an enemy soldier, then we are fighting the gods themselves because Tribune Macer was nowhere near the action."

A response of whispers and tittering spread through the tent. A quick smile and nod from Spurinna gave Quintus the confidence to go on. It took a few moments for him to relate his own version of events on the island that day. The more he spoke, the more the hatred grew in Macer's eyes.

"I do agree with the tribune on one important issue," he continued.

"The loss of our men was certainly unnecessary. However, the cause of that loss was not insubordination. It was cowardice and incompetence on the part of Tribune Macer."

The murmurs grew louder at the bold statement, but Quintus had one more point to make and raised his voice over the commotion.

"Last, I would like to comment on our victory in destroying the bridge last night. That causeway was set aflame as a result of a plan devised by me, the gladiators, and our best sagittarius. It was executed by brave men under my command. The tribune was nowhere to be seen during the action. I know the official record of the event was different . . ." He glared at Macer. ". . . because I was ordered to bear false witness to that report."

Macer jumped to his feet, his fury boiling over. "Enough lies! What proof does this gladiator scum offer for such ridiculous allegations?"

Quintus found himself enjoying putting Macer on the defensive, especially since he was prepared for just such a challenge.

"I offer as proof our own camp physician." A surprised look crossed the old man's face, and he suddenly sat tall on his bench as he became the focus of attention. "He has accompanied us this evening to tend to the tribune's wound. I ask him, was the wound caused by a gladius or axe like those being wielded by the Vitellian auxiliaries? Or was it caused by one of our own pila?"

The old man stammered, his eyes glancing quickly between Macer, Spurinna, and the emperor.

"We can have our own camp physician examine the wound," Spurinna said with a hint of suspicion.

The old physician lowered his eyes to the dirt. "It was caused by one of our own pila," he said quietly. "It was thrown in anger by one of our men as the tribune whipped the centurion after the battle."

"There was a near mutiny this morning, sir," Quintus clarified. "Fighting for the emperor and for Rome is one thing. But dying needlessly for Macer's ambition is different. My gladiators won't stand for it."

The emperor suddenly stood. "I've heard enough," he said loudly as he raised his arms theatrically to command the room. He stared directly at Macer, who took on the look of a scared dog. "Tribune Macer, it appears you have lost control of your unit. You have done nothing to gain the men's respect and, from what I've heard here tonight, your military decisions are more than questionable." The emperor turned to Spurinna. "Legate, I want this man replaced as leader of the gladiator unit."

"Yes, Caesar," Spurinna said with a bow. He turned to an older officer seated near the side wall of the tent. "Tribune Flavius Scipio, you are hereby assigned command of the gladiator unit near Cremona. Tribune Macer, leave this council."

Macer shook with rage as he stood and stared at Quintus. The young gladiator raised his chin slightly and allowed just the hint of a smile to cross his lips. Even the lash marks began to feel better. Macer threw open the tent flap and stomped from the council meeting.

"Good riddance," Otho said as he dropped back in his chair. "Now, perhaps we can get on to more critical matters."

Quintus took that as his cue to leave. He sighed with relief as he headed for the portal. He could not have asked for a better end to this meeting, although knowing what was about to be plotted in this tent would have been helpful. But he was content to wait for that information. He knew it would come to him eventually, now that he held the rank of centurio princeps.

"Centurion Romanus." It took Quintus a moment to realize he was being addressed by the legate. He stopped and looked back at Spurinna.

"Yes, sir?"

"Don't leave. I want you to hear this. Your men will be involved."

Quintus couldn't believe his ears. It was as if the legate had read his mind. "Yes, sir," he said, then moved from the aisle toward a wooden bench.

Spurinna called for his map. As Quintus sat, he felt many of the officers' eyes on him and glanced around. Most of the faces were hard. He sensed that while many enjoyed seeing Macer stripped of his command, the idea of the victory being handed to a gladiator didn't sit well with many inside the tent. But after a moment, a few offered a slight smile or a curt head nod. It wasn't many, but enough to allow him to regain his confidence.

Two aides scrambled in with four thick papyrus rolls. On a large table in front of the dais, the rolls were unfurled, positioned side-by-side, and secured at the ends with stones. The senior officers stood and moved toward the table. Quintus joined the junior officers standing on the benches and peering over the shoulders of the veterans. The map revealed an overview of the Po River region. The layout had been carefully drawn in dark ink, encompassing the area from their headquarters camp here in Bedriacum, west to the Vitellian camp at Cremona, and south to Otho's camp at Brixellum. Every road, forest, farm, and river ferry point in between was neatly detailed.

Using his dagger to indicate positions on the map, Spurinna began laying plans for an attack on the Vitellian camp at Cremona. What started as a general objective soon evolved into a detailed, spirited discussion as to the most effective strategies to employ. Quintus found it a fascinating process to witness. Although much of the terminology and tactics were well above his limited knowledge of military operations, he absorbed as many details as he could. Of the twenty-three officers in the tent, the majority of the discussion was between just four men, with occasional questions and input by Otho. From his queries, Quintus assumed that the new emperor's rise in politics did not include a long military career. This worked well for Quintus, since the explanations to the emperor also allowed him a better understanding of the plan.

"We must tread carefully," Spurinna said. "The Vitellian generals Valens and Caecina have joined up at Cremona."

One of the names rang loudly in Quintus's ears. *Caecina.* This was the general Castus and Petra had told him about. He could be a potential ally in Quintus's mission, if he was approached right. Quintus thought of a small note hidden in his tent, as Spurinna continued his warning.

"Their combined forces now number fifty thousand versus our thirty thousand. I think it's wise to wait for the legions from Moesia and the Danube who have pledged to support us."

"That could be weeks!" yelled a testy commander whose patience seemed to be wearing thin throughout the meeting. "You tread *too* carefully, Spurinna. We'll lose our momentum. From what I hear, Caecina doesn't even want to fight for Vitellius! Our men are ready to press forward after our victory on the Via Postumia. We have a good plan and the element of surprise. We need to push them now!"

Spurinna glanced from the emperor to the irritable commander. "Titianus, I realize you're anxious to protect your brother as emperor. But being too aggressive could cause disaster."

Quintus was surprised to hear that Otho's own brother was part of the military team fighting to keep him in power. The physical resemblance between the two became more apparent: same round chin, same fiery eyes, same bulky body—although Titianus's broad chest was mostly muscle, while the emperor's was mostly flab. Titianus also had a blind ambition that rivaled Macer's.

"Well, I say if we wait and do nothing, we're *inviting* disaster," Titianus said. "How about you, Proculus?"

Proculus, one of the other four commanders who controlled the discussion, nodded. "I have to agree with Titianus. We don't know when the support legions will be here. I say we go."

"I disagree," the fourth general interrupted. "We're too greatly outnumbered. I think we should wait for the eastern legions."

All four commanders looked at Otho. It was up to the emperor to break the deadlock. Otho nodded as he stroked at his chubby bare chin. "If we have reinforcements on the way, why should we not think Vitellius has them on the way as well? If we wait to increase our numbers, it might allow the Vitellian numbers to grow even larger."

"An excellent point, brother!" Titianus said, sensing a victory.

"I say we go now," Otho said, "just as soon as the men can be moved into position."

Spurinna shrugged as he replied. "Very well, Caesar. We shall make it work."

"I know it will work," Titianus said with a loud laugh, slapping Spurinna's back.

"We must be wary of these vineyards," Spurinna said as he ran the dagger point over the map rendering of farmlands just east of Cremona. "Our men will have no room to fight in the trellises, and our cavalry will not be able to maneuver their horses in there."

"Not to worry, Spurinna," Titianus said with a wink. "This will be *our* battle. *We'll* dictate where it's fought."

Spurinna ignored the commander's condescending attitude. "Caesar, I think it's best for you to remain at your camp in Brixellium. You're on the south bank protected by the Po there. We'll assign two hundred of the Praetorians to guard your camp. We can't spare more than that."

"Very well," the emperor replied.

"I want the rest of the Praetorians in the center, augmented by two hundred of Scipio's best gladiators." Spurinna leaned back and addressed Scipio directly. "I've seen this man fight and rally his troupe," he said pointing to Quintus. "He's a good man. Allow him to choose the gladiators who will fight alongside the Praetorians."

"Yes, Legate," Scipio answered. "And the other gladiators? How many are there?" he asked Quintus directly.

"After this morning, about eighteen hundred total."

"I want your sagittarii alongside our archers," Spurinna said to Scipio. "The rest of the gladiators will harass the enemy from the rear. Any questions on your role?"

Scipio looked at Quintus to see if he had any questions. The simple act suggested that things might be much different under this tribune. Perhaps the gladiators would finally earn the respect they were due. Quintus shook his head.

"No, sir. We're ready," Scipio replied.

"Very well. I'll get the full orders and timetable to you tomorrow. For now, get your aides and accompany the centurion back to the gladiator camp."

Quintus and his new commander saluted the emperor and generals and left the tent. It took an hour for Scipio to gather his junior tribunes and personal equipment. Quintus used the time to set his first plan of action firmly in his mind. Soon, they were on the road to the gladiator camp just south of Cremona.

"My gladiators are good men, one and all," Quintus said as they rode. "Macer just never gave us a chance. He wanted no part of us from the day his orders came through."

Scipio nodded. "How experienced are your men?"

"In the arena, they are mostly veterans. Tertius, secundus and primus palus, mainly."

"And on the battlefield?"

"They fought well at Bedriacum. The battle quickly turned to a rout. Many of these men were battle-hardened prisoners before they were sold to the ludus. They know the battlefield and train well. It's what we do day after day."

"Then that's all I need to know," Scipio replied. "Well-trained and disciplined fighters are all I care about. Kill more of the enemy than they kill of you, and you'll have no problem with me." Scipio took his eyes from the dark road and looked directly at Quintus. "But fuck up on my battle lines and Macer will look like a cute little house pet compared to me."

The intensity in the tribune's eyes was unmistakable. Yet Quintus sensed a smarter, more level-headed officer here than Macer had ever been. The hard, chiseled jawline showed dignity. And the two missing fingers of his sword hand showed this man did not hide from the action as Macer did, although the old wound probably kept him off the front lines now.

"My men will not disappoint you, Tribune," Quintus replied.

Scipio nodded. "Who's this sagittarius that helped bring down the Po bridge?"

"Lindani. He's from Ethiopia. The best archer I've ever seen. That plan would not have worked without him. He controlled the operation at the bridge."

"Then I want him to lead the sagittarii. I've always found archers work harder for one of their own."

"Very well, Tribune," Quintus said, wondering how Lindani would take the news.

The night was half over by the time they reached camp. Scipio took up residence in his predecessor's tent, and his aides woke Macer's three remaining junior tribunes and sent them to Bedriacum. Within a few moments all was quiet again on the south bank of the Po.

Quintus checked the perimeter guard list and spoke with one of the men scheduled for the next watch. He then crept into his tent and gently shook Amazonia awake. He jerked his head to motion her outside. As a centurion, Quintus was now entitled to his own private quarters, but as a show of unity, he had decided to remain with his original contubernium.

"What's up?" she whispered as they stepped away from the tent.

"We have a new tribune . . ." She smiled at the news. ". . . but that's not why I woke you. I need you to take guard duty."

Her forehead wrinkled in puzzlement. "It's not my night for guard duty."

"I know but I need a favor," he said glancing around. "Get your equipment and relieve the guard at the third position closest to the river. I already cancelled his scheduled relief. The watchword is 'virtue.'"

Amazonia shrugged, then fetched her armor and weapons, and walked toward the river. Quintus stripped off his new cuirass, helmet, and gladius, and laid them by the tent. He kept only the dagger that hung from his leather belt. He searched his kit for the small piece of cloth Castus had given him three months earlier. He found it at the bottom of his rations bag, folded it, and hid it securely under his belt. Once he saw the guard return to his tent, he crept down the path to the water's edge.

"What's going on?" Amazonia whispered as he approached.

"It's best you don't know at this point," he said quietly as he walked past her and stepped into the river.

"What are you doing?"

He would have laughed at the look of shock on her face had his mission not been so dangerous. "I'll be back soon. You never saw me here."

He submerged his large body into the dark water and stroked hard to propel himself out toward the center of the river. He kept his arms and feet underwater as he swam, trying not to create a splash. He felt overly buoyant after his last episode in the river. Amazing how much easier it is to swim without armor, he thought to himself with a smile. The current was swifter than he had anticipated, and he made a mental note to start his return trip farther upstream so he would land at Amazonia's post. She and Lindani were the only two he could trust right now. And he would have another task for Lindani tomorrow.

The river seemed even wider than it did from the high ridge. He paddled past the island that had cost so many lives earlier that day. The bodies of many of his men still littered the rocky shore, and he said a quick prayer in their honor. The Vitellian auxiliaries were nowhere to be seen.

He approached the north bank cautiously and strained his eyes to find the sentries. He spotted the silhouette of a legionary leaning against a tall dead tree about thirty feet to his right. He let the current carry him a bit farther down the bank. Once he was clear, he scurried up the bank and dropped behind the bushes. He listened for voices but heard only the chirp of crickets and the croak of frogs. Slowly, he drew the dagger from its sheath and approached the guard from the rear. In a swift, silent move, he slipped his hand over the guard's mouth and pressed the blade against the man's lower back just under his armor.

"Do not make a sound and you'll not be harmed," he whispered into the guard's ear. "I have information for Legate Caecina. Take me to him."

The man strained to nod under the pressure of Quintus's massive arm.

He pointed toward the trees, throwing his arm forward as if to say they had a long way to go.

"I'm going to release my hand from your mouth. You'll speak quietly. Any call of alarm and this blade will be up your ass. Understood?" Again the man nodded. "Now, quietly, where's Caecina?"

The man gasped for air, then spoke in a low voice. "He's in the main camp at Cremona. You'll never get in there without an escort. We should go to my centurion. He'll get you there."

"Fine. Lead the way." Quintus kept a tight hold on the top edge of the man's armor. He glanced around them as they walked to be sure they weren't followed. They entered the outpost camp, and the light of the campfire revealed two legionaries preparing for guard duty. They looked up at their approaching comrade, confusion evident on their faces. As they saw Quintus, they grabbed their javelins and charged forward.

"Leave him!" yelled the sentry. "He says he has information for Legate Caecina. Get the centurion."

Within seconds, the two were surrounded by a dozen legionaries, weapons drawn. The centurion crawled from his tent and rubbed his eyes.

"What the fuck is this?" he growled.

"I need to see Caecina," Quintus said, keeping hold on the sentry. "It's a matter that affects the lives of all your men."

The centurion scanned Quintus's wet red tunic. "Why don't you give me the message and I'll see he gets it?"

"No. This information is for the legate only."

The centurion studied Quintus's face. "You'll need to give me that pugio first. And you'll be bound and blindfolded until we get there."

"First, I want your word I'll be taken to the legate."

"You've got it," the centurion snapped as he stepped forward. "Now give me the knife."

As soon as Quintus relinquished the weapon, he was grabbed by three of the legionaries. His hands were tied in front, and the world went dark as his eyes were covered with a reeking black cloth. He stumbled as he was pushed forward. He wondered if he was now simply a prisoner-of-war or if the centurion would honor his word. The familiar smell and sound of horses came to him after a short walk. Someone raised his hands and placed them on a mane.

"Get up," the centurion said. "Keep your head down until we get to the main road."

Quintus threw his leg up on the horse blanket. He held tightly to the mane and ducked low as the horse was led into a trot by the centurion. He felt branches brush past him until the hooves clattered on the paving stones of the Via Postumia.

"Hold on," called the centurion, and the two horses broke into a gallop. They rode for what seemed like two or three miles before the horses slowed to a walk. The sounds and smells of a much larger camp surrounded Quintus.

"Get down," the centurion said. Then his voice turned away as he called to another. "Watch him. I'll be right back."

Quintus felt rough hands grab each of his arms. No words were spoken as he stood in total darkness wondering what the Vitellians' main camp looked like. After a moment, he heard footsteps approaching, then the centurion's voice again.

"Come with me."

Quintus was pulled down a dirt road and through the entrance flap of a tent. The sudden warmth felt good against his damp tunic. Strong hands continued to clench each of his bound arms.

Without a word, the cloth was pulled from his head. He looked around a command tent very much like the one he had left a few hours earlier. A tall middle-aged man stepped into view. His face bore a look of suspicion, but his eyes were friendly. A tuft of white hair lay in disarray above a weathered face that sprouted a week's growth of gray stubble.

"I'm Aulus Caecina Alienus. I hear you're looking for me." His voice was tired, but his interest seemed piqued.

"My name is Quintus Honorius Romanus. I'm centurio princeps of one of Otho's auxiliary units. I have information you'll want to hear." Quintus glanced at the guards, then back at Caecina. "It concerns news from Marcus Livius Castus."

Caecina's sleepy eyes brightened. "Unbind him, then leave us," he said to the centurion and his guards. He motioned for Quintus to sit at the large table in the center of the tent.

"Help yourself," he said, pointing to a decanter of wine and a half-eaten loaf of bread.

Quintus poured himself a cup of wine and waited for the sentries to clear the tent before he spoke. Caecina pulled up a small chair and joined Quintus at the table.

"Castus sends his regards," Quintus said quietly. "He told me you would have an open ear to what I have to say."

Caecina smiled. "That depends on what you have to say."

Quintus reached for his belt. Caecina's hand dropped quickly to the handle of the pugio that hung at his side.

"No need to be alarmed, Legate," Quintus said with a smile. "I think this will help put your mind at ease."

He unfolded the small, damp cloth and laid it in front of Caecina. The general lifted it and leaned toward the oil lamp at the center of the table. The squint in his eyes lightened as he read the few words: *Dolobra—Trust this man—MLC.*

Caecina laughed. "Castus has quite a memory to recall a nickname from so many years ago."

Quintus wondered how a legate had earned a moniker that equated him with a military pick axe, but it was not his place to ask.

"So what is your news, Quintus?"

"I think we might be able to help each other." Quintus paused for a moment. The old man sat forward, and Quintus lowered his voice so it did not pass beyond the goatskin walls. "Word has it your heart is not in this fight."

Caecina made no response. Quintus decided to come right to the point.

"I have a proposal that could bring this war to a quick end. I can provide you the battle strategy I just saw laid out in the Othonian command tent. But in return I need something from you."

"Go on," the legate said quietly.

"I need to know how you truly feel about this war."

Caecina's expression changed to one of surprise. He studied Quintus for a long moment, then sighed.

"Is civil war ever a good thing?" he began, his voice sounding weary once again. "Every man that falls is a Roman citizen or a Roman ally. There is no enemy blood spilt. And for what? The laws of Rome will not change regardless of who wins." He lowered his voice further and glanced at the tent flap to be sure it was closed. "This is not a war of beliefs and principles and better government. It's a war of egos. If this war was for the Empire, I would be first in line to fight the toughest battles. But I have a hard time standing first in line to fight for just a man. That's how I feel about this war. I'm fighting for just another man." A wistful look came to his face. "If I know Castus, and if he was still in the fight, he'd feel the same way. He was the best centurion who ever fought under me."

Quintus sat back. "Legate Caecina, do you know the governor of Judea, Vespasian?"

A twinkle lit the legate's eyes and he smiled. "I do."

Quintus returned the smile. "Then, sir, we need to talk."

Quintus spent the next hour laying out the details of two very different plans: the Othonian battle plan developed in Bedriacum and the larger plan developed by Castus and Petra months earlier in Pompeii. Caecina took it all in, quietly scrutinizing his canvas map attached to the tent wall as Quintus spoke. When the young gladiator was done, the legate studied his face one last time.

"I've known Marcus Castus for twenty years," Caecina said. "If he tells me I can trust you, then I guess I can take him at his word."

"Sir, I risked not only my life but the lives of men in my familia to come to you tonight. There is nobody in this campaign who wants to see this war end more than I do."

Images formed in Quintus's mind of Vespasian teaching him a new parry with a wooden gladius. Of his dear father blissfully reviewing the plans for two new ships. Of his crying mother being comforted by Vespasian.

He looked Caecina in the eye. "Besides, I have some very personal reasons for wanting to see Vespasian in power. I give you my word that I have not deceived you and will never deceive you."

Caecina watched him quietly for another moment before he spoke. "Very well. Then all that's missing is the timetable."

"I'll have that tomorrow. There's a tall dead tree near the sentry post where I came ashore tonight. Have the guards watch that tree. It will deliver the information you need."

Quintus stood to leave. "I'm sorry for those we will kill tomorrow. I assure you, it will be as few as possible. If I should fall to one of your men, remember what we've decided here tonight. It will mean a new and stronger Empire," he said, extending his hand to the legate.

"I pray to Jupiter we're on the right road to that new Empire," Caecina replied as he clasped Quintus's forearm.

The following day passed slowly for Quintus. He needed to get this battle behind him. The orders for the Cremona attack had arrived early in the morning, and Scipio had called a meeting with his junior legates, Quintus, and the senior gladiators from Rome and Capua. Their mission had been made clear and their roles in the battle had been reviewed in detail.

Quintus chose his best two hundred Pompeiian gladiators and drilled them throughout the afternoon. By twilight, the fighters were sent to their tents to rest and prepare for the midnight river crossing that would put them in position beside the Praetorians east of Cremona. The rest of the Pompeiians, along with the Rome and Capua gladiators, would cross the next morning and strike Cremona from the south. This time, there would be twenty river galleys to ferry the men, allowing many more fighters to hit the shore and cut through the protective ranks of Vitellian auxiliaries.

As the sun slipped behind the distant trees, Quintus strolled to the tent of his contubernium. He pulled back the flap and motioned for Lindani to meet him outside.

"Is your arm well enough to fire an arrow?" Quintus asked as they walked together.

"Yes," the hunter replied.

"Then get your bow and quiver, and meet me at the ridge near the catapult before the guards are posted." Quintus split off and headed toward the meeting place before Lindani could ask any questions. He positioned himself in the low bushes to the right of the artillery piece and studied the north bank in the rapidly dimming light. He spotted the leafless tree.

"What am I to do?" The voice startled Quintus. He found Lindani crouched beside him but, as usual, had not heard him approach. The African's tone seemed curt. Perhaps it was the lingering pain of his wounded arm, Quintus thought.

"See the dead tree across the river?"

Lindani scanned the far bank. "Just to the side of the island?"

"That's the one." Quintus reached up under his tunic and withdrew a small sheet of papyrus, neatly rolled and folded over, along with a short length of string. "Give me an arrow."

Lindani slid an arrow from his quiver and handed it to Quintus. "You want me to deliver a message, no?"

Quintus rolled the paper snugly around the shaft, then secured it with the string and a tight knot. "The less questions you ask, the better," he answered as he worked. "How's the arm?"

Lindani did not respond. Instead he laid the bow down in the dirt. "I will not do this," he said.

Quintus looked up from the arrow. "What?"

"I will not do this," Lindani repeated firmly.

The angry scowl looked out of place on Lindani's soft, friendly face. But the defiance in his eyes told Quintus this was no joke. Anger swelled in the pit of Quintus's stomach.

"You *will* fire this arrow."

Lindani sat motionless.

"That's an order, sagittarius." Quintus's voice was louder than he knew it should be.

Lindani remained still, his hard gaze never leaving Quintus's eyes. Finally, he spoke.

"Your rank of centurion allows you to order me, yes. But does our friendship not mean more than that?"

The question caught Quintus off guard. He did not know how to respond.

"There is much happening with you that I do not understand," Lindani continued. "Amazonia, too, is not at ease with this. Why do you not confide in your two trusted friends?"

There was so much Quintus wanted to say, but he could not. "The less you both know right now, the better."

Lindani shrugged and folded his arms, wincing slightly when he inadvertently touched the blood-stained bandage around his left forearm.

"Then you may fire your own arrow," the hunter said.

Quintus glanced up at the fading light. There was no time for this discussion right now. But he would not make the mistake of *ordering* Lindani to fire again.

"Look, we don't have much time, and this note is more urgent than you can possibly know."

"And that, my friend, is the point. Why can we not know this? Why can we not help you in this quest?"

"You *are* helping me. Both of you. But if you or Amazonia are ever captured, I can't risk this plan falling into the wrong hands."

Lindani's expression turned from defiance to anguish. "Do you feel we would turn against you?"

"Of course not," Quintus said, exasperation tainting his voice. "Not deliberately. But the Roman army has painful ways of making prisoners talk. If you don't know the details, then neither of us ever needs to worry about that." He put his hand on Lindani's shoulder. "Have I ever given you reason not to trust me?"

Lindani looked down and shook his head. Quintus picked up the bow and presented it to the hunter.

"Then do me this favor, Lindani. Fire the arrow."

The African hesitated for a moment, then took the bow and nocked the arrow with its surreptitious payload.

"The papyrus will affect the flight," Lindani said quietly as he lined up on the old gray wood of the trunk. "I do not know if I will hit the tree."

His tight lips revealed the pain in his bandaged bow arm.

Quintus smiled at him. "You'll hit the tree . . . even with that hole in your arm."

The twang of the bow string seemed loud in the silence of the wooded ridge. They both watched the shaft arc in the dim twilight. Quintus was sure it was going to fly too high and end up well beyond the target. He wondered if they had enough light to wrap another arrow and fire a second shot. But as he watched, the path of the arrow suddenly dropped, and a second later he saw it strike the trunk of the old tree. He looked at Lindani, who grinned.

"The weight of the papyrus is heavy, no? I must adjust for that."

Quintus smiled. "I guess I don't need these then," he said, pulling two more copies of the message from his tunic.

Lindani shook his head. "Why do you have no faith in Lindani?"

Quintus smacked the African's back as they rose, chastising himself for insulting his best friend twice in one evening. But Lindani's words echoed loudly inside his head. Until now, Quintus hadn't realized just how painful it was going to be to deceive his most trusted friends.

"Oh, one more thing . . ." Quintus said. "Scipio has put you in charge of the sagittarii."

Lindani stared at Quintus for a moment. "Why?"

"He feels the men will respond better to one of their own . . . especially one who can put an arrow in a tree from across the Po with a sheet of papyrus on it."

"But I know nothing of leading men."

Quintus smiled at him. "Neither did I."

He put his arm over his friend's shoulder as they walked back to camp.

XIII

April AD 69

THE TIERED STONE SEATS of the open-air theater at Caesarea were filled to capacity with five thousand Romans, Judeans, and Syrians. Laughter filled the night air as the sarcastic wit of *The Eunuch*, by Publius Terentius Afer, resonated with the receptive audience. Though written more than two hundred years earlier, the play always drew big crowds.

Lucius glanced at Vespasian seated to his left. He noticed the governor's heartiest laughs came as the performers poked fun at the Roman aristocracy. On his right, Julia's giggling fits were almost a show in themselves, breaking out at any line that referenced the title character's missing piece of anatomy. He had not seen her this relaxed for a long time.

The play ended with thunderous applause for the masked performers. As Vespasian and his guests rose from their front row seats, bodyguards appeared from nowhere and flanked him and Titus.

The governor turned to Lucius and Julia, a broad smile still on his face. "Terentius's works never get old, do they?" he asked.

"No they don't, Governor," Julia replied. "I certainly prefer him to Plautus."

Vespasian nodded as he walked. "I agree, although Plautus has written some fine comedy, too. A bit crude, perhaps, but very funny."

"Cruder than jokes about a man with no testicles?" Lucius said. He didn't mean it to be funny, but Vespasian found the comment hilarious.

"Walk with us to the palace," the governor said, putting an arm on both their shoulders. Titus walked alongside Julia. Lucius wondered what Vespasian had in mind. It was too late in the evening for a strategy meeting. And he didn't seem to be the type for orgies, but the vices of Roman politicians never ceased to surprise him.

They headed toward the promontory just beyond the walls of the theater. Once away from the crowd, on the private, secluded walkway linking the palace to the theater, the bodyguards fell tactfully behind and Vespasian came right to the point.

"I'd like to take you up on the offer to use your ship."

"Of course," Julia said without hesitation.

"Where will we be sailing?" Lucius asked, then added, ". . . if I may presume we're invited."

"Yes, of course you're invited," Vespasian replied. "In fact, I'll have need of you at our destination. We'll be heading to Nicopolis, near Alexandria."

"That's the headquarters for the legions of Egypt, isn't it?" Lucius asked.

Vespasian nodded. "Our time draws near to visit Julius Alexander and his armies. But the meeting must be discreet—more discreet than a war galley pulling into port will allow."

"That's not a problem, Governor," Julia replied. "My crew on *Juno* is well paid. They ask no questions and keep their mouths shut."

"Very good," Vespasian said. "I need to meet with Alexander face-to-face. I want to judge for myself what support we can muster outside my circle of influence here in Judea. It's one of the rules I live by: always know the true strength of your forces before you commit to conflict."

"A rule that applies as well in life as on the battlefield," Julia replied with a smile.

"Exactly," Vespasian said with a nod.

Sea mist filled the air as they strolled the paving stones that hugged the rocky coastline. A few restless gulls took flight, their cries echoing off the palace walls. After a moment, Vespasian spoke again.

"I sincerely hope these armies will not be necessary. The thought of adding to the death toll depresses me."

"Death and war go hand-in-hand, Governor," Lucius said with a shrug. "It's a necessary evil."

Vespasian looked at him for a moment. The hard gaze reminded Lucius that this man had seen more war than almost anyone in the Empire. He realized it was dumb thing to say.

"There are sometimes ways around it," the governor finally said. "In fact, you might be able to assist me there, as well."

"How's that?" Lucius asked quickly.

"I've devised a plan with Mucianus that will target Rome's economy rather than her legions."

They reached the palace gate and stopped walking. The bodyguards passed them and joined the guards at the gate. Both Lucius and Julia leaned forward, awaiting Vespasian's explanation.

"We'll establish a blockade of imports to Rome. As you well know, the majority of grain consumed by Rome comes from Egypt and North Africa. Preventing that grain from leaving the ports at Alexandria and Carthage would effectively lay siege to Rome from hundreds of miles away."

The simple genius of the plan struck Lucius right away. Any emperor would have a hard time controlling the impetuous population of Rome if the daily grain subsidies were curtailed or, the gods forbid, discontinued. The mob lived only for bread and arena games. The one thing that upset Lucius about the idea was that he didn't think of it first.

Julia spoke before Lucius could find the right words. "This is what happens when military intellect and common sense reign," she said with a broad smile. "Governor, how I look forward to the days of prosperity that will grace this Empire with you on the throne."

Vespasian laughed and waved off her praise.

"So we can count on your support then?" Titus asked pointedly.

"Absolutely," Lucius replied. "On your order, our captains will halt all shipments to the capital. We also have influence with many of the other ship owners as well. I can assure you the embargo will be effective."

Julia glanced at Lucius, but spoke to Vespasian. "Well, we don't want to *over* commit, Governor. I don't know if we can promise that every owner we know will honor the blockade. But we'll certainly do our best to show them justification for the temporary losses."

Vespasian nodded. "I can ask no more of you."

"This is something else we want to address with Julius Alexander in Egypt," Titus said. "Whoever the current emperor is, I'm sure he'll be offering substantial bribes to shipping owners to break the siege. We want to be sure the Egyptian legions will take control of the ports to prevent the ships from loading."

"When do we leave for Nicopolis?" Lucius asked.

Vespasian shook his head. "No date has been set. I agree with Castus that we should not make any drastic moves just yet. It would be foolish to fight both Otho and Vitellius. Let them finish their battles first. Castus knows both of these men well. He feels strongly that, no matter who wins, it won't take long for him to alienate the legions, the Senate, and the people of Rome. So, as soon as a victor emerges, we move—both with the blockade and our trip to Egypt."

"We can be ready to sail with a day's notice," Julia said.

Vespasian draped his arms once again on their shoulders, this time with a firm hug. "I knew I could depend on you two. Thank you." He gestured toward the gate. "I'd invite you in, but Titus and I have another long day of meetings tomorrow. Unfortunately, the Jewish revolt drags on."

"Understood, Governor," Julia said. "Thank you for a wonderful evening."

They watched Vespasian and his son disappear behind the gate. Julia took Lucius's hand and they walked toward the main road.

"I feel like walking tonight," she said. "Do you mind?"

Lucius had been tired and somewhat bored by the play, but he now felt as energized as Julia was. He called to their coach driver, who had spent the evening parked near the palace gate.

"Go on ahead. We're walking back." The man waved politely, snapped the reins, and drove the Romanus Shipping and Transport coach out of the waiting area and down the coastal road.

Julia sighed as she drew in the salty ocean air. "This is better than we could have dreamed! Who would have thought our shipping business would have played so well into Vespasian's plan."

"Now if we could only get our new ships in the water," Lucius said, "we'd double our fleet and have even more influence in the area."

"I think we should be careful about peddling our influence, Lucius." She nodded her head toward the waves lapping at the shoreline rocks beside them. "We're not the largest shipping fleet in that sea, you know."

"I'm well aware of that, Julia." Lucius hated when she scolded him like a child. "But the more support we offer now, the better our position later in Rome."

"I understand. But I don't want to promise what we can't deliver."

"Don't you realize the debt of gratitude that Vespasian will owe these shippers? How could they not agree to that?"

"We don't know the finances of every company who calls in Africa. How can we promise him they'll all honor the embargo?"

"Fine," Lucius snapped at her. "I was only trying to help."

Julia took his arm and placed her head on his shoulder. "It's a beautiful night. Let's not fight."

The softness of her voice surprised him. He expected another protracted argument, but instead, she had melted his anger with a few gentle words. He leaned toward her and glanced out over the black water. A half moon sat on the horizon, painting glistening stripes of yellow in the sea. He wondered if this was what it was like to be married—a quick argument followed by an even quicker resolution. Perhaps this is what happened when love and respect were involved.

If so, it would take getting used to.

XIV

April AD 69

T HE LEGATES Spurinna and Titianus gave the order, and their legions advanced down the Via Postumia, which lay before them like a gray ribbon in the dawn mist of the green Italian countryside.

Quintus's two hundred gladiators marched near the center of the large formation alongside the Praetorian Guard. To their rear, a group of fifty venatores led by Lindani followed with bows, slings, and quivers loaded with arrows. The young African seemed nervous about being put in charge of the venatores, but Quintus agreed with his tribune; there was nobody better suited for the job.

As they left behind the safety and security of their well-fortified camp at Bedriacum, Quintus kept his eye on the other centurions, who shouted encouragement to their men. He was torn between following their lead and honoring his promise to Caecina to kill as few men as possible. He kept mute as he marched.

They rounded a bend and caught sight of a Vitellian scouting party. The Vitellians spun their horses at the approach of the army and galloped back down the road toward their camp at Cremona.

Titianus let out a loud laugh. "Run you fucking babies!" he called after them. "Run back to your mother's warm tits!" His men cheered the taunts.

For more than a half-hour the Othonians marched on with no further enemy contact. Spurinna rode from right to left along his lines as they advanced. Quintus got the distinct impression the general was getting nervous. He watched Spurinna study the farmlands on either side of the road, his head jerking anxiously with every bird that took flight and each new sound.

The legate finally raised his right arm and called a halt. The order was relayed from century to century down the ranks.

"Why are we stopping?" Titianus yelled.

Spurinna looked down the road. "I don't like this. The Vitellians should have challenged us by now. We're getting too close to their camp, and we're getting too close to those damn vineyards." He pointed down the road to the expansive fields covered by wooden trellises. "This is exactly what we agreed we would not do. We can't fight in there."

"Pluto's balls, Spurinna! You're too wary to lead this army."

The legate gave Titianus a hard look. Disputes among officers were not to be had within earshot of the soldiers. But the loud-mouthed general went on.

"Those bastards are on the run. You saw them. For all we know, they've abandoned their entire camp by now. I'll bet a month's wages Cremona is ours already. They're probably running smack into our auxiliaries coming up from the south. We need to push forward. Now!"

Spurinna looked away from his counterpart and studied the sprawling vineyards again. He shook his head. "I don't like it. I say we hold here and let them come to us." He turned and called to one of his aids. "Tribune, send out a scouting party."

The Vitellians' plan was obvious to Quintus, but he dared not make a sound. In his late night discussion with Caecina, he had disclosed Spurinna's concern over the area's terrain and vineyards. Caecina had evidently taken that apprehension into consideration when designing his own plan of attack.

Titianus groused to himself as he sat on his horse. The morning sun rose higher and beat down on the army's helmets and armor as they stood in the open, waiting for their enemy to appear. Quintus's eyes stung as the sweat rolled from his forehead. Grumbles came from the

Praetorians, quiet at first but more pronounced as time wore on. After an hour, Titianus's irritation rose faster than the temperature, until he finally exploded.

"This is horseshit, Spurinna! We can't stand here broiling all day waiting for an enemy who may never come."

"We'll wait for the scouting party to return with information," Spurinna shot back, obviously losing patience with his aggressive counterpart.

"They've been gone too long. They were probably captured or killed."

"All the more reason to be cautious."

Titianus shook his head. "This sun will sap our strength faster than a pitched battle. To Hades with this! I'm moving my men forward."

He turned in his saddle and ordered his aquilifer forward. The men of his Praetorian legion followed their eagle and marched out ahead of the stationary cohorts.

"This is madness, Titianus!" Spurinna yelled after him. "We should not be splitting our forces."

"Then follow us to victory!" Titianus hollered back with a laugh.

Spurinna bit his lip in frustration but refused to give the order to move his men forward. Quintus watched the Praetorians march into the distance. As the last men in Titianus's long column took the distant bend, all hell broke loose. A cloud of dust rose from the distant countryside and the neat order of marching soldiers broke into disarray. The army had been ambushed.

Quintus looked at Spurinna, whose face had turned from a mask of frustration to one of horror. For the first time since he had met him, Quintus sensed that the legate did not know what to do. A general could not sit by idly and watch soldiers slaughtered by the hundreds. But marching forward in support of them could seal the fate of his own men. Spurinna closed his eyes for a moment, as if seeking divine guidance. His legionaries grew restless watching their comrades in battle as they dawdled on the roadway.

"Why are we waiting?" one yelled.

"They're being slaughtered. Let's go!" another hollered.

The jeers from the agitated warriors increased until, finally, the general's eyes opened.

"At the quick-step, march!" he yelled.

Like the start of a chariot race, the men on the front line broke into a full run.

"Hold the lines!" Spurinna called, but his men were beyond restraint. Rank after rank charged forward, draining energy with every step as they ran down the Via Postumia with almost forty pounds of armor, weapons, and gear.

Quintus had better command of his gladiators than the legate had on his trained legionaries. Holding their lines, they moved down the road at a slow trot.

"Easy men," Quintus called, just loudly enough for his group to hear. "Let's live to fight another day after this massacre. Let them take the brunt of this. We're just the hired help." He looked toward his fighters as they advanced slowly. Of the faces that glanced back, half reflected relief; the rest, puzzlement.

"I don't know what's running through that mind of yours, Quintus," Drusus responded with a laugh, "but you know how to cover our asses. And in a mess like this, that's all we could ask."

A murmur of agreement purred through the cohort. It seemed most of his familia understood he had an alternate plan in the works. Perhaps they had spoken among themselves and decided to give him the benefit of the doubt. They let hundreds of legionaries stream past them in passionate fervor, placing more and more bodies between them and the Vitellians.

As the sounds of battle drew closer, Quintus took a deep breath. He was determined to keep Taurus in check this day. Today he needed brains, not brawn. It was a lesson that had been seared into his mind at the Po River battle. He only hoped the blood, the screams, and the death struggle of the battlefield would not summon the warrior spirit against his will.

By the time Quintus and his troupe arrived at the battleground, the fighting was at fever pitch. It appeared one of the Othonian centuries had captured the eagle of the Vitellian Twenty-First Legion. But their conquest was short-lived as the unit was quickly overrun by an entire cohort of furious Vitellians.

Quintus directed his men up the slope of a vineyard along the left flank. It seemed a good place to remain close to the action, while keeping the fighters out of harm's way. But within minutes, he spotted a century of Vitellians making their way along the perimeter of the battle, apparently in hopes of attacking from the rear. The enemy wove their way through the very trellises Spurinna had warned about, coming straight at the gladiator unit.

"Lay low among the vines," Quintus ordered quietly. "Wait for my signal." He hoped the soldiers would pass without noticing them, but he knew hiding two hundred and fifty fighters at this close range was wishful thinking.

The gladiators and venatores spread out across the vineyard. Some lay flat in the dirt tracks between the orderly rows of vines; others crouched behind the thick uprights of the tall trellises; still others crawled into the shallow irrigation ditches. Quintus pushed aside a handful of leaves and purple berries to watch the approaching enemy. The sweet smell of the young grapes was a stark contrast to the stench of death rising from the road.

The Vitellian century crept forward, the legionaries' attention focused on the battle below. It appeared they would pass without incident. But suddenly a dozen gladiators sprang from a row of trellises and threw their pila. Quintus was as shocked as the Vitellian soldiers.

"Hit them!" he yelled.

The rest of his fighters charged the soldiers. Arrows flew from higher up the slope. Quintus engaged the Vitellian centurion, a well-built man with rage in his eyes. It was like fighting in front of a mirror. Once again, the enemy wore the same armor and helmets, and brandished identical weapons. This time, their shields even displayed golden wings similar to the Praetorians' but without the lightning bolts.

The speed of Quintus's sword arm drove the man back until he struck a trellis post. The determination in his eyes quickly turned to panic. Quintus pressed forward and crowded him, thrusting furiously with his gladius. The Vitellian rolled sideways to escape the trap. In the move, he lowered his scutum an inch. It was all the space Quintus needed. He thrust. A gush of blood flowed from the man's neck, and he dropped with a garbled scream.

Quintus stepped back and scanned the skirmish. Many of his men were using the same tactic, driving their enemy backward into the tangle of vines and trellises. It was not the style of combat for which a Roman legionary was trained. The gladiators were far more adaptable to the unusual fighting conditions. That experience, combined with their superior numbers, allowed them to quickly dominate the enemy. Within moments, the eighty Vitellians lay dead or wounded.

"I said to wait for my signal," Quintus yelled as his men reformed around him. He waved for them to get down, and they dropped once again between the rows of vines. "Now, who attacked these men?"

For a moment, there was silence. Then Vulcanus, the burly hoplomachus Quintus had once saved from the jaws of a crocodile, spoke up.

"I did." His arrogant tone angered Quintus. "They were going to see us anyway."

"You don't know that," Quintus shouted. "And it was not your decision to make."

"Look, Quintus, are we here to fight or hide in fields?" Vulcanus hollered back.

Quintus's rage boiled over. He crawled forward and grabbed the hoplomachus by the top of his cuirass. "It's 'Centurion' on the battlefield, Vulcanus. And you're here to do what I tell you to do, understand?"

"No, I don't understand," Vulcanus replied. "*None* of us understand. What in Hades are we doing here, Quintus?" The defiance had gone from his voice, and in its place Quintus sensed simple confusion.

He released the man's body armor. But before he had a chance to reply, a female voice came from beside him.

"He's just trying to keep us alive in this madness, Vulcanus," Amazonia yelled. "Or are you so anxious to die?"

"I'm no more anxious to die here than in the arena," Vulcanus shot back. "But at least in the arena I feel I'm fighting with *honor*, not hiding like a *coward*."

The words stung Quintus. He had thought by now, after all they'd been through together, his men were ready to follow him blindly, regardless of his orders. But inside he knew that these men had more heart, soul, and brains than most of the legionaries on this battlefield. Unless threatened by the whip at the ludus, many were not the type to follow anyone blindly.

"You're right," Quintus said. He averted his gaze toward the battle that raged on the road below them. "What we're doing does not seem honorable to many of you. It pains me to give these orders." He turned and looked Vulcanus in the eye. "But there's a reason for what I'm doing . . . a *good* reason. To lay out those details would be too dangerous. All I can do is ask you to trust in me."

"We're not in the arena now, Vulcanus," Drusus said with a sneer. "Who's going to see you fight out here, anyway? I'd rather live to fight another day on the sand, than lay dead on that road down there." He used his gladius to point to a pile of dead soldiers. "Nobody's ever heard of those poor bastards. But 'Vulcanus' is a name that will be back on everyone's lips in Pompeii someday." He slapped the gladiator's back. "But only if you let Quintus get us through this. I'm ready to follow. Who's with me?"

A shout came from the assembled fighters, and Quintus breathed a sigh of relief.

"I swore to Petra that I'd keep as many of you alive as possible. I make the same pledge to you. Just have faith in me and we'll get through this."

He looked down the hill toward Spurinna who was shouting orders that were relayed by the cornu horns. "Now spread out, and keep your heads down."

He crawled forward and peered through a clump of snail-eaten leaves. He was grateful for the support and common sense Drusus had shown, but was it enough to help him keep his men safe and his mission unhindered?

The charge of an Othonian cavalry unit pursuing a band of Vitellian slingers caught his eye. With stones loaded in their leather straps, the Vitellians ran into the vineyard adjacent to Quintus's position. The lead cavalry trooper rode hard with his lance held low, more intent on skewering his prey than on watching where he rode. He hit the crossbeam of an old sturdy trellis hard enough to knock him from his saddle. The beam had caught him in the throat and almost decapitated him. He was dead before he hit the ground. The dozen or so horsemen who followed pulled up short. They trotted back and forth, looking for a way in but were unable to reach their quarry. The scene reminded Quintus of field mice scurrying into a den, leaving the hawks to circle in frustration. The slingers unleashed a volley of missiles that struck with deadly accuracy. Quintus counted at least ten Othonian cavalry down in the blink of an eye. The slingers took off at a run, reloading their weapons as they went.

As he scanned the battle, Quintus saw similar scenes playing out across the vast region of wineries. Caecina had prepared his men well to capitalize on the terrain. The Othonian forces seemed in total disorder. The abundant trellises, irrigation ditches, and streams in the area made the disbursement and reinforcing of legions a nightmare. In short time, it became graphically obvious to Quintus why Spurinna considered such an innocuous area of farmland a certain killing ground.

Amazonia crawled up beside him. "What do we do now?" she asked. "We'll be spotted sitting here eventually."

"This will be the end of the first chapter of this cursed war. Trust me, we don't want to be embroiled in this fight."

"Hey baby, you don't have to tell me twice to keep my head down," Amazonia replied. "I'm with you. Sounds like the rest of these guys are, too. It's just a little hard to make two hundred fighters disappear."

A thought occurred to Quintus, and he glanced at Amazonia. "So let's make our own battle."

He jumped up and thrust his gladius at her. Instinctively, she raised her shield and easily countered the blow, but the look of confusion on her face made Quintus smile, despite the dire surroundings.

"Don't you get it?" he asked as he struck another light blow. "The commanders just need to see us fighting. With this much chaos, they can't tell *who* we're fighting. Everyone on this battlefield looks alike."

Smiles sprouted on every gladiator's face as it dawned on them what he was suggesting.

"Jupiter be praised," Memnon said with a laugh. "A centurion with brains!"

They stood, paired up, and began stepping through their standard ludus workout, this time with a metal sword instead of a wooden rudis.

Quintus glanced at them as he sparred with Amazonia. "Make it look good, men. Remember what Julianus always says: 'The appearance of danger is often better for the spectators than danger itself.'"

"Some of you drop your shields," Memnon shouted. "We can't have the Praetorian emblem on both sides of the battle." About half the shields hit the ground. A few fighters picked up discarded Vitellian shields to enhance the illusion.

"Good," Quintus said. "Lindani, have your men keep low in the fields and move constantly. Take a shot now and then to keep the missiles flying from our position." He raised his voice so the entire troupe could hear. "Now everyone keep a look out behind your opponent. If the Vitellians approach, shout a warning. And if our own legates approach, shout a louder warning."

The sham skirmish went on for almost an hour. Occasionally a gladiator would drop, crawl away, then reappear in another part of the wide vineyard. The fight had to look good to Scipio, Spurinna, or any of the other officers who might be watching from the road below.

"Careful," Amazonia called out as she cocked her head to the side. Quintus followed her motion and saw a line of about thirty Vitellian legionaries fighting their way toward the vineyard. Quintus kept an eye on them, and when the time was right, he shouted his order.

"Attack!"

The legionaries' faces showed their confusion when two hundred fighters, who had appeared to be locked in mortal combat, suddenly turned together and overwhelmed them. Most were killed in a matter of minutes; the wounded lay moaning in the fertile black earth.

An ugly thought occurred to Quintus. He looked down at the pitiful, bleeding soldiers. He had no option but to issue the order.

"We have to kill them," he said as calmly as he could muster. "We can't leave anyone alive to say what we were doing here."

Vulcanus looked at Quintus, his blank expression hard to read. A trickle of blood ran from the corner of his mouth. He made no move to kill the wounded man at his feet.

"Consider it a mandate from the mob and the games' editor," Quintus said quietly.

The hoplomachus continued to stare at Quintus, but his sword suddenly jerked downward and pierced the wounded soldier's neck. He relinquished his stare, spit blood on the ground, then resumed his mock combat with a fellow Pompeiian. Other arms thrust downward until the moaning stopped and the thirty Vitellians lay dead.

Quintus maneuvered Amazonia into a position where he could keep watch on the road. The Vitellians continued to dominate. The Via Postumia was once again littered with thousands of dead and dying soldiers, the majority of them Othonian. Ironically, it was now the dead Othonians who were causing the biggest problem for their comrades still fighting. While the Vitellians held their line firm, the Othonians continued to advance over the pile of corpses in the road. Many of them lost their footing in the puddles of blood and atop the slick shields and armor. The momentary mistake usually resulted in a blade to the face or throat and yet another Othonian in the growing pile.

As the afternoon wore on, it became obvious to Quintus the Othonian cause was lost. A wave of fresh Vitellians poured down the wide road from their nearby camp. Quintus seized the opportunity to make his move. He waved for Amazonia to stand down, then scanned the battlefield for Spurinna. He spotted him in the midst of battle on the far side of the road.

"Everyone start working your way down toward the road," he called loudly. "Stay alert for the retreat signal from the horns. It should be coming soon. Memnon, take command here." With that, he headed toward Spurinna's position, fighting the occasional challenger who stepped in his path.

Spurinna cleaved the bare head of a Germanian auxiliary fighter, then spun his horse and slapped its flank with the flat side of his bloody gladius. Quintus intercepted him as he galloped toward the rear of the fight.

"Legate, there's a fresh cohort headed this way from their camp," Quintus called out. Spurinna pulled to a stop and sat tall in the saddle to peer over the heads of the fighters in front of him. "I saw them from the slope on the other side of the road," Quintus continued.

"I wondered where your men ended up," Spurinna replied as he scanned the distant road. "By the gods, we'll never stand up to that horde!"

"I thought the Vitellian reserves would be tied up with Scipio and the rest of the gladiators to the south," Quintus said, fishing for more information.

"I got a report from Scipio's courier a while ago," the legate said as he continued to study the approaching legions. "The rear attack failed. They were wiped out by the same Batavian auxiliaries you fought on the Po island the other day."

Quintus was stunned. He pictured a field littered with dead gladiators, and he became angry. The senseless killing had gone on long enough.

"The men are faltering, Legate," he said. "We'll be overrun if we don't retreat."

Spurinna turned on him with violent eyes. "*I* decide when we retreat, Centurion. Got that?"

"Yes, sir," Quintus replied tightly, his anger and frustration growing.

Spurinna continued to assess his rapidly deteriorating forces. Quintus stared up at the general, watching his eyes shift between the bloody combat in front of him and the Vitellian reserves marching toward them. Quintus knew that each step brought him and his men closer to annihilation. Why couldn't this experienced general see it? Perhaps such experience deterred the ability to admit defeat. The muscles in Spurinna's neck contracted and his jaw tensed as he shook his head in anger. Quintus prepared for the rage to be unleashed on him, but the legate let out a yell toward the sky.

"May the gods damn that fool Titianus straight to Hades!" he hollered. "His impatience cost us this battle." Quintus knew it had cost them the war, but he said nothing. "Have the cornicen sound Retreat. We'll regroup down the road and return to our camp at Bedriacum."

"Very well, sir," Quintus said with authority. "Allow me to head for Brixellum to deliver the news to the emperor. I can bring good riders who can work as couriers to Bedriacum."

"Yes, fine," the legate yelled as he rode off.

Quintus relayed the orders to the trumpeter, then grabbed the mane of a horse wandering the rear lines unattended. The charger jumped at his touch, still skittish from the battle, but allowed him to mount. Quintus hoped the small wound in the animal's left flank would not hinder his ride. The notes of Retreat from the large round cornu horn trailed in Quintus's ears as he kicked the horse into a gallop and headed back across the road toward the sloping vineyard.

"Amazonia, Lindani, Vulcanus, and Flama, find horses and follow me. The rest of you regroup down the road. You're falling back to Bedriacum."

Lindani threw his bow over his shoulder and sprinted toward the horses that still lingered beside the dead cavalry troopers. He launched himself at the trellis near the edge of the vineyard, grabbed the heavy crossbeam, and swung up onto the back of the closest charger. The animal jittered in alarm, but the African had him under control quickly. He grabbed the bridles of two other horses and, herding another in front of him, drove all three animals toward the waiting gladiators.

"Your mounts await," he called down at them with a smile.

Quintus spun his horse and dug in his heels. The others mounted and followed him east toward Brixellum and Emperor Otho.

The sun had just dipped behind the tall trees as Quintus and his fighters led their horses off the river galley. By the time they arrived at the emperor's camp three miles from the south bank of the Po, the stars were bright in a dark sky. They were challenged by the guards, and Quintus gave the watchword.

"Where is the emperor?" he asked as he dismounted. "I have news from the battle lines." One of the soldiers pointed to a large, brown leather tent near the center of the compound. Quintus handed his reins to Lindani. "Stay ready. I might need a courier tonight."

Quintus walked down the wide path between the Praetorians' tents and approached the emperor's quarters. He made no attempt to wipe the caked gore from his hands, forearms, and armor. He wanted Otho to see the Roman blood the emperor had caused to be spilled this day. Four guards stationed near the flap blocked his path, but Quintus stepped up and stood toe-to-toe with the largest of the Praetorians.

"I have news from Legate Spurinna for the emperor," he said, puffing his already massive chest.

"Allow him in!" Otho's muffled voice yelled from inside.

Quintus threw back the flap and found the emperor seated alone, staring at a map of northern Italia spread on the large table before him. A tray of fish fillets and olives sat untouched beside the map; not so the generous decanter of wine, which was half empty. The emperor clutched a silver goblet in his trembling right hand. From his dejected manner, Quintus wondered if he had already heard the news.

"I bring word from Legate Spurinna," Quintus began.

"Fine, Centurion," Otho snapped. "Let the rancid words flow then."

"I'm afraid the battle is lost, Caesar. The legate was just sounding Retreat as I left the front lines. At least two-thirds of our men are gone."

The shaking in Otho's hands became worse as a hum within his throat turned to a growl. He flung the goblet across the tent, the few drops of wine it held splashing on the dark wall. "Damn the gods!" he yelled. "Why are the Fates not with me on this quest?" He continued staring at the map, as if searching for his next plan of action. "Why, Centurion? Why did we lose?"

Quintus hesitated.

"It was my brother, wasn't it?" Otho said, his words slow and slurred by the wine. "Titianus never had the patience to be a good commander. Jupiter only knows why I gave him that position." He slumped back in his wide seat and rested his chin in his hand.

Quintus glanced at the tent flap to be sure it had fallen closed after he had entered. He inched closer to the crestfallen emperor before he spoke. "Excellency, forgive me for saying so, but do you feel it's wise to prolong this war?" He paused to see the emperor's reaction, but there was none. "Vitellius and his legions now have an open road to Rome. They can use our captured galleys to ferry their men until they re-bridge the Po."

"What of the rest of your gladiators who were to attack from the south?" Otho raised his head, his eyes suddenly reflecting a glimmer of hope. "Were they successful?"

"I'm afraid not, Caesar. Tribune Scipio reported they were wiped out by the auxiliaries."

"Damn!" Otho yelled as he slumped back in his chair again. "Damn them all to Hades!" His foot struck out and clipped the leg of his table, shoving it violently sideways and spilling the metal tray onto the dirt floor. A young slave poked his head through the tent flap at the sound.

He rushed to pick up the mud-encrusted food but as he bent, Otho swung at him as well, knocking the teenaged boy into Quintus's legs. Quintus steadied the slave and helped him up.

"Please, Caesar," Quintus said softly. "Allow no more Roman blood to be spilled."

Otho looked up as the gladiator stood with his red-stained hands on the young boy's shoulders. The emperor did not utter a word, but the look in his eyes told Quintus the war was over. Quintus would have almost felt pity for the man, had he not been the cause of a thousand unnecessary deaths.

"Leave me," the emperor said, his voice now barely audible.

The slave ran from the tent, but Quintus walked slowly, looking back at the broken shell of a man who had tried to gain an empire. With his next step he walked into the barrel chest of Legate Titianus. The emperor's brother stood in the tent entranceway, a fresh scar across his scowling face dripping blood onto the front of his armor.

"What are you doing here, gladiator?" Titianus bellowed. "Why aren't you on the lines?"

Before Quintus could answer, Otho spoke, his voice now strong again with authority. "He delivered the news I knew was coming, Titianus. We cannot win this war. Today's events have proven that."

"Horseshit!" Titianus yelled. "This is just a setback. You heard Spurinna the other night. The Fourteenth Legion is marching from the north for us, the Danube legions are within four or five days, and the Moesian legions are right behind them."

"Yes, and now I realize we should have listened to Spurinna and waited for them," Otho shot back. "But the Fates have set our course."

Titianus pushed past Quintus and walked toward his brother. "We'll move you to the main camp at Bedriacum and barricade the entire town. We have enough men for that. Then we'll wait for the reinforcements. We can hold them!" His last words were punctuated with a loud fist on the table.

Otho looked at his brother for a moment, then shrugged. "I will sleep on it," he said finally, his voice low and soft again.

"No, we must move now," Titianus pushed. "Caecina has set his camp three miles from ours. By the morning they could have us surrounded."

Otho seemed unmoved. "I said I will sleep on it. Leave me now."

Titianus hovered over him without moving. The broken emperor stared at his brother with a look that demanded respect. "I said leave me," he hissed through clenched teeth.

Titianus turned and stormed toward the tent flap, roughly shoving Quintus aside. The gladiator looked at Otho. "You know the right decision, Caesar," he said quietly. He pulled back the flap with his bloody hand and left the emperor alone in the tent. As he walked away, he heard Otho's voice call out.

"Guards, I am not to be disturbed . . . by *anyone*."

Quintus found Lindani rubbing a homemade salve into the cut on his horse's flank. "I need you to deliver a message to Spurinna. Tell him Titianus is arguing to barricade Bedriacum and wait for the eastern legions, but Otho is leaning toward capitulation. As soon as I know Otho's final decision, I'll send another courier. That's it." Lindani nodded, then untied his horse's reins and hopped up on its back.

"Wait," Quintus said as the venator wheeled the horse around. "Tell him Otho wants him to remain in Bedriacum tonight in case there's another attack. He's not to come here to Brixellum."

The last thing Quintus wanted was another pair of eyes on Otho all night.

The clouds in the east grew red, painted with the sun's first rays. Quintus was already seated against a pole next to the emperor's tent, waiting for the camp to come fully to life. He had not gotten much sleep. Amazonia approached and sat beside him. Her swollen, red eyes told him she, too, had not slept much. She glanced at his hands, but before she said anything, the sound of hooves caught their attention.

They stood as five riders approached the camp's small central forum. Though they all wore the same armor, it appeared the tribune at the center of the formation was being escorted into the camp by the four cavalry troopers who surrounded him. The scabbards that normally held the tribune's sword and dagger were empty.

"Centurion, call your legate," the tribune called to Quintus as they pulled their horses to a stop. With Spurinna still across the river in Bedriacum, Quintus headed toward the Praetorian prefect's quarters. He preferred to keep Titianus and his violent temper out of what looked to be the final ultimatum. The prefect stepped from his tent just as Quintus got there.

"What is it?" the head Praetorian asked.

Before Quintus could reply, the tribune spoke for himself. "I carry a message from Legate Caecina on behalf of Vitellius."

"Approach," the prefect said.

The tribune dismounted and walked toward the officer. He handed him a small scroll bound with the wax seal of a Roman legate. The tribune spoke in a civil tone, but the resolute arrogance in his words was clear. "Our forces stand ready to attack once more. But Legate Caecina wishes to offer Otho a deal before the final blow is struck. He extends a pardon to all Othonian forces who lay down their arms and take the oath of allegiance to Aulus Vitellius. In addition, Otho must be turned over to us within the hour. Otherwise, your camp at Bedriacum will be laid to waste."

"Tell Caecina he can go fuck himself." The statement shocked both Quintus and the Praetorian prefect, neither of whom had yelled the insult. They turned to see Titianus standing defiantly in front of his tent. The wound across his face had stopped bleeding, but the gash, which had obviously been sewn by unskilled hands, was irritated and caked with scabs.

"Titianus . . ." the Vitellian tribune said with a patronizing smile, "only you could be so eloquent in the face of death. So be it."

The Vitellian turned toward his horse.

"Wait," the prefect called. "This man does not speak for the emperor."

The tribune smiled again as he remounted his charger. "As Otho's brother, I should think his words carry weight."

"Stand down for a moment," the prefect said. He cast a malicious glance at Titianus then walked toward the emperor's tent.

The four guards at the entrance hesitated in granting their own prefect admittance to the imperial quarters. The Praetorians took their job seriously and a direct order from the emperor himself was not easily disobeyed. After a few harsh words from the officer, the guards finally stood aside.

Quintus's hands tightened to fists in anticipation. A shout from the tent brought the four Praetorians, the cavalry troopers, and Titianus running. Quintus and Amazonia stood alone with the Vitellian tribune. Quintus felt Amazonia's gaze on him.

"He's dead, isn't he?" she whispered.

"It appears so," Quintus responded.

She glanced again at his hands. "I see you finally cleaned up last night."

Quintus unclenched his fists and rested his right hand on the hilt of his gladius. "We all have to wash the blood from our hands at some point," he replied quietly.

The flap to Otho's tent was thrown back, and the prefect emerged, the dawn's light revealing an ashen pallor on his face. He approached the tribune. "It appears Emperor Otho has taken his life. Tell Vitellius our men are his. I will send word to our camp in Bedriacum, and we will send couriers to meet the advancing eastern legions."

The tribune nodded and threw his leg up once again on his horse. With a quick kick he galloped down the path to the camp gate and disappeared. Amazonia nudged Quintus, and he followed her gaze back to the command tent. Titianus stepped through the portal carrying the dead body of his brother. The black hilt of the emperor's own dagger protruded from his chest, and scarlet stained the front of his white toga.

The disfigurement of Titianus's face was worsened by his grief. He slowly carried his older brother to the center of the square and laid him gently on the hard earth. Word spread rapidly through the camp, and within moments all two hundred Praetorians stood staring in disbelief at the pitiful scene.

"This is not right!" Titianus suddenly yelled, tears brimming in his eyes. "My brother would never take his own life so long as there was hope." He scanned the men who had gathered in the square. "Who did this?" he screamed.

The Praetorians all stared back in silence.

"Your brother did the honorable thing," the prefect said quietly. "Now he stands before Jupiter in glory."

Titianus looked down again at his brother's body. "I'll never believe this was done by his own hand," he said quietly. "But I want a pyre built in this forum within the hour. I want my brother honored as a hero would be honored, for he was the hero of Rome." He looked up at faces that stared back at him blankly. "Move!" he screamed at them. The Praetorian prefect nodded, which sent the men into a flurry of activity.

Titianus's gaze fell on Quintus, and his eyes narrowed to slits. Quintus could not tell if the look reflected anger or suspicion, but in either case, he knew it was time to leave.

"Prefect," he called, "I'll take my fighters and ride to Bedriacum with the news." He looked at Otho's body, then continued. "Spurinna will need an official dispatch from you on this. He won't take my word alone."

The officer grunted and headed for his tent. A group of soldiers arrived with the first of the wood and began laying the funeral pyre. Quintus sent Amazonia to gather Vulcanus and Flama, then followed the prefect to his tent, not wanting to remain alone in the square with Titianus.

Contending with a series of interruptions from his men, it took the prefect a while to compose and seal the dispatch to Spurinna. When he finally finished, he handed the scroll to Quintus, then pushed past him and exited the tent. With a grim smile, Quintus tapped the small papyrus roll in his hand. He stepped from the tent to find his three comrades mounted and ready to go. Behind them the funeral scene was set, and Titianus laid his brother's body onto the middle of the low wooden platform. Quintus mounted his horse and watched the solemn ceremony.

Titianus folded the dead monarch's hands on his chest just below the dagger's hilt. A Praetorian handed Titianus a torch, and the grief-stricken legate laid the first flames into the pyre.

"Take this man's spirit, oh Jupiter," Titianus called out toward the sky. "He lived only to serve you and the people of Rome. Hear the prayers of his faithful subjects." A column of ten senior Praetorians, including the prefect, carried torches to the pyre and each lit a small section. In seconds, the dry timber ignited and a roar of flame enveloped the body.

Quintus was surprised to see tears in the eyes of so many men. As he prepared to turn his horse and head toward the gate, a cry of grief came from someone in the assembled mass of Praetorians. One of the guards suddenly broke from the ranks and threw himself onto the burning pyre. The horses skittered as Quintus and his fighters stared, stupefied. The burning man screamed and squirmed within the flames. A second later, another followed his lead, then another. No officers stepped forward to stop the self-immolation, and no soldiers seemed startled or appalled at the ritual.

Quintus looked at Amazonia and his two gladiators. They stared at the fire, their eyes reflecting the same shock and disgust that sickened him.

"Let's go," he whispered.

"Gladly," Vulcanus replied with a shake of his head.

They walked the horses down the wide path to the gate, which now sat devoid of any sentries. A column of gray smoke rose behind them as the screams of yet another martyr shattered the peaceful morning.

"By the gods," Amazonia said, a numb look still etched on her face, ". . . and they call gladiators crazy."

Once through the gate, they kicked their horses into a gallop and headed north to Bedriacum.

• • •

The Othonian camp was still in a state of turmoil when Quintus and the three fighters arrived late in the morning. The smell of death hung heavy in the air, and the screams of those undergoing amputations and operations in the camp hospital assaulted their ears. They knew from experience that a cup of wine did not go far as an anesthetic.

As he maneuvered his horse slowly toward the administration area, Quintus looked down into the open ends of the legionaries' tents. Some sat stitching each other's gaping wounds. Others were stretched out motionless, either exhausted or dead. Still others sat staring out at the pathways with vacant eyes. The camp reeked of defeat.

Quintus found Spurinna pacing by his tent. The legate hurried toward him with expectant eyes.

"It's over," Quintus said, handing down the dispatch. "Otho is dead and it's over. Caecina will arrive shortly to address the men. They are all to be given amnesty."

The legate took a deep breath. Without another word he spun and walked toward his tent.

"There's Lindani." Amazonia pointed down a narrow aisle between the auxiliary tents. Quintus and Amazonia hopped down from their horses and walked toward the hunter, who sat alone in the dirt outside their shelter. Quintus's heart raced as he saw the depression on his friend's normally cheerful face. He knew what was coming.

"How are the rest of the men?" he asked right away.

Lindani shook his head. "It is not good, my friend. In our vineyard, only ten were lost. But Tribune Scipio's attack from the south was tragic."

"I know that, but what are the numbers?" Quintus snapped at him, instantly regretting his tone.

Lindani glanced at Amazonia, then back to Quintus. "He attacked with sixteen hundred fighters. I have heard only three hundred and thirty survived. Many have serious wounds."

Quintus was devastated. He had known the body count would be high since the attack was no surprise to the Vitellians after his clandestine meeting with Caecina. But he had not expected numbers like these.

"What of the Pompeiians who were with him?" he asked, not really wanting to hear the answer.

"They did not fare too badly, about fifteen killed," he said. "Riagall the Celt was among them."

Quintus hated to hear names associated with body counts. It made it too real. This one hit especially hard, for the fighter was part of his own contubernium—his own tent family. He thought back to the day he had faced Riagall in the Glevum arena. The Celt had fought well and the crowd granted him a missio. Quintus remembered running a victory lap after their bout and then holding Riagall's arm up to share in the ovation. The gesture might have breached arena protocol, but it was a memorable display of mutual respect and helped forge a bond among the fighters of the Britannia ludus. He would miss Riagall. Knowing the Celt's death was, in no small way, a result of Quintus's own duplicity made the loss that much harder for him to accept.

"I hope this is worth it," he said quietly, shaking his head as he walked away. "I hope Castus knows what he's doing." He walked down the dusty aisle seeking an empty tent in which he could be alone.

Within the hour, Caecina and the entire Vitellian infantry and cavalry were at the front gate of the Bedriacum camp. As Spurinna had ordered, all ambulatory Othonians had lined the main avenue into the camp as a show of respect and humility to the Vitellians. Although they were former enemies, they were all still Romans. He and Caecina had agreed that uniting the camps would reinforce that bond. Of course, it did not escape the notice of any soldier that the deployment was also an occupation of enemy territory.

Quintus stood at the head of his weary Pompeiian fighters halfway down the long avenue that led to the camp's central square. He could feel the tension in the air as the order was called to open the gates. But as the sentries swung the heavy wooden barricades open, the tense atmosphere dissolved quickly. The Vitellian legionaries were magnanimous. Most of their faces reflected friendship and relief, although a few of the older centurions and legionaries bore triumphant smirks. While there was no cheering for the victors, soldier greeted soldier as comrade, with forearms clasped and a friendly slap on the back.

Quintus couldn't help wonder if he and his gladiators would continue to be treated with the respect they had finally earned under Scipio—or would they once again be the scum of the Empire in the eyes of the Vitellian officers, centurions, and legionaries?

Caecina rode at the head of his men, nodding in a gracious manner to each group of Othonians he passed. The general's eyes met Quintus's, but neither acknowledged their previous encounter. Caecina seemed younger now than Quintus remembered, perhaps due to his freshly shaven face.

As the legate passed, the Othonians peeled from their ranks and joined the Vitellians in their walk toward the camp's central forum. Judging by the conversations Quintus heard around him, many of the former enemies had actually trained and fought together in previous campaigns.

Caecina entered the square and acknowledged his Othonian counterpart who awaited him by the command tent. Spurinna gave a crisp salute, then extended his hand as Caecina stepped from his horse. As their forearms joined in a strong handshake, a cheer rose from the assembled soldiers and auxiliaries. Spurinna gestured toward a wooden equipment crate that had been dragged into the square. Caecina mounted the makeshift podium and addressed the men in a clear, strong voice.

"I am Aulus Caecina Alienus, Legate of the Fourth Rhine Legion. I am sorry for the death of your previous commander." Quintus smiled at how the general carefully avoided referring to Otho as "emperor." "But this day we will be united under another. And we shall fight side-by-side once again against the enemies of Rome in distant lands, not against our own brothers." A loud shout of approval came from every man within the sound of his voice. "I will now administer the oath that will bind us once again as comrades-in-arms."

All the men who had fought hard for Otho over the past three months raised their hands and recited the oath of allegiance to Vitellius. They swore to obey the directives of the new emperor, to not desert their posts or their comrades, and to not refuse death on behalf of the Roman state. Quintus recited words that had no meaning to him. It was just as much a charade as his pledge had been to Otho three months earlier.

The soldiers cheered again as the recitation ended. Quintus was sure they celebrated more their survival of the civil war than their pride in allegiance to yet another megalomaniac looking to prosper at the cost of Rome. Caecina closed his oratory with more inspiring remarks, then ordered all centurions who had commanded Othonian units to line up for interviews. Quintus joined the line that formed beside him as Caecina climbed from the equipment crate and walked among the men.

"What's your name, your century, and your current head count?" a grizzled centurion asked as Quintus reached the head of the line.

"I am Quintus Honorius Romanus. I command a unit of gladiators and venatores from Pompeii. There are 247 of us left alive, although eighteen are in no condition to fight."

The centurion grunted. "Just what we need . . . a bunch of fucking gladiators fighting with us now. How many did you start with?"

"Three hundred," Quintus replied.

"Not a bad body count, Romanus," the centurion said as he made an entry into his ledger. "Either you command good fighters or you hide from the action." He stopped writing and looked Quintus in the eye. "And since they're all *gladiators*, my money says you hide from the action."

The man's tone infuriated Quintus, but he said nothing in reply.

The centurion laughed and went back to writing. "Next."

"I have a question," Quintus said without moving from the line. "We have thousands of dead on the Via Postumia. We need help burying them. Who do I see to organize that?"

The centurion looked up at Quintus. A moment passed and he said nothing. Then his head snapped back, and he let out a howling laugh that caught the attention of every soldier in the area.

"You must be joking, right?" he said as he caught his breath. Quintus let his silent stare answer the question. "First of all," the centurion continued, "even if they *could* be buried, it would not be a job for the victors. But that's not an issue because Emperor Vitellius himself has issued strict orders that the Othonian bodies are to be left on the road to rot." The centurion's smirk returned as he leaned forward. "You know . . . as a bit of a reminder to anyone else who might get an itch to declare himself emperor."

Quintus began to shake with rage as a murmur went up among all those who heard the centurion's heartless remarks. "Those are soldiers of Rome lying on that road," Quintus said, trying to keep his temper in check, "regardless of which emperor they fought for."

The centurion dropped his white feather quill onto his half-completed ledger and stood up, face-to-face with Quintus. "And I say they're Othonian pigs who deserve nothing more than the crows picking at their rotting corpses."

The murmurs grew to shouts and, before Quintus had a chance to respond, a young legionary dove at the centurion. "My father lies out there, you son of a whore!" he screamed as he crashed into the centurion. They both toppled backward into the dirt. Their struggle kicked up a cloud of dust, but it was over quickly, with the centurion's gladius buried in the young soldier's side. A dozen Vitellian legionaries quickly formed a protective ring around their centurion, swords and javelins lowered menacingly.

"Anyone else have a problem with this issue?" the centurion yelled as he yanked the sword from the body and wiped a stripe of fresh blood on the back of the dead man's tunic. He stared defiantly at Quintus, almost willing him to attack. But Quintus turned and walked away.

His body continued to tremble with rage and frustration as he headed toward the auxiliary tents where his gladiators were housed. But before he got there, he felt a hand on his thick arm. He turned and looked into the face of Legate Caecina.

"I'm sorry about all that," the legate said.

"About what?" Quintus asked harshly. "Yet another Roman killed unnecessarily? Or the fact that we cannot bury our dead?" He turned and kept walking. He was surprised that the general walked with him.

"About both. I warned Vitellius it was a mistake not to show compassion and honor to our fellow Roman warriors." The legate shrugged. "But fear runs rampant in the mind of every new emperor. And to them, it's best to fight fear with more fear. He thinks the edict will show strength against any potential rivals."

Quintus shook his head as they walked. "And this is the man you fight for?"

Caecina glanced around to be sure no other soldier was within listening distance. "As I said to you in Cremona that night," he replied in a low voice, "I don't think either of these men are worth fighting for. But let's not lose sight of the bigger plan at hand here, Quintus. Think of Castus . . . and Vespasian. You, yourself, helped put that in motion. Don't let the death of one more soldier divert you from your path."

Quintus stopped walking and looked the general in the eyes. "That's the problem, Legate. To you he was just 'one more soldier.' To me, he was a man with a name and a family." He turned and walked toward his tent, leaving Caecina alone on the pathway.

Amazonia and Lindani approached the tent from the opposite direction. "We just heard a centurion killed one of the Praetorians. Is that true?" Amazonia asked. Quintus nodded and Amazonia shook her head. "If Vitellius treats the Praetorian Guard that badly, how do you think the gladiators will fare under his hand?" she said, dropping into the tent.

Quintus turned and looked back at Caecina walking alone among the tents and fighters. "I don't know," he answered. "But I do know that our work here has just begun."

XV

June AD 69

A HARSH SUN glared on the bleached Egyptian sandstone of the forum at Nicopolis. Lucius used his hand to shade his eyes as he and Julia stood a few steps behind Tiberius Julius Alexander on the second-story balcony of the legions' administrative offices. Below them, soldiers from the two legions of Egypt marched into the forum in precise formations. The small town, three miles east of Alexandria, housed the headquarters of the ten thousand men of the Third Cyrenaica and Twenty-second Deiotariana Roman legions, tasked with keeping the peace in North Africa.

"These soldiers are among the best in the Empire," Alexander said over his shoulder to Lucius. "As prefect of Egypt, I am proud to lead them."

"As well you should be," Lucius said with enthusiasm. "They look ready to take on the world."

He knew Vespasian would have enjoyed nothing more than to see this army assemble before him, ready to pledge their allegiance to him. But the savvy governor had realized it would not be prudent for him to be seen personally inciting the legions against Emperor Vitellius. So Vespasian, his son Titus, and his ally, Governor Gaius Mucianus of Syria, were already headed back to Caesarea on Julia's merchant ship, the *Juno*. Their meeting with Julius Alexander had gone well. They had all agreed that the new emperor must go.

In the two months that had passed since he had wrenched control from Otho, Vitellius had earned a reputation that rivaled Nero's in decadence and self-centered debauchery. He had horrified much of the Senate with ill-chosen appointments made hastily from his temporary headquarters in north Italy. And he had enraged the Praetorian Guard by replacing their ranks with his own soldiers from the Rhine legions. For the ex-Praetorians, that meant a cut in pay to half their usual salary and a loss of status that was incalculable. The unprecedented insult of forbidding them to bury their dead at Cremona added to the tension and resulted in cohorts ready to mutiny at the slightest instigation. In Judea, Vespasian stood ready to capitalize on these critical mistakes.

As the legions assembled before him, Lucius considered the risks he and the others had taken over the past weeks. At any other time in Roman history, their plans would have been viewed as treason of the highest order, and their lives would have been snuffed out faster than an oil lamp. But instead they stood with armies ready to march for them.

The senior tribune stepped forward and signaled that the men were in place and ready to be addressed. Alexander spoke in a loud voice that easily reached the legionaries in the rear ranks.

"I have a letter I would like you to hear. It is addressed to the men of the Third and Twenty-second legions in Egypt from Flavius Vespasianus, the governor of Judea. It reads as follows: 'Fellow soldiers of Rome, by this letter and the voice of your prefect, I seek your support. For too long our Empire has suffered . . .'"

It took a while to read the entire text but not one legionary moved a muscle throughout the address. Lucius had expected an occasional outburst of cheering or some other response to many of the rallying calls Vespasian had written. But all was quiet. He looked across at Julia and sensed that she, too, was growing concerned that these legions were not yet ready to see a fourth emperor in less than a year.

Alexander came to the end of Vespasian's letter. "'. . . I therefore solicit your assistance in my quest to assume the principate. I do this under the eyes and guidance of almighty Jupiter, for the people of Rome and the strength of the Empire. Soldiers of Rome, do I have your support?'

The letter is signed: 'Flavius Vespasianus.'"

The prefect lowered the scroll and gazed out upon the mass of gleaming armor. There was the briefest pause before a loud chorus of cheers burst from the provincial forum. The sudden roar of ten thousand voices startled Lucius in its intensity. He met Julia's gaze and saw a broad smile break across her red lips. It was clear she was ready to return to Rome. And he was certainly ready to return to Roman politics. Under the protection of a new emperor with a debt of gratitude, the ghosts of his past would finally be buried.

A rare rainstorm descended on Caesarea as the *Juno* entered the harbor for the second time in a week. Lucius and Julia were met on the dock by their Judean office manager, Aram Kalyndu, who whisked them through the downpour in the company's covered carriage to the palace.

"I take it the good news has already reached here," Lucius said as he and Julia were ushered into the palace tablinum—the sparse private office where Vespasian held his most confidential meetings.

Vespasian, Titus, and Mucianus hovered around a polished cedar table in the center of the room. Maps and scrolls were heaped in piles on the table, some overflowing onto the beige and blue tiled floor. Vespasian looked up from a map of Italia.

"Yes, it did," he said, although his face showed no emotion. "A dispatch rider arrived a few days ago."

"Obviously, the legions here in Judea heard as well," Titus said, his face beaming. "My father's personal guards saluted him as 'Caesar' and 'Augustus.' And the formations followed suit in their camps the next day. A letter inviting further support is circulating throughout the legions of the East, all the way to the Danube."

"Congratulations, Caesar," Julia said to Vespasian with a sly wink.

"It's still too early for that title," he replied as he pulled another map into place on the table. Lucius could make out the whole of the eastern

Empire, with the bases of each legion highlighted and annotated in black ink.

Mucianus picked up where Titus left off. "With my Syrian legions, our army is at least as large as the Vitellians', probably larger. We'll also get word to the ex-Othonian Praetorian Guard who have been disbanded. With a promise of reinstatement, our forces will grow by another eight or nine thousand. Antonius Primus and the Seventh Galbiana are also vocal in their support."

Vespasian looked across the table at the Syrian governor. "And we hope by confronting Vitellius with those numbers, combined with the African blockade, we'll get him to surrender without further bloodshed. That's the way I want this approached. Understood?" There was a harshness to his words that Lucius had rarely heard.

"Of course, Flavius," Mucianus answered.

Vespasian seemed to regret the reprimand as soon as he had voiced it. "I just hate the thought of more Roman deaths in this war," he said with a sigh.

"We all do, Father," Titus said. "But you know it's unlikely Vitellius will give up without a fight, even faced with overwhelming odds."

Vespasian's aide entered and cleared his throat to interrupt as politely as possible. "Sir, Marcus Castus is here to see you."

"Bring him in," Vespasian said enthusiastically. It seemed to Lucius that just the mention of the old centurion's name always brightened Vespasian's mood. A dripping wet Castus soon entered the palace office. "Get this man a cloak right away, and some wine," the governor called to his servants.

The tough old centurion looked a wreck, but even the soiled, soggy tunic and rain-soaked hair did not dampen his spirits. "I bring good news from Rome," he said with a smile that revealed more than one missing tooth. "Our contact tells me that Caecina is secretly working against Vitellius. He plans to turn the Ravenna fleet to our side, then his own legions."

"By the gods, that's excellent news!" Vespasian said loudly, slapping the back of the old man's wet tunic. "Perhaps this *can* be done without blood-shed." He turned and called toward the door. "Helvia, never mind the cloak. Bring this man to my quarters and fetch him one of my dry tunics. Right away." He placed an arm over Castus's shoulder and looked him in the face as they walked toward the door. "And you're confident in the accuracy of the information from this contact?"

"I have no doubts whatsoever," the old man replied.

Vespasian smiled. "But his identity remains a mystery . . ."

Castus paused, considering the unspoken request. "I think it's best for now, Flavius," he replied. "There's still much for him to do. But you'll be pleased when you meet him . . . again."

Vespasian stopped walking, and his bushy eyebrows arched. "Ah, so I know this mystery man!"

Castus smiled. "You do, Flavius."

Vespasian laughed. "Well, now you've really piqued my curiosity, you old warhorse. Who is it?"

Castus shook his head. "It's best we wait."

Vespasian shrugged and slapped the man's back as he herded him out the door. "Get changed, my friend, then we'll have a good, warm meal."

Castus followed the slave girl down the hall, and Vespasian returned to the office table. It appeared the weight of the world had been lifted from the governor's stocky shoulders.

"Good old Caecina," Vespasian said rubbing his hands together. "I could see how the prospect of yet another battle of Roman against Roman would put him off."

Lucius looked around the room and caught a glance between Titus and Mucianus. Were they becoming skeptical of Castus's source of information? Since the reports were still flowing after Otho's death, the spy must now be in the Vitellian camp. For how many sides could one man fight? Was everyone in this room—not the least of which, Lucius himself—willing to allow this faceless mole to put them and their well-calculated plans at risk? It was time for someone to voice the concern that weighed on everyone's mind.

"Flavius, if I may . . ." Lucius said. "Do you really feel comfortable not knowing who this spy is? Suppose this is a trap or just a ploy to keep you at bay?"

Lucius saw Titus's eyes quickly dart to his father. As Lucius suspected, he wasn't the only one concerned. Vespasian looked up from the map of the eastern Empire and studied Lucius for a moment.

"First of all, I have known and fought with Marcus Livius Castus for many years. I trust him with my life. If he feels his source is trustworthy, then that's good enough for me." His eyes narrowed a bit, and he leaned forward slightly toward Lucius. "You've provided me with information yourself, Lucius. How do I know I can trust you and your sources?"

Lucius was taken aback by Vespasian's tone and realized he had overstepped his bounds. "I'm sorry."

"He meant no offense," Julia added.

"And none was taken," Vespasian replied, but his gaze never lightened on Lucius. "However, in unstable times like these, I always go with my gut instinct. It's never failed me before, and I trust it won't fail me now. I have faith in Castus."

Titus used the momentum of Lucius's question to steer the conversation. "That's all well and good, Father. But is it wise to just sit and wait, hoping for the game to play out in our favor?"

"I agree with Titus on this," Mucianus said quickly. "Now is the time to strike. We need to put pressure on Vitellius."

Vespasian had resumed his study of the map but paused and looked up at his guests with a quizzical expression. "Have you all forgotten that my background is the military?" His voice was calm and pleasant, but he seemed determined to put these questions of weakness or indecisiveness to rest. "Do you not see me studying the maps? Of course we will put pressure on Vitellius. And, no, we will not just sit idle and wait for the game to play out without us. I have always guided my own course in life."

He paused, as if debating whether or not to continue.

"We will march on Rome," Vespasian continued softly. The intense weight of the statement was almost lost in its casual delivery. Vespasian looked down again at the map, and they all excitedly followed his gaze. "Antonius Primus is already here," he said, pointing to an area just south of the Danube River. "I'll have him and the Seventh Legion advance first since they are weeks closer to Rome than we are. Castus will arrange a war council . . ." He studied the map further. ". . . here in Ptuj with the Thirteenth Legion. He and Primus will set the details. Mucianus, you can prepare your legions to march west to the Macedonian coast. Depending on events, you will either cross the Aegean in the war galleys Caecina will secure for us and march on Rome from the south, or you will follow Primus up and over the Alps and come in from the north." Vespasian looked up and studied the bright, eager faces around the table before he continued. "But nothing happens until we give our blockade time to work and we give our man on the front lines time to help Caecina negotiate a surrender."

"And what's my role in this, Father?" Titus asked. His voice betrayed his hurt at being left out of the plans so far.

"Have we all forgotten that the Jewish revolt in Jerusalem has not yet been put down?" Vespasian replied. "You and I will remain in Judea to finish this job once and for all. And if there's not time to crush it completely before I'm needed in Rome, than you will stay and finish it for me."

There was no hesitation in Titus's response. "Of course, Father."

Vespasian exhaled a long sigh. "Now, let us all retire to the triclinium for some dinner. I'm sure Castus is famished." He again scanned the faces of those in the room. "What we've set into motion here could alter the history of the Empire."

"And well it should," Lucius said proudly. The others in the room responded with a cheer.

"I have to say I agree, my friend," Vespasian said as he placed his hand on Lucius's shoulder. "I, for one, have had enough of emperors who focus more on themselves than on the citizens of Rome. The more I've seen and heard this year, the more sickened I've become. The people need someone to rid them once and for all of this unending procession of incompetent pretenders to the throne. Treasonous or not, I see that as my responsibility."

"Is it a crime," Lucius asked, "to want to restore dignity to the principate and a feeling of pride in our emperor?"

Julia grasped Lucius's hand and squeezed. He knew in her mind she was already reacquainting herself with a view of the Forum from her own personal balcony. "A Flavian dynasty is what the Empire needs now," Julia said, referring to Vespasian's family name. "An undisturbed lineage that will guarantee us all decades of peace and stability." She winked coyly at Titus, and he returned the smile.

Vespasian looked down at the map one last time before leaving the room. "Let us hope Minerva grants us the wisdom and vision to walk this path carefully." He thought for a moment, then continued. "And let us hope our man on the front lines can work out a peaceful resolution with Caecina's help."

XVI

July AD 69

MARCHING WITH THE LEGIONS along the Via Flamina into the heart of Rome was an empty experience for Quintus and his gladiators, despite the cheering throng. They felt like men without a cause. After reluctantly fighting for the Othonians, they were now an unwilling appendage of the army of Emperor Aulus Vitellius.

The procession had been followed for most of the day by more than a hundred thousand Roman citizens, servants, camp followers, and shopkeepers who had met the entourage at the pink cliffs north of the city walls. The emperor's gilded litter had led the long procession all the way from Cremona, where he had finally arrived forty days after the battle.

The folly of the imprudent new monarch had begun shortly after he had arrived from the Rhine. His comment at the grave of Otho—"A little grave for a little man"—did little to inspire the Othonians who had sworn to support him. His standing only grew worse among the legions as he toured the wretched Cremona battlefield, still littered with the bodies of the dead who had been refused burial rights by his own order. "The scent of death of a fellow Roman is very sweet," he had quipped to the accompanying legates and tribunes. The quote had spread through the camp like the stench from the battlefield itself.

Even the reports and rumors of a new army being assembled to place Vespasian on the throne did not seem to bother Vitellius. It appeared his only concern was the level of pomposity and flamboyance in his procession to Rome.

Quintus craned his neck and looked toward the head of the column in the far distance. The emperor had stepped from his transport at the city gate, donned his white and purple toga, and now led the procession on foot. Quintus trudged ahead, ambivalent about his military standing but happy to once again be in the city that he would always consider home. As they marched, the talk of the fighters around him focused on returning to their ludi at Pompeii and Capua. But he knew their work was far from over. Vitellius would never release them or any other auxiliaries until he and his political cronies held a firm grip on Rome. And he knew that Vespasian's army was on its way. But rather than contribute to a further drop in morale, he remained silent.

Within the hour they reached the Forum and were disbursed into groups to be billeted throughout the city. The gladiators and venatores were housed once again at the Ludus Magnus. The procurator of the imperial school, Tiberius Lupus, allowed Quintus the freedom to come and go from the ludus, since his centurio princeps rank required he be available for military conferences. Quintus managed to get Amazonia and Lindani out for an occasional saunter through the city as well.

From Pompeii, Cassius Petra sent his head physician, Agricola, to Rome to assist the medical staff at the Ludus Magnus in treating the plentiful war wounds. The crafty lanista knew the imperial procurator would look after the injured fighters from his own ludus first, and let his junior medical assistants practice their medicine on the fighters from Pompeii and Capua. Petra decided it was in his best interest to look after his own property. As Agricola healed the Pompeiians' wounds and broke their fevers, the imperial trainers paired the revitalized visiting gladiators with the Roman fighters in daily sparring matches. The doctores seemed impressed with the caliber of fighters being turned out by Petra and Julianus in Pompeii.

Quintus soon fell into a new routine. He split his time between training, exercise—unfortunately, without his homemade muscle-building apparatus sitting dormant at the Pompeii ludus—and the occasional military conference that required the presence of the centurion ranks. Days became weeks, and weeks became a month. The grumbling of the fighters from southern Italia grew louder with each passing day. Quintus did his best to soothe tensions but refused to provide more information than was absolutely necessary. He hoped Caecina would be able to work some magic and deliver the Empire to Vespasian without bloodshed. But as each day passed, that became less likely.

As July turned to August, the summer heat in the stifling city grew almost unbearable. Although many of the Vitellian soldiers who occupied Rome sought the cool waters of the Tiber for relief, Quintus knew to stay clear of the river and cautioned his fighters to do the same. As a child growing up in the large, dirty city, Quintus had heard many lectures about the ill effects of the foul river water. The effluent of hundreds of sewers, and even the bodies of criminals and Christians killed in the arena, ended up in the Tiber. Quintus was proven right when dozens of soldiers soon succumbed to chills and disease.

The heat also caused tensions to flare within the populace. Rome had become an overcrowded garrison town. On two different occasions, the gladiators were called into service to support Vitellian legionaries in quelling riots in the city. Rumors flew rampant throughout Rome that a long-distance blockade of grain from Egypt and Carthage would soon leave the State storehouses empty. Many in the lower class who depended on that grain to feed their families decided to let their feelings be known by torching some of those same State storehouses.

One warm evening in early September, shortly after dinner, the gladiators were herded onto the expansive training field of the Ludus Magnus.

"What's this all about?" Amazonia asked Quintus as she joined him, leaning against a palus training post. "They need us to kick around some more old men with torches?"

"Who knows?" Quintus said with a shrug. "I heard nothing at the conference today about expecting more trouble tonight."

"Gladiators and venatores," Tiberius Lupus shouted to the thousand or so who had assembled on the field. "Our new emperor, Aulus Vitellius, has called for games to celebrate his birthday in three days' time." A moan rose among the fighters. "The emperor feels the people of Rome need a . . . distraction . . . from the recent events. The doctores will now circulate with the pairings."

Quintus and Amazonia stared at each other in shock. "Oh, this asshole is something else," Amazonia said in disgust. "People are rioting in the streets, he has a blockade on his hands, and Vespasian is breathing down his neck . . . and he calls for games! What kind of an idiot is this man?"

Quintus shook his head in disbelief. "Every day the officers grumble about his inaction. They know that the legions in Egypt, Judea, and Syria have pledged to Vespasian. We'll soon have a hostile army approaching from the East. Yet instead of planning for battle—or surrender—he plans for his birthday celebration." He looked around and lowered his voice. "This is why Caecina wants to rid the Empire of this dolt. Unfortunately, Valens—his counterpart—still supports Vitellius. Something will need to be done. This madness can't go on much longer."

Their conversation came to an end as the murmillo trainer approached. "Amazonia, you will face Pugnax," he said, then turned to move on.

"Doctore," Quintus called after him, "my fighters and I do not belong to the Ludus Magnus. We should not be fighting in these games. You don't even know our rankings. How can you pair us up?"

The doctore stopped and glanced back. "All the best fighters fight, regardless of their home ludus. However, the procurator agreed that Rome fighters will face Rome fighters, Pompeii will fight Pompeii, and Capua will fight Capua." A sly smile crossed his lips before he turned away. "You're a part of the Vitellian army now, remember? You do what you're told. Besides, what difference if you die on a battlefield or in an arena? A gladiator is a gladiator, right?"

As the murmillo doctore walked away, another loud voice called out from across the field. "Taurus, you will fight Memnon," the Thracian trainer yelled.

Quintus didn't think it was possible for his morale to sink any lower, but hearing that he would now face his unofficial optio—his assistant and longtime comrade in the arena—managed to make him feel even worse. He glanced past Amazonia and saw Memnon watching him with an impassive look that was hard to read. After a long moment, they broke eye contact and each walked their separate ways. Quintus knew he needed to get Memnon alone at some point. In fact, he needed to speak with all the primus and secundus palus fighters from Pompeii before the games. He was done losing good men for this moronic emperor.

For the third time in his life, Quintus found himself looking up into the crowded cavea of the Amphitheater of Taurus. He walked the circuit of the arena in the opening pompa beside a topless and well-oiled Amazonia. As always, her stunning beauty caused a stir in the crowd as she passed each section of seats. Her auburn hair, now halfway to her shoulders, shimmered in the morning light. The deep blue of her subligaculum loincloth accented her bronze skin and the flowing golden cape she was given for the pompa. Even Quintus had a hard time keeping his eyes from the perfect body he had not seen uncovered in many months.

They both acknowledged the mob with perfunctory waves and nods, but neither showed the flashy bravado of their earlier pompas until the chants of "Taurus! Taurus!" spread from one rowdy section to half the cavea. Although in no mood for showmanship, Quintus realized that ignoring the crowd's wishes during a game was tantamount to an automatic death sentence. He stepped through a brief *wushu* display, his curved sica flashing in the bright, hot sunlight as it traveled with astonishing speed. The sword exercise—taught to him by Master Sheng during the Oriental's stay in Britannia—always excited the crowd and managed to help Quintus relax and allow his *chi* energy to flow. The permanent designs of the bull and the Gorgon that adorned his torso gleamed as his sweat began to run. A loud roar greeted the demonstration. He finished with a flourish of the sword and a brief bow, then walked on, following the procession along the stone arena wall.

"So this is the asshole we're fighting for," Amazonia whispered to Quintus as they approached the emperor's podium. It was the first opportunity they had had to be near the new ruler. Vitellius sat slouched on his imperial throne. Even the countless folds of his white and purple toga could not hide the abundance of his body. As was the custom, all eyes on the arena floor turned up to him upon passing the dais, but all they saw was the gray hair on the back of his head. The fleshy emperor was far more interested in the display of shellfish laid out behind him than in the fighters parading in front of him.

"Fat fuck," Amazonia muttered as she passed. "I hope he chokes on a clam."

Quintus bit his lip to stop from laughing out loud. They lined up with the other gladiators and hunters at the center of the arena. A distant door opened, and from the tunnel, three priests and four attendants led an ox into the arena.

"What's all this?" Quintus asked quietly.

Lindani turned from the rank in front of him. "We hunt only boars, stags, and bears today, so it must be a sacrifice."

The ox was walked into position in front of the podium and the Pontifex Maximus—the high priest—conducted a brief ritual. At first, Quintus was surprised to hear that the god being honored was in fact, Nero. But he then realized how similar in looks, character, and pure decadence Vitellius was to the hated emperor. The spectators murmured in disapproval, but Vitellius took no notice, nodding to the high priest to continue. One of the holy men raised his pole-ax and brought it down hard on the ox's head, stunning the animal. He then pulled a long, thin knife and slit the animal's throat. As the blood ran into the sand, the ox was rolled on its side, slit open, and its entrails removed. The high priest proclaimed loudly that the omens were favorable and Nero was pleased. Quintus had no doubt that even if the entrails had been putrefied, the omens would have been declared "favorable," and Nero would have been "pleased."

As the attendants dragged the bloody carcass from the arena, the fighters were marched back to the waiting cells beneath the cavea. Lindani and the other venatores opened the games with a massive group hunt. The crowd noise echoed through the holding area where Quintus quietly moved from fighter to fighter. He used the time to reiterate what he had discussed privately with each of them over the past three days in the ludus. "As Julianus often says: 'The appearance of danger is often better than danger itself,'" he reminded them. "It would be wise for you to both give and take in these bouts, something you're not used to doing. But by allowing both fighters to show strength and aggressiveness, the rate of missio will be much higher and very few Pompeiian gladiators will be sentenced to die today." He looked each of his gladiators in the eyes as he made his point. He was satisfied that they all understood and agreed with the plan. Now he just had to hope the new emperor abided by the wishes of the crowd and did not issue his own verdict on the vanquished fighters.

The afternoon brought higher temperatures along with the gladiator bouts. Quintus stood nervously at the portcullis gate leading to the arena. Amazonia's voice suddenly came from beside him. "The last time I stood here, I watched you tied to a post and Lindani save your life."

He studied her green eyes. "As I recall, you lifted this gate, dashed into an arena full of lions, and saved both our lives." He glanced down at the scar she had received that day which still marred her beautiful leg.

She looked through the open grating at the fight getting started on the sand. "A bond was formed that day among the three of us, you know," she said, "one that will never be broken."

"The bond was there long before that day," he replied. "We just had to look death in the face together to recognize it." Quintus watched her as she leaned against the gate. "Are you ready to fight today?" he asked, remembering the uncertainty during her last bout in Pompeii.

She looked at him and smiled. "I'm ready."

A sudden scream from the crowd drew Quintus's attention back to the arena. A Pompeiian retiarius had tossed his net at a secutor. The rete snagged the corner of the man's scutum, and the shield was ripped from his hand. Undaunted, the secutor advanced bravely with only his gladius. Quintus smiled. He knew the retiarius well and was certain the man could finish off a shieldless opponent in a matter of seconds. But, as Quintus had requested, the retiarius gave ground and offered the secutor his own opportunity to win the crowd. When the retiarius went back on the offensive and finally had the secutor at the point of his trident, the crowd immediately called for mercy. The secutor was spared, and both fighters left the arena alive. Quintus slapped their backs as they passed him in the tunnel. If the rest of the fights went as smoothly, the troupe would escape the day in good form.

Quintus remained at the gate all afternoon as bout after bout for the Pompeiians ended in missio, just as he had planned. Of course, a Roman mob was never happy without blood at their games, so some of the fighters from the Rome and Capua ludi found themselves in the honorable kneeling position with a gladius or pugio thrust into their necks.

Amazonia faced the thraex Pugnax in one of the final matches. She put on an excellent display of offensive and defensive maneuvers against the experienced fighter. Quintus was glad to see her confidence returning, knowing the high number of missiones on this day had eased her mind. It was always easier on a gladiator when the crowd was in a generous mood. And she had that crowd in the palm of her hand as she unleashed one of her screaming spin kicks that caught Pugnax square in the chest. He fell on his back and fought to catch the breath she had knocked from his lungs. Before he could recover, she dropped down on his hips and straddled him with her sword at his throat. As an added bonus, she seductively ground her hips and perfect bottom against his groin as she held him at bay with her sword. The crowd erupted in a climax of cheers and screams, not only granting Pugnax his life but envying his position on the arena floor.

"That was interesting," Quintus said flatly as she entered the tunnel, twirling the green victory palm in her right hand and tightly clutching the coin purse in her left.

"Is that a touch of jealousy I detect?" she replied with a wink and a sensual smile.

Suddenly flushed, Quintus turned back toward the arena. *Was* it a touch of jealousy?

Two more bouts were fought before Quintus donned his Thracian helmet. It had taken him many days of training at the ludus to once again get comfortable looking through a facemask. After months of his open centurion's helmet, the facemask seemed restricting, limiting his vision more than he remembered. But a few whacks with the wooden practice rudis reminded him of its importance.

He inhaled deeply and closed his eyes. Normally the energy would have been coursing through his veins, summoning Taurus from the depths of his being. But in this fight he needed cunning and deception, not the strength and power of his alter ego.

He felt a presence beside him at the gate and opened his eyes to see Memnon. The man seemed calm and professional, much different than the obnoxious, blustery façade he had presented the first time Quintus faced him at the Aquae Sulis arena. It had been Quintus's first arena combat, and he remembered every detail.

"Stick to the plan, Memnon," he said, "and we'll both be eating dinner together tonight at the ludus."

Memnon nodded, and the red horsehair plume that sprouted from the top of his murmillo helmet fluttered forward and back. The gate rose, and the praecone announced the final match of the afternoon as the fighters took their position in the middle of the arena. The crowd was on its feet as the referee dropped his arm, signaling the start of the match.

Quintus crouched and circled his opponent. Memnon attacked first, thrusting his gladius over the top of the small parmula toward Quintus's chest. Quintus easily parried the attack, then went on the offensive. He deliberately kept his speed down to pace the fight and draw out the action. The murmillo backed off, using his large shield to block the blows. Quintus pretended to stumble in the sand and whispered, "Attack me." Memnon obliged. He unleashed a blistering series of blows that clanged against Quintus's shield and curved sica. Quintus made a point to show effort in blocking the attack, although he could have defended himself blindfolded. The crowd responded with praise for Memnon.

As the murmillo came in with a high blow, Quintus forced his blade aside and stepped in close to Memnon. "Alright," he said, quietly enough so the referee could not hear. "Now keep your scutum raised." With a loud yell, he spun quickly and smacked his blade hard across Memnon's large red shield, the loud clash having the desired effect on the spectators. As the crowd noise rose, Quintus unleashed a blindingly fast assault. His arm and sica turned to a blur. But each blow was carefully aimed to connect with the shield, not the person.

Using subtle verbal cues, the action ebbed and flowed across the arena for another five minutes. Finally, Quintus felt the crowd had been worked into a sufficient frenzy. "You're going to win this now," he whispered to his opponent. "Strike at my parmula."

On Memnon's third stroke, Quintus let the small square shield fly from his hand. A gasp soared from the cavea. He continued to work his sword at the near-superhuman speed he had come to perfect. But he slowed just enough to allow Memnon to prick his sword arm and draw blood. He thrashed hard, forcing the seeping blood down his arm toward his hand. He soon felt the slickness on the hilt of his sword. With the next strike from Memnon, he loosened his grip just enough to let the sica fly from his grasp. The scream of the crowd told him he had played the part well. He made an effort to dive toward the lost weapon. But Memnon lowered his shoulder and rammed into Quintus's side, throwing him into the sand. By the time Quintus rolled and attempted to rise, Memnon's sword was at his throat.

Although Quintus had staged the fight himself, his view down the length of a gladius being wielded by a victorious opponent unnerved him. It was a sight he—or Taurus—had never experienced before. He stared dumbly at the blade.

"Your finger," Memnon said to him quietly.

Quintus looked up at him, puzzled.

Memnon glanced at the referee closing from the side. More words came, but they were muffled by his helmet and the growing crowd noise. Quintus continued to stare at him, trying to decipher the message.

"Hold up your finger for mercy," Memnon said, almost too loudly.

This time the words came clearly to Quintus's ears. His stupidity struck him like a blow to the head. He immediately raised his arm with his finger extended. But was it too late? Arrogant gladiators who were too proud to beg for mercy usually got the verdict they sought: death. Would the fickle mob think he was so conceited as to not seek their mercy as he lay in the sand?

He and Memnon both glanced at the section of the cavea above them. Quintus was shocked to see scowling faces with their thumbs turned down. He was frozen with panic. How could he possibly have let this carefully crafted plan backfire? He had volunteered to take the fall thinking his reputation would save him. It seemed a surer bet than risking Memnon's life. But now a stupid mistake, misinterpreted as an insult, was about to take *his* life instead. He heard the word "Missio" being shouted from the tunnel where Amazonia, Lindani, and dozens of other fighters had gathered, but he knew their opinions did not matter. He twisted his head in the sand and scanned the far side of the cavea. With relief, he saw white handkerchiefs fluttering. But were they enough to keep him alive? The noise was deafening as it echoed in his helmet. He strained to see Vitellius on the podium but could not twist his head back far enough. It seemed the cheering and the waiting went on forever. His mind raced uncontrollably. He wondered if he would soon be with his dead parents on the Elysian Fields. He watched Memnon for some sign of a decision, but the murmillo's facemask hid any hint of what was happening.

A sudden scream from the spectators sent a jolt up Quintus's spine, and he twitched in the sand. His heart pumped furiously. He looked for some reaction from Memnon. He saw the man's chest rise and fall with a deep sigh. What did it mean? Was it relief? Or was it regret for having to kill his comrade?

"Missio!" shouted the Roman referee as he pulled Memnon's gladius aside.

Memnon raised his arms and punched the sky. He walked from Quintus's field of vision as he headed toward the podium for his reward. Quintus could not move. He lay in the sand, understanding for the first time in his life what real fear was in an arena. Even the devastating shipwreck he had lived through and his near-drowning in the Po River did not compare with this past moment of his life. Now he knew the terror and panic and desperation of a vanquished gladiator. And he swore to himself that it would never happen again.

"You had me scared there!" Memnon yelled happily, slapping Quintus hard on the back as he joined him, Amazonia, and Lindani in the ludus mess hall.

Quintus jumped at the touch, still jittery from the afternoon's close call. "I had *you* scared? How do you think *I* felt?"

Memnon sat down and looked him squarely in the eye, a serious expression suddenly transforming his face. "I know *exactly* how you felt, Quintus. Do you not remember holding your sword at my throat in Aquae Sulis?"

Quintus had been so wrapped in self-pity, he had forgotten the outcome of his very first arena bout. The roles of the same two men had been precisely reversed.

"Of course. I'm sorry, Memnon," he replied quietly.

The murmillo burst out in his loud, showy laugh. "Don't fret it, Quintus. It's what we do. If they don't drag us out of the arena dead, then we walk out stronger, eh? The same assholes who ridicule us on the battlefield, cheer us in the arena. We're scum and hero all in one. It's the life of the gladiator!" He lifted his large cup of wine and goaded everyone at the long table into a toast to Quintus. "Here's to never having to look down the wrong end of a gladius again!" he shouted so the entire mess hall could hear. "May Hercules watch over us all!" The entire room responded with a loud cheer.

As the fighters and hunters dug into their meals, the door at the far end of the room opened and Tiberius Lupus, the procurator, entered. "Quintus Romanus! You're needed," he shouted.

Quintus looked across the table at Amazonia and Lindani. "Now what?" he muttered. He slurped a few more quick spoonfuls of barley and bean soup, then rose and walked to the door.

"Your tribune, Flavius Scipio, has called for you," Lupus said as he led him out the door. "There's a conference tonight at the north Praetorian barracks. He wants you there."

Quintus exited through the main gate of the ludus. The large open field of the Campus Martius and the narrow, squalid streets beyond were still clogged with festivities and drunken revelers celebrating Vitellius's birthday. Legionary patrols were everywhere, harshly dealing with any crowd that seemed bent on protesting the grain blockade. The crush of bodies, combined with his own drained energy from the arena bout, slowed him down. It took twice the usual time for Quintus to walk the two miles to the barracks.

Once there, he was admitted to the administrative conference room and took a seat next to Scipio near the middle of the crowded room. The conference space was similar in layout to the large field command tents, except the dark goatskin tent sidings were now thick walls painted a deep terra-cotta red.

Within moments, the Generals Caecina and Valens entered, and every man stood at attention. The legates nodded for the group to be seated, and Valens took the podium at the head of the room.

"Our scouts tell us that Flavian forces from the East, under the command of Antonius Primus, are about to enter Italia at the north border."

A drone of muttering voices rose in the room.

"Quiet!" yelled Valens. "The emperor has ordered us to march north and meet that threat. We leave in five days." Again, the murmur of voices began but settled to silence as two optios unfurled a large map and hung it on the side wall. Valens walked to the map and began outlining plans for the various legions, cavalry, and auxiliary units.

Quintus knew what many in the room were thinking: "What in Hades took so long?" The loyal Vitellian officers had waited weeks for marching orders to stop Vespasian. But not Legate Caecina. Quintus knew that he had hoped the news of the grain blockade, combined with the rumors of such large armies marching from Syria, Judea, and the Danube, would have forced Vitellius to capitulate. But it seemed Valens had won his push to fight.

Quintus sought the eye of Caecina, and the general responded with a tight smile. He casually scratched his forehead with two fingers, and Quintus knew what he had to do.

The conference attendees were dismissed after the plans and strategies had been discussed for more than two hours. Quintus walked through the open barrack gates, then disappeared into the shadows of the public park across the road until the street was clear of military personnel. Rather than head back to the Ludus Magnus, he walked up the dark alley behind the military compound and turned left at the second intersection. The narrow streets that separated the filthy insulae tenement buildings were not a safe place in the dark of night. But with Quintus's physique, he knew few bandits would consider him an easy target. He moved slowly, almost tripping over a body that lay in the street, either drunk or dead. The smell of stale vomit mingled with the stench of urine and feces that had been dumped from the apartment windows above.

He lingered beside a rough stone wall halfway up the alley. Within a few moments he was approached by a tall figure wearing a hooded cloak. Quintus reached for the handle of the pugio he had slipped into his belt before leaving the ludus. But as the man approached, he pulled back the hood just briefly enough to be identified. Quintus recognized him as Legate Caecina.

"I don't have long," Caecina said quietly, scanning the dark street around them. "Valens wants to fight. I need a way to delay him so I can lead both forces north myself without him."

Quintus thought quickly. "Do you have access to his food?"

Caecina nodded, then hesitated. "Yes, but I don't want to kill him. He's a good man. He's just fighting for the wrong person."

"I understand. I'll visit with my physician." Quintus hastily studied the rough stone wall beside them until he found a small ridge above eye level. "Tomorrow evening, I'll place whatever he gives me here," he said pointing to the high ledge. "Check it at this time tomorrow."

"Good," the general replied. His eyes never stopped scanning the fetid streets and alleys around them. "I also have a message for the courier. Tell him I will split the forces on the march north in order to defend the two bridges on the Po. From Bologna, half will go to Cremona and half to Hostilia. But first, I'll ride ahead to Ravenna on the coast to gain control of the fleet. My first discussion with Bassus, the fleet commander, was promising. I think his ships and crews will be ours. Tell Primus I'll send word to him from Hostilia."

Quintus paid close attention to every detail, knowing the fate of armies was being sealed with these words in this dark alley. "Very well. Is there anything else?"

"No," Caecina replied. "I'll leave the oil lamp in my room burning near the window. Hopefully the courier will see the signal and know to meet you."

Quintus smiled. "He'll see it."

Without another word, Caecina turned and disappeared down the alley, leaving Quintus alone once again on the black street.

• • •

The following evening after dinner, Quintus secured a tiny bag of hemlock to the drawstring of his undergarment. The small amount of poisonous herb seemed inadequate to put down a strong warrior like Valens, even temporarily. But Agricola had assured him the carefully measured dosage would put the aggressive general out of commission for at least two weeks, with no permanent aftereffects. Thankfully, the helpful physician—the same who had adorned Quintus's torso with the remarkable stigmates— had asked few questions. Petra had ordered him to support Quintus any way he could.

But frustration set in as Quintus heard his name called by the guard on duty. On this most important night, he had been rented out for the evening. So before he could make his drop for Caecina—a drop that could well change the outcome of this civil war—he had to first satisfy the sexual appetite of yet another wealthy Roman woman. He was hardly in the mood for lovemaking, but arrangements had been made that afternoon and a sizeable sum paid. He had little choice in the matter.

He walked the long hallway of the ludus cells and stopped abruptly as he reached the front gate. Rather than the usual brightly colored coach sent for most gladiators, an oversized litter awaited him. To the front and rear stood a total of twelve sturdy slaves, three manning each of the carrying poles that jutted from the ornate shelter.

The ludus guard had a grin on his face as he put a mark next to Quintus's name on his wax tablet. Under his breath the guard sang the same silly rhyme he had hummed each time Quintus left for such proceedings.

"Taurus makes the young girls cry. Taurus makes the old women sigh."

Quintus stared at the man and shook his head as if pitying a simpleton.

"Which will it be tonight, Taurus? A young beauty or an old hag?" The guard snickered at his own words like a schoolchild.

Before Quintus could think of a suitable retort, a husky female voice came from inside the litter. "I don't know, guard, which do you think?"

Quintus and the guard turned to see an attractive middle-aged woman draw back the deep red curtain and lean from the window of her litter. She laid her arms on the sill and let her considerable breasts, clearly visible through her sheer white stola, rest on her forearms.

"I wonder if the ludus procurator would find your question amusing," the woman continued, her radiant eyes burning a hole in the guard's forehead. "Shall we go inside and ask him?"

"My apologies, madam," the guard stammered. "I meant no disrespect. I was not aware that such a beautiful patron would be calling here personally."

The woman stared at the guard a moment longer, then leaned back into her couch with a melodic laugh. "Come along, Taurus," she called. "We have business to attend to."

Quintus smiled at the guard. He leaned closer to the man as he reached for the handle to open the litter door. "So tell me, Strabo," he whispered. "Who will you be fucking tonight?"

He stepped up into the spacious interior and chuckled as he closed the door behind him. With a quiet command, the slaves stooped as one and lifted the thick wooden poles, hoisting them with ease onto their shoulders. They strode with a smooth quick-step down the paving stones of the entrance road.

Quintus settled into the soft cushions opposite his patron. He had never ridden in a litter; his mother had always thought them too pretentious. The shelter was handsomely decorated in various shades of red with gold and bronze accents. The slight musty smell and the worn edges on the plush upholstery told him the transport had serviced this woman for many years.

He looked across the narrow knee space and found the woman studying him. Her pitch-black locks were pulled up in a nest of tight symmetrical curls layered high atop her head. The elaborate hairstyle framed an attractive face that had begun to show the slightest hints of age at the corners of her turquoise eyes. But even as he studied the ample curves of her body, his mind continued to drift back to his task for Caecina. Yes, this would be a most pleasurable assignment if only he didn't have the future of Rome tucked into his waistband.

"Good evening, madam," he finally said with a smile.

"Call me Juno." Her voice seemed even huskier than before.

"Well, Juno, so what—" His question was cut short by her two bare feet jerking up from the floorboard and sinking into the red cushion on either side of him. Her knees spread wider and she pulled the gown of her stola aside, revealing a triangle of dark hair.

"You shall be my Jupiter," she whispered, lust saturating her voice.

She undid the two clasps at her shoulders and let the white stola fall to her waist revealing pendulous breasts with large nipples, the tips of which rose like delicate brown raisins.

Her hand went to her pubic mound and she began rubbing herself in rhythm to the swaying transport. "I love the rhythm of a litter, don't you? It's like riding on twelve giant men at one time."

Quintus had a feeling that wasn't an empty analogy. He could easily see this woman handling twelve men at one time.

She moaned softly. "Just feel the movement. Isn't it wonderful?"

A thought crossed Quintus's mind. The quicker they could get down to business, the quicker he could be on his way to the alley and make the drop for Caecina.

"Have you ever made love in a litter before, Mistress Juno?" he asked in a whisper. "With a goddess like you so near me, I'm afraid I can't wait to reach your bedroom."

A spark ignited in her eyes. Quintus quickly pulled his tunic over his head. The woman whimpered and her hand gyrated faster as the stigmate of his Minotaur was revealed in all its glory. Seeing her reaction, he breathed deeply to animate the image on his chest. While her eyes were locked on the head of the bull, he slowly slipped his undergarment off, being careful not to dislodge the tiny bag tied to the drawstring. He rolled it into a bundle with his tunic and stuffed them beside the seat cushion. He sat back and watched the woman come to her first climax of the night.

"Come to me, my husband, Jupiter," she panted.

She reached for his cock. The warm wetness on her fingers brought him to full erection with a few strokes. She continued to whisper details of how she wished to be taken by the ruler of the gods. Quintus considered letting himself come quickly, but the last thing he needed was this wild woman bursting into the procurator's office demanding her money be refunded. He had to find the right balance of eagerness and endurance.

The woman knew how to use her hand and tongue, perhaps more skillfully than any patron he had ever had. It would take serious concentration to give her her money's worth. He thought about the hemlock in his pouch. He thought about how sick it would make the Legate Valens. He thought about anything to hold himself back from a massive climax as she worked her magic.

"Let me take you now, goddess," he finally whispered in her ear.

She rose from her knees and threw herself back on the couch with a feral eagerness. He leaned forward and slipped inside her. Her wetness offered an easy entry. He began pumping. She ran her hands up and down his broad chest, grabbing at the Minotaur and the rippling muscles beneath it. The deep breaths through her teeth turned to louder and louder moans of pleasure. After a few thrusts, she grabbed his ass with both hands and began ramming him into her. He felt the litter sway sideways and the oddest thought suddenly sprang into his mind. He wondered if the slaves could continue walking a straight line with their mistress getting pounded like a wild dog up on their shoulders. The image almost made him laugh out loud as he pumped faster and faster. He pictured the poor slaves zigzagging their way down the street. He pictured passersby stopping to listen to the moaning, while others wondered how much wine these slaves had drunk this evening.

The woman leaned forward and bit his ear lobe. "Faster, Jupiter. Please, faster, my husband."

Quintus pumped harder and faster. Her large breasts bounced violently. The swaying of the litter became like a small boat in a rough sea. Just as it appeared their transport would tumble sideways into some dark gutter, Quintus climaxed with a final hard thrust. The woman beneath him squealed with delight and held him tight inside her until he spilled his last drop.

He laid atop her, panting for a moment, then withdrew and sat back on the facing couch. The woman laid perfectly still.

"I've never ridden in a litter before," Quintus said with a grin. "Somehow I don't think I'll ever forget my first ride. Thank you for a memorable evening." As he spoke, he was already picturing the nook in the dark alley where he would hide the hemlock for Caecina.

The woman sat forward and tugged at the stola crumpled around her waist. But instead of pulling the top back up and straightening the gown, she pulled the white material over her head.

"Who said the memorable evening was over?" she said with a playful gleam in her eye. She reached out and began rubbing Quintus's wet, limp cock.

"Ahh, Mistress Juno. I think Master Jupiter has had enough holy coupling for the evening."

"Nonsense," the woman cooed. "We've just gotten started." She stroked his penis harder and faster. "The ruler of the gods should be good for at least one more fuck tonight, no?"

Quintus could hardly believe his ears.

"I've paid a hefty sum for you tonight, my Jupiter. Please don't make me complain at the ludus." Her voice was like a pleading child, but her message was unmistakable.

By the gods, he did not need this tonight. What if Caecina went to the wall and found nothing? Would he look again a second time? Or would he simply give up and assume Quintus had abandoned their cause? If Valens wasn't delayed on his march, it could mean the end of Vespasian's campaign. Everything hung on his making the delivery. And this one rich, oversexed bitch was standing—or kneeling—in the way of it all.

Quintus looked down at her speeding tongue as it ran up and down the length of his shaft. He tried to concentrate on giving this woman what she wanted. He watched her work, hoping the visual stimulation would help him replenish himself. While the image was more than attractive, it was just too soon. He closed his eyes. He tried to think of something, anything—or anyone—that would put him in the right frame of mind. Slowly, an image formed in the darkness. He felt the slight tingle that told him blood was beginning to flow once again to the right place. The image grew in intensity and clarity. He could feel himself getting hard again. The woman chuckled as she continued to work between his legs. But it was not this woman who was bringing him back to life; it was another. The image surprised him, yet in a way it seemed perfectly natural. He concentrated, and soon the crystal clear figure of Amazonia formed in his mind's eye.

He could see every detail of her body, most of which he knew well from their arena bouts. He began to see multiple visions of her at the same time. He was fully erect now, and the woman who called herself Juno moaned happily as she worked with both hands. But Quintus only thought of Amazonia's emerald eyes looking at him. Her auburn hair when it was still long enough to spill onto her bare shoulders. Her perfect breasts that seemed both youthful and mature at the same time. The sweet scent of her as she sweated in the harsh Italian sunlight.

The woman in the litter mounted him and began sliding up and down. But he remained focused on the beauty of Amazonia. In his mind, he saw her astride him. He watched her work herself up and down on him, throwing her head back in ecstasy. Not the false euphoria she created for her clients, but true sexual ecstasy. He responded by thrusting up to meet her. Her moans became louder with each thrust. He felt the woman in the litter tense and begin coming as she rocked faster and faster on his cock. Quintus opened his eyes. To his fascination, he continued to see only Amazonia. She was there with him, grabbing at his chest as they pumped against each other, crying out in pleasure. The sight—real or imagined—sent him over the edge. He came as strongly as he had just moments earlier playing his regal role of "Jupiter." But this time it was because he made love to the only person who could excite him more than Juno herself.

Slowly the image before him dissolved, and Amazonia's face was replaced by the sweating, spent visage of the woman in the litter. The transformation sent a shiver along his spine, not because the vision of this woman wasn't pleasant, but because the intensity of his fantasy shocked him beyond words. He lay still as the woman climbed off him.

"Not bad," she said with a smile. "I knew the great Taurus was good for one more." She parted the curtain and called to her head slave. "Atticus, take us back to the ludus."

Quintus was quiet during the ride back. He wasn't sure how to react to what had happened, but he let the pleasure of it play in his mind as he pulled his undergarment back on. He checked to be sure the tiny bag was still attached before he slipped his tunic back over his head.

"I must call for you again sometime soon," the woman said. "That was most enjoyable."

Quintus shrugged. "I can't promise I'll live up to the same performance. You must have gotten me on a good night."

As they approached the ludus and the litter slowed, the woman leaned forward and kissed Quintus hard on the lips. Her hand groped him one last time. "Until next time, then."

Quintus smiled. He felt the litter being lowered and the four legs gently touch the paving stones. He nodded, then slipped out the door. The litter was raised, and the slaves trotted forward. Although they never showed it, he was sure the twelve men were grateful for the lessened weight of their payload.

"So . . . how was she?" the guard asked as he approached Quintus.

"A bit more than you could ever handle," Quintus said with a straight face. "Listen, Strabo, don't sign me in yet. I got word while I was out that the tribune wants to meet with me. I need to go to the barracks. Let me borrow your pugio for safety. I'll be back shortly."

The guard did not hesitate as he handed over his small dagger. Quintus liked his double roll as both centurion and arena fighter.

He made his way toward the north Praetorian barracks, walking at a brisk pace but not running, which would have aroused suspicion. He played the events of the evening back in his mind a few times as he walked, alone with his thoughts. He stayed clear of the guards near the barracks gate, then quietly made his way toward the dark alley that ran behind the military compound. He slipped the tiny bag from under his tunic and placed it on a high ledge in the stone wall. He hoped with all his heart that Caecina had not yet checked the spot. But he could not wait around to see. He had to move on to his next task.

He made his way up the Vicus Minervi to a wooded area that bordered Rome's north wall. The secluded site, near the Porta Pinciana gate, had been selected months earlier as the spot for Quintus and Castus's courier to rendezvous whenever the gladiator unit was in Rome. He stepped carefully through the blackness of the forest, a thin white mist swirling around him as he moved. The only sounds to break the eerie stillness were the chirp of a cicada and the occasional hoot of a tawny owl. He found the poplar tree etched with a "V" and sat patiently, letting his eyes adjust to the darkness and his mind return to the pleasant vision of Amazonia.

After almost an hour, a gentle rustling of weeds sent his hand instinctively to the handle of the pugio. "Virtue," came a whispered voice from the darkness. Hearing the correct watchword, Quintus stepped from behind the tree and looked into the face of Julianus.

"It's good to see you, Doctore," Quintus said as he grasped the Pompeiian trainer's forearm.

"It's even better to see you alive," Julianus said with sincerity. "I saw you in the arena yesterday. I thought you'd had it."

"You were there?"

"In the high tiers, keeping a low profile," Julianus replied quietly.

"As soon as I heard Vitellius had called for games, I figured you'd be involved."

"What can I say? I'm not used to losing," Quintus said with a shrug. "My doctore trains me too well."

"And I know you too well to know you shouldn't have lost to Memnon." Before Quintus could explain, Julianus continued. "But I saw what you were all doing in there—letting both fighters take control of each match." The seasoned trainer nodded with a grin. "Nice plan. I knew you were the one we needed to lead this bunch."

Quintus felt a warmth in his chest, like he did when his father used to compliment him as a child.

"So, I saw the signal in Caecina's window," Julianus said. "What news is there for Castus?"

XVII

September AD 69

THE STREETS OF CAESAREA seemed darker than usual to Julia on this night. She watched Lucius's face as he stared out over the low doors of the bouncing carriage. The red glow from the torch they passed on a street corner revealed a glum look. There was a sudden lurch as the right front wheel dropped into another pothole.

"Damn it, why can't Vespasian keep these roads in better condition?" he grumbled. "We're pushing this man to run an empire, and he can't even keep his fucking roads repaired."

Julia did not respond. She knew better than to disagree with Lucius when he was in such a foul mood. Although he took it to an extreme as usual, she could understand his anger—not toward Vespasian's public works administration but toward the delays in getting the first of their new freighters launched. The meeting they had just concluded with the ship's designer and construction foreman had left them both frustrated. As accommodating and polite as these Syrians and Judeans were, their sense of speed and urgency could not compare with the work ethic in Rome. Another delay in obtaining the lead for the anchor stocks, and the parts needed for the capstan to raise and lower them, had pushed the launch date back another three weeks.

"The legionaries have many other duties besides road work, Master Lucius," Aram Kalyndu offered cheerfully as he drove the pair of horses expertly around a turn and headed toward the docks. "I am certain they will resume their repairs soon."

Lucius sneered at the driver's back, then looked at Julia and shook his head. "Fucking savages," he grumbled.

Julia tensed as Aram glanced over his shoulder, but the amiable Syrian said nothing further. She hated when Lucius maligned the local population so overtly, especially in front of the man who managed their Judean shipping operation.

"The shipyards near Antioch are a lot different than those of Ostia," Julia offered quietly. "You can't expect things to run as smoothly in the provinces as they do in the city."

"That's horseshit," Lucius shot back. "This delay is due to scheduling errors and poor management, not the availability of materials. You know that as well as I do. It's just another unnecessary holdup in expanding our fleet."

She had to admit he was right. Had the materials been ordered on time, the delays could have certainly been avoided. But Lucius's vicious scolding of the project foreman during their meeting would do little to improve the situation. In fact, it might have made things worse. She let the matter drop as they neared the end of their ride.

The carriage slowed as it approached the *Juno*'s gangway. Julia had petitioned to stay in their luxurious ship cabin during their time in Caesarea, rather than in the small, sparse apartment above the Romanus Shipping and Transport office. Wanting the ship kept available for her and Lucius, as well as for Vespasian's use at a moment's notice, she had cancelled all cargo runs for the *Juno* until further notice. The captain and crew were more than happy to oblige, favoring catering to their elite passengers over manhandling tons of amphorae and crates in the ship's hold. Had the new freighter been launched on time, it would certainly have helped offset her losses.

The fresh, salty breeze did little to raise Lucius's spirits. Aram jumped from the driver's seat, opened the small door, and offered his hand up for support. Lucius shoved the man's arm aside as he stepped from the carriage.

"Do you think I'll fall on the pier just stepping from a carriage?" he shouted.

"Lucius!" Julia snapped.

"It is quite alright, madam," Aram said with a smile. He bowed his head toward Lucius. "I meant no offense, Master Lucius. I understand how you feel about tonight's meeting. I, too, was frustrated."

Lucius grunted and turned away. Julia stood to leave the coach.

"I remember Master Caius Romanus having many such frustrations when he arrived to open his office here years ago," Aram continued as he offered his hand once again. This time it was taken by Julia. "But he was a man who respected the Syrians, and by that he got much accomplished."

Lucius stopped walking and spun toward the manager. Julia heard a loud crack and felt Aram's supporting hand give way. She almost toppled from the step that hung below the carriage door but grabbed the side in time to keep her balance. She looked up to see blood trickling from the edge of Aram's mouth.

"How dare you lecture me!" Lucius screamed. He drew his arm back to strike the man again with the back of his hand.

Julia lurched forward and stepped between them. "Stop it, Lucius!" she yelled. "He meant no harm." She looked at the Syrian. The shock on the man's face as he wiped the blood from his lower lip brought pity to her heart. "I'm so sorry, Aram."

Aram bowed to both of them. "It is I who was wrong, madam. My sincerest apologies." He adjusted his tall head wrap and climbed back up into the driver's seat. Without another word, he snapped the reins and drove the carriage from the dock.

She looked at Lucius and seethed. "You just can't keep that fucking temper of yours under control, can you?"

"What right does he have to talk to me like that?" Lucius yelled back at her.

"He was offering some simple advice, and it was *good* advice, if you'd only listen and stop being so damned paranoid all the time."

"So now we're taking business advice from a fucking Syrian!" Lucius screamed. He stepped toward Julia and grabbed her arms. "What in Hades is wrong with you, woman?" She could see the familiar look of unbridled rage start to overtake him and felt his fingers tighten on her upper arms. "Maybe we should put that Syrian dog in charge of getting these ships built! How's that for good advice?"

"Get your fucking hands off me." Her anger forced the words through her tightened lips. She stared defiantly through the fury in Lucius's eyes, daring him to strike her. His face flushed with anger.

"Is everything alright, madam?"

Julia glanced toward the ship and saw her captain and three crewmen standing at the rail. She looked back at Lucius. "Let go of me," she hissed. The words seemed to snap Lucius from his vindictive trance. She felt the blood once again course through her arms as he released his grip.

"Don't you dare step foot on this ship tonight," she said in a hoarse whisper, then pushed past him and climbed the slight incline of the gangway.

"Master Lucius will be staying in Caesarea this evening, Captain," she said as she headed toward the deckhouse door.

"Yes, madam."

There was a shuffling of feet on the deck behind her, but Julia did not turn back as she opened the door and stepped inside. She descended the stairs to her cabin, and her breathing increased with each step. She began to tremble as she opened the elaborately carved door to their private quarters. It was the suite she had shared with Lucius every night since she had rescued him from the African ludus. She shut the door and her eyes at the same moment. Tears streamed down her flushed cheeks. She shook with sobs and leaned back against the heavy door to steady herself.

It was the *realization* more than Lucius's actions that upset her so much. She knew a night like this would come. She knew the same damnable temper and frenzied paranoia that had cost them their lives of luxury in Rome would resurface. She had hoped he would change, that perhaps his year in the African ludus would have taught him a well-deserved lesson. Or, at the very least, he would have appreciated her more, considering the risk she took in delivering him from the vile prison. She had even thought the prospect of marriage might, in some small way, bolster stability and maturity. But deep inside she knew that was just a pathetic dream. Lucius Calidius would never change.

After a few moments, she wiped the streaks from her face and walked to their bed. Wrapping herself in the soft linens, she fought to clear her mind and suppress the emotions that had clouded her judgment for too long. The more she thought, the more her anger channeled away from Lucius and toward a much bigger issue: the social order of Rome. Although she had the same ambitions, with better business sense, shrewder cunning, and certainly more intelligence than many men in Rome, she was forced to follow the road to wealth and power by treading in a man's footsteps. The thought infuriated her, but such were the politics of Rome. The time for tears and regrets was over; the time for an alternate plan was at hand. She could no longer afford to put her fate solely in the unreliable hands of Lucius Calidius. She needed someone else—a new male minion—to escort her back to Roman society. But who?

She had come far since her husband's death and was moving in the right circles. Unfortunately, being in the hinterlands of the Empire limited her choices. She had already been drawn to Titus, Vespasian's son. He was smart, self-assured, and more than a bit desirable. But he would not be going to Rome. Vespasian had made it clear his son would remain in Judea until the Jewish revolt was put down for good. That could be years. Even the prospect of attaching herself to a future emperor could not overcome years—perhaps a decade—in another Roman province. She had had enough of the provincial life.

What about Vespasian himself? He had been married once but never re-wed after the death of his wife. He was one of the most confident and intelligent men Julia had ever met. But who was she kidding? The man was in the midst of fighting a civil war, and a long-distance war at that. His mind was on the throne and nothing else. Besides—and this was a point Julia found hard to admit to herself—he was simply out of her reach.

Then there was Gaius Mucianus, the governor of neighboring Syria and Vespasian's biggest supporter. But, like Titus, there was no guarantee he would relocate to the capital when the war was done. The same could be said for Julius Alexander, the prefect of Egypt. With the wealth and power available to him in Alexandria, she doubted he would take a new post in Rome.

Marcus Livius Castus was the last of their inner circle. But despite his current ties to the future emperor, he was still just a broken-down old soldier. The thought of spending her prime years on the arm of the grizzled ex-centurion, with his missing teeth and battle scars, sent a shiver down her spine. Even attaining the luxuries of Rome had its limits. Besides, his humble background—not to mention his gruff manner—would never allow him to be accepted into the high society of Rome.

As her mind continued to drift through the possibilities, a peculiar thought entered her head. She lay still in her bed, staring at the dim ceiling, as the idea formulated. It was a scheme that would take all her ingenuity to make happen. It would take time to play out. And she would need to keep Lucius on a string for a while longer.

The longer she thought, the more the plan crystallized. She would target the man that, perhaps more than any other, guided the current course of the Empire. He was certainly a man who would be owed a tremendous debt of gratitude—and a substantial reward—when this war was over. Of course, there was one small obstacle to overcome: she did not know this man's identity. She smiled, then heard herself giggle. It was still an inspired plan of genius. Who better to tie herself to than the very man who would place the next emperor on the throne?

The spy on the front lines.

And the only person in the region who knew the man's name was due at the governor's palace over the next few days. For this, she would overlook his shabby appearance, missing teeth, and battle scars. She would be sure to greet Marcus Castus warmly on his next visit.

XVIII

October AD 69

QUINTUS, Amazonia, and Lindani collapsed in a heap at the entrance to their tent in the new military camp at Hostilia. The late afternoon breeze off the Po River running beside the site helped soothe their aching and sweating bodies.

Their arrival in the northern Italia town that morning, after a twelve-day march from Rome, had been followed by backbreaking work building and fortifying another sprawling headquarters camp. Scouts reported Flavian forces just a few miles to the north, so the ramparts were built to a height of six feet and crowned with staked obstacles. A six-foot deep trench in front of the earthen walls increased their effective height to twelve feet.

This was the second camp Quintus and his gladiators had helped build, yet he was still amazed at how quickly the process went with twenty three thousand men all taking part in the construction. Although the perimeter walls ran for almost two miles, the entire camp had been laid out and built in under four hours. A similar but smaller camp had also been constructed by the ten thousand men in Caecina's army at Cremona, a hundred miles to the west. By evening, the two largest bridges across the Po were well protected.

The setting sun combined with the breeze to bring welcome relief to the entire army. Torches were lit along the main boulevard that ran the length of the camp and the two side streets that separated the auxiliaries from the legionaries and cavalry. Their orange light blended with the blue veil of a full moon to create a peaceful mood in the austere military setting.

A sudden bustle of activity along the main street caught Quintus's attention. "Legate Caecina returns," he said, watching the general ride in on his white charger with two aides a few paces behind. Caecina nodded to Quintus as he passed.

"Does he coordinate the attack of his two armies?" Lindani asked.

"No, he hasn't been to Cremona," Quintus answered. "Otherwise, he would not have returned for at least two days." He looked around and leaned forward. Lindani and Amazonia did the same. "I have a strong feeling there will be no battle," he said quietly. "I think this ugly episode in Rome's history is about to end peacefully."

Amazonia seemed surprised. "Why? Because Valens isn't here?"

Quintus smiled and nodded, pleased that the small bag he had left in the dark alley had obviously been found by Caecina later that night. Within a few days of the drop, Valens had come down with a mysterious stomach ailment, forcing him to turn over temporary command of his army to Caecina while he remained bedridden in Rome. The hemlock had worked its magic.

"Valens being laid up is only part of it," Quintus said as he watched the legate dismount and summon the tribunes into his tent. "Caecina's own plans seem to be taking root."

Amazonia and Lindani both offered a quizzical look. "So we make this march for nothing?" Lindani asked.

"No, it was very necessary," Quintus replied. "But should soldiers have to die in order for a march to be justified?"

"Not at all," the black hunter replied with his wide grin. "I am a man of peace, as well. I much prefer taking aim at lion and ostrich than at men. But a nonviolent truce is a different ending than most of Rome's campaigns."

A cornu horn sounded the officer's assembly call. "Let's see what the Fates have in store for us for the next few days," Quintus said as he rose. He walked down the row of gladiator tents and out onto the main boulevard where hundreds of centurions were making their way toward the small forum in front of the command tent.

Caecina wasted no time in emerging from his tent with a broad smile and mounting the podium. Quintus noticed that the tribunes following him did not all share his high spirits.

"Centurions, I want to repeat directly to you what I have just told your tribunes." He paused for a moment and scanned the expectant faces in the crowd. "There will be no fighting. The war is over."

Quintus was ready to bellow a cheer but sensed an aura of apprehension rather than optimism. He noticed that the officers who normally fought under Valens's control grumbled the loudest and seemed the most wary.

Undaunted, Caecina pressed on with his news. "This evening, I have negotiated a truce with Antonius Primus, commander of the Flavian army. We have agreed that the best person to lead our Empire to a glorious future and restore true power and wisdom to the principate is Flavius Vespasianus, Governor of Judea."

The name brought an increase in muttering among the centurions. The glow in Caecina's face faded, but his voice remained strong and resolute. "Three days ago, I spoke with Lucilius Bassus, commander of the fleet at Ravenna, and he agreed with me that enough Roman blood has been spilt. The fleet is now controlled by Vespasian."

Before the discontent grew any louder, Caecina quickly issued his orders. "I hereby command that all images of Aulus Vitellius be removed from our standards. All centurions will muster their legionaries before the next change of the sentry, and the tribunes will deliver the oath of allegiance to their men in the name of Flavius Vespasianus."

Quintus could see that the continued grumbling was wearing on Caecina. The spark of hope and promise that had lit the legate's eyes when he had started was now a smoldering ember of anger. "Are there any questions?" His hard face defied any further comments. "Fine. You're dismissed."

Quietly the centurions and tribunes dispersed back to their respective units. Quintus waited for a moment and watched the general study his officers as they melted back into the expansive camp, quietly mumbling to each other as they went. Caecina noticed Quintus staring at him. The troubled look on the general's face communicated his concern clearly. The legate stepped from the podium, threw back the flap of his tent, and disappeared into the large command space.

Quintus headed back down the main avenue toward the auxiliaries' and gladiators' tents. In the flickering torchlight he saw the news spreading through the camp like wildfire. Some legionaries simply showed surprise while others displayed unmistakable disdain. Quintus was surprised at the level of support in the camp for Vitellius. The emperor's loyal Rhine legions were still in Rome, now functioning as the new Praetorian Guard. But it seemed the allegiance he enjoyed from his armies on campaign, especially Valens's legions, was equally rabid. The sound level in the camp increased as heated voices reacted to the shocking turn of events. By the time Quintus reached the first of the gladiator tents, the news had already swept over his fighters.

"The men who fight for Valens are not pleased," Lindani said, his eyes scanning the camp behind Quintus, absorbing the tension that was rising faster than the temperature on a Roman summer's afternoon.

"That's an understatement," Amazonia offered. "It looks like we're going to have a full-blown mutiny here before the night's over."

Shouts began to punctuate the restlessness that grew across the camp. "No!" a legionary across the road hollered. "Vitellius is my emperor. I'll fight for no other!" Rather than take control of the situation, his grizzled centurion nodded in agreement.

Quintus gathered his six hundred gladiators and venatores into a sizeable circle around him. His voice was just loud enough to reach his men without drifting to the surrounding camp meetings. "I know it's not the popular sentiment in this camp right now, but Caecina is our legate and we'll support him any way we can. I told you many months ago that our work here had just begun. Now we find ourselves back on the banks of the Po in the middle of another power struggle. The difference is that this one will put an end to all the foolishness once and for all."

As usual, Drusus was quick to offer his support. "Like I said before, Quintus. You're a centurion with brains. You got us through the battle at Cremona alive, thanks to our little charade in the vineyard. So, why doubt you now?"

Quintus scanned the faces of his men and saw a look of agreement in each one he studied—except one.

"So it's *Vespasian* we fight for now," Vulcanus said with a wary look in his eyes.

Quintus should have expected such a blunt response from the man who had questioned their peculiar actions in the Cremona battle. The tactless disclosure angered him. But, he also realized his mission was no longer much of a secret. If he was encouraging them to support Caecina—and Caecina had already proposed capitulation to Vespasian—then Quintus obviously supported Vespasian. The candor of the cagey hoplomachus had presented him with the opportunity to unburden himself.

"It's always been Vespasian we've been fighting for, Vulcanus. But that's been too dangerous to say." Quintus glanced past his men to be sure no one else in camp was hearing this. "Castus and Petra know Vespasian well, as do I. Back at the ludus, we agreed that he's the man to lead this Empire. I've been working toward that goal since the day we left Pompeii."

A look of realization and enlightenment began to sweep across their faces. After a moment, Vulcanus spoke up.

"Then what do you need us to do?"

"Trust in me and stick with me," Quintus replied with all the sincerity in his heart. "But we *must* support Caecina. With his own cohorts camped at Cremona, he'll need all the help he can get here tonight."

A loud shout and the sudden clash of swords interrupted their gathering. A few hundred of Valens's devout legionaries and centurions had charged the command tent. Caecina's personal bodyguards put up some resistance, but seeing the overwhelming number of legionaries facing them, quickly laid down their arms and stepped aside.

"This doesn't look good," Quintus said, wondering if Caecina would emerge alive or if his body would be dragged from the tent.

Moments later, the tent flap was tossed back and the legate was shoved through the opening. He landed in a puff of dust in the middle of the square. An eerie hush fell over the camp as thousands of soldiers watched their general rise from the dirt. His hands had been tied in front of him and his arms bound tightly to his sides by a wrap of chain that encircled his body several times. After the initial shock wore off, a cheer came from the encampment of Valens's tough Fifth Legion. The riotous noise soon spread across the camp.

A cavalry officer lobbed a rope over Caecina and pulled it tight. He kicked his charger forward and the rope pulled tight, almost yanking the general off his feet. Quintus bit his lip. Caecina steadied himself as he was tugged along behind the horse. The officer laughed and cheered as he hauled his new prisoner down the main road of the camp.

"You're a fucking coward, Caecina!" one of the men of the Fifth Legion yelled. As the general passed him, the rowdy legionary stepped forward and spat in the old man's face. "Take that back to Vespasian for me."

Laughter erupted from the camp. A rock flew from the Fifth's encampment and struck Caecina in the face. The general staggered for a moment, then raised his chin and walked on. Blood streamed from his nose and clotted in the gray stubble of his chin.

Quintus's hands clenched to tight fists. Frustration and pity surged through him like a burning fever. How could they do this to this man? Why are they not cheering him as a hero of Rome instead of humiliating him like some barbarian prisoner? But Quintus could do nothing except stand mute at the roadside as Caecina stumbled past, his once-beaming face showing stunned disbelief.

Their eyes met for a brief moment. Quintus hoped the look on his face would convey both his sorrow and rage. Caecina's nod was barely perceptible, but it gave Quintus a small sense of comfort.

Caecina was dragged down the length of the main camp road, continuing to run a gauntlet of rowdy legionaries and auxiliaries who had lined the torch-lit avenue. The remainder of the men showed their ex-legate enough respect to hurl only insults and not stones. The captors quickly palisaded a corner of the horse corral, between the veterinarian's tent and the workshop, to house their new prisoner.

Quintus looked at Amazonia and Lindani, who had remained by his side as the other fighters drifted back to their tents. "This changes things," he said to them quietly. "I might need to ask your help again. Without the legate's assistance, I don't think I can do this alone."

"Shut up and ask," Amazonia said flatly. "At least now we know who we're really fighting for," she said.

"You know we both stand ready," Lindani said. "If the time is right, then we act."

Quintus put an arm over each of their shoulders as they walked back to the tent they shared with the others in their contubernium. Quintus asked Memnon, Drusus, and the others to give them a few minutes alone. Without hesitation, the men cleared the tent so he could speak in private.

"As my unofficial optio, Memnon has been a help to me on the fields of battle and in preparing for war," Quintus said softly. "But now what I need is diversion and stealth—roles that suit the two of you perfectly." He took a deep breath, then continued. "The camp commandant will probably call a war council soon to announce the new acting legate and to discuss our strategy against the Flavians. He'll have the centurions running all night. I can't risk disappearing for too long. Lindani, I'll need you to deliver information to Primus in the Flavian camp. They're just north of here, across the Tartaro River near Verona. Amazonia, I'll need you to help get him out of our camp."

Her lips parted with a shrewd smile. She reached up and grabbed a breast in each hand. "Looks like I'll need to put the sisters to work tonight."

Quintus was stumped for a response to that but was saved by another blast from the cornu horn calling the officers to council. Lindani crawled from the tent. Quintus moved to follow him out, but Amazonia grabbed his arm.

"You know we've been ready to help you all along," she said.

"I know," he replied. "I just didn't want you too wrapped up in this. Then if things went bad, there would be nothing for you to be questioned about."

"I understand. But we're all in it now. I'm here for you, Quintus. I'll always be here for you."

The tender look on her face told Quintus the statement was more than just a commitment to fight this battle. He nodded and they both climbed from the tent. Quintus stood and looked into the bottom of Lindani's jaw. The African's head was tilted back as he studied the heavens.

"It is an omen from the war god Mars perhaps?" the hunter asked.

Quintus tipped his head back and looked up at the full moon hovering over the camp. Amazonia gasped beside him. What was once a clear, bluish-white disc now reflected a ruddy complexion of deep red. At first, Quintus thought the smoke from the hundreds of torches was obscuring it. But a quick glance showed the smoke blowing in the opposite direction. He noticed that most of the soldiers were now studying the lunar event. Some just stared, but many seemed genuinely frightened.

"A blood moon foreshadows bad fortune," Lindani said.

"But for who," Amazonia asked, "us or the Flavians?"

"It depends how well we deliver this message, no?" he said with a smile.

Quintus smacked his friend's back, then walked with the other centurions to the command tent. The camp commandant was already huddled over a map with the commander of the Fifth Legion as the large tent filled to near capacity.

"Senior Tribune Fabullus from the Fifth Legion will replace the traitor Caecina," the commandant said without prologue.

Fabullus, a squat but stocky man, launched into the briefing. "We need to leave Hostilia. With Vespasian and Primus controlling the fleet, we are in a bad position here, caught between the Po to our south and the Tartaro to our north. The Flavians can easily launch an offensive by boarding the galleys and sailing up both rivers to surround us. I want a contingent of men from the Fifth on the banks of these rivers immediately. I want scouts with them ready to ride back and sound the alarm if the Flavians attack tonight. In the morning, we'll prepare to march to Cremona, but we won't leave until after dark tomorrow night. I want all the campfires and torches left burning. This will keep their scouts thinking we're still here. It'll give us a half-day jump on them."

Quintus nodded with the others. Even with his limited military training, he could see that Fabullus was a more aggressive tactician than Caecina. *Too bad this information will all be in the Flavians' hands before sunrise*, Quintus thought. He knew the result would be annihilation for most of the men in this tent, but once again, a bigger mission was at hand. Putting Vespasian on the throne was all that mattered now. And if it meant the lives of these foolish commanders and their rabid legionaries, then so be it.

"We'll cross the Po," Fabullus continued, "then head west, using the river as a defensive barrier against surprise attacks by Primus. Once we cross the river, we'll destroy the bridge, which will force Primus to head for the bridge at Cremona. And that's where we'll be waiting for him."

The council remained in session for a few more hours as the strategies of a second battle at Cremona were put forth and discussed. Quintus absorbed every detail. It was almost midnight when they were finally dismissed. As he left the tent, Quintus glanced skyward and saw the red blush was now gone from the face of the moon. He wondered if it was a coincidence that the heavenly blood ran only during their war council. Perhaps Mars *was* warning them of disaster. He said a silent prayer to the war god as he walked, wondering if his was the only plea from this camp for an *enemy* victory.

Activity was brisk, even at this late hour, as the legionaries from the Fifth and their scouts were assembled to march to the river banks. Quintus gently shook Lindani and Amazonia awake and they moved outside the tent. He quietly repeated the information from the command tent while he scribbled notes on a piece of papyrus he had pulled from his centurion's kit. He folded the paper and gave it to Lindani.

"The watchword that will get you to Primus is 'virtue,'" Quintus whispered to him. "Move quickly but be careful of our men lining the banks of the Tartaro."

"Do not worry," Lindani replied. "Just tell me how to get the horse outside the camp."

"Leave that to me," Quintus said. "I'll meet you where the Verona road enters the forest north of camp. Getting you back into camp will be more difficult."

"That you may leave to me," Lindani replied.

Quintus donned his armor and centurion helmet, then headed for the corral near the north gate. The horses snorted and stirred as he approached the two auxiliary troopers guarding the cavalry's mounts and Caecina in his corner of the enclosure.

"Saddle that horse for me now," he said sternly pointing to a spirited black mare.

The two men looked at each other in confusion before one responded. "But, Centurion, our orders . . ."

"Damn your orders, trooper!" Quintus interrupted. "I have a dispatch for the tribune with the Fifth who just left for the Po. It's urgent I catch them before they deploy. Now if you'd prefer, I'll have the acting legate, Fabullus, deal with you directly."

"No, sir. Right away." The troopers dropped their javelins and scurried to prep the horse.

As they worked, Quintus wandered toward the small cell that had been erected in the corner of the corral. He saw Caecina's eye watching him through a gap between the palisades that made up his new quarters.

"Our work continues," Quintus whispered as he nonchalantly leaned against the wall. "I'm sending word of Fabullus's plans right now to Primus."

He glanced at the open space and saw the wrinkled skin around the eye crinkle as the general smiled. "You're a good man, Quintus."

"I'm sorry I couldn't help you before," Quintus whispered. "The frustration was—"

"It would have been suicide," Caecina interrupted. "Do not worry about me. Vespasian is the only man you should be thinking about right now."

Quintus nodded. "Perhaps someday everyone in this camp who survives will realize you were right tonight. I wish it hadn't gone this way."

"Our fate is in your hands now," the old legate said quietly. "You're doing the right thing, Quintus. Never doubt that."

"She's ready, sir," the auxiliary called from the corral.

"May Hercules go with you," Caecina whispered.

"And Jupiter be with you," Quintus replied quietly.

In a moment, he was on the charger's back and trotting past the two sentries at the rear gate who pulled aside the wooden barrier.

From beside the empty hospital tent, Amazonia watched Quintus disappear into the black haze beyond the camp ramparts. She stepped from the shadows and plodded down the perimeter road, holding her stomach and moaning slightly as she approached the two sentries Quintus had just passed.

"Where in Hades did they dig the latrines?" she asked them in a friendly voice.

"Other side of the camp," the taller of the guards replied. A grin crept across his face. "We've heard about you. You're with the gladiators."

She pressed her legs together and fidgeted as she replied. "Yes, but right now I just need to find a place to pee without causing a riot." She glanced between the two guards into the darkness outside the gate. "How about letting me step out there? I can't make it all the way across camp."

The shorter sentry shook his head. "Sorry, nobody allowed in or out tonight unless they're an officer, or *with* an officer."

"Oh, don't make me go get my centurion just to take a pee." She made a point of glancing around before she continued. "Look . . . I'll tug my tunic off for you while I go, alright? Just let me pee."

The two sentries looked at each other, the eyes of the taller one pleading with his partner. The shorter one scanned the quiet tent area across the road. Seeing no one around, he cocked his head sideways as a signal for her to step past him.

"Quietly," he said to the taller guard, who almost tripped over his javelin as he rushed to draw back the wooden gate.

With a smile Amazonia slipped past them and took a few steps back toward the deep ditch in front of the rampart. They both followed her out, the shorter one periodically glancing over his shoulder back into the camp. She crossed her arms, grabbed the sides of her tunic, and pulled it over her head. Her sizeable breasts were tugged up by the wool material, then dropped back with a soft slap against her skin. She tipped her head seductively, making sure the eyes of both sentries were focused only on her for the next few moments. She slowly lowered her undergarment and stood naked before them.

"May I pee now?" she asked in a husky voice.

"Please do," the taller sentry replied, his grin still locked in place.

She squatted in the darkness and the gentle sound of her urine hitting the ground reached the sentries. Amazonia watched them impassively while they leered at every inch of her body as she sat on her heels in the dirt. The sudden flash of black that passed behind the two legionaries almost startled her. She faked a shiver and a smile to cover any inadvertent reaction they might have sensed.

"Oh, it's cold out here," she said as she rubbed her arms, then let her hands drift to her hard nipples. "See what I mean?"

The tall sentry licked his lips as he nudged his partner. Amazonia finished and stood up. She lingered for a moment, making sure Lindani was clear of the open area behind the sentries, before stepping back into her undergarment and slipping the red tunic back down over her head.

She approached the two sentries with her sexy smile in place. "Thanks, boys. Hope you liked the show." She ran her hands across each of their crotches as she passed. From what she felt, they had thoroughly enjoyed it.

Quintus handed the reins of his horse to Lindani as the hunter joined him in the dark woods near the road a half-mile north of camp.

"I am not sure," the African said as he hopped up on the back of the horse, "but I believe Amazonia was naked with the sentries as I left the camp."

"Well, we told her we needed a distraction," Quintus said, trying to hide the pang in his heart with a laugh. "Can you think of a better distraction than that?"

Lindani cackled. He raised his heels to spur the horse down the road, but before he kicked, a shout came from the woods behind them.

"Hold there!" a gravelly voice yelled.

Quintus spun. Three legionaries led by a grizzled optio rushed from the woods. The soldiers had their pila leveled at Quintus and Lindani. One prodded Quintus with the sharp metal point.

"What's going on here? Where's he going?" the optio growled.

Quintus cursed himself for not thinking that the main road to Verona would be guarded. His mind raced.

"I've given this man a message to deliver to the tribune of the Fifth," he said with authority. "You're delaying our mission, Optio. Allow him to pass."

The optio squinted. "The Fifth's been sent to secure the Po. That's south of here, not north."

"They've split their forces. Some have been sent to the Tartaro, and that's *north* of here," Quintus shot back.

The optio took a step closer to Quintus. "You're the gladiator," he said, loathing evident in his voice. "I don't take orders from a shit-eating gladiator, even if you do wear the armor of a centurion." He spun toward Lindani. "Get off that horse. Now!"

One of the guards snatched the reins from Lindani's hands. He punctuated his officer's command with a jab that drew a trickle of blood from the African's thigh. The mare snorted and stepped sideways, her large eye on the spear.

"So help me, I'll bring you up on charges!" Quintus yelled, stepping forward. The tips of two javelins clinked against his cuirass. "The Fifth has been assigned to *both* rivers, you idiot. This man carries a dispatch for the tribune at the Tartaro bridge."

"Shut up!" the optio yelled. "This is *my* road tonight, and I've heard nothing of the Fifth being on the Tartaro." Again he looked up at Lindani. "Now get off that fucking horse or you're a dead man."

Lindani looked at Quintus. The gladiator nodded, and he climbed down from the saddle.

"Search them," the optio ordered. A smile crossed his lips. "Arresting a couple of traitors should finally get me to centurion."

Quintus could not believe that this dense junior officer, who didn't even know where his own forces were stationed, was about to jeopardize the future of Rome. His mind continued to churn, but there was little he could do with two pila resting on his chest.

"I found something," one of the legionaries said as he pulled the small roll of papyrus from Lindani's waist band.

"That's for the tribune's eyes only," Quintus hollered. "Open it and you'll hang from a cross."

"If he speaks again, run him through," the optio ordered.

"Sir, you'd better look at this," the legionary said, reading Quintus's note.

Quintus's heart raced. He looked at Lindani standing behind the horse. With the slightest nod of his head, he said everything the hunter needed to know.

"To Legate *Primus* . . . !" the optio read out loud. His head jerked back to Quintus. "They *are* traitors. Arrest them!"

Lindani reached for the horse's rump and pinched hard. The charger reared up with a shriek. Lindani pushed her flank and the horse stumbled sideways, almost toppling onto the legionary holding the note. Lindani snatched the paper from his hand and took off running down the dark road.

"Get him!" the optio yelled.

The legionary dropped the reins and drew back his pilum to throw. In the commotion, Quintus drew his sword. The blade became a blur as it knocked aside the two iron points still held at his chest and struck the back of the pilum just as the guard released it. The slice sent the javelin flying into the woods. Quintus completed the arc of his swing against the horse's rump. The sting of the flat side of the blade jolted the animal into a charge.

"Your mount is on the way!" he called to Lindani.

He leapt sideways and felt the tip of a spear glance off the back of his helmet. He spun and sliced at the legs of the guard who charged past him. With a scream the soldier tumbled into the brush beside the road.

"Kill him!" the optio screamed as he pushed another guard forward.

Quintus dove for the wounded man's pilum, rolled, and came up facing the charging soldier. He cocked his arm and hurled the javelin. It pierced the man's throat with a force that drove the shank out the back of his neck. The soldier stumbled forward, dropping his javelin as he fell. Quintus snatched the pole before it hit the ground. He heard the last legionary charging his flank. With his eyes glued to the enraged face of the optio, he spun the pilum sideways and thrust. The unsuspecting soldier found the iron tip buried in his groin. He fell with a piercing squeal.

"I told you to let us pass," Quintus said without breaking his gaze from the optio. "Now you've caused the deaths of three good men."

The brash officer flew into a rage. He charged Quintus with sword drawn. Quintus held the pilum like a staff, the way he'd often used his trident in the arena. As the screaming, swearing optio ran closer, Quintus began spinning both the metal tip and wooden end of the javelin back and forth. The closer the optio got, the faster the ends spun. By the time the man was within striking distance, the pilum was a blur of deadly motion. The optio did not stand a chance. His first sword thrust became his last. The butt end of Quintus's javelin struck his face three times in the blink of an eye. The optio staggered backward, stunned. The point of the pilum cut a gash down his sword arm. The ripped tendons forced him to drop his gladius.

"You should have respected your superior officer," Quintus said through clenched teeth, "even if I *am* a gladiator." He then thrust the javelin forward, piercing the optio's forehead. The officer gasped and dropped dead on the Verona road.

"You should have let us pass," Quintus whispered again.

The moans of the wounded men surrounded him. He knew what had to be done. He turned and saw the moonlit silhouette of Lindani seated on the horse a hundred feet down the road.

"Are you hurt?" the hunter called.

"I'm fine. Go." Quintus replied. Lindani spun his mount and galloped north. In seconds, the black rider on the black animal disappeared into the night.

Quintus used the pilum to finish off the wounded soldiers. With each thrust, his heart sank lower. He tried to look on it as an honorable arena win, but the ruse did little to lift his spirit. He dragged the four bodies deep into the woods and covered them with undergrowth. Soon the chirp of cicadas was once again the only sound in the forest.

He said a silent prayer to Hercules, then returned to the camp. He approached the same two sentries at the rear gate, who were deep in discussion. Probably reliving their encounter with Amazonia, Quintus figured. They were startled as he approached out of the darkness.

"Halt," the taller one called. "Watchword!"

"The Emperor's Triumph," Quintus replied. The gate was pulled back, and he entered the camp at a quick-step.

"Centurion, what happened to your horse?" the taller guard asked.

"The centurion at the river needed it to check on his men through the night." Quintus kept walking as he spoke, acting as if he did not owe the sentries an explanation. He heard nothing further as he continued on to his tent.

"Everything go alright?" Amazonia asked as he crawled into their cramped shelter after removing his armor.

"Not really, but he got through," he whispered. "What's this I hear about you being naked with the guards?"

"Well . . ." she began with a smile.

The look in her green eyes radiated the same mischievous glint they had held in his sexual fantasy during the encounter in Juno's litter. Ever since picturing Amazonia so vividly in his mind's eye that night, he had not been able to see her quite the same as he used to. Bedding down next to her each night in the tight confines of their tent became more difficult. Having her so close—close enough to feel the heat from her body on the cool autumn nights—yet not being able to reach for her had become a special torture all its own.

"Romanus!" The loud voice came from outside the tent, interrupting his thoughts and Amazonia's explanation.

Her eyes grew wide. "Could they have seen you?" she asked quietly.

"We'll find out," he said as he exited the tent.

Their senior tribune, Flavius Scipio, stood outside with a junior tribune at his side. "Fabullus wants you to take a century of gladiators down to the bridge for the night, just in case. Apparently, you've gained a reputation for handling bridges over the Po. Get moving."

"Yes, sir," Quintus replied, then disappeared back into his tent.

"That was close," Amazonia whispered. "Now I see why you needed Lindani to go tonight."

"Want to go watch another bridge?" he asked with a smile.

"Sure, I didn't need more than a few moments' sleep tonight anyway."

• • •

Just before sunrise, the new sentries at the rear post got a surprise as a riderless black horse trotted up to the gate. The skittish mare reared back and whinnied as the barrier was drawn back. One of the guards took hold of the bridle and tried to calm the animal down. The other watched him lead her back to the corral, wondering where the horse had come from.

Neither saw the black figure slip through the gate behind them.

XIX

October AD 69

VESPASIAN was in a good mood. Julia noticed his demeanor always improved when Marcus Livius Castus arrived. The two men obviously had a fascinating history together.

"We'll eat in good time, Lucius," Vespasian said with a laugh.

Julia glanced beside her and saw Lucius ogling the mehiwet cakes laid out on the silver tray before them in the palace triclinium. She gave him the look a mother would give a disobedient child. He returned an impish grin, but Julia looked away. She could feel his eyes on her but refused to acknowledge him. She was surprised at how remarkably calm and reserved he had been since their fight on the dock two weeks earlier. But she had given it little thought over the past few days. She was too intent on launching the backup plan she had laid for herself.

"Ah, here he is!" Vespasian said as he jumped up from his couch. "The servants said you had arrived a while ago."

Vespasian walked quickly toward the door as Castus entered.

"I'm sorry, Flavius. It took me a while to clean up."

The emissary's visits had grown more frequent as the Flavian forces marched toward Rome. But the trips were clearly taking a toll on the old ex-centurion. Each time he arrived at the Judean palace, the man looked more gaunt and haggard.

Julia stood and glanced at Lucius, who rose beside her. "Don't you think it would be wise for you to go say hello," she whispered in as stern a voice as she could muster.

Lucius looked at her for a moment before walking around the gathering of couches and heading toward the door. She hoped her nervousness was not evident.

She kept a smile on her face and her eyes locked on the activity in the entrance foyer as she quickly reached down the low-cut neckline of her yellow stola. She retrieved the small pouch she had tucked between her breasts before leaving the *Juno*. She quickly pulled the top open, leaned across the small table, and poured the finely ground white powder into the goblet of wine that had been filled for Castus.

"We waited for you," Vespasian said, waving his arm toward the square of couches. "I'm afraid Titus is in Jerusalem for a while, so he won't be joining us. More trouble with the Jews. But I hope you bring good news."

Castus settled heavily on the couch adjacent to Vespasian and across from Julia and Lucius. Julia greeted him with a broad smile.

"Hello, Castus. You're looking well, considering the long ride," she lied.

"Thank you, Julia. Always nice to see your beaming face," Castus replied.

"So what's the latest news?" Vespasian asked as he lowered himself chest-first to his couch.

"The Vitellians have marched north to meet Primus. Battle lines are being drawn near Cremona once again. But Valens stayed behind in Rome." A mischievous smile added to the wrinkles on the old man's face. "Seems he came down with a sudden illness."

"Excellent," said Vespasian with a loud laugh. "So Caecina is in control."

The smile drifted from the centurion's face as quickly as it had appeared. "I'm afraid not. They're commanded by a senior tribune named Fabullus."

"Fabullus? What happened to Caecina?" Vespasian asked quickly.

"Caecina was thrown in chains when he proposed capitulation. The

Fifth Legion elected their own commander to lead the army."

Vespasian looked concerned. "This Fabullus will fight?"

"He will fight," Castus said quietly. "He's a staunch supporter of Vitellius. Almost as determined as Valens."

"Damn," Vespasian muttered. He grabbed a handful of sea mussels off the second tray that had been laid before them and began to eat in silence.

"Primus will prevail, Governor," Julia said. "You know that."

"Yes, but not without heavy casualties on both sides," Vespasian replied. "These are well-trained legions facing each other."

"Then let us offer a toast for their protection." She quickly snatched her cup and held it high. "Bacchus, god of wine, we ask you to petition the pantheon of gods to watch over those brave men at Cremona and spare as many Roman lives as they see fit. We drink in your honor."

She watched Castus closely over the rim of the cup. The old man drained the goblet in one long gulp. He winced slightly and looked at the governor. Julia's heart leapt.

"Not one of your better vintages, Flavius," he said with a smile.

The governor looked down at his own goblet. Julia's heart raced, and her hand tightened on her cup.

"Really?" Vespasian said. "Then we must get something else. Helvia . . . a different vintage."

"Yes, Dominus," the servant girl replied, then left the dining room.

Julia placed her cup on the table and breathed a sigh of relief. The beating in her chest subsided.

Over the next hour, four more courses of food and cakes appeared on the table before them. Vespasian's spirits eventually lightened as he drank and told more war stories about his days in Britannia fighting alongside Castus. The old man responded with laughter for a while, but then became listless and distracted.

"I think I must leave you for the evening," he finally slurred to

Vespasian. "I'm afraid I'm not feeling well."

He pushed up off the couch and winced in pain as he grabbed his stomach.

"Are you alright, my friend?" Vespasian asked, his bushy eyebrows arched in concern.

"I seem to have a touch of stomach pain." Castus swayed as he stood, still holding his stomach. "And a light head."

"Should I summon the physician?" Vespasian asked as he rose from his couch.

Julia waved her arm nonchalantly. "Do not trouble yourself, Governor. I could use some fresh air myself." She rose and took Castus by the arm. "I'll walk with him and get him to bed. I'm sure it's just the bounty of your banquet taking its toll on a tired, empty stomach."

Castus nodded to Vespasian. "I'll be fine," he said with a grimace.

Lucius rose next to Julia, but she turned quickly to cut him off. "And I'll be fine as well, Lucius, dear. Please stay and keep the governor company." She stared hard into his eyes to be sure there would be no discussion. Without a word, he dropped back onto the couch.

As they left the dining room and walked down the wide palace hallway, Castus began to sway and stagger.

"I do feel quite ill," the old man said with a tremble in his voice.

As she steadied him, Julia could feel a cold sweat break out on the man's arms. "Your room is right there," she said in a lilting voice, trying to keep him calm. "You probably just need a good night of rest."

By the time they entered the room, she practically had to carry him to the bed. She could feel the heat radiate off his body as his temperature rose dramatically. She dropped him onto the soft down mattress, then rushed to shut the door.

"The . . . room . . . is . . . spinning," Castus said in a weak voice.

"I know, dear. I know," Julia whispered as she approached the bed. She sat beside him and adjusted his legs into a comfortable position. "Is that better?"

"No . . . still . . . spinning . . . and . . . birds . . . I hear . . . birds . . ."
His voice trailed off to a whisper.

Julia stroked his forehead and was shocked at the heat she felt on the
palm of her hand. Sweat began pouring from the old man as he moaned.
A sudden pang of regret clutched her chest. The physician she had bribed
for the mushroom powder had assured her there would be no lasting effects. Fever, vivid illusions, and delirium were the most common effects,
perfect conditions for extracting information. But seeing Castus roll back
and forth in such agony was something she had not anticipated. She had
expected him to simply drift off to a half sleep, while she quietly pressed
him for answers. A loud yell from him made her jump, and she glanced at
the door, hoping it was thick enough to contain the sound.

She moved toward the head of the bed and pulled a chair up behind the
low headboard. She sat and began gently massaging the man's temples.

"Is that better, Castus?" she cooed in a light whisper. The only response was another moan, this one thankfully quiet. Then words began
flowing, incoherent and rambling.

"The horse . . . watch out for the . . . sun is too . . . bright . . . I can't
. . . do it now . . ."

Julia leaned close to his left ear as she continued to rub the sides of his
head. "Castus," she whispered, "do you know where you are?"

"But I . . . I have to . . . the battle is . . . won . . . if I . . ." He moaned
quietly again.

"If you what, Castus? How will you win the battle?"

"Men . . . will fight . . . Primus will . . . win . . . if I . . ."

"Are you there now, Castus? Are you with your men on the battle
lines?"

"Men . . . not with . . . men . . . don't see . . . men . . . no . . . no! . . . NO!
Get them off me!" His voice quickly rose to a piercing cry, and he twitched
in the sweat-soaked bed linen.

"Shhhh, you're alright, Castus. You're alright," Julia said, trying her
best to keep her voice calm as she glanced at the door. She ran her fingers

through the damp strands of his matted hair. "I'm here with you. Tell me, Castus. Tell me where you are."

There was silence, except for the man's heavy breathing which had become quite shallow.

"Castus, tell me how Primus will know him."

"Primus . . . good general . . . good man . . ."

"Yes, Castus. Primus is a good man. But how will he know your man? How will he know not to kill your man on the lines?"

"Primus . . . is a . . . good . . . man . . . fights . . . hard . . ."

She whispered in his ear with a voice as soothing as she could muster. "Yes, Castus, Primus is a good general. But you don't want him to kill your man on the front lines, do you? How will he know him? Who is he?"

"Primus . . . horse . . . his sword . . . seeks . . . the bull . . . his sword . . ."

"What horse? What bull, Castus? What will he do with the sword?" Julia leaned closer, having a hard time hearing the words.

"No . . . sword . . . bull . . . the bull . . . he seeks . . . the bull . . ."

Julia sat up and thought for a moment. The words were not making sense. Why would a general look for a bull on a battlefield? She leaned down again as the man's moans grew louder.

"Alright. It's alright, Castus," she whispered as she rubbed his head. She moved her hands to his chest and gently stroked the tunic that was now sopping wet with perspiration. His moaning subsided.

"What bull, Castus? How will Primus find a bull on a battlefield?"

"The . . . bull . . . walking . . . fighting . . . the bull . . . Taurus . . ."

The word sent a sudden jolt through Julia.

"The bull, Castus. Is the bull called Taurus?"

"The bull . . . Taurus . . . the . . . bull . . ." The old man's words were barely discernable.

Julia began to tremble. She leaned forward and put her lips next to the man's ear.

"Taurus the Bull, Castus. Is your man the gladiator they call Taurus the Bull?"

The man's words came as brief whispers. "Taurus . . . the . . . bull . . . Quin . . ."

Julia's heart pounded. "What's his name, Castus? What's the bull's name. Say it." She laid her ear close to the man's trembling mouth.

"Taurus . . . bull . . . Quintus . . . Roman . . . Romanus . . ."

Julia leapt from the chair. It scooted backward and tipped over. She stood staring at the sweating wreck of a man in the bed before her. His words had been barely audible, but she had heard them as clearly as the peal of a bell.

Could it be? Was it possible that her very own nephew was the spy on the front lines? It had to be. Why else would the name have come from Castus's lips?

The corrupt physician was worth every sesterce of the sizeable sum she had paid for both the drug and his silence. The yield was more valuable than she could have ever dreamed. Now she only needed to decide how it would best work for her.

Reestablishing relations with her dear, estranged nephew was certainly an undertaking worthy of her charms. The trick would be to do it while keeping Lucius in the dark. For if he ever discovered that his fate was once again tied to his lifelong nemesis, it would surely push him beyond all reasonable thought.

Julia smiled as she looked down on the sweating, trembling body on the bed.

"I'm sorry, Castus, but this was well worth the price we've both paid."

XX

October AD 69

CohorS GLADIATORUM, take the flank!" the senior tribune yelled, his voice carrying clearly over the clatter of military boots on the paving stones.

Quintus acknowledged the order as he led his men at the quick-step alongside the cavalry. But his attention was elsewhere as he looked desperately for some way to keep his men safe. Unfortunately, with a canal levee to their right and the rest of the Vitellian army to their left, there was simply no place to go but straight ahead into the waiting ranks of Flavians.

As he advanced, Quintus noticed the burgundy stains on the bleached stones of the Via Postumia—remnants of the last battle they had fought on this very road six months earlier. Without Valens or Caecina for support, Fabullus had consolidated his forces at Cremona. Leaving the bulk of his fifty thousand men in reserve, he now marched a force of ten thousand—including all the gladiators—forward to probe the strength of Primus and the advancing Flavian legions. Quintus knew this could well be the final chapter of the war.

They drew closer to the Flavians. He tensed, fighting to keep his anxiety in check. He could not afford to have Taurus emerge now. He had to keep a clear head. Taurus would cloud his judgment and cause carnage he did not want.

Within seconds, they crashed into the Flavian line. Swords thrust out at them viciously from behind a wall of shields. Quintus felt a blade nick his forearm as he beat against the barrier of red shields. To his left, his gladiators pressed into the enemy defenses. The line wavered but did not break.

Quintus hated killing Flavians in battle, but he hated to see his men die even more. He shouted encouragement to his fighters. The banshee cry of Amazonia cut through the battle noise, and two Flavians fell from the line. They were quickly replaced by legionaries from the supporting ranks behind them. But the strength and endurance of the veteran gladiators proved too much for the Flavian legionaries. Slowly, their line began to buckle.

Quintus knew the fighting instincts of his gladiators had taken hold as they saw themselves gaining the upper hand. The tips of their gladii sought each speck of flesh presented, and they exploited every foot of ground given up by the weakening soldiers. More and more of the Flavians dropped as the gladiators' momentum built. But every Flavian who fell pained Quintus. He considered ordering his men to slow down, but their well-honed instincts now had them gripped in the frenzy of survival.

He lashed out at another Flavian who rushed him. The man dropped with his throat slit open. Quintus almost wished it was his own throat that had been slashed, for he had caused the death of yet another brave soldier who had aligned behind a good man—the man Quintus knew was destined to become emperor. The frustration of this deadly paradox was becoming too much.

To his surprise, a Flavian signifer, wearing the fur and skull of a brown bear and carrying the standard of the Seventh Galbiana legion, appeared directly in front of him. Another dilemma flew through Quintus's mind: Would killing this man and capturing the standard stoke a fire in the Vitellians and help lead to a rout he did not want? Or would it enrage Primus and encourage his Flavians to fight harder, forcing Quintus to kill even more good men? There was no time to weigh the consequences.

"I don't want to kill you," he yelled at the signifer. The man looked at him with a puzzled expression, contrasting with the fierce bear's head atop his helmet. "Drop your standard and fall. Then you will live."

Quintus could see the understanding finally register in the man's eyes. But instead of complying, the signifer hefted the heavy staff sideways and swung it at Quintus's face. Sensing the man's assault, he ducked. The curved blade mounted at the bottom of the pole flew over his head, creasing the red crest on his centurion helmet.

"I'm sorry, Signifer," Quintus said as he buried his gladius in the man's groin. "You're a brave but stupid man."

The standard bearer's shriek mingled with the cacophony of the battle, and he hit the ground. The standard fell at Quintus's feet. He picked up the pole bearing the golden laurel, five silver discs, and a crescent moon. As much as he did not want to spur the Vitellians behind him, he turned to wave the captured standard at the senior tribune. He hoped, once he showed progress, he could start moving his gladiators back to a safer position.

He was shocked to see how far into the enemy lines they had penetrated. It only took him a second to realize why. As his gladiators had been advancing, many of the other Vitellian units had been retreating. Although fired with spirit at the outset, the Vitellian legionaries could not sustain their attack against a force almost twice their size. To his horror, Quintus saw that his men were about to be stranded and surrounded.

"Break off and fall back!" he shouted.

He dropped the newly captured standard, and it landed with a clink on the armor of the dead signifer. Quintus spun his own standard bearer around and shoved him toward the rear ranks. The man had a difficult time pushing his way through the crush of his own men still surging toward the battle line. With continuous shouts, he relayed Quintus's "Retreat" order. Finally, the confused fighters obeyed the command and followed their banner into a retreat.

Quintus faced the enemy as they backed away. At first, the battered Flavians seemed unsure about their pursuit. They spent time regrouping their forces, giving Quintus the few precious moments he needed to get his men out of harm's way. He glanced at the bodies of the dead being left behind in the retreat. With the same armor and helmets worn by both friend and foe, it was impossible to tell how many of his gladiators had fallen in the brief battle.

He took another step back and froze in horror. The bloody face of Drusus looked up at him from the battlefield. A dying heart pumped the last few surges of blood from the wide hole in the side of his neck. Despite the advancing Flavians, Quintus knelt beside him.

"I'm sorry . . ." Drusus rasped. "I failed you."

With every word, Quintus could see the life spirit drift from the man's eyes. He remembered the good-natured jeers aimed at this man the day he had lost a sparring match to a new recruit called Amazonia. He remembered the man's undying support and bravery through every battle of this cursed war.

"You've failed no one, Drusus," he whispered as he touched the man's cheek. "It's I who am sorry."

"Keep the men safe," Drusus said, his voice barely audible.

The Flavians were closing quickly, and Quintus had no choice but to resume his retreat.

"I vow on your soul that our tactics will change, here and now," he called out as he stepped backward.

Drusus reached out to him as he died. Quintus let the image of his friend—his *contubernalis*—sear into his memory. He made a pledge to himself and Drusus. He would not cause the loss of one more gladiator or venator in the name of Vitellius, and he would not move to attack one more Flavian soldier. This useless slaughter of good men would now come to an end.

The blast of a nearby trumpet jarred Quintus from his thoughts. The senior tribune shouted commands to keep the Vitellian retreat orderly. Quintus kept his fighters to the right flank and watched the withdrawal become a tentative cat and mouse game. The Flavians continued to shadow the Vitellian forces, but at a distance of two to three hundred feet. The pace of retreat became more urgent with each mile.

"Why does Primus not charge and wipe us out?" Lindani wondered out loud. The panting in his voice revealed that even the well-toned African was growing weary of the fast stride.

"He's probably waiting for the rest of his army from Bedriacum to catch up," Quintus guessed. Only one thing was clear to him: with each step they took toward Cremona, the closer the Flavians came to suffering devastating losses under the barrage of artillery that awaited them. The thought of heavy boulders and oversized arrows fired point-blank into the ranks of Flavians did not paint a welcome scene in Quintus's mind.

Cheers soon came from the rear lines of the retreating Vitellians. Quintus's cohort rounded the bend and he saw the legions of Fabullus come into view. In orderly patchwork squares, the army was an imposing sight—forty thousand legionaries, auxiliaries, and cavalry sprawled across the road and well into the farm fields on either side. The force seemed to stretch halfway to the distant horizon, where the palisades of their Cremona fort were backlit against the late afternoon sun. As Quintus had feared, the heavy artillery was in place and ready to fire.

The five thousand battle-weary Vitellians wove through the open patchwork of fresh soldiers and made their way toward the rear. Quintus turned to watch the next melee begin. The cohorts on the front lines stood taut and ready for the Flavian onslaught. But to Quintus's relief, none of the Flavians followed. Instead, they held at the bend, then slowly fell back to regroup and wait for their reinforcements from Bedriacum.

Quintus sent his walking wounded on to Cremona, then reformed his remaining fighters behind the rear ranks.

"We lost Drusus," he said.

The look of alarm on Amazonia's face told him he should not have been so blunt. Though accustomed to death in the arena, the rapid loss of life on the battlefield was hard even for a gladiator to accept.

"Damn this fucking war to Hades," Memnon muttered.

"How many more have we lost?" Quintus asked.

"About eighteen gladiators; all the venatores are fine," Memnon answered.

Quintus nodded. "I have pledged on the soul of Drusus that our days of fighting for Vitellius have come to an end. From this moment on, we take no more Flavian lives."

"We're all fine with that. But now what?" Amazonia asked.

"We lay low for now," Quintus responded, looking toward Lindani. "Then at nightfall we send our emissary, here, through the dark woods and into the Flavian lines to arrange the deliverance of our cohort to the army of Vespasian. He'll—"

Quintus was interrupted by a harsh call from the senior tribune. "Romanus!" the officer yelled as he approached. "Report to Legate Fabullus at the quick-step, and bring your Ethiopian friend."

Lindani threw Quintus a concerned look as they rose and trotted toward the circle of high-ranking officers that had formed around a campfire nearby.

"Centurion, has your African ever done reconnaissance work?" the gruff legate asked without preamble.

"Yes, General," Quintus lied. "He was our eyes and ears along the Po River a few months back. He's the quietest and fastest we have. And he's invisible at night."

Quintus's mind raced to find a way to make the orders he sensed were coming work to his favor.

"Good. We need him. Some of the tribunes are petitioning to attack tonight rather than wait for the morning sun. I think it's madness when both armies wear the same uniform. But they raise a good point about the Flavian reinforcements. I need to know when they'll arrive. If they're almost here anyway, I'll hold the attack until morning. But if they're still a ways off, we attack tonight." The legate looked Lindani over but spoke to Quintus. "Does he speak Latin?"

"Better than most of your auxiliaries," Lindani answered in fluid Latin before Quintus could reply.

The legate gave him a harsh stare. "Fine. Be ready to leave at nightfall. Report directly to me on your return. And make it fast."

"Yes, sir, he will," Quintus replied, quickly pushing Lindani back toward the gladiator cohort.

"Does he think I am a savage?" Lindani fumed once they were outside the legate's earshot.

"He's just pissed that you're sharper than most of his own legionaries," Quintus said quietly. "But he did just make our job that much easier. Listen, use the watchword to get to Primus. First tell him to get those reinforcements up to the lines at the quick-step and to expect an attack shortly after nightfall. Then draw him a copy of the banner you designed as our vexillum, but make sure he understands that once the battle begins, we'll probably get split up. We'll fight wherever we can do him the most good behind our lines. And when you get back to Fabullus, the answer is: 'No, the reinforcements are nowhere near their lines yet.' I want this battle to happen tonight. The darkness will work in our favor."

They rejoined their fellow fighters, who had moved farther to the rear and started a campfire of their own to heat a pot of grain porridge. Memnon and Valentinus rubbed flat stones from their kit over their gladii to restore the edge, while Amazonia repaired some broken links in her mail shirt. Quintus sat near Amazonia and welcomed the fire's warmth against the autumn chill. Lindani slid one of the burning sticks from the fire and tapped it absentmindedly while staring into the flames. Quintus quietly laid out his and Lindani's plan to his fighters.

"What if we're separated from our standard bearer?" Valentinus asked when Quintus finished.

"He's right," Amazonia said. "How will the Flavians recognize us then?"

"I'm still working on that," Quintus admitted. "Maybe we could—"

"Like this . . ." Lindani interrupted, reaching for one of the red shields lying next to the campfire. He blew out the small flame at the end of the stick in his hand and used the charred end to draw a large black gladius across the front of the scutum. Surrounded by the yellow laurel already emblazoned on the shield's face, the image almost perfectly matched the banner Lindani had designed many months ago. "Now we each have our own vexillum to fight under, eh?" he said with his characteristic grin.

Quintus shook his head and slapped the African's back. "Simple, yet effective—just like you!"

He waited for the African's cackling to cease before he continued.

"Now, here's what we do in battle . . ."

The sun had been down for hours when Lindani finally returned to the Vitellian lines. A flurry of activity began as soon as the hunter reported his "findings" to Fabullus. By the time Lindani joined Quintus, the gladiators were already forming their lines at the head of the second wave, just behind the Third Cohort of the Twelfth Legion.

"I assume everything went well since they're ordering us into formation already," Quintus said.

Lindani looked around, then leaned toward Quintus, keeping his voice low. "Primus has ordered his men not to attack any fighter with a black gladius added to his scutum." He looked down the row of gladiators making up the front line of their formation. Each held a javelin beside a shield bearing a crude image of a black sword. "Some of the men are not such good artists, eh?"

"They're good enough to impress our illustrious tribune. He congratulated us for the spirit of solidarity we showed in marking our scuta." Quintus and Lindani shared a smile. "I just hope the marks can be seen in the darkness," Quintus added.

"A crescent moon will rise in the east soon," Lindani said peering into the dark sky. "That will cast light on the front of our shields."

Quintus glanced at the artillery area to the rear, where a row of ten catapults stood armed and ready to fire. The throwing arm of the center artillery piece, much larger than the others, held a boulder of at least three hundred pounds. To either side of the catapults sat a dozen or more ballistae—giant crossbows—armed with their oversized arrows. Quintus dreaded the furrows of destruction and carnage the missiles would plow.

A sudden blast came from the cornu horns. The frontline Vitellians began their march down the Via Postumia. The artillery pieces fired as one, creating a thunderous boom that echoed off the surrounding hills. The rumble was followed by an eerie silence as the boulders, giant arrows, and flaming balls of pine pitch sailed quietly through the night air. Quintus looked up and followed the path of the lethal comets to their unlucky targets almost a quarter-mile away. The balls of flame lit up the expanse of Flavian forces. Quintus was relieved to see they were in formation and well prepared for the attack, thanks to Lindani's visit. Unfortunately, no army could truly prepare for the devastation of heavy artillery. Fireballs erupted an instant before the sound of their impact reached Quintus. The screams of men on fire and those maimed by the missiles shattered the cool autumn evening. Without catapults and ballistae of their own, the Flavians could only endure and begin their own advance.

"Everyone remember your assignments," Quintus called to his fighters as they marched forward. "What we do here tonight may not seem honorable to many of you. The gods know it is not an honorable way for anyone to fight. But it is necessary. You saw with your own eyes that these men will not listen to reason. Legate Caecina did everything he could to avoid this night. But they brought it on themselves. That's why we must do what we do tonight. Are you with me?"

A shout of approval rose from six hundred arena fighters.

Quintus nodded with tight lips. Now if he could only convince himself of those same words.

With both armies on the move, the distance between the opposing forces closed quickly. As they drew near, the front ranks of both forces unleashed a volley of pila. The javelins rained down on both the Flavian and Vitellian cohorts, embedding in flesh and wood. Quintus thanked Hercules that the initial barrage did not reach back to his auxiliary ranks. But many of the legionaries in front of them dropped. Those who didn't scurried for the shields of their dead comrades to replace their own, rendered useless by the heavy javelins embedded deep in the painted wood.

The second wave of formations, including Cohors Gladiatorum, were ordered to ready their pila. Quintus's gladiators raised their javelins.

"Remember the plan," he said to those within hearing distance.

The command to throw was shouted by the other centurions, and Quintus echoed the order. But his men hurled their pila short. Most fell harmlessly in the dead zone between the two armies, but a few embedded in the shoulders of their own forward ranks. The shocked legionaries were too close to the enemy to turn to see what morons had impaled their own comrades. The clash of the two front lines came with a sudden clamor of hundreds of swords against hundreds of shields.

Rather than maintain battle formation, which would have kept the ranks open for freedom of movement and quick withdrawals by the leading lines, Quintus pressed his fighters forward into the turmoil of battle. In such close quarters, their murderous actions would be obscured by the mass of bodies and confusion.

Quintus was first to strike. His gladius thrust forward into the back of the naked neck, just beneath the helmet guard, of the Vitellian legionary in front of him. The soldier dropped, never knowing what had caused his death. The thrust was familiar to every gladiator. It was the fatal blow taught in every ludus and dealt to every gladiator who had the verdict of death imposed upon him in an arena. It severed the spinal column from the brain and caused an immediate and painless end.

Quintus stepped over the body and approached the back of the next soldier in front of him. To his left, Vitellian soldiers dropped like so many sacrificial lambs. He fought the urge to close his eyes. The ease of the killing heightened the ugliness of their deed. For Quintus, each thrust seared another scar into his own soul. He tried thinking of all the lives they were saving by their plan this night. He thought of a war shortened by weeks or perhaps months. He thought of Vespasian reuniting a country ripped apart by megalomaniacs. He thought of honoring a debt to the man who had helped his mother and father. He thought of wise leadership and the new wave of prosperity that would soon envelop the Empire. But no matter what he thought, he could not escape the debauchery of driving a gladius into the neck of an unsuspecting soldier from behind.

Within moments, the front line of Cohors Gladiatorum had advanced more than halfway through the Vitellian formation in front of them. The crush of bodies worked in concert with the darkness and the swift thrusts to conceal their actions, even from the cohorts advancing on their flanks. The forward ranks of the Twelfth Legion's Third Cohort were soon only three deep.

As they approached the front line, a Vitellian soldier who had been in the heat of battle since the initial encounter stepped back to draw a breath. The look of shock on his face when he saw the gladiators rather than his own cohort behind him was almost comical. Quintus approached him and, without warning, buried his bloody gladius deep in the soldier's throat.

The gladiators now faced a line of Flavian soldiers. There was an awkward pause as the Flavians saw the marked shields and stood stupidly on the battlefield, not knowing what to do or whom to attack next. But the gladiators solved their dilemma. Quintus bellowed his orders, and the gladiators turned and beat a hasty retreat. Since the ranks that had marched behind them had not kept pace with their swift advance, a wide gap opened in the right center of the Vitellian line. The Flavians gave a rallying cry and poured into the breach. The cohorts to the right and left of the gladiators tried to fill the break, but were overwhelmed by the momentum of the Flavian charge.

Some of the Vitellians grasped the situation and realized the gladiators had betrayed them. They moved to attack the arena fighters, but

Lindani and his archers stood ready for just such a situation. From their position a hundred feet to the rear, they fired on anyone who challenged their gladiators. Dozens fell, and Quintus's troupe escaped unscathed.

"Now we split," Quintus yelled as they ran. "Memnon, take your men to the farm on the north. Priedens, take your group to the vineyard on the south. Keep low and have the archers pick off whatever Vitellian officers they can. My unit, follow me."

Most of the fighters surged into the field behind Memnon. Quintus was followed by Lindani, ten of his sagittarii, and a dozen gladiators, including Amazonia. They kept to the dark woods and circled wide around the battlefield. They emerged between the rear ranks of Vitellians and the city walls of Cremona, their new targets laid out neatly in front of them—the artillery.

Quintus watched the two-man ballista teams load and fire their oversized bolts. The catapults next to the ballistae continued to leap off the ground every time the throwing arms smacked against the heavy crossbeams. In the center of the road, the brawny four-man team at the giant center catapult hefted another colossal boulder into the bowl and prepared to yank the release cord.

Quintus pointed to the line of woods along the southern shoulder of the road. "If you move up along this tree line, will that get you close enough to take out the artillerymen?" he whispered to Lindani.

"Yes, at least most of them."

"Alright, start with this first ballista on the right. Amazonia and I will take it from there. Wait for my signal."

Lindani nodded, then motioned his archers forward. They held their arrow shafts secure in the quivers to avoid the clicking of wood as they took up positions behind the roadside trees. Amazonia and the gladiators followed Quintus back through the woods as they made their way closer to the first ballista.

"Just me and Amazonia for now," he explained to the small force. "We'll try to keep a low profile. But if all Hades breaks loose, charge the artillerymen." The fighters nodded their understanding. Quintus untied the cord at his chin and removed his crested helmet as he spoke to Amazonia. "Work with me to cut the ropes on the firing arms," he explained. "We'll go back and cut the torsion skeins later. Leave your scutum here. It'll be too hard to work with it."

He signaled Lindani with a wave of his gladius just beyond the tree line. A stream of arrows shot from the woods, each striking an artilleryman working on the south side of the road. The adjoining crews shouted a warning and drew their swords. The machines at the far north continued firing as the nearby crews slowly approached the dark woods.

"Let's go," he whispered. He and Amazonia used the large wooden frames of the ballistae to shield themselves from view as they approached the artillery area. Quintus raised his sword and hacked at the first firing rope. On the third blow, the fibers of the thick rope gave way. Amazonia was already working on the second ballista when another cloud of arrows flew from the woods. More artillerymen dropped with a scream. Amazonia's rope finally gave way, and she stepped into the shadows as more legionaries ran toward their fallen comrades. Piece by piece, she and Quintus worked their way toward the catapults in the center of the road, which were left unattended as more and more crewmen ran to investigate the hidden threat in the woods.

"What do we do with these?" Amazonia asked as she approached the first of the smaller stone-throwers.

"Cut the drawback ropes for now," Quintus answered as he ran to the second catapult. "If they can't wind the arms back, they can't load the stones."

Another group of artillerymen ran past them, swords drawn, headed toward the woods. Quintus was in mid-stroke as one of the Vitellians stopped, apparently sensing the motion. He turned and stared blankly into Quintus's face. For a brief moment, he wore a look of confusion, then opened his mouth to shout an alarm. Quintus thrust his gladius into the gaping jaws. The man fell before he could make a sound, but the clank of his body armor hitting the paving stones caught the attention of two more soldiers. They called out, and the charging artillerymen stopped and turned.

"It's the gladiator! He's a fucking traitor!" one of them yelled. Without hesitation, all seven charged Quintus with swords flashing.

Quintus wondered if leaving his shield in the woods had been a good idea. He called to his men in reserve, then took on the first attacker, parrying the man's thrust and pressing the gladius aside. He grabbed the man's sword arm and, in a lightning-fast strike, thrust his gladius into the side of the man's neck. Blood spurted from the severed jugular, covering Quintus's arm. Quintus pulled the soldier in front of him, using the dead body to block the blows of the next attacker.

Over the dead man's shoulder Quintus saw Amazonia engage another Vitellian. In the distance, his small force of gladiators charged from the woods. As if the dead man in his arms sought one last chance at vengeance, a stream of blood suddenly pumped from the gaping neck wound and covered Quintus's face. Seizing the opportunity, the second attacker thrust high at Quintus. Sensing the move more than seeing it, Quintus jerked his head to the left. The shiny blade pierced the crimson spray of blood, barely missing his right eye, but creasing the side of his head just above the ear. A momentary feeling of helplessness and frustration hampered his instincts. His heart leapt and fire surged through his veins as rage ignited inside him. In the split second it took his attacker to ready a second thrust, Taurus emerged, triumphant at being allowed to fight again.

With a primal yell, Taurus tossed the dead body at his attacker like a child's rag doll. The weight drove the Vitellian back a step and gave Taurus the room he needed. Although still almost blinded by the blood in his eyes, his gladius streaked forward with a blur and caught the soldier in the center of the throat. He toppled backward, landing with a thud atop the body of his dead comrade.

Taurus spit into his hand and used the saliva to wipe as much blood as he could from his eyes. His vision cleared just in time to see Amazonia hack the hand off the sword arm of her assailant. The man's gladius—his fist still clutching tightly to the hilt—clanged on the paving stones. His scream blended with the wail of a banshee, as Amazonia's perfect body spun in a whirlwind. Her extended leg caught the handless soldier on the left cheek guard of his helmet. His head snapped back with an audible crack as the bones of his neck shattered.

Another artilleryman dropped with one of Lindani's arrows embedded in his head, while the remaining three were quickly overrun by the reserve gladiators.

"Lindani! Clear the other catapults!" Taurus yelled, pointing down the row of war machines with his dripping gladius.

Arrows flew across the road, and one-by-one, more of the artillery crews fell. Taurus turned to resume hacking the catapult ropes when a call of alarm came from the north side of the road.

"Traitors! The gladiators have turned on us!" The cries came from the senior tribune, who had ridden back to check on the dwindling artillery fire. "Ninth Auxiliaries, turn and attack!" The order was shouted with such vigor and hatred, it easily carried over the din to the century of rear auxiliaries being held in reserve 150 feet in front of the artillery line. Their centurion and standard bearer ran to the rear, and eighty men charged behind them. "Kill them all before—" An arrow through the neck from Lindani's bow turned the tribune's last words into an incoherent burble.

"Lindani, move up and cover us!" Taurus called. He turned to the group of eleven gladiators who were already forming a barrier between the charging auxiliaries and the artillery area. "Flama, get the others from the south vineyard! Quickly!" One of the fighters broke off, threw his shield aside, and sprinted for the vineyard. "Keep working on the catapult ropes," Taurus called to Amazonia. He moved toward the empty slot where Flama had stood.

"Bullshit!" she replied and stepped into the gap herself. "Taurus can cut through these damn ropes a lot faster than I can." She turned with a grin and faced the charging century. "Besides, I never liked these fucking barbarians anyway."

Before Taurus could reply, a small cloud of arrows flew at the charging horde from Lindani's archers. Protected behind their mobile wall of shields, only three auxiliaries fell.

"Cut, will you!" Amazonia shouted.

The loud boom of the giant catapult firing punctuated her shout and jarred Taurus into action. He snatched a second gladius from the road as the first rank of auxiliaries collided with the shields of the gladiator barrier. Taurus's enhanced speed and power were focused on a single mission: to destroy every weapon of war assembled on this line. The blades of the swords twitched with anticipation as he approached the first catapult. This time, it took only one mighty blow from each blade to sever the heavy drawback ropes. Like a man possessed, Taurus sprinted from one artillery piece to the next, leaving a wake of frayed rope in his path. But by the time he reached the center of the Via Postumia, the easy work was over.

Now he studied the four brawny artillerymen who were about to lift another massive boulder from the rows of missiles that had been laid out behind their oversized catapult. He remained in the shadows, biding his time. He would allow the forces of nature to help him defeat these four.

He used the moment to glance back at the pitched battle in front of the artillery line. It was evident that the hastily-trained auxiliaries were no match for the veteran gladiators' swordsmanship. But his fighters were heavily outnumbered, and there was still no sign of reinforcements from the vineyard. A loud grunt turned his attention back to the catapult team. The four men had just hefted another three-hundred-pound rock on to their shoulders. The time was right.

With the full force of the bull emblazoned on his massive chest, Taurus ran directly at the back of the man in the rear. He plowed into him, smashing the man's face against the jagged rock, splitting his forehead, and breaking his nose. The momentum sent the boulder teetering forward. The two men on the flanks fell sideways, and the massive stone dropped onto the leading artilleryman as he stumbled and fell. His scream was cut short as his spine and ribcage were pulverized. The twin blades in Taurus's hands began spinning. One slashed out and decapitated the rear carrier, the stunned expression still etched on the bloody face as the head landed on the road. Taurus stepped toward the first of the two remaining crewmen. Before the man could draw his sword, both arms were hacked to ribbons by the twin flashing gladii. The last man jumped up with his weapon ready. With a cry of anger, he charged. Taurus caught the artilleryman's gladius in the angle made by his two crossed swords and pressed the point toward the ground. As their two bodies came together, Taurus snapped his head forward. His forehead connected with the man's nose, sending another spray of blood into Taurus's face. The stunned crewman staggered backward, grabbing his flattened nose. Taurus sliced hard, severing the man's hand and slicing his throat open. Before the crewman hit the ground, Taurus was already hacking at the thick cord attached to the release mechanism of the giant catapult. With the third hard blow, the throwing arm of the machine sprang forward for the final time, the empty bowl throwing nothing but a whoosh of air.

The flailing ropes caught the attention of the neighboring crew. Taurus no longer had the covering fire of Lindani and his archers to clear out the artillerymen. From here on, he was on his own. He took a step, then paused, concerned about his outnumbered comrades still fighting to hold a protective barrier between him and the century of auxiliaries. He decided the war machines on the north side of the road could wait. But as he turned to join the battle, he saw two hundred gladiators charging from the woods. Amazonia looked back at him with a confident smile as the first of the reinforcements crashed into the battle. Her grin suddenly faded and she shouted: "Drop!"

Without hesitation, he dove for the paving stones and heard the thud of a javelin striking the wooden catapult behind him. He rolled forward and came up with both swords swinging. Another crewman hurled his pilum. Taurus made quick work of sidestepping the threat and knocking the javelin from the air with a swift slice as it passed. He sheathed one of his swords and retrieved the pilum from the road. His arm drew back as he ran toward the smaller catapult. A look of terror crossed the faces of both crewmen. His arm snapped forward with a speed that nearly matched the throwing arm of the catapult. The slender pyramidal spearhead pierced the belly of the closer soldier, then caught the forearm of the one behind as he attempted to jump aside. Both were pinned to the frame of their catapult.

"Lindani teach you that trick?" Amazonia said as she ran up to Taurus.

"You can't help but learn from the boy," Taurus replied. As he reached the moaning artillerymen, he put both out of their misery, then dispatched the last with a thrust hard enough to pierce one of the segmented bands of his body armor. The man fell at his feet.

Taurus looked at the body for a moment. He realized then that Taurus did not feel the same pangs of regret that Quintus had earlier in the battle. Knowing what still had to be done, the thought was both comforting and terrifying. Taurus would get this job done now, but Quintus's conscience would pay the price later.

Taurus looked up at Amazonia. "Let's finish this thing," he said in a hoarse whisper.

He drew his second sword, inhaled deeply, and closed his eyes for a moment. He recalled the *wushu* teachings of Master Sheng. He felt the *chi* flow. He willed the energy through his thick arms, into his hands, then into the twin blades. The swords became one with his arms. He visualized every artilleryman on the north side of the Via Postumia dead at his feet. He let the air escape from his lungs, and the silent breath built to an animal-like growl. He leaned forward and let the momentum carry him into a trot. The heavy breathing beside him told him Amazonia was with him step-for-step. Soon a growl came from her throat as well. He sensed that she was feeding on his energy, that somehow his *chi* had flowed through to her. The deep rumble in her voice was hypnotic, almost sensual. Their trot became a run. Their growls turned to a fierce war cry. Within moments, they reached the first of the artillerymen still firing their deadly missiles.

They took on the closest of the three-man crews, thrusting at necks, faces, arms, and legs—anywhere flesh was exposed. Their blades raged like a tempest. In seconds, the crew lay dead. Taurus and Amazonia moved from catapult to catapult, covering the thirty feet between them quickly. By the time each artillery crew spotted the assailants, it was too late. Severed limbs fell to the ground. Bodies dropped and guts spilled. One crew after another succumbed to the vicious onslaught. By the time they reached the last dozen ballistae, the two gladiators had developed a macabre rhythm to their killing. Taurus went for the head and neck, while Amazonia—perhaps in subconscious, sadistic revenge for her years as a whore—thrust upward into each groin. Both were drenched in blood from head to toe, presenting an even fiercer image to the few remaining artillerymen. By the time they reached the last ballista, the crew had dropped their ammunition and fled without a fight. The two warriors stood panting like dogs, covered in gore so thick they were barely recognizable.

"So that's what it's like to be 'Taurus,'" she said in a husky voice.

"You felt it, didn't you?"

She looked at him for a moment, her beautiful emerald eyes incongruous within her blood-spattered face. She nodded. "I'm glad I never had to face you in the arena. There's no defense against that."

"Let's finish off this artillery," he said. "Now we cut the sinew that creates the torsion. There'll be no repairing them then."

All the gladiators hacked at the skeins until the night air was filled with the pops and cracks of the tightly wound animal tendons ripping apart. The few Vitellian officers at the rear who came to investigate the noises and the sudden lack of artillery fire were cut down by Lindani's arrows.

With the carnage over for the moment, Taurus breathed deeply and allowed his calmer, more rational alter ego to emerge.

"How many did we lose?" Quintus asked.

"Five," Flama answered. "Not bad, considering the odds."

Quintus shook his head. "It's five too many . . . Back to the vineyard. The venatores can continue to pick off the officers from there. We'll lay low until morning."

Throughout the night, the battle raged. Arrows and slinging stones flew surreptitiously from the vineyard, dropping a centurion here and a tribune there. The eagle bearers, standard bearers, and cornicen trumpeters were also prime targets. Without them, communication on the battlefield was virtually impossible.

At one point, a sharp-eyed centurion noticed the arrows flying from the trellises of the dark vineyard. He took a patrol in to investigate, but the small unit was annihilated in minutes, ambushed by the well-hidden gladiators Quintus had placed throughout the field to protect the venatores.

Finally the eastern sky turned an indigo blue. The first rays of sun painted pink highlights on the undersides of the clouds, and within moments the bright disc broke the horizon. From the rise of the vineyard, Quintus wondered how such a beautiful event could unveil such a ghastly scene.

"That is a sight I would expect to see only in the bowels of Hades itself," Lindani said as he crouched beside Quintus and Amazonia.

"We've all seen hundreds die in the arena," Quintus said, never taking his eyes from the unholy vision at the bottom of the rise. "But I've never seen anything like that."

The length of the Via Postumia and its surrounding countryside—from the newly lit eastern horizon to as far as the smoke would permit vision to the west—was littered with tens of thousands of bodies. Even at a distance, the large pools of red staining the white road and its green borders were clearly visible. Hundreds of crows and vultures circled silently, drawn by the scent of blood, offal, defecation, and vomit rising from the nightmarish landscape. Large pockets of battle still persisted. Thousands of blood-soaked legionaries on both sides continued to wage war, while thousands more sat behind the lines recuperating, waiting for their rotation back to the front.

"Do you see Primus?" he asked Lindani, not sure what the Flavian general looked like.

The African scanned the battlefield. Quintus hoped beyond words the legate had survived the night. But before Lindani could answer, a sudden noise interrupted the search. Cheering rose from the rear ranks of the Flavian army. The joyous shouting grew until it overwhelmed the battlefield. Quintus strained his eyes to see why so many of the Flavians had suddenly turned to the east and started cheering.

"Are not many of Primus's men from Syria?" Lindani asked.

"Yes, mostly Syria and the Danube region," Quintus replied.

"Then that is the reason for the cheering. The Syrians have a tradition of honoring the sun each morning with a cheer."

Quintus looked from Lindani to Amazonia, who shrugged with a baffled expression. He turned back to the battlefield and was surprised to see most of the surviving Vitellians stop fighting. They craned their necks to look eastward down the road and called to each other with animated gestures, clearly concerned about the enemy's celebration.

A thought occurred to Quintus and a smile crossed his lips for the first time in days. "This is our chance to bring this thing to a halt right now," he said as he jumped up. "Follow me, but don't bunch together."

He took off running down the rise toward the road. "Reinforcements!" he hollered as he reached the first of the Vitellians. "We saw a column that stretches to the horizon! Don't you hear them cheering their arrival? Vespasian's Judean legions have arrived!"

With only a few centurions and even fewer tribunes left to control the panicking soldiers, the Vitellians turned and ran. Seeing the results of Quintus's ploy, the rest of his fighters followed suit, spreading the word "reinforcements" through the ranks. The tentative mood on the battlefield quickly grew to a full retreat, then a chaotic rout, as thousands of

Vitellian legionaries and auxiliaries ran for the safety of the palisaded fort at Cremona.

Quintus worked his way through the crush of bodies to the north side of the road. He ran into the farm field and signaled Memnon. His optio rose from behind a stack of recently harvested wheat and waved him forward. Memnon called "Cease fire!" to the well-placed archers and slingers around him. Quintus turned and gestured for his fighters from the vineyard to follow. Soon he stood with almost his entire cohort and supporting venatores once again.

"Now is the time to deliver ourselves to Primus," Quintus called to the troupe, "but we need to be careful or we could end up as the final casualties of this battle. Lindani, stick close to me. Primus knows *your* face, not mine."

"You assume the general is still alive," Lindani said quietly. "Let us hope it is so."

Quintus kept the troupe low in the field, out of the main action. Between the wisps of smoke from the burning trees, houses, and bodies, he watched the last fanatical Vitellians battle to the death.

Lindani scanned the road desperately for Primus. "There!" the hunter finally said. "Primus approaches."

A few seconds later, the sound of hooves clattered on the paving stones, and Primus rode through a swirl of smoke into a small clearing at the edge of the field. He was followed by an entourage of senior tribunes, aides, and Praetorian bodyguards.

Quintus removed the belt that held his gladius and pugio, then undid the leather ties on his body armor and let the cuirass drop into the field. "Now's our chance," he said quietly to the African. "Move slowly and hold your hands out so they see we're unarmed." Lindani slipped the quiver strap off his shoulder and laid his bow in the black dirt.

The two stepped out from behind the stack of wheat and walked slowly toward the road. An alert Praetorian shouted an alarm, and charged into the field, sword drawn. Five more guards were on his heels.

"The watchword is 'virtue,'" Quintus shouted before they reached them. "I seek Primus!"

"Leave them!" Primus called to his guards. His eyes darted from Lindani to Quintus. "I seek the bull," he said.

Quintus reached up and ripped open the front of his red tunic. He let the top fall to his waist, revealing the stigmate of the Minotaur across his barrel chest. Primus grinned, then let out a loud laugh.

"Minerva's holy tits! Castus told me 'the bull' would make sense, but I didn't expect a walking mural. Welcome, Quintus. And you, Lindani."

"Thank you, Legate," Quintus replied. He turned and signaled to Memnon. More than five hundred fighters rose in the field behind Quintus. "I am proud to deliver myself and my men to you. We are the best fighters on this field and are prepared to swear our allegiance to the true savior of Rome, Emperor Vespasian."

Quintus's heart raced knowing this war was almost over and he was another step closer to repaying a debt of honor he thought he'd never fulfill.

XXI

November AD 69

LUCIUS GALLOPED along the coastal road, with the blue waters of the Mare Internum on his left and the endless beige sand dunes of Egypt on his right. He tugged his head wrap free, welcoming the relief from the heat that the late afternoon brought. He scratched at the short stubble of his freshly cut hair. As his return to Rome grew closer, he thought it wise to disguise himself from the few officials who might remember the fiasco at his arena games two years earlier. Thanks to the violent encounter with the latrine bucket tossed by his old ludus dispensator, his wider, flatter nose helped in that respect. Julia felt the shorter hairstyle made a nice finishing touch.

The cloud of dust on the eastern horizon told him Vespasian's column was near. This time, Lucius knew he would be the first to deliver his news to the Judean governor. Over the past few months, he could not fathom the speed at which Vespasian often received information. Lucius only knew that the governor had established an efficient dispatch system with Castus and the mysterious spy within the ranks of the Vitellians. But out here, in the middle of the desert wasteland between Caesarea and Alexandria, Lucius was certain the governor had not yet gotten the latest word of his army's progress in Italia. And Lucius knew that the more fresh and useful information he was able to deliver now, the better his standing would be when the new political pecking order was established under Vespasian.

Within another few minutes, the column was plainly in sight.

Brilliant white flashes danced on the taupe dunes as the sun glinted off polished armor. Lucius was intercepted by a small party of mounted advance scouts, one of whom accompanied him directly to Vespasian. The governor rode a roan stallion at the head of the column alongside his son Titus. His senior officers followed close behind. Two hundred cavalry troopers, along with a dozen baggage and equipment carts, made up the bulk of the force.

"Welcome to Egypt, Governor. I bring good news from Alexandria!" Lucius said, buoyant with enthusiasm despite his four-hour journey.

"It *must* be good, Lucius, for you to ride out into the hot Egyptian frontier to tell me," Vespasian said with a calm smile. He tugged his horse to a stop, and the entire column ground to a halt.

"Primus has defeated the Vitellians at Cremona. He now marches on Rome."

Vespasian's smile turned to a laugh, and he reached across and smacked Lucius on the arm. "Excellent! I guess that *was* worth riding out here for."

"Congratulations, Father," Titus said. "Or should I say . . . 'Your Excellency'?" The three tribunes riding behind offered a stiff salute and a cheer of "Hail, Augustus Caesar!"

Vespasian shook his head and waved his hand to silence the officers. "It's a bit early for that, gentlemen. We'll continue on to Alexandria to reinforce the blockade as planned. The more desperate Vitellius becomes, the more money he'll offer to entice blockade runners." Vespasian kicked his stallion back into a slow walk. "Ride with me, Lucius, and tell me what you know."

Lucius spun his horse and kept pace with the governor. His position at the head of the powerful column of cavalry made his stomach flutter with excitement. "This news comes from one of my ships that arrived from Ostia this morning. The captain says the battle was ferocious, with heavy casualties on both sides." At this, Vespasian's lips tightened with tension. "Obviously, the numbers were worse for the Vitellians than for Primus."

"Did Caecina survive?" Vespasian asked. "He's a good man."

"Yes, sir. Primus released him as soon as he took the fort at Cremona. There was also a battle for the walled city, and that fell to us, too."

"Then the road to Rome is wide open," Titus offered, "especially once Mucianus reinforces Primus. Now we only have to rid ourselves of that asshole, Valens."

Lucius smiled. "I think not," he replied. He loved dragging news out and delivering it with dramatic effect. "Valens is dead, though he never made it to Cremona."

"Dead? How? Where?" Titus asked.

"Near Narni. It was one of the last Vitellian strongholds, until their legionaries and officers began defecting in droves. The last holdouts were waiting for Valens to relieve them. Instead, they got Valens's head delivered to them on a pike by our cavalry." Lucius let that image set in before he continued. "Rumors are rampant throughout Rome that, right now, your brother Sabinus, as Prefect of Rome, is negotiating a surrender with Vitellius."

Vespasian looked at his son with raised eyebrows and an optimistic smile. "Perhaps the end of this war is closer than we thought."

They rode westward until the sun was close to touching the distant dunes. They made camp and completed their journey to Alexandria the following day.

Julia leaned over the wall of her Alexandria balcony in anticipation of the procession. A bustling, enthusiastic crowd lined Canopic Street, the main boulevard that ran the entire length of the city. Although a full hundred feet wide, with a series of fountains aligned down the center, only the southern half of the street was passable due to the crush of well-wishers crowding the northern lane.

As the honor guard of cavalry riders entered the Gate of the Sun in the distance, Julia once again adjusted the purple, gold, and white fabric that adorned the balcony walls of Romanus Shipping and Transport. She leaned out farther and looked down to be sure the giant banner was in place. The words "Welcome Caesar" appeared upside down from her vantage point but were unobstructed by the bunting.

She looked out across the thousands of enthusiastic, cheering Alexandrians. As the breeze blew her long white palla, she couldn't help but feel like the graceful figurehead of an elegant ship afloat on a sea of smiling faces. The jubilant atmosphere reflected her own mood perfectly.

A thunderous roar echoed down the boulevard as Vespasian rode his stallion through the entrance portal. The crowd waved white handkerchiefs and streamers that shimmered in the harsh Egyptian sun. But their brilliance paled beside the polished armor of the soldiers who followed Vespasian. A detachment of the Third Cyrenaica Legion had joined Vespasian's cavalry troopers at Nicopolis, just east of Alexandria. The five cohorts—twenty-four hundred soldiers in all—now marched in perfect rank and file behind the horsemen. They had been the first legionaries to declare their allegiance to Vespasian, so the governor felt it appropriate to include them in his first show of force in the region.

Between Vespasian and the soldiers rode his son Titus and a number of aides, Lucius among them. Even at a distance, Julia could see the smug, content look on his face. She knew he was as anxious for this day as she had been. The pleasure of planning the Alexandria celebration had soothed his violent temper. That, combined with the launch of their new freighter near Antioch, had helped put him in a manageable frame of mind once again. She wondered how long it would last. How long before his next malicious outburst would put her vision of returning to Roman society at risk once again?

As much as that thought used to worry her, it was now tempered by a viable alternative. Her backup plan had developed better than she could have imagined. Castus's delirious, fever-driven rantings that night in Caesarea had revealed much. Of course, once he had recovered the following morning, there was no mention of his words to anyone, including Lucius. While she watched the procession slowly approach the Romanus shipping office, she thought back to the mission she had given her most trusted ship captain: find the whereabouts of the acclaimed gladiator Taurus. Thankfully, the people of Pompeii had been more than forthcoming with gripes about the lack of games since their best arena fighters had been marched off to war. The women were especially anxious to see Taurus fight once again. It was all the confirmation she had needed.

Her second strategy was quick to plan: Get to Quintus when they reached Rome; offer her nephew heartfelt congratulations, along with part ownership in the shipping empire; and help him find a good wife to settle down with—someone Julia could control, of course.

But these generous offers would be made only if the unpredictable Lucius forced her hand. So long as he kept a level head, remaining attached to him would be the easier, and less costly, route to an elevated status. Perhaps she would even still consider their marriage plans. But if his ill-timed fits of rage once again threatened her new lifestyle, the offers would be made to Quintus—along with one other: she would deliver Lucius to him. From there, Lucius's return to the African prison would be just a matter of time.

She smiled as the options danced through her head, her return to high society now assured. The growing cheers of the crowd brought her back to the moment at hand. Vespasian and Titus approached the balcony, with Lucius right behind them.

Lucius looked up at Julia and pulled his horse to a stop. She was radiant, appearing even more buoyant than she had been for the past few weeks. He wondered if it was Vespasian's success that had put her in such a good mood. Somehow, he sensed there was something else.

She waved to him, Vespasian, and Titus with a gleaming smile. They all returned the greeting and dismounted. Behind them, the five cohorts turned right and marched down the road leading to the Great Harbor. The crisp formations, the ranks of red shields, the thousands of javelins pointing skyward, and the pounding of their hobnails on the road all combined to exemplify the military might that had made the Roman army the most feared and respected force in the world. If there was any question as to who was in charge of commerce between Rome and Africa, this scene surely put it to rest. Until further notice, these men would live at and guard the largest harbor in North Africa. Julia had agreed to convert one of her sizeable dockside warehouses into barracks for the cohorts. She had even installed cooking pits and ovens, which would work as both kitchen facilities and heaters on cool nights.

"Welcome to Alexandria, Caesar!" she called down to Vespasian.

The riotous cheer that followed seemed to embarrass the governor. He waved again to the crowd, then mockingly shook his finger at Julia. She offered another smile and headed for the stairs.

Lucius knew she lived for just such an occasion. As a show of gratitude for their support, Vespasian had publicly acknowledged her and Lucius and allowed them to host his welcoming celebration. It was sure to be Alexandria's social event of the year.

Julia appeared in the doorway and welcomed the governor and his son graciously, then gave Lucius a quick kiss. They lingered on the portico with their guests and Tiberius Julius Alexander, the prefect of Egypt, allowing the throng to take in the scene.

After a few moments, Lucius caught Julia's eye and motioned toward the door. She ushered the guests upstairs and into a sprawling feast of food and entertainment. The aroma of roasting meats greeted them at the door of the vast apartment, which was elaborately decorated with more purple and gold bunting and garlands of flowers. The news from Cremona had spread quickly the previous day, and a long line of dignitaries jostled to be among the first to offer congratulations for what was sure to be Vespasian's final step to the Imperial Palace. The festivities went on for hours and included the most exotic foods, the best Egyptian performers and musicians, and the most beautiful dancers within a hundred miles of the Nile.

Lucius noticed that Titus managed to disappear with at least three of the dancers at different times throughout the evening. Vespasian, too, smiled each time he saw his son scurry from the banquet hall with another beauty but seemed too worn out from the long trip to be interested himself. Lucius watched the governor stifle a yawn and decided it was time to bring the festivities to a close. He stood up from his dining couch.

"Friends and guests, may I have your attention?" he said in a loud voice. The musicians quieted and the room settled to near silence. "I would like to propose a toast to our next emperor, Vespasian." As one, the assembly lifted their goblets of fine Egyptian wine. Lucius cleared his throat. "May Minerva grant him the wisdom to govern wisely; May Mars grant him the strength to conquer all enemies; And may Cupid grant his son Titus the endurance to bed yet another dancing wench."

The guests broke into laughter, none louder than Vespasian and a flushed Titus. The goblets were emptied and one last cheer of "Hail, Caesar!" rose from the crowd.

"Now I'm afraid we've kept our honored guests from their soft beds in the prefect's palace much too long," Lucius continued.

On Lucius's cue, the servants stood together hand-in-hand and opened a corridor through the tightly packed revelers. Lucius and Julia accompanied Vespasian and his son as they walked the path through the applauding and cheering crowd, a flood of good wishes pouring from both sides of the aisle. They waved from the doorway, then descended the marble stairs and walked through the offices to the front door. The Romanus coach waited in front of the portico. The inferno atop the Pharos lighthouse cast an undulating orange glow on the matched white horses and the buildings across the wide avenue.

"A beautiful feast and a joyous welcome to Alexandria," Vespasian said as he reached for the door of the coach. "I sincerely thank you both."

"Actually, Governor, we were hoping you would indulge us for just a few more moments," Julia said in a perky voice. "We'd like to show you something before you leave for the palace. It's just across the street."

Vespasian's curiosity overcame his sleepiness. "How can I refuse such gracious hosts? Lead the way."

The four crossed the deserted intersection and walked partway up the street leading to Lake Mareotis. "I think you'll enjoy this," Lucius said. "It might provide a bit of . . . inspiration."

They entered a walled garden and passed a number of mausoleums with the name "Ptolemy" emblazoned over the entrances. Lucius led them to an ornate building with a pyramidal roof and marble façade. The word above this entrance was different—*Soma.*

"It means 'the body' in Greek," Lucius explained. Titus spoke fluent Greek and nodded in agreement.

"The Tomb!" Vespasian said with excitement as he suddenly realized their location. "I told Titus I wanted to visit here during this trip."

"We've arranged entrance although the hour is late," Lucius said with a smile. He held out his arm, offering their guests the honor of entering first.

Two Roman sentries in the antechamber snapped to attention as Vespasian entered. He and Titus studied the exquisite works of art that adorned the walls of the small square room. Murals featured scenes from Macedonia, Babylon, Persia, and India. Marble reliefs focused on the battle of Gaugamela, the sack of Persepolis, and the siege of Tyre.

"Shall we?" Lucius said, standing beside an inner doorway that led to a long flight of steps.

They descended the staircase, the few torches along the walls barely throwing enough illumination for safe footing. From the bottom came a bright, warm glow of flickering light, although the temperature seemed to drop with each step down they took. The sweet scent of incense drifted halfway up the stairs to meet them. An anxious Vespasian was first to enter the burial chamber, followed closely by Titus.

An audible gasp came from both guests. Julia looked toward Lucius with a smile and a wink. "Quite a sight, isn't it?" she said.

Before them, on a low platform covered with fine Persian carpets, lay a large sarcophagus of translucent alabaster. The light from the torch on the wall behind the tomb silhouetted the body within. The four of them stepped forward and peered into the open top at the preserved body of Alexander the Great.

"Amazing," Vespasian whispered.

A moment passed as they all stared in reverent silence at the champion of Macedonia. Titus leaned forward and studied the gaunt face. The skin had a slight leathery appearance, but the features still clearly revealed the handsome visage of a thirty-two-year-old man. "The preservation is unbelievable," he said. "He's been dead, what? Close to four hundred years? Yet he looks like he was laid here a week ago."

"A fine example of the wonderful and mysterious embalming process of the Egyptians," Lucius replied.

Titus's brow wrinkled as he studied the face further. His hand rose slowly and his finger extended over the lip of the translucent coffin. "His nose is cracked."

Vespasian looked at his son for a moment, then shook his head. "Leave it to my pragmatic Titus to stand in the presence of the greatest military genius the world has ever known and point to a crack in his nose."

Lucius and Julia chuckled, the sound echoing in the stillness and adding a touch of life to the burial chamber.

"Actually," Julia said, "legend has it that Augustus Caesar himself caused that during a visit to this mausoleum. He'd placed a wreath on Alexander's head, and when he moved to kiss him, he accidentally knocked his nose off."

Vespasian looked at Julia. Lucius could see the governor's tight lips quiver. Unable to hold it in any longer, Vespasian began to snicker. The sound was contagious, and in seconds the four of them were howling with laughter. The two guards looked down the stairwell with stern expressions, making Lucius feel like a mischievous child who could not help laughing at a funeral. The thought made him laugh all the more.

After a moment, Julia wiped a tear from her eye. "I hope Alexander's spirit has a sense of humor. I'd hate to be haunted by his vengeful ghost for this."

"I don't think you need to worry about Alexander," Vespasian said, gazing again at the body in the sarcophagus. "I've studied him all my life. He was a good and honest man who treated his friends, and even his enemies, with respect. He shared his wealth and power, especially with those most loyal to him."

It was just the opportunity Lucius was waiting for. "A trait I'm sure you'll exhibit in your rise to the principate," he said pointedly.

Vespasian turned to Lucius. His look was friendly, but after a long moment Lucius began to feel uncomfortable. Perhaps he had overstepped his bounds once again. Vespasian seemed to be debating some issue in his mind. Finally he spoke.

"I'm not out to conquer the world as he did, just restore some civility to the Empire. But, you're right. That's not a job to be done alone." Lucius's heartbeat intensified. "Publicly, I've been discreet and unassuming about the prospect of leading the Empire. I didn't want to appear overconfident in this campaign. But privately, Titus and I have been assembling a list of staff positions." Vespasian smiled at him. "I believe I saw your name on the list beside the title of 'Praefectus Annonae.'" Lucius's heart raced. The praefectus annonae managed the food and grain commerce of Rome, in particular the grain supplies from Egypt and North Africa. It was one of the highest offices attainable by a Roman citizen. Thankfully, thought Lucius, Vespasian did not know his true background. As an ex-slave, Lucius was not even a citizen, let alone eligible for such a position of power.

"I . . . I don't know what to say," Lucius muttered, the shock still coursing through his body. The reward was so much more than he had hoped for. He glanced at Julia and saw her beaming face.

"It's settled then," Vespasian said, slapping Lucius on the back. "We'll discuss your earnings when we get to Rome, but I'm sure you'll be more than pleased." He threw a beefy arm over the shoulders of both Lucius and Julia. "It's the least I can do for two people who have provided us with so much help and information. You have proven your loyalty time and again." He glanced back at the body of Alexander the Great. "Like that man there, I reward allegiance."

He stepped back and turned toward the stairs. Lucius saw Julia's eyes pool with tears and knew the same images were flowing through her mind as his: a beautiful house in Rome, social gatherings, political contacts at the highest levels, and an imperial position with power and influence. Their dream had returned with a vengeance, and they were starting with a clean slate.

"Thank you, Caesar," Julia said, wiping the tears from her cheeks.

Vespasian held up his hand. "No, Julia. Like I told my men, that title will have to wait until this campaign is over. We still have to win Rome itself."

XXII

December AD 69

I TOO GROW WEARY waiting for Mucianus," General Primus said disgustedly. "When we reached the Alps four months ago, I was told to wait for him. If we had, we would have lost at Cremona." The thirty-two military officers assembled in the command tent grunted in agreement. Primus raised the scroll of papyrus he held in his hand. "But those are my orders from Vespasian."

"But Vespasian is not here," argued the senior tribune from Seventh Galbiana. "He's not aware that his own brother and his youngest son are trapped on the Capitoline Hill. Would he wish us to just stand by on the outskirts of Rome while his family is threatened?"

Quintus watched the debate from his bench near the rear of the tent. Even at a distance, he could see the frustration building in Primus's face. The general tossed the dispatch scroll onto the map of Rome that had been unfurled atop the broad table at the head of the tent. "What do you wish me to do?" he yelled. "Disobey orders again? Even though we won Cremona, I still got my ass chewed for not waiting for Mucianus." Primus paused and took a deep breath. "Look, Vespasian is just trying to put numbers on his side. If we're going to attack Rome—and it looks like Vitellius is leaving us no choice—then Vespasian wants the odds stacked heavily in our favor. Mucianus left weeks after we did and he had a longer march. He's doing his best to catch up. For now, I think it's best we wait."

The decision caused a murmur to grow in the tent. The aggressive tribune stood again. "But what about—" He was cut short by Primus's upraised hand as an aide arrived and pulled the general away for a private consultation.

Quintus leaned toward the centurion seated next to him. "Why are Vespasian's brother and son trapped on the Capitol?" he whispered.

"I heard that his brother, Sabinus, was trying to convince Vitellius to abdicate. Vitellius finally agreed, but his Praetorians and a mob of fanatics wouldn't accept the resignation. They chased Sabinus out of the area, and he took sanctuary in the Temple of Jupiter. Sabinus is Domitian's uncle and guardian. The kid just happened to be in the wrong place at the wrong time."

"Gentlemen . . ." Primus called loudly, gaining the attention of the mumbling officers. Quintus saw greater strain on the leader's face. ". . . I have bad news. The Temple of Jupiter has been burned to the ground. Sabinus is dead and Domitian is missing." An immediate outcry vibrated the leather walls of the tent. The senior tribune was back on his feet, yelling for vengeance and gaining more supporters by the second.

"Silence!" shouted Primus in a booming voice that cut cleanly through the din. The uproar stilled, but tension remained thick in the air. "In light of these developments, we will make plans to take Rome immediately." A cheer burst from the room that reminded Quintus of the arena when a final thrust was made. Primus removed the papyrus scroll from the map, and the senior officers gathered around the table. Quintus and the other chief centurions moved forward and stepped up on the front benches to get a better view over their commanders' shoulders.

"We outnumber the Vitellians, but they're animals backed into a corner," Primus began. "Vitellius's Praetorians will fight like wild men, not only for him but for their own positions. They know if they lose, it's back to the Germanian frontier with them."

"Our own Praetorians want their jobs back," said the prefect of the original Guard who had been displaced by Vitellius. "Believe me, General, my men will most assuredly fight harder."

Primus nodded. The officers spent the next few hours discussing the details of their strategy. Quintus's attention drifted between the battle plans and a plan that was formulating in his own head. If he could make it work, it would be an action that would allow him to express the true depth of his gratitude to Vespasian.

By the end of the meeting, each officer knew his role in what was termed the "liberation" of their capital city. But Quintus had not had an opportunity to propose his plan.

"I want Vitellius taken alive," Primus said to end the council. "After what happened today, I'm sure Vespasian will want to deal with him personally. Plus, the citizens of Rome need to see the man punished."

"You know there's a good chance he'll take his own life before we ever get near him," said the Praetorian prefect, "which is a shame, since I'd give my left ball to dish out that punishment myself." A murmur of agreement rose among the officers.

Quintus saw his chance. "My gladiators can help." Every eye in the command tent turned toward him.

"How's that?" Primus asked.

"As you know from Cremona, sir, my men work well in secret operations. I'd like permission to take a small group of them in to find Vespasian's missing son. I think I know a way we can get to both him and Vitellius while your legions storm the city gates."

Primus motioned toward the map of Rome. "We're all ears, Centurion."

Quintus stepped from the bench and approached the table. "It will involve going underground . . . literally."

Quintus sat in the brush along the banks of the Tiber River waiting to give the signal to move. The force of fifty handpicked gladiators and venatores beside him were barely visible in the predawn darkness. The only sounds were an occasional cicada chirp and the gentle lapping of the water against the hulls of ten small boats held in place before them.

"The sun will rise soon," he whispered to Lindani, seated next to him.

"We'll be vulnerable to their archers." Lindani nodded but kept silent.

A twig snapped behind them, and Quintus glanced over his shoulder. "What are we waiting for?" came a female voice.

"We're to wait until we hear the splashing of the cavalry crossing upstream. That'll be the start of the offensive in the north. The Seventh Legion will attack the Milvian Bridge as the cavalry circles behind the Vitellians on the far bank. While that's going on, we head downriver."

"Well, they'd better get a move on before that sun rises," Amazonia said.

"I was just saying the same—"

"Listen," Lindani interrupted. The sound of splashing drifted down the river from the shallow ford around the bend. "I think it is time to go," the African said quietly.

Quintus gave the signal and the fighters boarded the rowboats, five to a boat, and shoved off the bank. Their weapons, helmets, and shields shared the cramped decks with the pitch-soaked torches they would soon need. Quintus kept a sharp eye on the city to their left, while Amazonia and Memnon rowed silently southward. Lindani sat near the stern, as did an archer in each boat, with an arrow nocked on his bowstring. Quintus spotted an occasional guard at the watchtowers, vaguely outlined against the hint of blue in the eastern sky. With no moon to reflect on the river, the boats were virtually invisible as they floated on the dark waters.

The northern point of Tiber Island soon came into view. In the lead boat, Quintus led his team through the western channel and under the deserted Cestius Bridge. He scanned the windows of the insulae apartments on the island to be sure no early riser spotted their procession. Luckily, all the windows were shuttered tight. He knew the prospect of killing a civilian in his own home was not the way Lindani would want to start this mission. They passed out of the channel beside the long narrow island, and the larger buildings of the city appeared on their left.

"We're close," Quintus whispered. "Hug the bank so we don't pass it."

The ten boats pulled to port and slipped under the first span of the

Aemilian Bridge. Quintus scanned the shoreline, now just a few feet to their left. A gaping black hole, outlined with brick and half submerged in the murky water, soon came into view.

"There . . ." Quintus pointed. "The entrance to the Cloaca Maxima."

Amazonia and Memnon glanced over their shoulders and carefully guided the prow of the rowboat into the opening. The ten-foot-wide sewer swallowed each boat in quick succession. Once inside, the oars were pulled in. The stench of human waste and decomposing organic matter assaulted their noses. A gentle twittering noise echoed off the stone walls, backed by the constant dripping of water.

"If you breathe through your mouth it's not as bad," Quintus said as he reached for a torch.

Amazonia stood and began to pole the boat down the dark passageway, pushing against the stone bottom with her oar. Her auburn hair, which had grown back to near shoulder length, came close to the ceiling of the tunnel. A sudden fluttering by her ear startled her.

Quintus used a flint to spark a flame on his torch. The flickering light revealed a ceiling covered with bats. The flood of illumination startled the creatures and, as one, hundreds dropped from the low ceiling and took flight. Amazonia let out a muted squeal and ducked as the bats flashed past her. In a few seconds, there was only the dripping water to be heard. Quintus looked at her with an amused smile.

"What? I don't like bats and I don't like rats, alright?" she said in an annoyed tone.

"Amazing." Lindani snickered, seated at her feet. "You will look down the throat of a lion in the arena without a second thought, but a bat frightens you."

Amazonia shrugged and resumed poling. "The lion frightened me, too. I just had more to lose then." She winked at Quintus with a quick smile.

He returned the smile, then turned and held out his torch to look down the long tunnel. The travertine blocks that made up the walls and barrel vaulted roof disappeared into a black abyss beyond the reach of the flame. Behind them, the small flotilla of rowboats was bathed in pools of torchlight. The boats crept slowly past the endless gray stones that had been stained green with algae. Occasional side tunnels split off to the right and left, the torches revealing only a few feet of their length.

"How do you know where you're going in this labyrinth?" Amazonia asked, her last few words repeating in an eerie echo.

"We just stick to the main corridor," Quintus replied. "I came down here once when I was a child. I found an open gate and went exploring. The workers who were doing repairs gave me a good scare, and that was the last time I ventured down here. But I know where the access stairs come out. It's right at the Forum."

"Just so long as you know where we're going," Amazonia said as she watched a long black water snake slither past the boat. "I'd hate to get lost down here."

The farther beneath the city they went, the more strange noises swirled around them. Echoed voices drifted from side tunnels that led to rain gutters or sewer gratings at ground level. At first the tone of the voices seemed calm and unaffected, but after a while, shouts of alarm could be heard. A woman's scream startled them all, then children crying. The rumble of running feet echoed like thunder in a summer storm.

"The battle has begun," Quintus said.

It took another half hour on the underground river to get to the Forum area. Quintus knew they were in the vicinity by the glow that shone from some of the side tunnels. The cones of sunlight had an ethereal look as they lit the musty air in perfectly aligned rows of ten to forty shafts.

"What a beautiful sight in such an ugly place," Amazonia said as they passed the first of the strange spectacles.

"I wouldn't go under there," Quintus said with a laugh. "Those are the public latrines at the shops near the Forum." As if on cue, one of the rays darkened and a stream of urine splashed into the water.

Amazonia wrinkled her nose. "Damn. That ruined it pretty quick."

"I think we're coming up to the steps at the Forum," Quintus said.

A small platform appeared out of the darkness along the left wall. Off the back of the landing, a narrow walkway led to steps that were dimly lit by filtered sunlight. Quintus pulled their boat against the landing and the first five fighters gathered their helmets and weapons and climbed out.

"Help unload the rest," Quintus said to Memnon and Amazonia. "Lindani, come with me and we'll check the gate. Hopefully, it won't be locked."

He led the African up the stairs toward the daylight. As they made the last turn in the stairwell, the sudden blast of early morning sunlight hurt Quintus's eyes. He let his sight adjust for a few seconds, then crept toward the gate. He gazed past the rusted bars into a deserted alley between the Basilica Julia—one of two courthouses on the Forum—and the Temple of Castor and Pollux. The voice of a centurion shouting orders and the unmistakable crunch of legionary hobnailed boots drifted down the alley. Quintus pushed on the gate, but it remained firmly shut.

"It's locked," he whispered. He reached through the bars and felt the keyhole in the iron lock. "Let me have one of your arrows," he said to Lindani. He fed the shaft between the bars and used the barbed tip to try to pick open the lock. A few clicks gave him hope he had succeeded, but the door refused to budge.

"Our mission is over before it has begun, eh?" Lindani asked.

Quintus looked at his friend with a deliberately pained expression. "After all these years, do you still have no faith in me?"

Lindani's stark white teeth reflected the morning sun as he smiled. "Of course. I just enjoy taunting the great Taurus."

Quintus grinned. "And it is exactly the great Taurus who will get us out of this stinking sewer. The gate will just have to come down the hard way." With that, he stood back from the opening and closed his eyes. His hands moved slowly before him as he summoned his *chi* and channeled the inner energy to his legs. Deep breaths filled his lungs with fresh air. His legs tingled. Then he visualized a broken gate. With a growl, his right leg kicked up, and the studded sole of his caliga smacked hard

against the rusted bars. Dust fell from the stones around the entranceway. A second kick sent the gate swinging outward, and it smacked hard
against the outside stone wall.

"After you," Taurus said with a crooked smile. "Rome awaits."

"So . . . Taurus the Bull *does* make an appearance today," Lindani said
with a satisfied nod. He stepped through the portal, and they both inched
their way from one column to the next under the arches at the southern
side of the basilica.

They heard a voice in the Forum. "Do we have men down there? I
heard a crash."

"Check it out," yelled another. "Then I want you at the Flamina gate."

"Damn, I thought they'd gone," Taurus whispered. "Get back to the
stairs." They turned and scuttled back down the alley.

"Halt!" the voice demanded.

Taurus's mind raced. He spun and saw a young optio headed toward
him, followed by at least a dozen legionaries.

"I heard a noise, Optio," Taurus said with authority, hoping his centurion uniform would intimidate the junior officer. "I took an archer and
came to investigate."

The optio eyed him suspiciously. "I need the watchword, Centurion."

Taurus didn't have a clue what the Vitellian watchword of the day was.
His stall gave the optio reason to study Lindani.

"And which of our legions has African auxiliaries?"

Taurus's trained eye could see the man's arm muscles tighten as he prepared to attack. He'd seen it thousands of times in the arena and ludus.

"The watchword is . . . *gladius.*" In a blur, Taurus's sword thrust forward, pierced the man's mouth, and exited the back of his head. The
soldiers stared as the body of their officer dropped in front of them. Their
split-second hesitation was time enough for Lindani to raise his bow and
fire. The arrow embedded in the forehead of the closest soldier. Lindani
and Taurus dove back through the sewer entrance. They were chased
down the narrow stairs by a file of enraged legionaries.

"Clear the stairs!" Taurus shouted as he neared the bottom. "Take them on the landing."

He and Lindani burst out of the tight stairway with a burly legionary at their heels. Amazonia used the pommel of her sword to connect with the man's chin as he charged through the portal. The blow shattered his jawbone and most of his teeth. She kicked him over the line of boats and into the river of sewer water. Two gladiators who had yet to unload from their rowboats dove on top of him, swords bared.

Taurus spun and took on the next soldier through the portal. Although the man was an experienced fighter, the veteran gladiator made quick work of him. The legionaries continued to stream into the sewer. The crush of bodies quickly overflowed the small platform and spilled into the underground river. The gladiators, who had been in the midst of disembarking, waged battle from their rocking boats. Taurus and Amazonia did their best to protect the vulnerable men, but two were knocked overboard with serious gashes in arms and legs. The gladiators and venatores in the rear boats jumped into the sewage and waded forward, pushing their way through the foul waist-deep water. The clash of swords and shields amplified tenfold off the bare stone walls. The fighting space became so cramped, Lindani and the other archers could offer little support.

Taurus saw two more soldiers come through the door. They faced Amazonia's back as she battled one of the larger Vitellians who had knocked a gladiator from his boat. As they drew back to strike, Taurus launched himself into the breach. With a mighty parry, he sent both thrusts toward the floor. The soldiers recovered quickly and engaged the new threat. Taurus's gladius fanned from one combatant to the other. He never yielded an inch of platform space.

Beside him, Amazonia landed a kick to her opponent's husky chest. The man staggered backward and lost his footing at the edge of the landing. He fell with a thump on the bow of an empty rowboat then toppled into the water.

At the same time, one of Taurus's opponents dove sideways to attempt a flanking strike against his sizeable adversary. The quick move inadvertently bumped Amazonia hard in the back. She tumbled forward into the water atop the burly legionary, striking her head on the brow ridge of his helmet.

Taurus saw her dazed look from the corner of his eye. His heart raced and blood pumped. He needed to get to her. With a yell, the speed of his gladius increased and he surged forward. He caught one of the soldiers on his sword arm, inflicting a gash deep enough to cut tendons. On his next strike, the man's weapon flew from his hand. Taurus kicked hard against the soldier's shield and sent him careening into the second legionary. Both staggered back and fell half on the landing and half into an empty rowboat. In two steps, Taurus loomed over them, delivering fatal thrusts into their groins.

He turned toward the splashing in the fetid water beyond the boats. Amazonia's head broke the surface but was quickly pulled under again by a bloody arm, its fingers entangled in her wet hair. Taurus dropped his shield and shoved his way through the thinning mass on the platform. As he had in the Pompeii arena when he challenged a raging crocodile, he spun his gladius so he could wield it as a large dagger and dove into the water.

The soldier's helmet splashed up in front of him. Taurus grabbed the brow ridge and yanked backward. The force was enough to pull the large man off Amazonia. Taurus was about to drive the point of his gladius into the man's exposed throat when the chin strap snapped and the helmet pulled free in his hand. The soldier again dove at Amazonia, who was coughing up vile brown liquid. In a rage, Taurus raised the helmet high and threw it with all his might. The iron bowl connected with the back of the legionary's head and split open his skull. A spray of blood and brain matter splattered into Amazonia's face. The man dropped face-first into the sewer stream and drifted away on the gentle current.

Taurus waded forward and took Amazonia by the arm. "You alright?" he asked.

"Fuck!" she yelled, then ejected a copious wad of brown spit. "This shit tastes worse than it smells."

"I've had the pleasure myself," Taurus said, wiping the dark liquid from around his mouth.

One final struggle persisted in the water downstream from Taurus. Lindani took careful aim in the dim torchlight and placed an arrow into the Vitellian's arm, forcing him to drop his sword. Two gladiators finished the man in seconds.

The soaked and reeking gladiators made their way back to the landing. Amazonia sliced at a rat that swam toward her as she waded.

"I think I would have rather stormed the city walls," she said, then wrung a puddle of foul water from her sticky hair and tenderly touched the welt growing on her forehead.

"I'm starting to think the same thing," Taurus replied as he hoisted himself up onto the platform. He stood silent for a moment, feeling his pulse slacken and his muscles relax. He let Taurus slip away, back to his inner chamber, until his Herculean speed and killer instincts would be needed again.

Lindani covered his nose and mouth. "We can keep to the shadows of the Forum, but that will not hide the stench."

"It'll just make them fear us all the more," Quintus replied. "Those with wounds too bad to continue, take a boat and return to the far side of the Tiber. The rest follow me." He snatched up his shield and led the way back up the stairs.

He went alone down the alley and peered into the Forum from behind the wide corner column of the basilica. He could not remember ever seeing the public square so empty. A few citizens and house slaves scurried through the morning shadows. To his right, the white marble stairs of the Temple of Castor and Pollux were deserted. Just beyond them, the passageway under the Arch of Augustus spanning the south entrance of the Forum also appeared desolate. In the distance, an occasional unit of Praetorians could be seen on a quick march from the Palatine Hill.

Good, Quintus thought, that meant fewer guards at the palace on top of the hill.

He glanced to the left, in the direction of their first mission. Toward the north, the full length of the Forum was visible. Quintus noticed details usually invisible in the mass of bodies that normally filled the plaza. The square flagstones formed a perfect geometric pattern of lines that converged at the base of the Temple of Concord on the north border. The raised platform for public speaking, known proudly to Romans as the Rostra, sat silent. The line of ships' prows that ringed the edge of the platform—captured trophies from momentous Roman sea battles—looked strangely abandoned in the unnatural stillness.

But the image that took Quintus's breath away sat beyond the Forum, at the summit of the Capitoline Hill. The Temple of Jupiter, the most important house of worship in Rome, built to honor the Optimus Maximus of all the gods, lay in smoldering ruins. The morning breeze brought the smell of the embers down into the Forum. Gargantuan columns held up only an ornate frieze. Missing was the beautiful pediment and gabled roof that had once borne so many golden statues. Although not an overly religious man, the scene of desecration sickened Quintus and fortified his resolve to deliver Vitellius to Legate Primus before the day was done.

He turned and waved his troupe forward. Two-by-two, forty-six fighters filed into the alley and ran toward the corner. "We need to get to the Gemonian Steps," Quintus said, pointing to a long staircase that ran up the Capitoline beside the Temple of Concord. "The last place Domitian was seen alive was in those ruins at the top. There's a good chance the Praetorians who were after Sabinus weren't even aware Domitian was with him. He might still be hiding in the rubble there."

Quintus glanced right and, through the Arch of Augustus, saw another Praetorian Guard unit on the march. "Let's stick to the basilica," he said and climbed the three steps to the open arcade that acted as a gallery for the legal proceedings. They trotted down the spacious passageway under a vaulted ceiling adorned with square patterns of red and blue. To their left sat the vacant nave of the basilica. On a normal day—when the city was not under assault—the vast hall would be filled with hundreds of jurists, praetors, and advocates pleading their cases. But on this morning, it acted only as an echo chamber for the cadence of the fighters' footsteps.

Quintus stopped at the north end of the colonnade and surveyed the surrounding streets and alleys. Even the few private citizens had gone. He waved his team onward, and they crossed the Vicus Iugarius and approached the Temple of Concord. At the foot of the Gemonian Steps lay a white toga in a crumpled heap. The purple bands along its edge signified a position of prominence. A streak of crimson leading down the stairs to the toga told him the bundle was more than just discarded apparel. It was a body, bloated and decaying in the street. The head had been cut clean from the torso. There was no question in Quintus's mind whose body lay before him. It was Vespasian's brother, Flavius Sabinus. The indignity of the act was well known in Rome. The hurling of the deceased's headless body down the Gemonian Steps was the greatest insult that could befall a man of public office who was deemed an enemy of the State.

He lifted the body and placed it in a more honorable position before the Temple of Concord, pausing to say a quick prayer for the man he never knew. He then charged up the long flight of steps with his fighters in tow. As he climbed, he continued to glance over both shoulders, scanning the Forum for any sign of a challenge. There was none.

The stairs bored through an arched opening in the low castellated wall surrounding the summit of the hill. Quintus reached the top and crouched on the step to catch his breath and survey the temple plaza. Flames continued to devour the thick wooden ceiling beams that had collapsed into the temple. White marble Corinthian columns were now streaked black with soot and the massive golden doors, severely warped by the heat, were stuck open. Giant statues of Jupiter, Juno, and Minerva, seated majestically upon towering thrones, graced the center of the temple, but their gold and ivory embellishments were now covered in gray and black ash. A burning beam still lay across the lap and arm of Juno, the heat from the flames disfiguring her delicate face and melting her golden crown. Surprisingly, there was no sign of activity in the ruins, not even an opportunistic vagabond from the nearby insulae scouring for remnants of value. Such was the mystique and sanctity of the temple.

Quintus turned and spoke to his team crouched in a line on the steps behind him. "Venatores, form a protective ring along the walls and keep a sharp eye. I want half the gladiators with me searching the left side of the temple. The rest take the right side."

The troupe moved quickly through the arched gate and into their assigned positions. Quintus led his group across the courtyard where the bulls and other offerings were sacrificed by the high priests, then up the ten steps to the temple's main floor. Cinders rained down on their helmets. Within minutes, the red crest of Quintus's centurion plume turned gray with ash. Thankfully, the comfortable, homey smell of the charred wood masked the lingering odor of the sewer.

Quintus and Amazonia entered through the far left door. Mounds of statues and other relics were piled near each door. "It looks like they used these to barricade themselves in," Quintus said. They stepped carefully through the scattering of burnt human remains on the stone floor along the left wall.

"Any of these could be Domitian," Amazonia said.

"That's true," Quintus replied as he walked, "but if there's any chance he survived, let's do our best to find him."

"I don't see how anyone could have survived this," Amazonia said. "I wonder how Sabinus ended up outside, although his fate was no better out there."

"The mob or the Praetorians probably caught him and dragged him out before the fire got too bad," Quintus theorized. "Either that, or he tried to run and was caught somewhere else."

"You think he would have run with Domitian still trapped in here?"

Quintus stopped searching for a moment. "That's a good point." He stood still and scanned the debris-covered floor closely. "If I wanted to protect my nephew from both the fire and the mob, I'd look to hide him someplace, then do what I could to draw attention away from that place." He stepped forward slowly and called out to all his fighters in the temple. "Check for any hidden doors or cellar entrances."

Within a few minutes a voice came from the far side of the building. "I think I've found a cellar."

Quintus and Amazonia hurried across the temple, winding through the burning beams and passing directly in front of the three seated statues. In the northeast corner, Quintus saw an iron door set flat into the stone floor. A dozen men struggled with two charred beams that lay across it. With their hands, arms, and legs covered in black, they finally managed to expose the full entryway. Quintus and two others lifted the edge of the door. The hinges creaked loudly until the iron panel fell with a crash onto the charred flagstones. The angle of the morning sun was still too oblique to light the hole. The first two steps were visible, but without torches, the rest of the cellar remained hidden.

"Anyone down there?" Quintus called. His own words echoing back from the darkness was the only response. He paused a second. "Domitian, are you there? We're not here to hurt you. We're fighting for your father." He thought he heard a noise. "Come on out, son. We'll keep you safe. The Vitellians' hours are numbered."

There was movement in the cellar, and a moment later a teenaged boy appeared in the opening, his face streaked with black soot and his eyes squinting in the light. He climbed the steps, followed by a middle-aged servant.

"I am Titus Flavius Domitianus, son of Flavius Vespasianus," the teenager said in a firm, proud voice. "Who are you?"

"I'm Quintus Honorius Romanus, a gladiator fighting as a centurion in your father's army. We're here to get you out."

"My father sent a *gladiator* to rescue me?" the boy replied with a hint of both repugnance and suspicion.

Quintus glanced at Amazonia, then back at Domitian. "Your father doesn't know you and Sabinus were trapped up here. Our legions have not yet taken Rome, but we came in through the sewers to find you and get you to safety."

"That explains the stench," the boy said, wrinkling his nose.

"Look," Amazonia replied in a testy voice, "we just risked our fucking lives to get you out of here. If you don't like the way we look or smell, we'll be happy to stick you back in that hole and be done with it."

"I'm very sorry, madam" the older man interrupted. "Our nerves are quite shattered. We didn't expect the door to get blocked. We should have been out of here last night."

"It's alright," Quintus said. "But now we have to work on getting you out of Rome without the Vitellians catching on to who you are."

"We're not going out through the sewer, are we?" Domitian asked, his tone more pleading than brazen.

"That's a strong possibility," Quintus replied, "unless you have a better idea."

The slave spoke up again. "I do, but I will need time to arrange it."

"How much time?" Amazonia asked.

"Give me until midday," he said. "If you remain hidden, you should be fine. Very few people know Master Domitian came up here."

Quintus thought for a minute, then spoke to Domitian. "I don't like it. If Vitellius gets word you're here, there could be trouble. You'd make an excellent hostage and bargaining token to help him save his own skin."

"Yes," said the slave, "Master Sabinus knew this. There's a plan in place to get Master Domitian free of the city. But I must make contact with those who will help him."

Quintus rubbed his chin and took a deep breath. "I'll give you until midday. If you're not back when the shadows reach their shortest measure, we're going out *our* way."

"Thank you, Centurion. I will not fail Master Domitian."

Quintus walked with the slave toward a rear entrance in the wall. He called instructions to the venatores to let the man go and to watch for his return. The slave disappeared through the portal and down the narrow street that ran along the back of the Capitoline Hill.

Quintus directed Memnon to distribute more men along the walls at the best vantage points to watch for signs of an assault on the hill. Quintus, Amazonia, and five other gladiators remained inside the temple with Domitian. As soon as Quintus sat, Domitian asked the question Quintus was dreading: "Where's my uncle?"

Quintus hesitated, then looked at Amazonia before he responded. "Sabinus is—"

"He's dead, isn't he?" Domitian interrupted.

"Yes."

"I figured as much." His response did not hint of any sorrow whatsoever. In fact, Quintus thought, the teenager seemed more upset that his rescue team had not been led by a senior tribune, or possibly Legate Primus himself, than he did about his uncle being murdered.

The boy remained quiet while they waited. Quintus guessed his age at about seventeen or eighteen, the same age he was when he first stepped into an arena. But by the kid's behavior, he figured Domitian was about as far from adventurous as one could get. It was also clear his ungrateful attitude continued to eat at Amazonia. The glances she threw the boy while she tapped her blade on the stone floor could have rekindled the temple fire.

"I don't like this," Amazonia finally said after an hour of waiting. "This is taking too long. If we're attacked, we could become trapped up here just like they were." She looked toward the front temple entrance where the noises of battle continued to grow louder. "The battle for Rome is raging, and we're sitting here babysitting." Domitian continued to stare at the floor, ignoring her and the rest of the gladiators.

"The slave asked us to give him until midday," Quintus replied. "It's just a bit longer."

"How do we know we can trust this slave?" Amazonia fired back.

"He's been in my uncle's household since he was a boy," Domitian said without looking up. "You can trust him." He finally looked at Amazonia with obstinate eyes. "Besides, I'm *not* going out through a sewer."

Quintus was about to grab Amazonia's arm to diffuse the situation, when a shout came from the rear entrance of the temple. The slave had returned. A moment later the servant walked through the portal holding two long, white linen robes with hoods trimmed in gold bands.

"A disguise?" Quintus asked.

"The best kind of disguise," the servant panted, still out of breath from his run up the hill. "In a few moments, the priests of Isis will walk in procession through the Forum, across the Aurelia Bridge, and out of Rome before the battle gets any closer to the city center. The two of us will join them. The priests will not be stopped or challenged by any of the guards."

Quintus thought for a moment. "What do you think?" he asked Amazonia.

"Seems fine to me."

He wondered if she just wanted to rid herself of the obnoxious teen. On the other hand, the plan *would* free up more of his men to get on with their search for Vitellius, rather than accompany the kid back through the sewer system.

"Maybe we should send two of our men with them," Quintus said. "Are there any more robes?"

"No, there is no time," the slave said, becoming flustered. "We must hurry. The priests of Isis will be passing very soon."

"Alright," Quintus finally said, "go ahead." He wasn't happy letting the boy out of his sight before delivering him to Legate Primus, but if Sabinus had arranged this escape, he was fairly confident the passage would be safe.

The slave helped Domitian into the robe, then pulled the hood low over the boy's face. The servant donned his own robe, and the two headed toward the rear portal in the Capitol wall. Quintus and his six fighters moved to accompany them down to the lower roadway.

"It's probably best we do this alone, Centurion," the slave said.

Quintus hesitated, then nodded. "May Hercules be with you."

Domitian turned before he walked through the portal. "I prefer Jupiter over the patron of gladiators," he said, then added: "But thank you, Quintus, for saving our lives."

Before Quintus could respond, Domitian turned and headed down the hill with his servant close at his heels. Quintus and Amazonia climbed the stairs to the walkway along the top of the wall.

"It would be a real shame if he got captured and killed," Amazonia said, the sarcasm dripping from her voice.

Quintus laughed. "He *was* a bit of a pompous ass, wasn't he? But let's remember, he is our future emperor's son, like it or not."

"It's scary to think that he might be emperor himself someday," Amazonia said.

Quintus looked at her. "By the gods, I never thought of that! Let's hope he remembers the day we saved his life."

Near the bottom of the hill, the two figures disappeared into a small clump of bushes at the side of the road. After a few minutes, the line of priests dressed in identical linen robes appeared along the Via Lata, the street bordering the eastern Capitoline. Quintus watched the two figures slip into line behind the priests and walk slowly toward the Forum. As they passed the decapitated body lying in front of the Temple of Concord, one of the two men paused for a brief moment. From a distance, Quintus could not tell which one it was, but he would wager a hefty sum it was the dead man's slave and not his obnoxious nephew. The procession turned toward the Tiber River and disappeared from view.

Quintus looked down the row of fighters that crouched beside him along the top of the wall. "Now Vitellius," he said with a grin.

XXIII

December AD 69

THE SOUNDS of the battle grew louder as the team of gladiators moved through the temple courtyard to the main gate and down the Gemonian Steps. As always, Quintus led the way, with Memnon, as company optio, in the rear position. Their new objective was the Imperial Palace atop the Palatine Hill, which rose at the opposite end of the Forum.

In small groups they dashed back across the street to the relative safety of the Basilica Julia. Quintus surveyed the area from his earlier vantage point. Groups of Vitellius's Praetorian Guards continued to stream from the Palatine area. This told Quintus the fight was going well for the Flavians. The Praetorians were being called out of the palace to help defend the north end of the city. More citizens and slaves now ran through the Forum in a panic, refugees from the besieged neighborhoods in the north districts.

"We need to move quickly," Quintus said. "I don't know how long Vitellius will stay at the palace if his guards are gone. Keep your eyes open. If we meet his coach or litter coming down, we attack. And we take him alive. Understood?"

The fighters nodded. They stepped from behind the corner column and ran toward the Arch of Augustus. A few citizens in the Forum stopped and watched the string of warriors on the move but said nothing. He slowed under the arch to allow his forces to gather behind him. The venatores covered the surrounding streets, while the gladiators moved across the small open square beyond the arch. They took refuge against the circular wall of the Temple of Vesta, home of the Vestal Virgins and the holy fire of Rome. It was perhaps the only building still occupied at the Forum. At least one of the six Vestals was required to tend the hearth day and night, during war or peace.

Quintus used his gladius to point at the stairs running up the hill behind the round temple. "Those steps will start us up the Palatine. They join with the Clivus Victoriae, which leads to the palace. Lindani, keep your venatores ready. We'll need support if we run into the guards."

The African nodded, and the sagittarii placed arrows on bowstrings. The two slingers loaded their deadly missiles into their sling pouches. Quintus took one last look across the square, then ran for the steps. The flight was half the length of the Gemonian Steps and Quintus reached the top quickly. He crouched and looked up the road. Seeing no one, he raised his arm to signal his troupe forward when a sudden shout startled him.

"Flavian soldiers! They're over here!" came the voice.

It took a moment to locate the person shouting the warning.

"Hurry! They're headed for the palace!"

Finally, Quintus saw him. A middle-aged man leaned from the window of his insula apartment opposite the hillside. He shouted up the hill, beyond Quintus's line of sight, and pointed frantically at him and his men on the steps. Quintus had to assume there was another unit of Praetorians now headed their way.

"Lindani, if that asshole makes another sound, kill him," Quintus said. He stood to move up the road to meet the defenders.

"They're on the steps!" yelled the man.

Quintus turned and looked at Lindani. The African had his bow drawn back tightly, the arrow tip pointing at the apartment window. But he did not fire.

"What are you waiting for?" asked Quintus. "You want him to give them our numbers, too? Kill him!"

The bow quivered slightly, but Lindani's fingers did not release the bowstring.

"Danaos, take care of it," Quintus ordered in an irritated tone. The venator beside Lindani drew back his bow and fired. The man let out a short cry, then fell from the two-story window into the street below.

Lindani released the tension on his bow and looked at Quintus with apologetic eyes. "I am sorry. An enemy soldier I can justify to my gods and to myself. But not a civilian. I cannot do it."

The sincerity in Lindani's voice melted any trace of anger Quintus felt. Amazonia put her hand on Lindani's shoulder. "Don't worry about it," she said quietly. "I don't think I could have done it either."

Quintus led the group onto the road. "Gladiators, form three ranks. Venatores in the fourth rank. Stay armed and ready to fire." The road ahead of them curved to the right. "Roscius, check up ahead."

As the troupe moved forward cautiously, Roscius climbed a few feet down the steep slope to the left. He made his way quickly through the low brush until he was in position to see farther up the curved road. He waved his hand at Quintus and their advance halted. Quintus watched the man's hand signals carefully. Roscius flashed all his fingers twice, then the fingers on one hand once. "Twenty-five soldiers," Quintus said quietly. The scout raised one finger and touched the top of his head. "One officer," Quintus translated. Roscius then crossed two figures in an "X" and mimicked firing a bow. "No archers."

Quintus ordered Lindani and one other sagittarius over the edge of the slope with quick instructions. He lined the gladiators against the retaining wall on the right side of the road with the remaining venatores to the rear.

The squad of Praetorian Guards approached slowly, heeding the warning of the now-dead Vitellius supporter in the window. Quintus gave the silent signal to fire when ready. Lindani and his partner crawled into position near Roscius, took aim, and after a few seconds, released. Quintus heard two bodies hit the paved road around the bend. He hoped one was the officer, as he had directed. There was a scuffling of feet and shouting of orders. Lindani and the second archer continued to fire, taking down as many Praetorians as they could before the men charged. Quintus heard a battle cry and the thud of running feet. He waved his men forward, and the gladiators reformed in three ranks across the road. He gave the order to charge, then watched the closing distance carefully, waiting for the right time to spring his second surprise.

"Gladiators . . . down!" he shouted. As one, the fighters dropped to one knee. The venatores hidden behind them remained standing. The instant their field of fire cleared, they unleashed a volley of arrows and stones, exactly as they had drilled. Most struck just above the top edge of the shields, into necks, faces, and foreheads. A slinger's rock struck one soldier in the temple, denting his cheek guard and dropping him instantly. A few arrows embedded in shields and one glanced off a lucky soldier's helmet. As the Praetorians struggled to step over their downed comrades, the gladiators struck.

Quintus engaged the first soldier on the right, thrusting with lightning-quick speed at his neck, arms, and face. The Praetorian was a well-trained, seasoned fighter. As Primus had predicted, the Guard put up a fierce defense of their emperor. As hard as he tried, Quintus could not inflict anything worse than a graze. His own shield moved swiftly as he anticipated the moves of the soldier, just as he would in the arena. The stalemate went on for more than a minute—an eternity for a single bout on the battlefield. Quintus deliberately let his shield slide to the left, exposing his sword arm and chest. The feint worked. The Praetorian lunged. As soon as Quintus saw the man commit to the move, his shield flew back in place and his gladius fired over the top at the man's exposed throat. His blade connected and the Praetorian staggered backward, dropping his scutum and grabbing at the hole in his windpipe. He attempted one more thrust but dropped on the street instead.

Quintus scanned the skirmish. More than half the Praetorians were down, but so, too, were many of his men. He sought out Amazonia. She was holding her own against another tough fighter on the far side of the road. The archers and slingers continued to fire into the fight, carefully controlling their missiles to seek out the enemy among the like-uniformed gladiators.

Quintus charged a soldier who had just sliced a gash into the leg of Balbus, a senior fighter from the original Britannia ludus. The two gladiators together finally dropped the aggressive Praetorian.

"Venatores, stand ready!" Quintus yelled as he attacked his third Praetorian.

"Gladiators . . . drop!" Again, the fighters dropped to a knee, this time behind raised shields. They only gave the archers a second to fire, before they rose back from their vulnerable positions. But it was all the time needed. Most came up to face a mortally wounded adversary. They quickly turned their attention to the six remaining Praetorians still in the fight.

"Lay down your arms!" Quintus shouted at them. "There's no need to die for a lost cause."

The surviving Praetorians backed off, glancing at each other and instinctively forming a tight circle. The gladiators and venatores quickly surrounded them. "Drop your weapons and walk away," Quintus said to the bloodied, panting men. "I give you my word you will not be harmed."

The Praetorians looked at each other and seemed to consider the offer. Their response was not what Quintus had expected. Every second man dropped his weapon and looked skyward, exposing his neck. Without hesitation, their comrades placed swords at their throats and thrust. Three men fell dead. Then two more. The last Praetorian standing looked defiantly at Quintus.

"We would rather die than live under the shadow of Vespasian," he said with venom in his voice. He grinned at Quintus as he raised the point of his gladius and thrust it into his own throat. Amazingly, the man continued to stand staring at Quintus with the blade lodged in his neck and the grin still etched on his face. Finally, he staggered, his eyes rolled back, and he dropped beside his comrades.

"Crazy bastards," Amazonia said as she stared at the pile of bodies in the road. "They burned themselves to death for Otho, and they cut each other's throats for Vitellius. Do the emperors cast some magic spell over these Praetorian assholes?"

"Just the same promise of power and wealth that drives every Praetorian," Quintus said, shaking his head. "Pull our wounded to the side and reform the lines. Let's get—"

A sudden scream and the thunder of running feet came from the area below them. The troupe moved to the edge of the road and looked down the north face of the Palatine. Through the Imperial fora and markets in the distance came a stampede of people dashing into the city center.

"Primus must have broken through in the north," Quintus said with relief.

The flood of people poured into the Roman Forum below them, followed closely by at least three Flavian centuries. Quintus and his gladiators cheered and waved their weapons at their comrades below, who responded with enthusiastic cries of victory. Many seemed ready to charge up the Palatine alongside the gladiators, until a mounted tribune arrived and called the centurions together. The legionaries were quickly ordered into rank and file, and marched at the quick-step back up Clivus Orbius toward the northeast suburbs. Quintus smiled to himself. The centuries were marching up the street that had once led to his own home. His pleasant thoughts were interrupted by the sound of the tribune's horse galloping up the Palatine Road to where they stood.

"Centurion Romanus, we need your men," the tribune yelled.

"But, sir, our orders are to locate and arrest Vitellius," Quintus replied.

"Not any more. We need reinforcements, every man we can get, at the Praetorian barracks. Now!"

"We'll lose Vitellius if you pull us from our mission," Quintus argued. "We may never get this chance again."

The tribune spun his horse. "He's probably long gone, but take five men and search the palace. The rest come with me."

Quintus thought quickly. He could not assault a guarded palace with five men. If there was strong resistance, he would have to wait for reinforcements anyway. If there was no resistance, he did not need five men. Only the two he trusted most of all.

"Amazonia, Lindani, come with me," he said. "Memnon, take the rest and follow the tribune."

Memnon's face showed disappointment. "Fine," he said with mock drama. "We'll take the barracks while you three swim in the emperor's pool."

Quintus smiled at his loyal optio. "I'll make it up to you."

The gladiators and venatores followed the mounted tribune back down the hill, across the Forum, and up Clivus Orbius, leaving the three fighters standing alone on the road among twenty-five dead Praetorians.

"Well, this should be interesting," Amazonia said. "I've never assaulted an imperial palace with three people before. Come to think of it, I've never assaulted an imperial palace before. Fuck it, let's get this asshole." Quintus smiled and shook his head at her. He had never met a more reckless woman in his life. But he had never met a more exciting woman either.

They worked their way farther up the curved street that led to the summit of the Palatine Hill. Lindani stayed well ahead of Quintus and Amazonia on the outside slope where he could watch the road ahead. The upper portion of the boulevard was deserted.

As they crept around the final turn, the complex of the imperial palace came into view. To the right side of the wide expanse stood the Palace of Tiberius, a two-story structure built in the classic Republican form with a square layout and frontal staircase. The walls were predominantly of white stone, with two levels of colonnades supporting a roof of terra-cotta tile. To the left lay a three-story wing added by Nero, only slightly more elaborate with a graceful curve to the front façade. Although sizeable, the buildings were not as ornate as a Roman citizen might expect of the imperial residence. Perhaps, thought Quintus, this was why the eccentric Nero had decided to build his own "Golden House" below the Palatine. The three emperors since Nero's death, however, had rejected the garish, extravagant Domus Aurea and taken up residence in the more modest palace atop the hill.

The three warriors studied the grounds from the road before moving forward. The palace seemed deserted. "I think we're too late," Quintus said. "An emperor wouldn't be found alone in a vacant palace with no guards, especially with enemy troops flooding into the city."

"Perhaps there are some inside we could persuade to tell where he has gone," suggested Lindani.

"Only one way to find out." Quintus moved toward the wide portico that spanned the width of the main building and climbed the stairs. Amazonia and Lindani kept a few steps behind, weapons at the ready.

The main door sat open under the center arch of the colonnade. Quintus stood to the side of the portal and looked in. The colorful design of the grand vestibule more than made up for the bland exterior. Various patterns of brown, cream, and green marble, polished to a mirror-like finish, covered the walls. The same marble, cut into small tiles, was arranged in a vivid geometric pattern across the spacious floor. Twelve niches around the room held tall statues of the gods, beautifully carved in black basalt.

Quintus motioned with his head and the three entered the foyer. They stepped lightly, sensitive to the clicking of their caligae on the tiled floor. The sound of trickling water blended with their echoed footsteps. The room led out to the largest peristyle Quintus had ever seen. The open-air garden, surrounded by dozens of pink columns, was dominated by a huge fountain. Water sprayed from a fish at the apex and cascaded down tiers of oversized seashells into a wide octagonal pool. Still there was no sign of guards or an emperor.

On the south side of the peristyle, Quintus pushed open another oversized door and scanned the interior of the imperial triclinium, the banquet hall that had seen fifty years of political intrigue, orgies, entertainment, and murder. Although it now lay deserted, it showed the first evidence they had yet seen of recent use. Food still lay on tables in front of sumptuous couches. Some of the trays had been knocked over, spilling loaves of bread, vegetables, and shellfish across the marble floor.

"Looks like someone left in a hurry," Amazonia said.

"And they have left recently," Lindani said, studying the tray of vegetables. "Even the flies have not had time to feast on the wasted food." He picked up a radish and tossed it in his mouth.

"I think it's time we search the living quarters," Quintus said.

They went back through the peristyle and took another hallway, this one leading to the larger wing that appeared to be the private residence of the emperor. The first three rooms, an office and two guest bedchambers, were empty. They moved a few steps farther down the long hallway. Lindani suddenly froze. Quintus and Amazonia followed his lead.

"What is it?" she asked.

The African tipped his head slightly, listening to a sound neither Quintus or Amazonia could hear. "There is an animal present here," he finally said. "It has sensed us. I can hear the growl."

The three raised the tips of their weapons. Lindani checked to be sure his arrow sat tightly against the bowstring. They stepped carefully down the hall. Near the end, the wide passageway turned to the right. Now Quintus, too, could hear the low rumble of a growl. It came from around the corner. They stepped to the left side of the hall to stay clear of the opening. Quintus leaned forward to peer down the secondary hallway.

A fierce bark split the silence. They jumped. A bulky mastiff stood just beyond the corner. The dog charged. Quintus crouched and raised his scutum. The beast leapt but never reached the shield. It howled and fell to the floor with Lindani's arrow in its head.

"Shit, that'll get your attention," Amazonia said with a shiver.

"It would not have reached us anyway." Lindani pointed to the long chain that bound the animal to the broad double doors at the end of the second hallway.

"Looks like someone doesn't want us in there," Quintus said.

They moved forward, weapons still raised. Quintus gently pushed at the door, but it did not budge. The distinct shuffle of feet came from the closed room. He looked at his two comrades and nodded. He mouthed the words "On three," then counted silently as he bobbed his head. On the final number, they crashed their collective weight into the barrier. The double doors flew open, toppling a large cabinet that had been wedged against them. Quintus heard a high-pitched squeal. The three warriors stood in a tight semicircle and scanned the room for a threat. None came.

The sound of nervous whimpering drifted from the far side of the room. They moved cautiously around the spacious bed. In the dim light, Quintus saw the form of a man cowering in the corner, trembling arms covering his head. The heavyset man wore the simple blue tunic of a household slave. The thinning gray hair on his head marked him as one of the senior servants.

"This is some reception for an imperial palace," Amazonia said. She approached him and tapped his arm with the flat of her blade. He jumped as if she had branded him with a hot iron. "Come on, old man. Get up. We're not going to hurt you."

The man slowly looked up, his face a mask of fear and anguish. "Don't hurt me, please," he begged in a wavering voice.

"Well, that depends on whether you cooperate," Quintus replied calmly. "Who are you?"

"Thoranius. I am the personal valet of Emperor Vitellius."

"Are you alone?"

"Yes. At least, I think so. The others left this morning. The emperor ordered me to care for the palace until he returned." The man lowered his head in shame. "But I became scared when I heard all the fighting. I fetched the dog and closed myself in here."

"Where is the emperor?"

"I don't know where they've gone. He left in his litter, along with his staff and a unit of Praetorians."

Amazonia stepped forward and touched the edge of her gladius to the side of the man's face. "We want to know where he's gone," she said slowly.

The man began to tremble again. "I don't know! I swear it! They went down the Clivus Victoriae and disappeared. The emperor has a country villa . . . Ariccia . . . in the hills to the east of Rome. Perhaps they went there."

Quintus became more dejected with each word. He wanted desperately to complete this mission successfully for Primus and Vespasian, but the quest was slipping further and further from his grasp.

"Tie his hands and take him with us," he said in a clipped, annoyed tone. "If nothing else, he can lead Primus to the country villa."

"But . . . but . . . I can't . . ." the old man stammered.

Amazonia pulled him to his feet. "Save it for the general, old man."

She used a curtain cord to bind his hands in front of him, then marched him past the broken doors. Lindani held the slave in the hallway while Quintus and Amazonia checked the other rooms in the residence. All were empty.

"That's just great," Quintus lamented as he pushed the man out through the peristyle. "All that planning and work, good men dead, and all we end up with is a fat old slave who knows nothing."

"We got Domitian out safely," Amazonia replied. "I'm sure that's more important to Vespasian right now. Vitellius won't be free for long."

"Yes, but I wanted *us* to grab him."

They moved in silence through the large vestibule and out into the courtyard.

"More of our men arrive," Lindani said, peering out toward the Forum as they started down the main road. "I think the fight for Rome has been won, eh?"

"Thank the gods. Now, hopefully, we can all return home and get on with our lives." The thought of facing an adversary one-on-one in the arena again was comforting to Quintus.

Near the bottom of the hill, they descended the stairway toward the Forum. They passed under the Arch of Augustus and approached a senior tribune who was ordering his cohorts into formation in the middle of the public square as a show of strength.

"Tribune, have we taken the barracks yet?" Quintus asked as he approached.

"Yes, we . . ." The tribune turned and looked at the three fighters and their captive slave. "Jupiter's balls! Good work, Centurion!"

Quintus stood silent, staring at the officer.

"Legate Primus will be more than pleased," the tribune said happily. He approached the prisoner. "I wouldn't wish your fate on my worst enemy, Vitellius."

The name hit Quintus like a blacksmith's hammer. He glanced toward his friends and saw wide eyes and gaping mouths.

The tribune's voice came again, but Quintus was in such a fog he didn't hear the words. He did feel Amazonia's foot kick his shin. He snapped to attention. "Sorry, sir," was all he could think of to say.

"Sorry for what?" the tribune replied. "I asked where you found him."

"Oh . . . ah . . . in the palace." Quintus looked at Amazonia, wondering what else to say.

"Where else would you find an emperor?" Amazonia said with a casual shrug.

"Did his Praetorians put up a fight?"

"Like wild dogs," Lindani said, "but we overcame them."

Quintus had to bite his lip to stifle a laugh.

"Well, good," the tribune said, slapping Quintus on the shoulder. "You're the gladiator, right? 'Taurus,' is it?"

"Yes, sir."

"I just want to be sure who to credit with this capture, Taurus." The tribune grabbed Vitellius roughly by the arm and dragged him toward the Basilica Julia, calling for a dispatch rider as he walked. Vitellius stared into Quintus's eyes as he was pulled away. The look of the nervous, cowering slave had gone. In its place was defiance and hatred.

"Well," Quintus finally managed to say, "for an emperor, he's a damned good actor."

XXIV

January AD 70

I T SEEMED all of Rome had turned out to welcome their new emperor to the city. Senators, magistrates, and other dignitaries filled the Forum Romanum, alongside the best of the military cohorts who had fought bravely for this day. The general population of citizens cheered from the perimeter. Their numbers overflowed into the adjoining Forum of Augustus and Forum of Julius Caesar. Basilicas and temples were adorned with green bands of garland and purple banners that fluttered in the cool morning breeze.

Quintus stood nervously but proudly at the head of his gladiators and venatores. He wished the rules preventing the wearing of military gear within the pomerium—the sacred boundary of the city of Rome—had been lifted for just this one day. He would have liked to have worn his crested helmet and polished armor for this occasion.

But his civilian attire could not hinder the pride he felt for his Cohors Gladiatorum. They stood in perfect rank and file in their place of honor at the foot of the Rostra. His anticipation swelled as the crowd's cheering increased. He could hear the clap of hooves from the four horses that pulled Vespasian's chariot. But, standing at attention, he was forbidden from turning his head to watch the approaching spectacle. He had to be content with the glimpses he could catch from the corner of his eye.

He wondered how Vespasian had changed over the years. But more than that, he wondered if the emperor would recognize him. He and Castus had decided to let his identity be a surprise for Vespasian—one more bit of good news on such a wonderful day. But now Quintus grew impatient. He wanted desperately to show this great man how, after ten years, he had finally been able to repay him for the loving support he had shown his family.

At last, the chariot rolled past him. He was astonished at Vespasian's appearance. Other than carrying a few more pounds, it seemed the man had not aged a day over the past decade. His white and purple toga flowed beautifully in the light breeze. But Quintus still had to stifle a laugh. Even presented with such a tremendous outpouring of love, the man's tight lips and arched eyebrows still held the same strained expression Quintus remembered so clearly as a child. After their first meeting, Quintus had laughed to his father how this new business associate seemed to be relieving himself as he sat with them in the peristyle garden. He could still hear his father's laughter. As the thought faded, he watched Vespasian wave to the crowd. Under his arched eyebrows, the twinkle in the man's eyes revealed an unmistakable delight over the grand festivities.

The chariot halted at the Rostra, and the new emperor stepped from the vehicle and climbed the steps to the speaker's podium. The requisite swarm of imperial staff and attendants followed him up the stairs and almost filled the sixty-foot-wide platform. To Quintus's ears, the cheering was at least as loud as that in the amphitheater. It seemed the people of Rome had finally all agreed upon one leader.

Support for Vespasian had swelled after the brutal death of Vitellius, which occurred on the very day Quintus, Amazonia, and Lindani had delivered the deposed emperor to the legions. Once word had spread of his capture, a mob had gathered in front of the Basilica Julia and demanded Vitellius be handed over to them. To pacify the crowd, the tribune had displayed the broken man to them with a rope around his neck and a gladius point under his chin. But their bloodlust was powerful and, rather than pacify them, the display had incited them all the more. They rushed the tribune and snatched Vitellius. Before the legions could restore order, the ex-emperor had been hauled to the bottom of the Gemonian Steps and beaten to death. Using hooks, his body was then dragged to the Aemilian Bridge and tossed into the river Tiber. The tribune had been reprimanded for bad judgment, but Vespasian had been so pleased to hear of the rescue of his youngest son, the incident was soon forgotten.

Vespasian now glowed with exuberance as he waved to the crowd. Quintus breached military protocol and cocked his head just enough to watch the podium. Rather than subside, the cheering grew louder by the minute. Quintus glanced across the lane that had been kept clear for Vespasian's chariot and scanned the happy faces. He spotted Marcus Livius Castus, the man whose actions had led to this day. Even at a distance, Quintus could see tears flowing freely down the weatherworn cheeks. The old centurion cheered alongside Petra and Julianus in the special section reserved for honored dignitaries. Although dressed in their finest tunics, the tough look of Castus and Petra still betrayed them as ex-centurions. A few of the polished socialites in the group cast the occasional smug glance their way. Quintus wondered what the snobs would say if they knew the critical role these courageous men had played in their future and the future of Rome itself.

Vespasian finally waved the crowd to silence. "Citizens of Rome, I am honored to be your emperor." The simple statement prompted another long chorus of cheers. The words of his speech were short and meaningful. The way a good general addresses his army, Quintus thought. As Vespasian closed his remarks, he brought to the Rostra Legate Primus and Legate Caecina. Their reception was equally enthusiastic. Quintus was pleased to see Caecina looking proud and fit again—a much different man than the one who was unjustly bound in chains and locked in a horse corral. Today he finally received his rightful acclaim.

Vespasian also acknowledged Legate Mucianus, who had arrived after the battle for Rome had been won but was instrumental in attending to the daily governing of the Empire until Vespasian arrived.

The new emperor then prepared for one final presentation.

• • •

"Oh, get on with it," Lucius whispered just loud enough for Julia to hear standing next to him. "We've got a new life to start."

Julia glared at him. "Will you settle down?" she whispered back in a harsh tone. "This man just gave you that new life. You could show him the respect he deserves."

Lucius did not respond. He tapped his foot on the Rostra flagstones in anxious anticipation. As a senior staff member, he was part of the supporting cast that stood behind Vespasian on the platform. He had quietly pulled Julia up beside him. He knew she would enjoy the feeling of power looking down on the people from the Rostra. But now, he was anxious to see their new house provided by the State. Although he was certain it would be a grand residence, he had already determined that renovations would be in order. He had always wanted to design his own home, especially when money was no object. Besides a handsome starting bonus—"to keep you for the first few months in Rome," Vespasian had said—Lucius's State salary would be half a million sesterces per year, almost double what he had earned as an Imperial Advisor to Nero. The salary would nicely supplement the income stream already flowing from the shipping business. Yes, he wanted to see their new home, visit the baths, acquire his household servants, and generally luxuriate in the greatness of Rome. Perhaps, if he could find time this week, he might even meet with the current commerce staff and begin planning for his new role as prefect.

But right now, he simply wanted off this fucking podium. Julia glanced at him, as if reading his mind. This time, she sent him a sexy smile. "He's almost done," she whispered. "Then we'll check out our new bedroom."

So that's what's been running through *her* mind up here, he thought. He knew deep down, she was just as excited to be back in Rome as he was. Perhaps, more than excited—stimulated.

"And then we can set a date," she continued in a whisper.

The statement didn't register with him, and that must have shown in a blank expression. Julia looked at him as if he were a scatterbrained child.

". . . for the marriage," she said.

In the hectic excitement of the trip to Rome, he had all but forgotten about the arrangement they had agreed upon. Once the maneuvering with Vespasian was complete and they were back in Rome, it was time to drop the pretense and get married for real—quietly, of course, so as not to alert Vespasian to the charade. The reality of impending nuptials did not panic him as much as he had thought it would. Perhaps he was finally ready to commit to spending his life with this woman. With her money and his new title, it would be a good life indeed.

"Lastly . . ." Vespasian said loudly.

Oh, thank the gods, thought Lucius.

"I want to acknowledge a special team of warriors who have helped my cause more than anyone will ever know. These men are not legionaries. In fact, most of them are not even citizens. They are a team of gladiators."

A murmur went through the audience. Lucius glanced at Julia. He almost thought he detected a smile on her lips.

"They were recruited from the ludus in Pompeii . . ."

With every word, Lucius's heart beat faster.

". . . and are among the best fighters in the arena."

Lucius quickly scanned the ranks of soldiers before him.

"You saw them here in Rome, during the famous Rome vs. Pompeii Challenge some years ago."

Lucius could now actually hear his own heart thumping.

"Today I honor the man who led this team so valiantly, and who personally rescued my son and captured Vitellius."

Don't say it, Lucius thought. *Don't you fucking say it.*

"I give you the man they call 'Taurus!'"

An earsplitting roar rose from the crowd, especially from the commoners along the perimeter. But Lucius didn't hear a thing. He felt as if he couldn't breathe; like a weight he had exorcised from his chest a year ago had, in the blink of an eye, returned in full force. He looked at Julia. Again, he thought he caught the vaguest hint of a smile. It was almost as though she had expected to hear the name.

But before he could say anything, a hand touched his shoulder and gently nudged him to the side. A well-built man in a red tunic—hitched up high at the belt, the way a soldier wore his tunic—stepped past him and approached Vespasian. The man dropped to one knee and the emperor placed a small wreath of oak leaves and acorns on his head—the corona civica, the rarest of awards for the common soldier. The man's head tipped back as he looked up into the emperor's eyes. Lucius nearly passed out. The face was instantly recognizable. The hard jawline, the close-set brown eyes, the long lashes. This was Quintus! The man who had destroyed his life! The specter from a horrible nightmare that the cursed gods forced him to keep repeating! Lucius held tight to the banister in front of him to stop from falling over. It seemed the entire Forum had begun to spin.

Quintus looked up at Vespasian and smiled. He saw the slightest change in Vespasian's expression. The emperor's head tipped slightly to one side, and he stared into Quintus's eyes like a curious puppy. His arched eyebrows scrunched a bit closer together.

"Do we know each other?" Vespasian's words were barely audible over the noisy crowd. "Castus tells me we do."

"Yes, sir, he is correct. You once showed me and my mother a kindness I could never repay . . . until today." It was the moment he had waited for all year. "I am Quintus, son of Caius Honorius Romanus."

Vespasian's mouth dropped open, and his eyes grew to the size of large coins. "By the gods . . . It *is* you! Quintus Romanus!"

He tugged Quintus up off his knee with a mighty jerk and hugged him hard enough to crush his ribs. Quintus gasped for breath. Vespasian straightened his arms again and gazed at Quintus. The look of pure joy on the emperor's face was something Quintus knew he would remember for the rest of his life. His only regret was that his parents were not here to witness this.

"But . . . I was told you were dead," Vespasian said. "I heard . . . stories."

Quintus smiled. "All lies, I'm afraid. Someday, when you have the time, I'll tell you the *real* story."

"Thank you, Quintus," Vespasian said. "To know it was you who helped end this war and saved the life of my son fills me with a happiness beyond words. You will always be an honored guest in my home."

"The honor is mine, Caesar," Quintus replied. "It was the least I could do for you. My men and I will always stand ready to support you."

Vespasian nodded, then raised Quintus's hand in his own and together they faced the cheering crowd. Quintus pointed to Castus and Petra, then acknowledged his cohort of gladiators and venatores, who abandoned their stiff military bearing for the moment and joined in the cheering. Although Quintus was used to having the adulation of thousands heaped upon him, this was different. Perhaps it was because the prediction of Petra, Castus, and Julianus had come true. He *had* made a difference in Rome's destiny. But more than that, it was the joy of repaying Vespasian that made this day more special than any day in an arena.

He bowed his head and stepped back. Vespasian released his wrist, called for quiet, and began to wrap up his address. Quintus turned to leave down the steps at the back of the Rostra. He sought the same path through the crowd of staff members on the platform. The first man he came to smiled and stepped aside. The movement revealed a face that seemed to be torn in anguish. Quintus wondered what was familiar about the face. Then the realization hit him. He stopped as if he had walked into a stone wall. He studied the distressed man before him. The curly brown hair was now cut short, and the face seemed slightly different. But he was sure of it just the same. This was *Lucius Calidius!* But how could that be? Lucius Calidius—the slave who had stolen his identity and tried to have him killed—was rotting away in an African ludus. This could not *possibly* be the same man.

A flash of blue caught his eye just behind the man. Quintus tore his gaze away and looked into the eyes of his Aunt Julia Melita. Now there was no question as to the man's identity.

Lucius continued to hold tight to the Rostra railing with a bewildered look, but Julia seemed well composed. "Hello, Quintus," she said in a pleasant voice. "So good to see you again."

Quintus's mind raced with a hundred possible ways to react. First on the list was drawing his gladius and burying it to the hilt in Lucius's stomach. But he would not stain Vespasian's inauguration with this bastard's blood. Then he had a better idea.

He stepped forward and leaned toward Lucius. He reached out, as if to hug an old friend, then jerked Lucius's head close to his own. He whispered harshly into his right ear: "I don't know how you got out of there, but believe me when I tell you that you most certainly *will* return to that African ludus."

He released his grip on the back of Lucius's head and stared into his eyes for a moment. A mixture of terror and rage shone back. Before he stepped away, Quintus was pleased to see a visible shiver run down the spine of his lifelong rival.

That evening, as the rest of Rome celebrated, Lucius descended the narrow stairs to the carcer—the city's prison. He handed a one-hundred-sesterce bribe to the head jailer and motioned for the man to leave the cell area. The jailer looked around and stepped outside the door. Lucius closed it behind him, then walked down the brick aisle that separated the two rows of cells. The sights and smells brought back dreadful images of the African ludus: the very place his sworn enemy had now vowed to return him. But Lucius's course was set in his mind. He would *not* be returning there; Quintus would *not* win again. He just needed to gather information, set a plan, and go on the offensive. And the first accomplices to help him down that path sat in these reeking cells.

"Listen up," he yelled loud enough to be heard in all twenty cells. "I have a deal to make with one of you. Let's see who it's going to be." He paced slowly down the aisle, studying the men who sat in tattered, filthy military tunics. "All of you fought for Vitellius and have refused to take the oath of allegiance to Vespasian."

"We'd rather rot in here!" came a rabid voice from an unseen cell. Others shouted in agreement.

"Fine, but perhaps I can get one of you out *without* having to take that oath." The prison became very quiet. "Who here knows the gladiator they call 'Taurus'?"

There was a pause, then a voice came from the last cell in the line. "I know who he is."

Lucius walked to the end of the aisle. He looked in on three young men who appeared to have not shaved, cleaned, or eaten more than bread morsels for at least a month.

"Describe him," Lucius said.

"He's a big fucker, with the markings of a bull on his chest. Why?"

"Tell me what else you know about him. Did he fight with your legion?"

The ex-soldier grinned, revealing a mouth full of brown, rotting teeth. "That bastard fought with *everyone's* legions. That's the problem. He's a traitor. He can't be trusted."

Lucius nodded. "Why do you say that?"

"We first fought against him and his gladiators when they supported Otho at Bedriacum. Then he turned on Otho. Word has it he, himself, murdered the emperor. Then he convinced our legate that he would fight for us. But at Cremona, he turned against us, too. Destroyed our own artillery, from what I heard." The prisoner leaned an inch closer to Lucius and squinted his eyes for emphasis. "So how long you think his loyalty to Vespasian will last? He's a fucking mercenary, and all mercenaries blow with the wind. He'll support whoever pays his lanista the most."

Lucius thought for a moment. This was more than he'd hoped for.

The ex-soldier glanced at his cellmates then turned back to Lucius and lowered his voice. "So, what's the story? You looking to get rid of

Vespasian already? Get us all out of here, and we'll raise a whole fucking army for you."

Lucius looked at the man like he was inspecting an insect crawling on his arm. "I don't need a whole fucking army, asshole. I just needed information." He turned and walked back down the aisle. The prisoner jumped up and grabbed the bars of his cell.

"What about my deal?" he yelled after Lucius. "When are you getting me out of here?"

Lucius laughed as he pulled open the heavy wooden door to leave. "Take it up with the emperor," he yelled back.

XXV

January AD 70

THE IMPERIAL BANQUET was well under way in the palace triclinium by the time Lucius arrived. He stepped from the peristyle courtyard with its tiered fountain, through the double doors, and into the crowded banquet hall. The size of the hall was impressive, although Lucius remembered the triclinium in Nero's Golden House as being larger. The room was flanked by five arched alcoves on either side, the center three housing tall effigies of the major gods in black basalt and the two end recesses framing huge doorways. The maroon, beige, and golden hues of the polished floor marble were arranged in sizeable rectangular patterns that established the positioning of the couches. Trays of food were set along the end walls and arranged neatly throughout the couch clusters. Dozens of servants scurried through the hall, replenishing the fare as quickly as it was devoured.

Lucius weaved through the crush of luminaries. He estimated at least five hundred people in the room. Some stood engaged in animated conversation, while others lay stomach-down on the large red couches arranged three-to-a-group in open squares.

He spotted Castus speaking with the Pompeiian lanista, Petra, and his gladiator trainer. He was relieved to see that Quintus was nowhere in sight. Thankfully, the pomp and protocol of the imperial ceremony precluded any gladiators or other scum from attending.

Music flowed from the horns and stringed instruments of the small orchestra set in a corner of the hall. A large audience had gathered to watch a dance troupe in the piazza at the center of the hall. A juggler and two acrobats kept a smaller group of guests entertained in the opposite corner.

Lucius skirted past the piazza and spotted Julia on a nearby couch, laughing and flirting with a young senator and his wife. Her ability to bond instantly with the most attractive and influential patricians always amazed Lucius. Of course, she had had years to perfect the art, and she certainly had the physical charms to gain attention. This evening, her low-cut green stola revealed quite a bit of those charms as she lay on the couch. He approached her from behind and gently pinched her ass.

"Ah, Lucius, there you are!" she said with a bright smile. He sprawled out on his stomach next to her. "Say hello to Senator Saenus and his beautiful wife, Thuria."

The foursome exchanged pleasantries for a few minutes, then Julia leaned close to Lucius's ear. "Where in Hades have you been? You think it's wise to be late for your first imperial banquet?"

"I had information to gather," he replied.

"On what? The Quintus situation?" She lowered her voice even further. "I thought we agreed to let that go until tomorrow."

Lucius sighed and worked to keep his temper in check. "No, *you* said to let it go. *I* still feel something needs to be done quickly. You saw Vespasian's reaction to him on the Rostra." He felt Julia squeeze his arm and realized his voice was rising. He took a breath and continued at a lower volume. "The longer the gladiator is here, the tighter he becomes with Vespasian. We must do something *now*." He felt as though he was explaining the situation to a six-year-old. Although she seemed to want to, Julia did not reply.

Lucius kept an eye on the imperial couch on the dais to their left. The emperor seemed in good spirits, laughing heartily with two of the senior senators and a group of praetors. An aide approached and waited patiently for the emperor to finish his conversation. Vespasian stood and took a few steps back from his couch to speak with the assistant. Now would be the time to approach, thought Lucius. He nudged Julia. She excused herself from her conversation and walked with him toward the emperor.

"Ah, Lucius and the lovely Mistress Melita," Vespasian said warmly after the aide bowed and left. "I hope your new home is to your liking."

"It's absolutely wonderful, Caesar," Julia replied. "I love being in the heart of the city. I've missed this excitement for too long."

"I know how you feel," Vespasian replied. "Caesarea is a long way from Rome, and I don't just mean in distance." They laughed and Vespasian turned to take his place again on his couch. Lucius saw his opportunity slipping away. He boldly touched the emperor's arm. Vespasian glanced down at the hand on his bicep but seemed to take the breach of etiquette in stride. "Is there something more before I return to this magnificent food and drink?"

Lucius forced the smile from his face and leaned closer to the emperor. "Caesar, I'm afraid this is not good news."

Vespasian's look turned to one of concern. "Does it regard Titus in Jerusalem?" Leaving his older son behind in Judea to fight the Jewish revolt had been the emperor's only anxiety in relocating to Rome.

"No, Caesar. It has to do with your own security. As you know, my sources have always been very good." Vespasian nodded. "It appears there are some who are plotting against you already."

Vespasian shrugged. "We've just ended a civil war, Lucius. *Of course* there will be those who are at odds with me."

"This is more than that," Lucius continued, keeping his voice low. "This is a conspiracy within your own military. And it's led by a man who already has the blood of one emperor on his hands."

Vespasian looked skeptical. "My legions are strongly behind me, Lucius. I'm certain of that."

"The legions, perhaps. But what about the auxiliaries, especially the mercenaries?"

The emperor considered the question. "The gladiators?"

Lucius nodded. "Their leader . . . this man they call 'Taurus.' He is a danger."

Vespasian paused for a moment, then scanned Lucius and Julia. "Are you referring to Quintus Romanus . . . the man you told me was dead?"

Julia spoke up quickly. "That was the rumor I had heard, Caesar. We were as surprised to see him as you were."

Vespasian's eyes narrowed. "Yes, I'll bet you were. I should think at the very least his appearance would raise a few legal issues with your shipping fleet."

"Now that he's made his whereabouts known," Julia replied confidently, "I'm sure we'll work that out."

Lucius's heart raced again. "That's not the issue here," he said, perhaps a bit too loudly. "This man is not stable. He's a serious danger to you."

Vespasian's face lightened once again, and he laughed. "A danger? Quintus? I knew him and his father for years. And because of that, he put his life on the line for me and Domitian. Lucius, the only ones who need to fear the great 'Taurus' are his arena opponents."

"But, Caesar—"

"Not another word of this nonsense, Lucius." The emperor gestured toward the dancers and musicians. "It's a time for celebration tonight. Put these ridiculous thoughts aside and enjoy the evening." With that, the emperor reclined on his sofa and resumed his conversation with the praetors.

Lucius and Julia were left standing awkwardly alone. Lucius had known the first attempt at this stratagem would not be easy, but he had not expected such a firm rebuke. He took a half step toward the emperor's couch when a hand firmly grabbed his arm.

"Don't you dare!" Julia snapped. "I told you this was neither the time nor the place to bring this up. Let it go."

Reluctantly, Lucius followed Julia as she started back to their cluster of couches. Halfway there, a short middle-aged woman stepped in front of them.

"Julia? Quintus?" the woman asked.

The name sent a jolt through Lucius's already taut body.

"It is you, isn't it?" the woman pressed.

"Drusilla?" Julia asked, her voice quavering a bit.

As soon as Julia said the name, the images flooded back to Lucius. This was the wife of Senator Publius Nerva. She and her husband had been companions and political allies of his and Julia's during his first appointment in Rome by Nero three years earlier. Unfortunately, they had also been seated next to him and Julia on the podium of the arena the day he released the bulls. It was most certainly a day this woman would not easily forget.

"I thought it was you," the woman said, "but, Quintus . . . you look different."

Lucius glanced at Julia. They had discussed the possibility of being recognized in Rome, although they felt the chances were slim. Nero's staff and political cronies had been swept away by the succession of emperors who followed. But here, on their first evening in Rome, the specter of his past continued to overshadow their future. He had hoped their days of lies and deceit were behind them. But here was yet another lie they were going to have to live. It was the perfect end to this vile day.

"Oh, Drusilla . . ." Julia laughed. "This isn't Quintus. This is Lucius. He's Quintus's brother from Britannia. Everyone has always remarked on the resemblance."

The woman appeared to study him for a moment. "Yes, a different nose, but those same dark eyes," Drusilla said with a laugh. She leaned closer to Julia. "So what ever happened to Quintus after that day in the arena, dear? He went quite mad, didn't he?"

"You don't know the half of it," Julia said in an equally conspiring tone. "Why I ever associated with that man is beyond me." She reached out and took Lucius's arm. "Lucius came from Britannia to help me run the shipping business when his brother disappeared. He's been sent by the gods. Smart, supportive . . . Remarkable how siblings can be so different."

Julia's acting skills never ceased to amaze Lucius. The most feeble stories rang with the truth of Minerva when they sprung from Julia's lips. Now she just needed to change the subject.

"So tell me about the Senator," Julia continued. "Is he well?"

Perfect, thought Lucius.

"I'm afraid he's gone, Julia."

"Gone?"

"He disappeared after Nero's death and I never saw him again," Drusilla explained. Tears welled in her eyes.

"I'm so sorry," Julia said as she hugged the woman close. "I've lost my husband as well. We must get together soon and discuss it. I have some ideas that will help you forget those dreadful days of the past. A bit of a journey, perhaps?"

"A journey?" Drusilla replied with a gleam in her eye. "Sounds exciting."

Julia glanced over the woman's shoulder and nodded. Lucius followed her gaze and realized there was nobody there.

"I'm sorry, Drusilla. I've left some friends. Are you still at the State apartments, dear? No, of course not."

"I'm in the apartments alongside the Forum of Julius Caesar now. Number nine."

Julia began walking before Drusilla finished, tugging Lucius's arm. "I'll call on you in a few days, dear. We have lots to discuss. Enjoy the beautiful evening."

They left the woman standing alone and wove their way through the crowd until she was out of sight.

"Just our fucking luck," Lucius spat.

"We said that might happen," Julia said quietly. "Anyone with any connections at all in this city is here tonight. If she's the only one in this room to recognize us, then our days in Rome will be fine."

"All it takes is one wrong word from a person like that and our life crumbles like dry earth again. You do realize that?"

The flame of annoyance in Julia's eye rekindled. "Of course I realize that. But I'm sick of you always thinking the worst. Our story worked for now. I'll follow up in a few days and have her on her way to Carthage aboard the *Juno*. What's the problem?"

"A few days? She could ruin our lives in a few hours!"

Julia's face pulled taut with anger. "What do you want me to say, Lucius? That we'll kill her?"

Her voice was louder than it should have been, and it forced Lucius to glance around. "Alright, *alright*, damn you. I'll deal with it in the morning."

Julia stared at him for a moment. "You're not serious . . . You're . . . You're actually going to *kill* her?"

"I said *I'll* deal with it. Forget about her." He tugged Julia toward the couch before she asked any more questions.

Senator Saenus and his wife welcomed them back warmly. The laughter and conversation was lively, but Lucius took no notice. His mind wandered. He kept replaying the images of Quintus Romanus brushing past him on the podium; of Vespasian's reaction when he recognized Quintus; of the emperor hugging him so tightly; of Quintus's threat to return him to the ludus. His hands shook as he forced the images from his mind. But he couldn't concentrate. He began sorting through his options. What should his next move be? Up until that morning, he had had the next few years of his life laid out so perfectly. Now, uncertainty ran rampant. And why? Because, once again, a gladiator had snatched his dreams away. That same damned gladiator. That same damned, *fucking* gladiator—

"Lucius!" Julia's voice came strongly in his ear.

He looked up and realized Senator Saenus and his wife were staring at him from the adjoining couch.

"What is it, man?" the senator said with a laugh. "I haven't heard growling like that outside a lion hunt in the arena!"

Lucius glanced nervously at Julia, then smiled and wiped the perspiration from his forehead. "So sorry, Senator. I've got a lot on my mind."

Thankfully, two servants stepped between them and placed another massive food platter on the low table. "Stay with us, dear," Julia whispered, then reached toward the table and ripped a leg from the display of fowl at the center of the tray.

"Try this roast pheasant," she said, waving the limb at Lucius. "It's exquisite." Lucius could tell by the slurring she was probably on her fifth or sixth goblet of wine. He shook his head. "Fine . . . more for me," she said, then burst out in a loud giggle.

At the dais, the emperor's son Domitian stood and clapped his hands loudly. "Your attention, please," he said with a haughty air.

Lucius looked up and decided immediately he did not like the boy.

"If you would all clear the center floor, I have ordered a special performance for my father this evening." The boy turned toward the emperor on the adjoining couch and raised a goblet of wine. "Father, in honor of your triumphant return to Rome from Judea, I present to you a dance from the East. As my gift, I give you the Dance of the Seven Veils."

The few in the audience who had heard the fable of the dance performed by Salome for King Herod applauded wildly, knowing what was to come. The band struck up an exotic tune with quivering flutes. A beautiful young dancer, draped in layers of sheer purple silk, floated to the central square.

"This should be interesting," Julia mused with a sly grin on her face.

The exotic look of the young, olive-skinned dancer caught Lucius's eye and finally pulled him from his slump. He guessed her to be eighteen or nineteen, probably from Judea or Syria, but much more attractive than any of the local girls he had seen during his time there. She was just what he needed to occupy his mind and distract his thoughts from the day's events.

She began her performance with elegant undulations of her arms and hands. It seemed each of her ten fingers were controlled by a separate mind. In beat with the music, her graceful moves were punctuated by high kicks, quick spins, and a violent shaking of hips and belly. After a few moments, she began plucking the sheer fabric sashes from her belt and necklace. Most piled on the marble floor at her feet, but a few she draped over the heads of leering young men on the nearest sofas. Slowly, her curvaceous body became more and more visible. The fever of the crowd rose with every veil that dropped. A rhythmic clapping began, in beat to the Eastern music. With a few more stanzas, the dancer's breasts were bare. She moved across the open square so every eye could get the best view. The clapping and cheering increased, and soon the seventh veil fell. A cheer rose from the men in the hall, while the women gasped. The dancer's pubic mound had been shaved bare, presenting the illusion of a girl even younger than the dancer's teenaged years.

With the crowd's reaction, Lucius glanced at the dais. Vespasian was smiling but clearly ill-at-ease with the nude dancer.

"He's a bit different than our past monarchs when it comes to his taste in entertainment," Lucius said quietly to Julia, who had yet to pry her eyes from the dancer. "If this had been Nero's banquet, this Syrian tart would have sparked an orgy by now."

Julia shook her head in disappointment as the dancer writhed on the marble floor, her legs tucked under her splayed knees. "Too bad," she replied quietly. "Where's Nero when we really need him?"

The music grew to a climax, then an abrupt end. The applause came with loud shouts for an encore. But the dancer rose, bowed toward the emperor, and made for the corner door with the same poise she had exhibited in her performance. The crowd settled down, and all eyes turned to Vespasian. Lucius was curious to see how he would follow such an act.

The emperor rose a bit sheepishly from his couch and cleared his throat. "Well . . . I know of no other father who's ever received such a gift from his son." The guests applauded Domitian's entertainment selection with gusto before Vespasian continued. "I was going to say that the days of the depraved Claudians are over. But thanks to my son, I'm not so sure." The crowd laughed, and Vespasian took a deep breath. As his chest swelled, Lucius sensed the man's pride suddenly grow. "But I will say this . . ." he continued. "Tonight, a Flavian dynasty begins." The statement sparked a powerful cheer. "Friends, you honor me with your presence here tonight. And now it is *my* turn to present you some entertainment. I think you will find this equally fascinating. It embodies the power of Rome's military might, the creativity of her citizens, and the precision of her engineers and architects." A murmur grew, as did Lucius's curiosity. "Now, despite what you're about to see, I assure you there will be no blood spilled tonight. We shall leave that for the arena. But that doesn't mean we can't have a little violence." The crowd laughed and applauded. "Friends, I present to you one of the most remarkable gladiators of the Empire . . ."

Lucius's heart sank for the second time that evening. Before the name was even announced, he slumped back into a state that hovered between depression and rage.

". . . the magnificent Taurus!"

The banquet hall doors were pulled open to a musical flourish. Taurus's flawless profile stood silhouetted against a vast rack of candles that had been precisely aligned outside the doorway. Dressed in a dark blue tunic, he was armed as a dimachaerus—a twin-bladed fighter. In each hand he held a sica, the curved sword of Thracian gladiators, one over his head and the other extended before him. From the hilt of each hung a purple sash. He wore no helmet, but his black hair was held back with a golden headband. The scene brought wild applause.

Julia placed her hand on Lucius's arm, but he was too numb to notice. His recurring nightmare had returned. Once again, his adversary was the center of attention before an emperor Lucius depended on for his new life. Would this never end?

Taurus turned and stepped into the room. He glided across the marble floor with the same grace as the exotic dancer, but the bearing and presence of a bull. His bare feet made no sound, and his twin swords swung in slow figures to his right and left. He suddenly picked up speed as he stepped into the piazza, then somersaulted across the floor and came up with a loud cry that rang over the music and persistent applause. His swords crossed in front of his face as he grabbed the neck of his tunic with his index fingers. With a mighty yank, he ripped open the top, revealing the beautiful stigmate of the Minotaur on his chest and the scarred Gorgon on his back. His well-oiled skin glistened. The candle-light played on his rippling muscles and gave life to the mythological images. The tunic dropped to the floor, and he stood clad in a violet sub-ligaculum loincloth that matched the sashes on his swords.

The ovation of the crowd rattled the walls of the banquet hall and rang in Lucius's ears like discordant music. As much as he loathed the man before him, he too was awestruck by the spectacular display of the perfect human form. He could tell by the tightening grip of Julia's hand that she was equally captivated.

The music changed to a freeform melody with no distinct beat or rhythm that became a delicate backdrop for the fluid movements begun by Taurus. His two sicas twirled in unison, the purple sashes flowing behind like colorful clouds. His arms sprang forward in a series of thrusts, and he began an elegant battle against a horde of imaginary opponents. He advanced with blades whirling in a smear of silver, then froze with arms and weapons extended in a pose that shamed the statues ringing the edge of the room. After the briefest pause, he tumbled backward and came up in blazing combat with another invisible foe.

Lucius sat in stunned fascination as the display progressed. He watched Taurus's eyes burn with intensity as the gladiator worked his way back and forth across the piazza with practiced precision. In such close proximity, Lucius could clearly see that Taurus was indeed a different person than the Quintus he knew. The power of a beast, the passion of a man possessed, and the god-like speed marked him as a truly dangerous adversary. Lucius's eyes were locked to his rival's face as Taurus began another swift advance, this time toward Lucius's couch. The blades crossed and spun. He broke into a run across the open square, arms whirling in controlled slices and thrusts. He leapt into the air and tucked his head under. He came down gracefully on his shoulders, somersaulted

across the maroon and beige marble, and rose to his knees with the tips
of both swords less than a foot from Lucius's head. Julia let out a yelp.
Lucius winced and drew back on his couch. He looked from the blade
tips into the eyes of Taurus. The reflection of a candle chandelier gave
the impression the gladiator's eyes were on fire. Lucius felt the intense
stare pressing down on him like a physical weight. He shuddered, which
brought the slightest hint of a grin to Taurus's lips. Then, as quickly as
he had appeared, the massive fighter was gone, blazing another trail of
mock combat across the piazza. Lucius took a deep breath. He glanced
around him and noticed the others in his couch cluster laughing at his
horrified reaction.

"Not to worry, Lucius," Senator Saenus chuckled. "As the emperor said
. . . no bloodshed tonight."

Lucius's humiliation grew, but Julia squeezed his arm tightly, as if
knowing he was about to reply with a response they would both regret.
Little did this senator know that the slightest provocation could have resulted in the blades piercing each of Lucius's eyes. Lucius looked to the
floor and bit his lip. His shattered nerves twitched violently at the sudden
roar of approval that greeted Taurus's final pose.

Taurus remained in his final stance for a moment, savoring the look of
pure terror he had just seen in Lucius's eyes. He had used the distraction
of the naked dancer to seek out Lucius's couch from the doorway before
he entered. He decided the result had been well worth the effort.

His thoughts and the guests' passionate applause were interrupted by
the banshee wail of Amazonia. In the dramatic motion he had practiced
as part of Vespasian's tribute, Taurus spun and faced the main double
doorway. As anticipated, all five hundred pairs of eyes followed his gaze.
Once again, the heavy bronze doors were pulled open to reveal a beautiful
specimen. Amazonia's shapely body, beautifully rimmed by the flickering light of the candle rack, stood in the portal with two straight swords
crossed over her chest. From a thin gold belt low on her waist hung two

white strips of sheer fabric, one at the front and one at the rear. She slowly lowered the gladius she held in each hand, revealing another sheer white strip tied across her breasts which concealed very little. Her auburn hair glowed like burgundy wine in the candlelight. It was held back from her face by a golden headband that matched Taurus's.

Although they had rehearsed the entrance many times at the Ludus Magnus, the sight of her in costume bathed in the warm candlelight took Taurus's breath away. He detected a quick wink in her eye before she stepped forward and entered the hall with the grace of a gazelle. He stepped backward and set his curved blades into slow swirls. Halfway to the open piazza, Amazonia screamed and broke into a run. On cue, the musicians commenced a fast rhythmic chant, backed only by cymbals and drums. Amazonia planted a bare foot on a couch at the edge of the piazza and vaulted into the open square. She executed a perfect mid-air flip and landed squarely on her feet in front of Taurus. She used her momentum to launch a blistering attack. Taurus gave ground across the open square. The clang of the four swords echoed raucously off the marble walls of the great hall. Guests jumped to their feet and screamed encouragement, gripped by the action. But Taurus concentrated on the detailed choreography of each slice and thrust. He allowed Amazonia to take the lead, since neither she nor any other fighter at the ludus could match his reflexes. Now, even if a planned move was not properly executed, the lightning-quick instincts of Taurus would prevent injury.

The gladii in Amazonia's hands windmilled across the room in pursuit of her mock-adversary. He parried each slice with the edge of his curved blades, then slowed his retreat. He gave the nod that was the signal for the tide to turn. He yelled and hammered at her swords, careful to strike at the weapon and not the arm. As she retreated, he swung at her head, and she ducked. He swung at her legs, and she jumped. He kept up the seemingly vicious assault until she neared the edge of the open square. He relented just enough for her to launch one of her trademark spin kicks. Having never fought as her opponent, Taurus had never been on the receiving end of an Amazonia kick. As he ducked and her bare foot flew past his head, he realized she had been holding back in rehearsal. The blistering speed and power in her move would have easily knocked him unconscious in a true match. The realization excited him.

Amazonia used the split second it took him to recover to commence another offensive. But this time, Taurus felt different. His arms worked in perfect synchronization with hers, blocking her thrusts as she parried his. He could hear her breathing increase. He sensed a special look in her eyes. Perhaps she felt it, too. Her sweat blended with the olive oil on her skin and created a musty smell that filled Taurus's nose. As he continued his planned retreat, he realized he was becoming physically aroused.

She ended her charge with a wail. Her right arm rose, poised for a powerful down thrust. Although distracted by this sudden urge to envelop rather than fight his opponent, he dropped his two swords as planned. They clanged on the marble floor. His left hand grabbed her wrist as it came down at him, and his right grabbed the front of the white fabric that covered her breasts. He fell backward, dragging her with him. He considered just allowing her to fall on top of him, but forced himself to stick to the script. He lifted his legs as he dropped and planted his bare feet on her abdomen. His back hit the floor with a smack, and he flipped her over, never releasing his grip on the white material. She landed topless, sprawled on the floor directly in front of the dais. She let one of her swords slip from her grasp. Taurus arched his back and sprang forward, landing upright with Amazonia's top in his right hand. He moved toward one of his two sicas, but Amazonia flipped to her stomach, reached out and grabbed his foot. He fell on his side, and in an instant Amazonia was on top of him. He held her wrist tightly, keeping her one remaining gladius at bay. They rolled entwined across the floor. The cold marble did nothing to cool the heat generated by the two sweating bodies. Amazonia breathed heavily in Taurus's face, her breath sweet with wine. He could feel her oiled breasts pressing against his chest as they struggled on the floor. The shouting of the audience was now a distant echo in Taurus's ears. The astonishing strength of the woman on top of him was intoxicating. As she straddled him, the pressure of his stiff cock pressed between her legs. The fantasy he had envisioned in the litter that night suddenly flooded his mind. With the exception of their thin loincloths, here was his fantasy come true.

Amazonia smiled at him. "So it's the rough stuff you like, eh?" she whispered so only he could hear.

Before he could answer, he was shocked to feel her mouth clamping down on his. Her tongue probed deep into his throat. If this was part of the choreography, he thought he certainly would have remembered it. The strength and power of Taurus slipped from him like water down a drain.

Quintus barely heard the roar of approval from the crowd. Amazonia finally disengaged and looked down at him with a broad smile. He lay still, foolishly staring up at her. He could not begin to remember how this fight was supposed to end. Without a hint of hesitation, Amazonia drew back her arm and smacked him across the face with the back of her hand. She then raised the gladius he had forgotten about and, with a dramatic flourish, pointed its tip at Quintus's throat. The roar of the crowd grew to a new level. But the only things on Quintus's mind were the lingering thought of her kiss and the pleasant sting of her hand across his cheek.

"Well, done!" Vespasian yelled over the crowd. The sound of the emperor's voice brought Quintus from his spell. He accepted Amazonia's hand as they both rose and faced the dais. He sincerely hoped his erection was not visible under his subligaculum. He glanced to the left and saw Petra and Julianus slowly applauding, the surprised look on their faces paling in comparison to the shock that still resonated in his body.

"This is exactly what I meant when I spoke of the creativity of our people," Vespasian continued as he strode from his couch and joined them in the open square. "Your message was clear. It is the end of the civil war, and those who were once enemies must now work hard to become as one again."

"Precisely, Caesar," Amazonia responded in her husky voice. She grinned at Quintus as the emperor raised his arm to solicit another round of applause from the guests.

"Excellent!" Vespasian said. With his arms over their shoulders, he walked them back toward the dais. "You already earned my trust and respect during the war. Tonight you've delivered an extraordinary message of peace to the citizens of Rome. For that, you have earned my eternal gratitude."

Quintus could not have timed the statement better if he had said it himself. He glanced down at a nearby couch as they walked and saw Lucius and Julia following their every step and listening to every word Vespasian said. Quintus reached behind Vespasian and nudged Amazonia. She looked across at them and winked. Quintus grinned over his shoulder, then took his place on a couch beside the emperor's dais. Once settled in, he glanced again toward Lucius's couch. The space was empty.

He caught the blur of Julia's green stola as she slinked across the banquet hall. Lucius, his face as red as the table wine, was heading toward the bronze doors, tugging Julia behind him.

XXVI

January AD 70

VESPASIAN CALLED his first staff meeting two days after the banquet. Lucius was among the first to enter the Aula Regia—the throne room. His footsteps echoed from the polished marble and gold surfaces as he walked. The majesty of the surroundings had the desired humbling effect on those who entered.

A colonnade of white Corinthian columns lined three of the walls, their height working to stretch the room to appear even loftier than it was. The far wall of maroon and yellow marble held a semicircular alcove topped by an ornate half-dome. The throne itself—a dark wood chair upholstered in maroon and detailed with gold braid and precious stones—was wide enough to hold even the most corpulent emperor. It was centered in the alcove, resting on a platform two steps above the gray marble floor.

Lucius took a seat near the middle of the massive U-shaped table that had been set for the occasion. The open end faced the throne so Vespasian would have an unobstructed view of each of his advisors, who were now filtering in, in small groups. Besides Primus, Mucianus, and a few other high-ranking military officers, the rest of the thirty-two advisors were well-educated patricians, mostly businessmen carefully selected for their specialized knowledge in everything from finance and trade to the arts and engineering. Aside from the Senate, this was the inner circle of the elite, each of whom had daily access to the emperor himself. Looking round the table, Lucius's spirits rose for the first time in two days.

He had spent the first few hours after the banquet dealing with the Drusilla issue. As much as he had detested bargaining with the two scum thugs he unearthed in the grimy streets of the insulae tenements, silencing her was a necessary effort. He would protect his new life at all costs.

Virtually every other hour of the past two days he had agonized over the words Vespasian had spoken to Quintus at the banquet. The gladiator was too dangerous for him to simply ignore, yet the magical spell Quintus seemed to hold over the emperor was going to be difficult to break. Despite Julia's warnings, Lucius was determined to drive a wedge between the gladiator and the emperor. He could then eliminate Quintus Honorius Romanus from his life once and for all.

Julia had offered to meet with Quintus—"to better judge his state of mind," she had said. But Lucius refused. This was an issue he alone had to deal with. Besides, he had a nagging sense that Julia had some ulterior motive for the meeting. He had enough problems in his life right now without opening another battlefront.

The sound of approaching footsteps brought his attention back to the present. Everyone rose as Vespasian entered the hall. He approached the low stage that held the throne and shook his head with a sigh.

"This is a bit much, don't you think?" He addressed the question to the assembly in general.

"Not at all, your majesty," said a smarmy man Lucius didn't recognize. "It *is* protocol, after all."

Vespasian shrugged, climbed the two steps, and dropped onto the throne. "Very well. Let's get started."

The meeting took most of the morning. Each advisor introduced himself to the rest at the table and spoke briefly of the goals for his position. It appeared most of the staff already knew each other and had worked with Vespasian before. Lucius began to feel more and more like an outsider but was determined to make an impression. He had consulted with Julia the day before on a plan that he knew would get everyone's attention. When his turn came, he stood, outlined his background—omitting,

of course, the majority of his twenty-two years spent as a kitchen slave—
and then presented the key points of a bold shipping and commerce plan.
He made the impression he sought when he concluded with a promise to restore the gross tonnage of grain imports from North Africa to
their pre-blockade levels within just two months. A few scoffed, but
Vespasian's enthusiasm quickly quieted the nay-sayers.

At noon, the emperor called for a food break. As the servants brought
in the first trays, Vespasian rose and walked to the spread of shellfish along
the west wall. Lucius saw his opportunity to catch the emperor's ear.

"That's quite an ambitious plan you've set for yourself, Lucius," the
emperor said as Lucius approached. "But you have a good head for sched-
ules and efficiency. If anyone can handle it, I'm sure it's you."

"Thank you, Caesar. Your confidence is an honor. I won't let you
down." Lucius glanced around and saw most of the staff were standing throughout the throne room in small groups, deep in discussion. He
lowered his voice. "I would, however, be remiss if I didn't once again try
to bring a serious problem to your attention."

Vespasian raised a shaggy eyebrow. "Not this Quintus situation
again . . ."

"Caesar, he is a serious threat to you. My sources tell me that the man
led his gladiators against the armies of three different emperors, including your own!"

"It's not what you think, Lucius."

"I've heard talk from reliable people that he himself murdered
Otho."

Vespasian shrugged. "So what if he did? Is that supposed to convince
me this man is a menace to me?"

"If he was cunning enough to get to that well-guarded emperor, why
do you not think he will come after you?"

Vespasian chuckled and turned his attention again to the shellfish.

The sound irritated Lucius. He could feel his heart begin to race.
"How can you be so sure of his loyalty? This is *not* the boy you once

knew. How can I convince you of that? He's a gladiator, and all gladiators are mercenaries. He made secret deals throughout this war with anyone who paid enough money. By the gods, he destroyed his own artillery in one battle! How can you trust a man like that? For the right price, he'd just as quickly put a knife in *your* back, too. He needs to be *eliminated*."

Lucius's voice rose, and Vespasian glanced around to be sure no one else could hear. He put down a bowl of raw oysters, took Lucius by the arm, and pulled him toward a vacant corner of the room. "Look, I'm well aware of everything he and his men did during this war. In fact, I know more about it than anyone else, including you. I trust him with my life."

Lucius's frustration rose. He could not fathom why Vespasian would show such loyalty to a fucking gladiator. "He is a danger, Caesar! Why can't you see that?"

For the first time, Lucius saw anger rise in Vespasian's face. Or was it suspicion?

"What has this man done to you, Lucius? Why do you hate him so?"

Lucius panicked. "And why do you *protect* him so?" he yelled. "He's a scum gladiator and a known traitor!" The instant he finished the sentence, Lucius knew he had crossed the line. The entire staff and many of the servants stared at him in stunned silence. Primus's hand moved to the hilt of his sword.

"Leave us!" Vespasian shouted. At first Lucius wasn't sure to whom he was speaking. But as the staff and servants quickly headed for the doors, he knew this would not be good. He began to tremble. Would Quintus once again cost him a high-ranking imperial position?

Vespasian nodded to Primus, who was the last to leave the room. He then stepped nose-to-nose with Lucius. "For a smart man, how can you be so stupid? Don't you realize that Quintus and his gladiators have been working for me all along? Who do you think my spy was within the ranks? Yes, he fought for Otho, but just to eliminate more Vitellians. Yes, he killed Otho, and then staged it to look like a suicide. Those were my orders! That one death saved countless Roman lives. And yes, it was he who negotiated with Caecina. He was the first one to talk peace with the general. Damn it, Lucius, I myself didn't even know it was Quintus doing all this until we were on the Rostra together. All I knew was we needed an emissary we could trust, and when loyal friends like Titus Cassius Petra and Marcus Livius Castus tell me I can trust a man, I *believe* them. And now that I know it was Quintus Romanus, I know why they were so sure."

Lucius's knees began to rattle. The thought of Quintus personally playing such a monumental role in the outcome of this war was overwhelming. To his horror, Vespasian wasn't finished. The emperor pushed even closer to Lucius's face.

"Yes, he and his men had to kill a few of my men. They had no choice. But as far as I'm concerned their acts proved their loyalty and secured amnesty for every damned one of them. And they will continue to be housed at the Ludus Magnus as my auxiliary security force until I feel the streets of Rome are secure. Do you understand now why I do not see this man as a threat? I don't want to hear another word about Quintus and his gladiators. Nor do I expect to have to explain myself to you again!" Vespasian squinted, making the pained expression on his face even more pronounced. "You'll make a good praefectus annonae, Lucius. But, by the gods, I'll put you on one of your own damned freighters and ship you back to Egypt if this matter is ever raised again. Do I make myself clear?"

The harsh threats swirled around Lucius's head like a whirlwind on the high seas. But he couldn't back down. He knew that Quintus would not let him live in peace, not after all that had happened. No, he couldn't let the gladiator win this fight. He couldn't live with that sword dangling over him any longer.

"What of *my* loyalty to you?" he shouted back at the emperor. "Julia and I have provided you with valuable information and transportation all year. We were among the first to push you to assume the principate. We financed your march to Rome! Does that not stand for something? Does that not show *our* loyalty to you?"

Vespasian studied Lucius for a moment before answering. "What it shows is your ambition to back a candidate to whom you have ties. Nothing more . . . especially after all this."

Lucius could have screamed and strangled the emperor right there. But before he said another word, Vespasian's expression changed. The emperor's eyes became tiny slits.

"And don't think I'm not checking this situation out, Lucius. I'm still not sure what happened that day at the games."

"What games?" Lucius asked as nonchalantly as he could muster.

"When the bulls were let loose and trampled hundreds of spectators. You remember the incident, don't you?" Vespasian's condescending tone struck Lucius like a slap in the face. "The story I heard," the emperor continued, "was that Quintus Romanus was the editor of the games that day, and that he went mad and released the bulls. Now, how could that have been Quintus Romanus if Quintus Romanus was fighting in the arena that day as a gladiator?" Vespasian's words came more slowly, and his eyes seemed to burn two holes into Lucius's forehead. "Unfortunately, I was with Nero in Greece when it happened. But I *will* find out who the editor of the games really was that day. I know damn well it wasn't Quintus Romanus, and I owe it to him to clear his name."

Lucius fought to control himself, but as much as he tried, he could not keep the quiver from his voice. "I . . . I don't know who sat on the podium that day. Julia and I were not there either."

Lucius felt Vespasian's eyes probe even deeper.

"Interesting . . ." the emperor said. "An advisor to the emperor and you were not at the games?"

"We . . . We had other business," Lucius stammered. "I believe we were—"

Vespasian suddenly raised his hand in Lucius's face. "It doesn't matter. I have no time for this now." The emperor turned and walked away as he called to his legate. "Primus!"

Lucius trembled violently. He wondered if he was about to be arrested on the spot. The legate quickly stepped into the room, his hand still firmly on the hilt of his sword.

"Call the staff back," Vespasian continued. "Let us dine and finish the meeting."

On shaky legs, Lucius hobbled to his seat. Although the food was plentiful, he could not eat. The staff members stayed clear of him during lunch, sensing the tension in the air and wary of any repercussions.

Lucius hardly noticed. Nor did he utter another word for the rest of the afternoon. His mind was preoccupied with a hundred random thoughts, all of them nauseating. He struggled to keep his hands from shaking and his feet from tapping against the tiled floor. Like a schoolchild impatiently waiting for recess, he counted the moments until he could leave the room.

Then he and Julia could plot the death of Quintus Romanus.

Julia sat in the peristyle of her new house. The late afternoon breeze brought a winter chill to the garden setting, but it did not cool Julia's buoyant enthusiasm. Opposite her, two young designers, recommended by Senator Saenus's wife Thuria, were matching bolts of fabric to tile and marble samples. Decorating was always Julia's favorite part of relocation. The city home could not match her sprawling country villa in Britannia, but this prime location, on the slopes of the imperial Palatine Hill in the heart of Rome, more than made up for the reduced square footage. Julia had a clear vision of what this new home should be, and the two designers were doing an excellent job of bringing her ideas to reality.

"Let's talk about the bedroom," she said. "Those dark hues have to go. I'm thinking—"

The crash of the front door slamming against the inside wall startled the three of them. "Julia!" Lucius's voice screamed. It had the high-pitched tone that told her he was in one of his foul moods again.

"Out here, Lucius."

He roughly shoved one of the kitchen servant girls out of the way as he entered the peristyle, causing her to drop the tray she had just retrieved from the terrace. "We need to talk."

Julia was incensed. As usual, *his* issues were more important than anything she was doing. Well, not this time. "It'll have to wait. I'm in the middle of redoing our house."

He approached, and she saw the manic look in his eyes that meant trouble. Serious trouble. She hadn't seen him this intense since the day Quintus had come to their State apartment and carted him off to the African ludus. Lucius hovered over the three of them for a moment, then picked up two bolts of fabric and threw them into the fountain pool with a scream.

"Fuck the house! We may not have it long enough for you to decorate it!"

He turned to the two designers, who had scampered toward the pond, attempting to salvage their expensive material. "Leave us!" he screamed, his face almost purple with rage.

"I'm so sorry," Julia called to them as they hurried toward the door, empty handed. "We'll pay for the ruined material, and I'll have your samples returned tomorrow."

Lucius grabbed her by the arms and she cried out.

"Will you forget the fucking decorating! We have a big problem."

"You're hurting me! Calm down, will you?"

Lucius released his grip, kicked at the stack of tiles, and dropped heavily into the cushioned chair the servants had placed for Julia. She sat on the low fountain wall next to him.

"Now take a breath and tell me what happened."

Slowly and deliberately, Lucius spelled out the lurid details of his encounter with Vespasian that morning. With every word, Julia saw her new home and social standing drift further and further away. When he was done, they both sat in silence. The darkening evening sky reflected her life perfectly, Julia thought. Every time she saw sun-filled skies ahead, twilight always stole away her bright future. But it wasn't Apollo or Pluto or any of the other gods who interfered. It was always Lucius with his hot temper and big mouth. Now, once again, she would need to take control before the twilight became the pitch blackness of midnight. Her mind raced. She needed to fix this for the night, then get to Quintus in the morning. It was time to put her backup plan into action.

"We're finished," Lucius mumbled, staring at the scattered tiles. "Once again, that asshole of a gladiator is beating me." He looked up at Julia. His panic had simmered to a dark seething anger. "I'll tell you this. I will *not* return to that stinking cesspool of a ludus again. I would rather *die* than see that cell again."

Julia forced herself to focus, despite her anger. She struggled for a temporary solution, something to soothe Lucius, even if just for the evening. A thought began to form.

"You know . . . why do you think you'll be singled out in any wrong doing here?" She paused and looked at his flushed face. "Think about it . . . Just because Vespasian's suspicious that it wasn't really Quintus Romanus on the editor's podium that day in the arena, why should he think it was you?"

"Because he knows Quintus, and Quintus will tell him it was me."

"So what? It's our word against his. Nobody in Vespasian's inner circle was part of Nero's administration. Out with the Claudians, in with the Flavians, right?"

Lucius's eyes widened. "That's true. Nobody he knows can place me on that podium that day. Drusilla's been dealt with, I saw to that two days ago."

Julia's heart skipped a beat. "You didn't . . ."

Lucius simply stared at her, and she knew the answer. By the gods, they were now involved in the cold-blooded murder of an innocent woman! When would the melodrama end with this man? She took a breath and forced herself to focus on the issue at hand—keeping Lucius calm.

She stroked his arm as she spoke. "Maybe we can even keep Quintus quiet . . . with enough money. One thing Vespasian *does* know is that Quintus is entitled to inherit the shipping line. But what would a gladiator do with a transport business? I'll develop a plan to share profits with Quintus. Even a small share will certainly pay more than any arena fights. And the money will keep flowing only as long as he keeps his mouth shut."

Lucius continued to stare at her, but she saw the spark in his eyes that had kindled so briefly go out. After a few seconds, he stared once again at the dark floor and the jumble of colored tiles.

"Oh, what's the fucking point? We'll fix this problem, and there will just be another, and another after that." His head snapped up, and he looked her in the eyes. She could see the demon inside had returned again. "The only way to stop this nightmare is to see that man *dead* once and for all."

"Wrong!" Julia yelled. "Once again, you're overestimating his power. He's just a *gladiator*. What can he do to us? He has no proof of anything."

"He has the emperor's ear! And from what I've seen, Vespasian is listening."

Julia stood. She had had enough of Lucius's paranoia for one evening. "I say we just lay low for a while. I'll wager that this whole thing will be forgotten in a few days. That is, unless *you* keep bringing it up!"

She walked across the garden and headed for their upstairs bedroom, wringing her hands to stop them from shaking. She hoped her words had done enough to get her through another day or two without Lucius having a complete breakdown. She stopped and looked back at the broken figure sitting alone in the dark. As much as she hated his childish tantrums that continued to place them in jeopardy, she pitied him for the torment she knew was tearing him apart. In a way, she wished she felt closer to him, so she could truly soothe him. But she knew now that day would never come. There would be no marriage. There would be no more chances. There would be no more Lucius Calidius in her life.

• • •

For hours Lucius lay awake, staring at the tiny crack in the ceiling above their bed. He knew he would not sleep at all this night. His mind played back every word of his argument with Vespasian over and over again. The more he recalled the emperor's affection for the bastard gladiator, the more he returned to the same conclusion: the only answer was murder. But this time it would be done right. He would not leave the task to some dim-witted arena manager like last time. This time his plan would succeed. This time he would deliver the blow himself. No, he wasn't a trained fighter like Quintus. No, he hadn't killed a hundred men. Just one. But that one was a gladiator also. The thought made him smile. They all have a weakness. It's just a matter of finding it and exploiting it to maximum effect. He spent the next hour exploring every angle, probing every possibility. Soon, a plan formed in his head, each piece dropping into place like a perfect mosaic mural.

He rolled over and shook Julia vigorously. "Wake up! I've seen it! I've seen the death of the gladiator!" He could not bring himself to even say the man's name.

"What's the matter with you?" she replied in a groggy voice. "I thought we were done with this. Go back to sleep."

Lucius's fervor quickly turned to rage. "Sleep? You think I've been sleeping tonight? My fucking eyes haven't shut for a moment! While you've been snoring your ass off, I've been worrying about our future!"

Julia sat up and covered herself with the white bedsheet. "You mean you've been worrying about how to fix another colossal fuck-up you've brought on yourself!" she screamed. "When will it end, Lucius?"

"It won't end until he's dead and you know it!"

"All I know is, you've screwed with my life for the last time, you bastard." He was stunned at the hatred that suddenly appeared in her eyes. "I want no part of whatever this new insane scheme of yours is. Count me out."

Lucius was livid. "Count you out?" He laughed, despite his urge to scream. "I'm afraid not, Julia. It's just like the last time. If I go down, we both go down together."

Now it was Julia's turn to laugh. She knelt on the bed and faced him. "Oh, not this time, sweet Lucius. I've looked after *myself* this time. I've . . ."

She hesitated. Lucius eyed her suspiciously.

"You've what? Decided to buy another low-cut stola?" He roughly grabbed her right breast. "You think these tits alone are going to get you where you want to be?"

She knocked his hand away. "I've made a plan of my own." Her chin rose in defiance as she said the words. Then a smile crossed her lips. "I've known all along that Quintus was Vespasian's man on the front lines. I knew he'd be the hero of this war. That's why I've decided to . . . let's say, reestablish my family relations." Her eyes narrowed. "Alone."

Lucius forced out a laugh to cover his shock. "And what makes you think that bastard will have anything to do with you?"

The hatred in her eyes intensified. "Because when it comes to family, you know as well as I how Quintus is. A whispered reminder of his mother—my sister-in-law—should do it. A few tender stories from the old days and he'll be like clay in my hands."

Lucius was speechless. His own partner, in both life and business—the woman he shared a bed with! The woman he was about to marry!—had been working behind his back. The bitch had lived under his wing all the way from Africa to Judea to Rome, and she thanked him by planning a secret alliance with the most hated enemy of all?

"Oh, you're not *hurt,* are you, Lucius?" she continued. The condescending grin grew across her caustic face. "You didn't confuse this marriage idea with *love,* did you? Surely you realized it was just a convenient business arrangement. After all, how far could a woman get in Rome on her own, even a *rich* woman like me?"

Lucius heard the words as if they were distant, spoken in a vast cave. The room began to spin. A wave of fury rose inside him like he had never felt before. He stared at her defiant face. All he saw was the smug grin, mocking him and laughing at his gullibility. It was too much. His arm sprang forward, and he slapped her hard enough to knock her from the bed. Her naked body hit the wooden floor with a thud. The sound was a hollow echo in his ears. The room suddenly became foggy, but his mind was clear. He would deal with her, then he would deal with Quintus—alone if he had to. He crawled across the wool-stuffed mattress. But before he reached the side, Julia's head slowly appeared above the edge of the bed, her hateful eyes glued to him. A trickle of blood ran from her mouth. Beside her head rose the point of the dagger she held in her right hand. The wide blade reflected the moonlight that shone through the window. Lucius froze in the middle of the bed.

Julia's voice came like the whispered hiss of a serpent. "I'll be goddamned if I'm going to let you drag me into Hades with you again. It's over, Lucius. I'd rather die a pauper than live another day with a pig like you. Now, *get out.*"

Lucius knelt motionless on the bed, not understanding how his entire world could be crumbling around him once again. All the nights he had lain awake in the African ludus—just like tonight—and wondered what he could have done differently to keep his life on course . . . they all amounted to nothing. For some unknown reason, the gods had ordered him to repeat the same horrid existence over and over again until he was dead. Now, perhaps, that time had finally come. He would welcome it. But he wasn't about to die alone. By all the gods in the heavens, he would take the gladiator with him.

"Get out!"

Her scream made him jump. Without another word, he stood and lifted a tunic from the tortoise-shell bedpost. He walked down the stairs, through the atrium, and out the front door. The cold January wind whipped his naked body. But he felt no pain or discomfort. Just numbness as he walked down the Clivus Victoriae and into the darkness.

XXVII

January AD 70

THE BANG of the wooden rudis against his opponent's shield was a welcome sound to Quintus. It had been far too long since he fought for sport rather than survival. He cheerfully faced off against a primus palus murmillo from the Rome school. His Pompeiian comrades and many of the Roman fighters had gathered at the edge of the miniature arena in the heart of the Ludus Magnus. A few fortunate spectators were in the small cavea to witness the event. They were the rabid fans who lingered each morning near the ludus gate in hopes of being admitted to watch the day's training sessions. The savvy procurator of Rome's ludus used the eager fans wisely. Nothing filled an arena faster than the word of mouth they would spread about the latest up-and-coming heroes.

Quintus wanted to be sure the name "Taurus" was on the lips of these aficionados. While he didn't summon his warrior spirit for sparring bouts, he did put on an exhilarating display of speed and power. He was surprised at how well his opponent kept him at bay and even managed to force him into a few short retreats. The cheering of the Rome and Pompeii fighters quickly overpowered the small enthusiastic audience. By the intensity of his comrades' shouting, Quintus knew substantial wagers had been placed on him.

After a strenuous ten minutes, he decided to bring the bout to a close. He willed the speed he needed into his right arm, and the thrusts and slices doubled in intensity. Even in the cool afternoon breeze, the Roman murmillo quickly drained of all energy. Within moments, he was on his back with Quintus's wooden sica at his chest. Julianus, working as referee and Thracian trainer, called a "Halt." The murmillo pounded the sand in frustration as a loud cheer erupted from the Pompeiian fighters, who immediately looked to collect their winnings.

"Don't fret, Attilius," Quintus said, offering his hand to help raise the gladiator from the sand. "I'm unusually swift this day. It's just the euphoria of fighting once again in an arena. I can't help it."

Attilius grunted and allowed himself to be hauled to his feet. He pulled the helmet from his head and inspected the three large red welts on his right arm and left leg. "I'd hate to face that speed with a metal sica in your hand," he said.

"And you only fought 'Quintus,'" Julianus said as he slapped the vanquished murmillo's back. "You've yet to face 'Taurus.'" The senior trainer looked up into the small cavea and nodded a smile to Petra, who had been watching the afternoon sessions. "Alright, that's it for today," Julianus called to his men. "I want all Pompeiian fighters gathered in front of Dominus Petra now."

The Roman gladiators left the arena and filtered toward their barracks. As the spectators were ushered out by the ludus workers, shouts of "Hail, Taurus" rose from some of the more enthusiastic fans. Quintus looked up and smiled. It was good to be back. He joined Amazonia and Lindani along the low stone wall in front of their lanista.

"I saw some nice fighting today, ladies," Petra growled in the gravelly voice Quintus had come to love. The lanista's upbeat manner and temperament reminded Quintus of the old days back in the Britannia ludus. He wondered if it was due to the end of the war, or the fact that Petra was on his own in Rome and not constricted by his dictatorial partner, Facilix, who had remained at the Pompeii ludus. Either way, it was a welcome sight.

"I'm glad to see your time on the battlefield hasn't diminished your skills," Petra continued. "Now I don't have to waste time retraining all you assholes." The troupe laughed. "Except for you, Cavell. You still look like a fucking monkey with a gladius. Keep that damned shield working or you're going to lose that lethargic left arm of yours. Julianus, see that he does."

"Yes, Dominus," came the senior trainer's immediate response.

"All right then," Petra continued as he paced along the front row of wooden seats. "Tonight I want you all to say two prayers to Hercules: one for all the good men we lost in the war, and the second for yourself, to thank him that you weren't one of them."

The men mumbled in agreement. As their centurion, Quintus felt partially responsible for every one of those deaths. He decided he would say fifty-two prayers tonight, mentioning each lost comrade by name to Hercules.

Petra's voice rang out again. "I got word this morning that the emperor has called for games to celebrate his new dynasty. He has decided on another Rome vs. Pompeii Challenge, since the last match was such a success—apart from the incident with the idiot editor and his bulls, of course." An expectant murmur rose from the assembled fighters. "Now, Julianus and I debated about telling you this next bit of information, but we decided to set your minds at ease. Vespasian has made it clear that, as a reward for your role in his victory, none of you will be sentenced to death." The murmur quickly grew to a loud cheer. "But for the sake of your purses, which I understand will be substantial, and the honor of the Pompeii ludus, you *will* fight your best. Is that understood, ladies?"

A rousing "Yes, Dominus" came from the fighters.

"I said, is that understood?" Petra repeated.

This time Quintus was certain the response could be heard on the far side of the Campus Martius.

"Who do we honor in the arena?" Quintus yelled.

"Ave Vespasian!" the crowd of fighters replied.

"And who do we honor in our ludus?"

"Ave Dominus Petra!" they responded as one. The lanista's name was followed by a rousing cheer. Quintus smiled. He was glad to see that the spirit of their ludus had remained intact throughout the war.

A rare grin flashed on Petra's lips but was gone just as quickly. "Settle down," he ordered. "Lastly . . . Amazonia, Vulcanus, and Flama, see Julianus before you head to the barracks. The rest of you are dismissed."

"Ah, shit," Amazonia said to Quintus and Lindani as the group dispersed. "You know what that means."

"You have made the sex list, eh?" Lindani said with a cackle.

Quintus felt a pang of jealousy singe his heart but stood steadfast while Amazonia vented. "Yeah, just like my whoring days with my fucking pimp father."

"It's not that bad," Quintus said with a nudge, trying to make the news a little less painful for them both. "At least here you get to keep half the money. And, I'll tell you, from the parties I've been rented to this week, there are worse duties in the Empire."

Amazonia's eyes rose and met his. The hurt there surprised him. Then she shrugged and walked away. He watched her lithe body float across the sand. The pleasant vision was interrupted by Julianus calling his name.

"I have a message for you from the front gate," the trainer said as he handed the last of the practice equipment to a young ludus slave. "The guard says a woman named Julia was asking to meet with you this morning. Isn't that your aunt from Britannia?"

"It is." Quintus's suspicions rose quickly. "Did she say what she wanted?"

Julianus shook his head. "She was insistent, but the guards were firm about no interruptions during training. She said she'd be back tonight."

"Thank you, Doctore. I'm sure it's nothing."

But Quintus knew that everything involving Julia or Lucius always led to something. What were they planning now?

Amazonia heard her name ring down the hallway that separated the ludus holding cells. She adjusted the same sheer white top she had worn at Vespasian's banquet. The costume had been specifically requested by her client. She added a deep red dye of crushed berries to her lips, accentuating their fullness, just as she had done before servicing the wealthy Pompeiians who had rented her from her father so many years ago.

She pushed open the unlocked cell door and walked the length of the cold, dark hallway alone. The guard at the front gate checked her off the roster under the light of a wall-mounted torch, then handed the wax tablet to the coach driver who made his mark alongside her name. The burly driver opened the coach door, and Amazonia sighed as she stepped up into a luxurious interior. At least the ride to the house would be pleasant, she thought. But this was always the part of these visits she hated most, when her mind ran through the possibilities of what her night might hold. Usually it was a rather boring experience—a bit of awkward foreplay followed by a rather quick session of dull sex in two or three positions. About half the time, she would service couples, usually together but sometimes individually while the other watched. Occasionally, things would get rough or too depraved even for her liberal boundaries. So far, her physical strength and cunning mind had kept her safe. On rare occasions, the night would actually be a pleasurable experience, ending in a heated, synchronized climax for both her and her customer. But this would be her first sexual encounter since leaving Pompeii. She drummed her long fingers on the red upholstery and wondered why she felt so repulsed by something she had been doing all her life. Perhaps, she thought, it was because she now looked at Quintus so differently.

The coach left the Campus Martius, which housed the Ludus Magnus alongside the Amphitheater of Taurus. It turned left and drove along the darkened Vicus Aesculeti. Other carts passed them, beginning their evening deliveries of food, wine, supplies, and other necessities to shops throughout Rome. Aside from the tenement insulae apartment buildings, the houses they passed grew larger and more opulent the closer the carriage rolled toward the Forum Romanum and the city center.

After a few more turns, the driver pulled his horses to a stop. She heard his boots drop onto the smooth paving stones, and an instant later her door opened.

"That way, please," the man said, pointing toward the double front doors. He followed her though a small garden as she approached the ornately carved wooden entryway. A servant standing outside turned and pushed open the left door. Amazonia was impressed at the hefty build of the slaves. To afford such fine specimens, this must be a very wealthy family.

She stepped inside a dimly lit atrium. The sound of water trickling into the square pool at the center gave the home a pleasant, welcoming atmosphere. The burly driver placed his hand on her back and gently guided her around the pool and toward the stairs near the rear peristyle. A second fountain in the garden, surrounded by a low wall, continued the peaceful whisper of running water. The moan of a woman came from an upstairs room. It sounded as if they'd started without her, Amazonia thought.

She climbed the first few stairs, then noticed a shadow appear at the top landing.

"Good evening, Amazonia," came a young man's voice. "I've been looking forward to this."

Amazonia squinted in the dim light. Although the voice quavered, it had a familiar tone to it. "Do I know you?" she asked.

"I believe you have seen me once or twice before," the silhouette replied.

As she approached the wide landing, the man stepped into the pool of light cast by the triple oil lamp in the corner. The shadows were wiped from his face, and Amazonia froze in shock.

"*You!* You called me here tonight?"

Lucius Calidius grinned. "And why not? I admired your performance at the banquet. Most captivating." His grin turned to a hateful sneer. "Especially when you planted a lingering kiss on the lips of that . . . *gladiator.*"

Amazonia's heart pounded. The closer she stepped to Lucius, the clearer the madness showed in his eyes. Her survival instincts rose and she looked for an avenue of escape. She could hear both the coachman and the bodyguard climbing the stairs behind her. She glanced at the open door behind Lucius, wondering what was under the outside window on the far wall. Could she survive a jump?

A movement on the bed below the window caught her eye. She saw a naked body splayed across the mattress, arms and legs bound to the four bedposts with rope. She recognized the woman as Quintus's aunt, Julia Melita, although her delicate features were bruised and swollen, and her mouth was gagged. The woman moaned again, and Amazonia realized it was a moan of pain, not pleasure. Even in the dim light of the oil lamp, the white sheets glistened red with fresh blood between Julia's legs. The woman's eyes reflected pure terror as she stared helplessly at Amazonia.

Lucius stepped forward. His trembling voice lowered to a whisper as he neared Amazonia. "I especially enjoyed your arena performance during my Rome versus Pompeii match." He reached out and gently stroked her auburn hair. "That was quite a daring feat, lifting that gate and running into an arena full of lions . . . Just to save that *gladiator*." He screamed the last word into her face, grabbing a handful of hair in a vicious tug.

Amazonia swiped his hand away and drew back to swing her powerful fist at his head. But her arm was hooked by the bodyguard. She pulled the man forward and flipped him over her shoulder. He hit the wooden floor at Lucius's feet. With a wail she stomped on the man's groin, then lunged again toward Lucius. The husky coachman leapt forward and grabbed her around the waist, lifting her off her feet. Three more men, each with the massive arms and chest of a professional fighter, poured through the bedroom door. In a second, she was overwhelmed. Her arms were immobile, but she kicked frantically at both Lucius and her attackers. Soon, she was on the floor beside the groaning bodyguard with four large men on top of her.

The coachman pulled hard on her hair, and she screamed as he yanked her up onto her knees. Lucius's grinning face appeared just inches from her nose. The crazed look in his eyes frightened her almost as much as her first arena battle. But she steeled herself against his madness. Before he could say a word, she spit in his face.

"Fuck you, Lucius," she screamed. "Do what you want with me, but Quintus will win. You know he'll always beat you, no matter what."

Lucius did not attempt to wipe the saliva from his cheek. Instead, he leaned back and punched her hard on the jaw. Although pain seared through her face, she stared defiantly at him without flinching.

He grabbed her swelling chin and held her face close to his. His words came through teeth clenched tight enough to snap a gladius in half. "You listen to me, you fucking bitch. That gladiator should be dead now. If it wasn't for you and that African savage, he would have been a lion's meal two years ago. Well, you have interfered in my life for the last time. Tonight your gladiator friend dies. And then you die." An evil smile crossed his face. "But first, we'll have some fun."

XXVIII

January AD 70

QUINTUS SHOOK the small bones in his cup, then let the sheep knuckles roll against the stone wall of the barracks building. For the third time that night, all four dice showed a different side—the highest score possible. A cheer went up from the dozen or so fighters who had bet on another winning roll from the gladiator.

"Another *Venus!*" yelled a wide Thracian who had wagered against him. "I want to see those bones. You've fixed them!"

Quintus laughed and gladly threw the man the tali dice. "Have a good look, Tigris, then pay the winners."

Quintus looked past the Thracian and out the barracks door, expecting a guard to call for him at any moment. But the dimly lit hallway was vacant. He wondered why Julia had not yet returned. He was certainly wary of her intentions, but curiosity was getting the better of him. Besides, she was family—maybe not by blood, but by the laws of marriage. And she was the *only* family he had who was still alive. If she needed his help, he was ready to hear her out.

His thoughts were abruptly interrupted by a slap on his back and loud cackle from Lindani. "That is four times I win big on you today," the African said with a laugh, "three times in the barracks and once in the practice arena. The goddess Fortuna is with you today, my friend."

"It would seem she is, Lindani," Quintus replied. "It's been a good day."

The Thracian grunted and dropped the bones back in the cup. "Well, Fortuna has stuck a gladius up *my* ass tonight. I'm done." He threw his forty sesterces down on the dirt floor and walked away.

Quintus looked up and winked at Lindani as he gathered his winnings and dropped the coins into his leather pouch with a clink. "Yes, the gods favor the bull tonight." He shook the cup again. "So who's next?"

"Quintus," a guard's voice yelled from the door, "there's a coach waiting for you at the front gate."

Finally, he thought. "Is there a woman inside? Middle-aged, attractive?"

"No, just the driver. He insists on seeing you. I checked with Dominus Petra and he said to let you know and see what you wanted to do."

Quintus looked at Lindani. "Julia came here this morning looking for me. She said she'd return tonight but never showed."

The African shrugged. "Perhaps this is her coachman. Or, perhaps a woman of Rome looks to be rammed by Taurus the bull tonight, eh?"

"By the gods, I hope not. Not after the one last night." Quintus grabbed a blanket off his mat, then headed toward the door. Lindani was right next to him.

"I must see who insists on stroking Taurus's rudis tonight," he said with his wide grin.

In the pool of torchlight near the front gate, Petra stood talking with a burly coach driver in a black cloak. Quintus arrived in the middle of their conversation.

"He says his lady insists on having you tonight," Petra said. "She's offering a thousand sesterces. That's a nice sum for both of us, but I'll leave it up to you."

Quintus was disappointed the driver had not been sent by Julia. He stretched and yawned as he glanced past the driver into the sumptuous red interior of the coach. But the bitter night breeze seemed frigid after the warmth of the barracks. He pulled the blanket tighter over his shoulders. "Too cold and too tired," he said. "Besides, my luck is running hot with the tali tonight. Tell your lady, maybe tomorrow."

Petra shrugged at the driver and Quintus turned to leave. Before he took a step, he felt a firm hand grasp his bicep. The strength and audacity of the coachman surprised him. He turned and looked the man in the eye, ready to throw him to the ground if he dared persist. But there was something about the expression on the gruff man's face. The driver turned his back to Petra and Lindani. He opened his cloak and revealed something in his hand to Quintus.

"I think you should reconsider," he whispered in a hoarse voice.

Quintus studied the furry object in the driver's hand for a moment. Slowly, he recognized the item for what it was: a lock of hair. Auburn hair. Amazonia's hair. And it was streaked with fresh blood that stained the driver's palm red.

Quintus looked up at the coachman. "Where is she?"

"Get in the coach," the man whispered. "Alone, or she dies."

Quintus felt his fury surge. He was ready to strangle the captor on the spot, but kept his temper in check for Amazonia's sake. "I've changed my mind, Dominus," he said, dropping the blanket from his shoulders. "I'll go."

Without another word, he stepped into the carriage. The driver shut the door and climbed up into his seat. He tossed a large bag of coins at Petra's feet, then snapped the reins. Quintus glanced out the window as the coach pulled away. He saw puzzled looks on the two men left standing in the dust. He stared into Lindani's eyes. It was only the briefest instant, but he hoped the African got the message.

The carriage ride was short. They turned off the paved road from the ludus and headed across the fields that surrounded the Amphitheater of Taurus. In a few moments, they stopped on the far side of the arena.

"Inside," the coachman said as he jumped from the driver's seat. He pointed at one of the arched entrances with the gladius he now held in his right hand. From the way his fingers played on the hilt, Quintus could tell the man was a seasoned fighter.

Quintus entered the passageway and stepped past a gate that had been broken open. The coachman was a step behind him. Torchlight glowed at the far end of the dark inclined corridor. Quintus's pulse and breathing increased with every step he took. Finally he passed through the portal and entered the cavea at mid-level. He looked down into the arena and stood paralyzed.

In the center of the oval, Amazonia lay naked and bleeding in the sand. Her arms and legs were spread wide, tied to the base of four lit torches that had been driven deep into the sand. Purple welts and fresh cuts enveloped her body. Quintus could not see her face, as she stared toward the man who stood between her legs.

Lucius Calidius raised the front of his tunic and stroked his engorged penis. He looked up at Quintus and a malicious smile crossed his face. "We've been waiting for you," he called out.

Amazonia's head tipped back and she looked, upside down, toward Quintus. Both her eyes were blackened and swollen almost shut. An angry bruise distorted the beautiful symmetry of her face. "Run, Quintus. It's a trap," she yelled. "They'll kill you!"

Running was the furthest thing from his mind. He took a step forward, but the tip of the coachman's sword jabbed at his back hard enough to pierce the skin. The sudden sting made Quintus jump.

"Easy, Roscius, easy," Lucius called out, as if scolding a disobedient child. "Not too rough. We want our guest to enjoy this." Lucius continued to stroke himself as he spoke. "The whore prefers multiple cocks inside her. Why not come down and join us, gladiator?"

Quintus's heart thumped so loudly in his ears it almost concealed Lucius's words. The madman dropped to his knees between Amazonia's spread legs.

"Don't you fucking do it," Quintus said. "It'll be your death if you do."

Lucius stared at him for a moment. "Don't do what, gladiator? *This...*" He thrust his hips forward and entered her violently. Amazonia struggled with her ropes but remained bound and helpless. Quintus took another step forward, but the move only earned him a second gash in his back. "This is quite pleasurable, gladiator." Lucius continued to ram into her again and again as he spoke. "She's the best fuck in the city. At least, that's what all my friends tell me."

The sight triggered a wave of anger and hate that Quintus had never before experienced. With it came the rush of fury that called his deadly alter ego from his lair. Quintus trembled with rage. A low growl began in the pit of his stomach and roared from his throat like a wounded tiger. The fighting machine known as Taurus emerged with a vengeance.

Ignoring the blade at his back, Taurus spun on the coachman. The gladius cut a long slice along Taurus's waist, but there was no pain. His elbow rose and caught the man full in the mouth. Teeth shattered and blood sprayed. The burly man staggered back. Taurus grabbed the hilt of the gladius, and with the man's hand pinned firmly beneath his own, drove the sword upward into the soft skin beneath the man's chin. The force drove the blade through the front of the man's face, and the tip exited where his right eye once was. With a mighty yank, Taurus pulled the sword free and let the body drop to the floor.

He spun and faced the arena. Lucius continued to pound into Amazonia without the slightest reaction to what had just happened. "Very good, gladiator. Nicely done," the madman yelled into the empty seats. "Now come join us!"

With a howl of anger and frustration, Taurus leapt from seat to seat down the sloping cavea, taking three rows at a bound. As he flew, he pictured Lucius at his feet, groveling for mercy as he plunged the sword into the back of the bastard's neck. He planted his foot onto the first row seat and launched himself over the retaining wall. It was then he saw the eight other stout mercenaries pressed against the arena wall.

The instant his feet touched the sand, they charged. Taurus turned to meet the attack. Behind him, Lucius broke into maniacal laughter. The first five men surrounded him, swords drawn. The last three, holding a large black cargo net and three spears, stood in reserve. Taurus did not wait for the attack. He went on the offensive. His blade was a silver streak. He targeted one of the sword-wielding assailants. Within a second, he cut a wide gash from wrist to bicep. Tendons ripped and the man's hand went useless. With an upward slice, Taurus knocked the man's gladius in the air and grabbed the hilt with his left hand before it hit the ground.

Spinning both blades to keep the circle of fighters at bay, Taurus selected his second and third victims. As a ruse, he charged the man standing between them. When the two dropped their guard ever so slightly, Taurus struck. He spun like a whirlwind and slashed with both swords as he came around. Stunned, the two men grabbed at the wide gashes opened in their throats, then dropped face-first into the sand. The fighter between them never faltered. He charged in a frontal assault, while his comrade attacked from the rear. Taurus sensed the attack before it came. He already had both blades spinning. His head tossed back and forth as he fought two separate sword battles simultaneously, one right-handed, one left-handed. Although well-trained, the mercenaries would have been no match for Taurus one-on-one. But together, it took all his concentration and instinct to keep them engaged. The clash of the four blades went on, mixed with the laughing and intensified groans of sexual pleasure that continued to radiate from Lucius. The sounds sickened Taurus but also gave him strength. He could not let Amazonia's rape continue. He willed more energy into his arms. His twin swords gathered speed. Finally, one struck a wrist. As the fighter screamed, Taurus lunged. He buried his left gladius in the man's stomach. He turned and brought both swords to bear on his remaining opponent. As he prepared to attack, his eyes searched for the three remaining fighters. They were gone. He controlled his panic but knew he was in trouble.

The net flew over his head from behind, then swept him off his feet. He cursed his own stupidity as he hit the sand face-first. Lucius's tactic had worked. He had distracted Taurus just enough with his theatrics to cause a mistake. The net was wider and heavier than a retiarius rete. With the added weight of the four fighters pinning him to the ground, he could barely move. But he still had his swords. He directed all the power in his body to his arms and legs. Slowly, he pushed up off the sand, bringing the four men with him. He gained just enough space to thrust his right sword through one of the wide squares of the net. The move caused him to collapse again, but not before his blade had penetrated a jugular vein. A man screamed and blood poured down from above. Then Taurus felt pain, a severe sting in his thigh. He looked down and saw the tip of a hunting spear imbedded in his upper leg.

Lucius's voice penetrated the bedlam once again. "I'm coming, gladiator! I'm coming!" His panting rose to a fever pitch. "Ah, yes! I'm shooting my seed into your lovely Amazonia. And she's loving every drop."

The words and image sent Taurus over the edge. With a vicious roar, he pushed up from the arena floor and the pile of bodies rose. But another spear pierced the cargo net and tore into his arm. As much as he tried to ignore the searing pain, his arm collapsed and, once again, the tremendous weight pushed him into the sand.

"Now she dies," Lucius screeched. "I've had my fuck for the evening, dear gladiator. Now the whore bitch *dies! Do it!*" The order was screamed with such intensity, it seemed to rip Lucius's throat. One of the fighters jumped from the pile atop Taurus and ran toward Amazonia's prone body.

"No!" Taurus bellowed. A streak of energy surged through his body. He pushed himself off the ground with such a force that the two remaining mercenaries and one dead body flew through the air. He ripped the spear from his thigh and stood with the cargo net still draped over him. The fighter had reached Amazonia.

"Kill her!" Lucius screamed in an unearthly voice, as he stepped back from his victim.

Taurus's world suddenly turned to a nightmare in which he could move only in slow motion. He had to stop this. He had to reach Amazonia. He tried to pull the net from his body and run, but it clung to him like a wet blanket. One of the fallen mercenaries grabbed at his legs. Taurus sliced at the clutching hand. On the first stroke, he severed it cleanly from the forearm and broke free. But his feet still seemed imbedded in quicksand. There was too much distance, too many steps. The mercenary stood over Amazonia and raised his spear. No! A scream came from Taurus's throat. By all the gods, she cannot die! Not like this!

An arrow suddenly burrowed into the mercenary's right temple with a thump. Then another, striking just behind his ear. The man dropped his weapon and toppled forward onto the naked woman below him. His blood poured across her chest.

Lucius stood frozen. The only mercenary still in fighting condition whirled around to face the new threat. Taurus didn't need to look. He already knew the only man who could place two arrows in a man's head from across an arena. He crossed the last thirty feet of sand and reached Amazonia just as the last mercenary fell dead in the sand behind him.

Taurus rolled the body off her and cut through the thick ropes with four powerful slices. As he knelt beside her, Amazonia threw her arms around his neck. He hugged her tightly, desperately wishing he could take away her pain. But he was torn between comforting her and quenching the fury that raged inside him at what had been done to her. His decision was made when her hand slapped his back.

"Lucius! He's getting away!"

Taurus leaned back and looked at her. "Lindani!" he called out, never taking his gaze from Amazonia's emerald eyes. The whack of a fourth arrow striking its target was followed by a high-pitched wail. Taurus helped Amazonia stand on unsteady legs. He picked up the swords, and together they turned toward the animal who had just tried to ruin their lives for the last time.

Lucius lay in the sand near the far wall of the arena. An arrow protruded from the side of his left knee. He rolled back and forth, screaming. Taurus and Amazonia walked together across the oval toward the wounded creature.

With effort, Quintus forced his alter ego to recede. This was Quintus's fight, and Quintus's foe. *This* victory did not belong to Taurus.

A dozen scenarios ran through his mind. Should they send Lucius back to Petra's African ludus? Should they sell him into slavery and let him return to his proper roots? Should they hand him over to Vespasian with the full details of his sordid background? Or should they simply kill him, right here, right now?

His thoughts were interrupted by Amazonia's hand. She wrenched one of the two swords from his grasp.

"I am a prefect in the service of Emperor Vespasian," Lucius shouted as they approached. "Roman law demands that I be turned over to the imperial court for proper justice. I'll take this matter up with the emperor himself." He crawled as he ranted, leaving a trail of bloody sand in his wake.

Amazonia raised her sword. But rather than thrust, she smacked the side of her blade against his ribs. The loud slap was enhanced by the unmistakable crack of a bone. Lucius screamed.

Quintus nodded. "I see, Lucius . . . Is that what Roman law demands? Well, tell me, what did Roman law demand the last time we met in this arena? Was it Roman law that sentenced me to the lions? Was it Roman law that almost killed my two friends?" Quintus reached down and grabbed a handful of short, curly hair. He yanked Lucius's head back with a jerk. "And was it Roman law that murdered my friend Aulus Libo? Or was it you and your greed, and your blind ambition?"

Amazonia swung again, whacking the side of Lucius's face with the flat of her gladius. A gash opened on the welt that sprang from his cheek. "And where was your fucking law when I was being beaten tonight?" she screamed. "And when you were sticking that disgusting prick of yours in me? Was that justice? Was that Roman law?"

Quintus released his grip, and Lucius's head bobbed forward for a moment, then shot up with a defiant look in his crazed eyes. "You're slaves. You have no rights. Roman law doesn't pertain to scum like you." His mouth twisted into a spiteful smile. He suddenly threw his head back and screamed a maniacal laugh. "I can fuck you up the ass all night long, you stinking bitch, and there's not a goddamned thing you can do about it. You're no better than a dog in the gutter." He spit at their feet, and he laughed again.

Quintus looked at Amazonia. She was already looking at him. They read each other's mind like a roll of papyrus. Now it was Quintus's turn to smile.

"Here's what we think of your Roman law," he said quietly. His arm struck like lightning. Lucius's expression went from demented joy to shock. He looked down at the hilt of the gladius sticking from his stomach. He tipped his head back and tried to speak, but instead a gush of blood spewed from his mouth.

"Welcome to Hades," Amazonia said. She drew back her sword and swung hard at his neck. At first nothing moved. But as his body began to lean forward, Lucius's head dropped from his shoulders. Before it hit the sand, an arrow struck it in the temple.

Quintus and Amazonia turned. Lindani stood near the arena wall, his bow still rigid in front of him. "I could not let him pass from this world without saying good-bye myself," he said. He lowered the bow and walked toward them, handing Amazonia a red tribal robe he had thrown over his shoulder.

Quintus stared at the head of the man who had been his lifelong nemesis. The mad eyes stared back in terror, but Quintus felt no remorse. "Now he's Pluto's problem," he said. "Let him revel in the underworld."

He broke his gaze and looked at Lindani. "And where in Hades have *you* been? I could have used you a bit earlier." He rubbed at the bleeding, aching hole in his thigh.

"A hunter can do little without his weapons. I run like the cheetah, but even the cheetah takes some time to cross the plain, no?"

"I'm just glad you found your target," Amazonia said, wiping the blood from her breasts and wrapping the robe around herself. She looked up at the hunter. "Thank you, Lindani."

A broad smile flashed in the torchlight and Lindani beamed.

Quintus reached out and placed his arm over the African's shoulder. "Better late than never, my friend. How did you find us?"

Lindani's face took on the overly dramatic, pained expression Quintus loved. "You insult Lindani on this night? Does it take a tracker of such skill to follow the ruts of a wagon through a field of soft earth?"

Quintus looked at Amazonia and shrugged with a smile. "Just asking . . ."

Lindani cocked his head up toward the cavea. "The dominus comes. He, too, sensed a problem with the coachman."

A moment later, Quintus heard footsteps drifting from the mid-level entrance ramp to the cavea. Petra and Julianus were the first through the portal, followed by a dozen Pompeiian fighters armed with swords and spears. They scanned the arena, studying the carnage in the sand. Petra waved for his fighters to stay put, then descended the steps with Julianus. Lindani, a bleeding Quintus, and a battered and bleeding Amazonia met him at the wall.

"I've seen you two look better," he said. He looked past them at the severed head in the sand. "Is that who I think it is?" Quintus nodded. "Good" was Petra's only response.

Quintus lifted Amazonia over the wall and Julianus helped her to the front row bench. "What do we do with all this?" Quintus said, leaning his head back toward the carnage.

Petra turned and yelled up toward his men. "Memnon, take two men and get a dozen shovels. If anyone asks, we're digging a cesspool." Memnon waved and left the amphitheater with two fighters in tow. The lanista looked at Quintus. "The arena is as good a place as any to bury some bodies." He pointed toward Lucius's head with his chin. "Plus there's an odd sense of justice in sticking him beneath the sand of the arena."

Quintus rubbed his aching thigh and bit back a gasp of pain. "I guess tomorrow I'll visit my Aunt Julia to have a little talk about her role in all this again."

"She's not involved this time," Amazonia said. "Lucius beat and raped her, too. She's still tied to their bed. We'd better get someone there to cut her loose."

"I'll go," Quintus said.

"No, you can see her tomorrow," Petra said. "Amazonia, give the directions to Julianus. He can get her out. Quintus, I want the physicians to look at those wounds tonight. You, too, Amazonia. Go."

Quintus hopped the wall with some effort. "I'd better see Vespasian myself with Julia," he said. "It'll take a while to explain all this."

XXIX

January AD 70

A N ENTHUSIASTIC CROWD lined the main street of Pompeii to welcome home their heroes. The parade of fighters and equipment carts entered through the Vesuvio Gate and stretched for a quarter mile along the Via di Stabia. Quintus, Amazonia, and Lindani waved from the first cart in line.

"It's good to be home," Quintus said, acknowledging a cluster of four pretty girls who screamed his name. The zealous cheering seemed like a continuation of the celebration two days earlier, when the Pompeii fighters had met their Rome counterparts in the inter-city challenge to honor Vespasian.

Quintus thought back to his arena bout with Attilius, which had closed the show. The incredible energy that had radiated from the capacity crowd had only generated half his power that day. The other half had come from knowing that in the sand beneath his feet rotted the headless body of Lucius Calidius.

He reached up and touched the small terra-cotta icon that hung around his neck. He smiled at Amazonia and slapped Lindani on his sleek back.

"Yes, it's good to be home."

Afterword & Historical Notes

The maxim "truth is stranger than fiction" certainly holds true for the story of the Year of the Four Emperors. I would be remiss if I did not at least briefly attempt to separate fact from fiction within this story line.

AD 69 was, without question, one of the most turbulent periods of an already chaotic Empire. Virtually all of the events in this book did, in fact, occur during that year.

Gladiators were recruited into Otho's forces, and they were led by the tribune, Martius Macer. The use of gladiators on the battlefield was not a new concept. Among others, Tiberius and Julius Caesar had also recruited arena fighters into their ranks for temporary duty. However, unlike the heroes of our story, the ancient historian Tacitus tells us that the gladiators' performance in war was often dubious, many not being able to cope with the intensity and bedlam of the battlefield.

In terms of the succession of emperors through the year, Galba was murdered in January, eight months into his rule. Otho committed suicide in April. And Vitellius was beaten to death by the mob in Rome in December. I have taken liberties by suggesting that Otho's death was anything more than a suicide.

The battle at Bedriacum and the two battles near Cremona also occurred much as they are portrayed in the story, including the incident of sabotaged artillery and the panic raised by the Syrians cheering the sunrise. However, the killing of the Vitellian legionaries by the gladiator cohort in formation behind them was fabricated for the story.

The pontoon bridge over the Po was destroyed as it was in the story—by boats of fire being floated down the river. The resulting Po island battle with the Batavians and Germanic auxiliaries also happened mostly as portrayed.

Legate Aulus Caecina Alienus did try to surrender his army to Vespasian and was thrown in chains by his own men for doing so. Vespasian's primary support came from the legions in Egypt and Syria, along with his own legions in Judea. During a trip to Alexandria to solidify that support, he visited the tomb of Alexander the Great, whose mummified nose was—according to legend—knocked off by Caesar Augustus during an earlier visit. Vespasian's brother was killed on the Capitoline as presented, and his young son Domitian escaped the city by posing as a priest of Isis.

Perhaps most interesting was the bizarre fact that Vitellius actually *was* found alone in his palace by Vespasian's soldiers near the end of the battle for Rome. He posed as one of his own slaves to try to avoid capture and used one of the palace watchdogs for protection. I couldn't help having Quintus, Amazonia, and Lindani be the ones to find him. Their use of the Cloaca Maxima sewer system to gain entry to the heart of Rome was a work of fiction, although the underground tunnel was in fact large enough to navigate in small boats.

Throughout the book, I have woven the *Gladiators of the Empire* characters into actual historical events, often portraying them as the impetus to key decisions and actions of the emperors and their legions. To that end, I felt these decisions were certainly discussed and made by *someone,* so the roles of "instigator" and "mastermind" were assigned to some of the main characters of the series.

In a few instances, time was also compressed to help the flow of the story. For example, Vespasian did not arrive in Rome until the autumn of AD 70—almost a year after he wrenched control of the Empire. But obviously this time lag would have slowed the story line considerably.

Lastly, as in *Sand of the Arena* (Book One of this series), I have used the "thumbs down" motion in the arena to call for the death of a gladiator. The actual motion used by the mob and the games' editor has never been conclusively determined. Ancient writings include only the phrase ". . . with thumb turned." Some historians feel it was actually a "thumbs up" motion that signified death. Since I felt this might be somewhat confusing to readers, I have yielded to the Hollywood directors and used the hand signal we most associate with death in the arena. To signify mercy, I have the mob waving white handkerchiefs or the hems of their togas, which seems to be accepted as historically accurate by most Roman scholars.

For a detailed, historical account of the events of AD 69, I heartily recommend *The Year of the Four Emperors* by Kenneth Wellesley and *69 AD: The Year of the Four Emperors* by Gwyn Morgan. These works were of tremendous value in the development of this book.